Gutter Mind

Smoke Valley MC

K.A. Merikan

Acerbi & Villani Ltd.

Cover design by
Natasha Snow
http://natashasnow.com

Editing by No Stone Unturned
https://www.facebook.com/NoStoneUnturnedEditingServices/

TABLE OF CONTENTS

Chapter 1 - Mike

Mike stifled a yelp when the back of his head collided with a shelf and knocked off plastic bottles that vaguely smelled of bleach. But there was no going back when Mona snuck in behind him and pressed her soft chest against his arm so they could both fit into the tiny maintenance closet at the back of the store.

He'd been away for two weeks and had kind of assumed that the whole Harlyn debacle would have blown over by now, but her brothers had reappeared ten minutes after Mike's arrival. They were out for a ring on their sister's finger and Mike sure as hell wasn't going to give them what they wanted.

So here he was, squashed in the maintenance closet and hiding as if his lover's husband had just come in and she'd been forced to put Mike away *somewhere*.

That had been fun only once.

Mona shifted against him, and Mike had to bite his lips to stop a comment about her boobs pressing into him. "Can't you just go fuck them up so this is over with?" she whispered, pronouncing words in the sweet cadence of her Italian accent.

Mike scowled. If it only were that simple.

"It would have made a mess in the shop. I've been back for less than an hour, and the last thing I want is Mom on my back."

Mona groaned. "Some outlaw biker. Afraid of his mom. You just wanna feel me up."

Mike's lips stretched. "Come on, you're my sister's wife. I would *never*," he said in a tone that suggested he would have, even though he'd pretty much classified Mona as a sister once Rain had put that ring on her finger. Throughout their trip, they'd been sleeping in the same hotel rooms—sometimes in the same bed if it was cheaper—and he'd kept it kosher.

Mike could swear he heard Mona snort in the darkness, but focused on Shay's raspy voice out in the shop.

"I already told you Mike's away. If you're not buying anything, you should leave," she said sternly. She was a small woman, frail despite her wild black hair, and the tattoos covering most of the skin she showed, but she faced the Jaren brothers with confidence, as if she were disciplining one of her four kids. The Jarens weren't breaking her, but if they tried, Mike would have to ignore the possible damage to the store and fuck them up whatever the cost, because as the old lady of another MC brother, Shay was family.

She was also the first woman who'd managed to put reins on Mike's cousin, Kane, which made her a treasure that needed to be protected at all cost.

But she didn't need anyone's aid and stood her ground. "Go on. Out. And don't try anything stupid. We've got cameras all over the place."

The three men went silent, and Mike imagined them sharing uncertain glances. They damn well knew there would be hell to pay if they as much as stepped on Shay's toes.

He held his breath, listening to the silence hanging in the air just outside the closet.

The most outspoken of the brothers, Eric, raised his voice with no prelude. "A slut like you won't see we're only doing this for our sister's sake! She was untouched until he put his dirty hands on her, and he *will* marry her, or he'll dry out in the desert, with a hole in his head!"

Wow. That had escalated quickly.

Shay was unfazed. "I'll pass on the message."

One of the brothers huffed like an angry bear, but the short statement was followed by stomping, which meant they were leaving. Mike couldn't even enjoy Mona's breasts anymore, itching to get out of the dusty confines.

Finally, after what felt like forever, the door to the closet opened, and Shay gestured at them to come out, adjusting the cup of her bra, which peeked out from under her tank top.

"They're gone. But you know they'll be back. Hope Harlyn's V was worth the unboxing," she said in her low, raspy voice.

Mike rolled his eyes and opened one of the store's fridges to pull out a can of beer. It came from a local brewery, and while more expensive than big brands, it was Dad's favorite, so they always had it in stock. "Hey, I didn't coerce her into it. That girl is like a pussycat in heat, and I bet the only reason why she'd even want to marry me would be to get the hell out from under her family's 'protection'," he said and took a sip of the cool lager.

The shop belonged to the Heller family as well as the rest of the gas station, the garage, and the Smoke Valley MC clubhouse which housed a private bar and numerous rooms, including Mike's. He was the oldest of the siblings to still live at the compound, as it was a rite of passage to move out once you started a family. Which meant Mike would stay forever, and he wasn't complaining. The clubhouse was a constant stream of parties and pussy, with the added perk of being close to family within the safe confines of a tall concrete wall that kept away jealous husbands. What more could a man want?

He winked at his reflection in the glass door of the fridge. At thirty-seven he didn't look his age, courtesy of avoiding the kind of baggage some of his brothers had saddled themselves with. Kids, a house, and a woman to keep happy. Even Rain, his *lesbian* sister, for some reason had decided it was time to 'settle down', and now her and Mona were mothers to twins. Mike still had a little chip on his shoulder over not being their first choice of sperm donor, but it was only his ego talking, because he didn't actually want the responsibility. Their brother, Leo, could have it.

He pulled at the blond beard that had become a bit too bushy during the trip. What he did want after two weeks on the road was a visit to the barber's. Tanned, ripped, with blue eyes that made women pay attention, and Smokey patches on the back of his vest, he could easily live this way into his sixties. Their sergeant at arms, Admiral never 'settled down' and it was working out just fine for him.

Mona cleared her throat and poked Mike's side. "Are you checking yourself out?"

Shay snorted, but before she could have added her own snarky remark, the back door burst open and Kane rushed in, looking around with the eyes of a rabid pitbull. Shirtless, his flaming red hair wet, all the circus-themed ink on show, he was the human equivalent of a comet arriving to smash into anything that could hurt his old lady.

Mike waved him off. "Chill, they're gone."

"They shouldn't have come here to harass my Shay in the first place," Kane roared, getting into Mike's face.

Yikes. And this was the guy who used to claim it was his destiny to sow his seeds in any field that needed plowing? He'd really fallen hard. Mike saw this pattern all around. His older brother, Jack, had married his favorite stripper just two years back, and Leo had followed not long after, marrying a *man* when no girl would accept his ring. The world had turned on its head, and Mike wasn't joining that crazy train any time soon.

"And this is my fault how? Since when is it a crime to fuck a willing chick?" Mike asked, leaning against the closet door.

Kane snarled. "Since her family is some backwards dumbasses who worship aliens and lock up their women's pussies like they're filled with diamonds. Sort. This. Out." Droplets of spittle landed on Mike's cheek, but he'd let that slide for the sake of their family bond.

Mike hummed. "They don't *worship* aliens. They make figurines of little green men for a living. Jesus." Which reminded him that he needed to get rid of the ashtray Harlyn had given him as a present, claiming she'd made it herself.

Mona rolled her eyes and adjusted the Gucci biker jacket she often wore when riding. She'd grown up in wealth, and Daddy wouldn't let her go without. Living in the Nevada desert hadn't changed her fashion sense, even if she was so much freer out from under the wings of her mafia family. "So... I'll be going. Thanks for the trip Mike, I needed that."

He showed her his teeth in a wide smile. "Back to the mommy grinder? Bet you can't wait to change diapers again."

Mona laughed. "Why do you think we got Leo as an extra parent?" She waved and was off, swaying her full hips on the way out.

Kane tugged on Mike's beard. "I'm talking to you, man! One hair falls off—"

"Why's Shay working here anyway? Weren't you supposed to hire help?"

"We have help," Shay said and pointed her chin toward the front of the store.

A woman stood in the sunshine, facing the vast expanse of dry shrubs and pale brown hills stretching on the other side of the road. Petite yet not too short, she was the perfect size to pick up and carry around. Her legs were long and slender, like a gazelle's, and her hair styled into two cutesy buns just above her nape. She had it dyed too—platinum blonde at the top and dipped in color at the tips, with mint on one side and baby pink on the other. Someone needed to *water* her or she'd dry out in the merciless midday sun.

Mike hadn't seen her face yet and already knew he wanted to tap that.

"Who. Is. That?" he asked, quickly finishing his beer and stepping to the side in a bid to see more.

Kane exchanged glances with Shay, but Mike couldn't decipher what the silent communication meant. Other than Kane being jealous that Mike wasn't tied down, and could fuck whoever he pleased, of course.

"Arden. I guess you should go meet her. We hired her the day after you left for your trip with Mona," Kane said, crossing his arms, and making the clown on his bicep scowl.

But all of Mike's attention was on the pert ass packed into tight skinny jeans. Arden paired those with lilac high top sneakers, a studded belt in the same shade, and a white crop top that revealed the small of her back, as pale as her arms covered in colorful tattoos.

"I'm going in," he said with a grin.

Shay snorted. "Don't let me stop you."

Mike guzzled down the beer, dropped the can into the trash and walked out of the store with his smoothest gait. He approached the pretty fae adjusting a newspaper in a stand at the front of the shop, and when he looked at her pristine nape from up close, his instinct told him to lick the sheen of sweat off the smooth skin.

But that might have been too much for starters, so he settled on swatting one of the round buttocks instead. "I hear you're the new girl, pretty thing."

She twirled around, and before Mike knew it, a slap landed on... his beard. It had been clearly meant for his cheek, but Arden hadn't accounted for this much of a height difference. Not the tiniest girl Mike ever hit on, but she was twig-skinny, and when Mike stole a glance at her chest, there wasn't much there to write home about. Flat as an asphalt road in a desert. But Mike was all for equal opportunities, since flat chicks gave blowjobs no worse than girls with huge racks.

Arden stepped back and frantically pulled out what Mike at first thought was a key, but then it opened into the cutest little butterfly knife. It trembled in her slim fingers with nails painted glitter pink. If that wasn't the most adorable attempt at a threat, Mike didn't know what was.

Arden took one more second to assess him from top to bottom, and their eyes met. Hers were pale blue, as big as a doe's, with long dark lashes, but her expression was no less determined just because she had the face of a doll.

"Step. Away."

Mike's hands already went up in surrender—because a filly needed to want being ridden if it was to be any fun—but as Arden's warning echoed in Mike's head, his smile dropped, because he realized something.

Arden did not sound like a girl at all.

In fact, the voice that came from the plump mouth dipped in lip gloss, while not particularly low, was most definitely male. And as Mike's gaze gravitated lower, down the little protrusion at Arden's throat, over the planes of the chest, to the package at the front of Arden's jeans, one thing became abundantly clear.

The pretty thing that should have been another of his conquests was a boy. Or was he? She? They? Those things could get confusing nowadays. Mike would go with *he* for now.

"Don't hurt yourself with that," Mike said, nodding at the butterfly knife.

"Oh, I know how to use it," Arden said despite his breath hitching as if he were facing a lion. "I might not be able to kill you, but I will take an eye, you... caveman."

Mike's eyes grew wider, and he found himself staring at Arden's lips again, as if his brain refused to register Kane had intentionally pushed him at someone who wasn't on Mike's usual menu. "Take my eye? Now why would you want to hurt such a handsome face?" he asked with a wide smile.

Arden lowered his puny weapon, but watched Mike's every move like a baby hawk. And despite his voice, the Adam's apple, and the cock in those tight pants, Mike's brain refused to register that Arden shouldn't be a sex object for him. The pretty thing even smelled like a girl. Flowers and bubblegum.

"You are... neutral to me." Arden frowned, drawing Mike's gaze to his eyebrows. They were cute and manicured, and the fact that the boy wore the kind of delicate makeup that gave skin a luminous, angelic appearance left Mike with a deepening sense of confusion.

Arden made a damn stunning girl, regardless of what hid in his pants, and Mike found himself weirdly fascinated with the ambiguity of the person standing in front of him. "I'm definitely not neutral to you. You look better than my last ex."

The tiny knife lowered farther. Bad move, if Mike were actually up to no good, but Arden didn't look like someone with experience in fighting. With his smooth face and tiny frame he could've still been in his teens.

Arden glanced up at him, and Mike kept noticing new details about his face, like the crystal stud in his shapely nose, or the tiny spade symbol drawn above the side of his eyebrow. How did a person like this end up working at the gas station of the Smoke Valley MC in Hawk Springs, Nevada?

"Um... Thank you? But yeah, you're not my type."

Mike frowned, glancing all the way to Arden's nipples, hardened against the white fabric. "You're straight?" he asked, because, as incredible as that would have been, it wasn't impossible.

"N-no." Arden finally hid the knife back in his pocket, but grabbed a newspaper off the stand next to him to fan himself, as if he needed something in his hand to swat Mike if push came to shove.

Mike *was* straight, so he shouldn't care some gay boy wasn't interested in him, but it stung his pride, and the fact that Kane and Shay were not far away, sniggering to each other didn't make the situation any better. And then there was the way Arden watched him with widened pupils and fluttering lashes. There was interest there, dammit!

"And you want me to believe that a boy like you wouldn't want a piece of this?" Mike asked and pulled up his shirt, revealing his abs and pecs. He did make sure they were hard and tense once the curtain of fabric went up.

The flush blooming on Arden's face was a satisfactory answer, but Mike wouldn't let it go until he heard the correct words from the pretty lips.

"Nope," Arden said sternly, but still tickled Mike's chest with his gaze. "You can put that away."

Mike blinked. "This isn't a department store. Nobody would fire you for sleeping with the boss," he said, even though Mom was the de facto owner of the business.

Arden's lips parted, and the pink hue reached his ears. "You're gay?"

"No, but you look my type. Cute and compact. With a nice ass," Mike teased, taking a step closer while his eyes pinned Arden in place as if he were a butterfly. So he was straight, but nothing about this feminine boy threatened his identity.

Arden squinted and stepped back, hitting the shelves with car lubricants close to the entrance. "And you look like the kind of guy who always gets what he wants. Must be a tough thing to hear, so I'll repeat. You're not. My. Type."

Mike laughed, and the way Arden's eyes were instantly drawn to his lips told him *everything*. "You're lying. We both know I'm everyone's type."

Arden shook his head and the flowery smell he carried about him only got more intense, pulling Mike in. It was as if his mind didn't fully register Arden's sex. The petite form ticked all of Mike's boxes, and the rejection made the predator inside him all the more eager for a chase.

"What is it to you if you're not gay?"

"You don't look like a guy," Mike said, his instincts going awry from this confusing situation. His brain kept short circuiting as it flashed images of the glittery nails scraping Mike's back and the soft lips moaning his name.

Arden's frown deepened, and he crossed his arms over a chest so flat it might have been pressed with an iron. "I don't care. I wear what I like and I'm cute the way I am."

Mike nodded, struck by the allure of the strange creature before him and unable to look away. "How about I get you a drink?"

The boy's eyes flashed. "No! What the hell?"

Mike noticed one of the tats on Arden's arms was blurry, as if something had rubbed it off, and then he realized all the colorful patterns, ponies, skulls, and pink sharks were body stickers.

He probably wanted the look but was afraid of pain. How cute.

"Don't get so worked up, honey pie. No need to play coy with me when we both know you're not being honest with yourself."

Mike spotted Kane in the corner of his eye. Too soon. He wasn't done here. Kane had never exactly been gay-friendly, but maybe Shay had softened him up in that regard as well.

"You're exactly the kind of guy I'd never date!" Arden exclaimed.

Kane patted Mike on the shoulder. "Not going so well?"

Damn it. "It's only a matter of time," Mike said, staring straight into Arden's huge eyes. They were a pale blue, like tropical waters around a crater about to erupt with burning lava.

Damn, this...person was hot. And the rejection somehow made Mike even more eager to see what hid under Arden's clothes, whether he'd end up liking it or not. One of his brothers was gay, and so was his sister. What was the harm in a bit of experimenting? It wasn't like getting into a guy's pants would keep him from the girls.

Kane shrugged. "Should have told you New Girl's a bit frigid."

Arden squinted. "Don't call me that."

"How do you know? You wanted to bring Arden into your and Shay's bed?" Mike asked, eyeing Arden with a smile when he spotted the boy staring at his pecs.

"Only extra dicks in our bed are rubber," Kane said, waving his heavily tattooed hand. "Enough laughing. Now come, let's have a drink and you'll tell me about all the pussy you tapped in Texas."

There hadn't been any, for Mona's comfort, but Kane didn't need to know that.

"You goin' with me or what?" Mike tried once more, but Arden spun around without a word, and returned to his duties at the newspaper stand.

"What's up with him?" Mike asked as Kane nudged him forward and past a car being fueled at the family gas station.

Kane shrugged. "Don't know really. I thought he was trans or something, but he claims that's not the case. Why dress like a girl and then claim you're not one? Burns through my circuits, man."

The gates into the compound were open during the day, so family and friends, as well as customers of the garage could come and go. Mike left his bike for the prospect to deal with and led the way into the large, elongated courtyard with blocky, no-frills buildings on either side. He used to live at his parents' bungalow until he was old enough to move out, but since he could remember, the clubhouse had been his real home.

Its smooth, dusty walls were parched by the sun on the outside but thick enough to keep the rooms pleasant without the need for excessive use of aircon. This was where he'd had his first fight, where he'd first tasted liquor, and where he'd lost his virginity. This was where those closest to him all worked together.

It was *his* place in the world.

The garage was at the very end, to the left, with parking for twenty cars stretching all the way to the boundary of the property, and Mike noticed someone waving at him from there. Leo had been sweating into his overalls since morning, but he was a top notch mechanic, who earned the club a lot of legal cash. Out of all of Mike's brothers, Mike wouldn't have pinned him as the gay one. With firm muscles and a crew cut, he was the antithesis of someone like Arden. Then again, Leo's husband, Zolt, was even more butch, and that didn't make him any less gay.

But those were the only two gay men he knew, so without a better frame of reference, his mind raced to fill in the blanks about a person like Arden.

"You had a good vacation, lazy ass?" Leo yelled from across the dusty yard. If it wasn't for the ink adorning his arms, he could've been the boy next door all grown up. A wholesome and responsible family man. But no. He had an equally tattooed husband with a past, and lived at the back of a pawn shop.

"Pretty good. Had fun with the mother of your children while you took care of the brats," Mike said, changing direction to join Leo by the car he was working on.

Leo laughed, wiping some motor oil on his cheek. "They're fuckin' *angels*, man. When they grow up, I'll be keeping them away from guys like you."

Kane sat in the sunshine outside the garage and yelled for a hangaround to get them some beers. Mike leaned against a side table where some of the tools were laid out, and lit a cigarette, watching Leo pour coolant.

"So... you know Arden?" he asked, watching Leo for a reaction.

"Who?"

Kane snort-laughed. "You know who."

Leo gave them both a level glare. "Why would you ask *me*?"

Mike rolled his eyes and filled his lungs with warm smoke. "Because you're both gay. It only makes sense for you to befriend him."

Leo groaned. "First of all, I'm not gay, which I told you a million times. Secondly, I'm a married man with kids, who works as a mechanic at a biker club. I've got no business befriending a pastel-haired teenager who loves sparklers and makeup. Why do you care anyway?"

Kane sniggered. "Mike's in love."

But Mike wouldn't give him the satisfaction of expressing annoyance and waved off the dumb joke.

Leo raised his eyebrows and stopped working to get a better look at Mike. "What's this stupid shit about?"

"Mike got the cold shoulder from Arden," Kane sniggered, accepting one of the beers the hangaround brought over without a word.

Mike took his and pressed the cool, damp bottle to his sweaty forehead. Damn, they really should get some air conditioning in the garage, because the place was an oven, but Dad was too cheap to organize it. "I did not. The boy's clearly playing hard to get. You saw how he looked at me!"

Leo unzipped the top part of his overalls before tying the sleeves around his waist. "Why were you teasing him in the first place? You're a grown ass man, so act like one."

Kane laughed out loud and poked Mike with his elbow. "Gonna let your little brother talk to you like that?"

Mike exhaled the smoke through his nose and had a sip of the cool liquid that made everything better. "I know you're all about that husband, children, picket fences, and the mother of your children, who also happens to be our sister's wife, but some of us don't want to be tied down in modern patchwork families, *Leo*. I'm too hot to resign myself to mediocrity."

Kane laughed even harder, but Leo kicked his shoe. "What's so funny? Your old lady's a camgirl who made you a step-father to four." Leo then turned to Mike. "Go and find a different target. Arden's under Rain's protection. She brought him here two weeks back, gave him the job, and there you have it. The kid's got some issues at home or something, and he's living at the compound for now. Rain won't say anything else, and Dad's lips are sealed too."

Bingo. That was potentially useful information, but it wasn't like Rain could tell him what was attractive to men. Which left Mike with Leo. Again.

"So what should I do to make him suck me off? Is it true guys do it better?"

Leo spread his arms so fast he spilled some beer down his tattooed chest "The fuck's wrong with you? Just told you to stay away from the kid."

Kane had tears in his eyes. "I mean, Leo married one after dating women all his life, so it must be half-decent."

"Why, is he a minor?" Mike challenged.

That shut Leo down, and he lowered his beer. "No, but—"

"There's no buts. If he didn't want to get some, he wouldn't be making all that effort to look like the finest girl in town. I just need to know how to break through that icy facade."

Leo rubbed his big nose. "Why do you even—? What? What's going on here? Because it feels like I've stepped into another dimension."

Kane was eager to fill in the details. "Mike got his ego rubbed the wrong way. He won't go through with shit. He just wants to know he can. Arden told him he wasn't his type, and that's what got him so worked up."

The reminder was like a brand at the back of Mike's skull. "I'm just pointing out it's a complete lie. I'm every guy's type. Even Leo's husband tried to get into my pants!"

Leo groaned and had a big gulp of beer. "It was a long time ago. Besides, you're not Zolt's wet dream, so get over yourself. He just thought you'd be easy."

Mike snorted, amused that Leo would think this was a slight. "Everyone knows how easy I am. I just wouldn't want all that hair touching me, you know. Or does the beard feel good on your balls?" he teased. It was too much of a temptation with Leo, who took everything so seriously.

This time, though, Leo fired right back. "Maybe you should go for Arden after all, give him head, and then ask him. But as I've heard, the boy won't let you anywhere near him."

Kane downed his beer and grinned with the mischievous twinkle in his eyes, which was surely what had landed him Shay. "Fifty bucks you can't get the boy to admit he likes you."

Hell yeah. Of course he could do that. He so loved a challenge.

Mike walked up to Kane and grabbed his hand, shaking it. "Fifty that I can."

Leo rolled his eyes. "This is gonna end up so badly," he grumbled, put down his beer, and got back to the work at hand. Just because he resented fun didn't mean Mike couldn't have any. Hell, he'd be the gayest straight guy the world has ever seen.

Chapter 2 - Arden

"I'm dying here, Kaley. Withering away." Arden slurped on his milkshake, enjoying the cool drink not far from the gas station, yet far away enough to be alone. "Next time we meet, I'll be just a shadow..."

"Wow. That's a dramatic way to say you're not fucking anyone. You know you're supposed to lay low, right? Living in Hawk Springs, the boring shithole, is still better than rotting in prison."

Arden scowled. Couldn't he just forget what happened and start a new life? Wasn't that why he'd come here in the first place?

Only what kind of new life could he hope for in Hawk Springs? There was *nothing* going on here. Its closeness to Reno, and his sister, Kaley, was this place's one advantage, because the town itself was a maze of streets with stand-alone houses that looked as if they'd come from the very same factory. Their lawns were dried out, dust spiraled everywhere, and the lone tree within sight had yellowish leaves despite it not yet being time for a change of color. But worst of all, once Arden was done working for the day, he either went back to his tiny room with a mattress for furniture or walked around aimlessly. Maybe he should have crossed state lines after all and hidden somewhere far away instead of relying on a biker club for protection?

"So what? I'm supposed to never get my roots done?"

"Who do you want to beautify yourself for, huh? You're with an MC, in a town that's pretty much in the middle of nowhere," Kaley said, chewing something on her end of the line.

On his trek along the road, Arden got to a lone bus stop with a rusted bench facing the local bank and some industrial buildings obscuring the hills surrounding the town, but it would have to do, since its single park—if the bit of grass could be called that—in Hawk Springs was three miles away. He wished he'd taken his sketchbook so that he could pour all his stifled arousal onto its pages, because the light here was much better than in his tiny room.

"I mean... there's *people*. I just want to be presentable."

People like the stupidly hot biker with a patch announcing to the world his name was *Mike*. Arden had been replaying their encounter in his head for hours now despite knowing Mike was the kind of man Arden should stay away from. And yet, here he was, trying to distract himself because all he could think of was Mike's dick spurting cum at the back of his throat.

Which couldn't happen. Because Arden was done with sex, men, and especially sex with men like Mike. He'd been burned too many times to count.

"Handsome people?" Kaley asked in a low tone. "Much older than you and charming? Is that what this is about?"

Arden sighed, wiggling his feet in the gravel under the bench while the sun scorched his head. He should have worn a hat, but he'd put too much effort into the buns to ruin them.

"It's not like that. There's this one guy I met today, Mike, and I don't *want* him. It's just that he was so full of himself, showing off. I know he's straight and posturing in front of his buddies, but I…"

What? What am I trying to do?

"Oh, Ardy," Kaley said, and Arden could almost see her shaking her head. "I *know* Mike. Charming, hot, good in bed. But he'll squeeze you for all you're worth and leave. He's a player, Arden. Don't fall for his pretty smile. He actually bet Rain over which one of them would get in my pants. Can you believe that?"

Arden sat up straighter. "What? You slept with him? Who won? When was this?"

"Excuse me? What does it matter? Just believe me when I say he's bad news! Keep your head down until you can safely leave," she said just as a bus rolled into the stop, its wheels sending a gray cloud into the air. No one got off, and Arden had to wave the driver to signal he wasn't waiting for transportation.

"But I won't do anything. He's straight and just being an ass, saying I'm prettier than his ex and all that." Okay, so he was bragging a bit, but it had been a tough two weeks.

"Of course he's saying that if he wants to get into your pants. Jesus. Just think for once, Arden, please." She exhaled. "Look, I gotta go dancing now. If you absolutely cannot wait to see a stylist, ask Rain to take you. Pay her or something."

Arden got to his feet and walked along the dusty road. "I fucked up my life haven't I?"

He could hear shuffling as she gathered her things in the apartment they shared in Reno, which now felt so endlessly far away. "You made it difficult. I told you Luke was bad news. But no, you had to think with your dick," she said in frustration.

"He seemed nice..." Arden kicked an invisible rock.

"No, he didn't. He seemed hot and dangerous. He proved to be exactly what was on the box, so please learn from this. I really gotta go, but if you need to call me about anything important, I'll always answer. Bye!"

Arden managed to say half a goodbye until he got cut off, but his mood was plummeting fast. Luke had seemed like Arden's dream come true three years ago. Older, sexy, he'd showered Arden with gifts and excitement. But Kaley was right in saying that he'd never been perfect. Luke lots of demands, and was jealous even when they had relationship breaks, but to Arden that used to be a sign of masculine confidence and added to Luke's appeal.

Too bad Luke had proved himself to be a complete and utter cunt. Arden should have just run away from danger, gone into a public place and called the police, but in the heat of the moment, panicking for his life, he'd hit Luke over the head with a lamp. Now he was stuck in exile, hoping cops didn't find out about his crime once the body was discovered.

He hated Luke so much.

Arden walked past the gym owned by Mother Heller and was nearing the MC compound when Rain appeared like a godsend, walking alongside her pretty Italian wife, who pushed a double stroller with the twins.

She was the opposite of Arden. Where he tried to emulate an angelic softness, Rain was the coolest of biker chicks, just as tough as her brothers, even if smaller, and he trusted her to protect him if she said she would. Whatever had transpired with Kaley years ago, the two of them were still friends, and Rain had been Arden's ticket into biker protective custody.

The money he'd stolen from Luke after smashing his head in had surely helped motivate her whole club too.

"Hey, Rain!" He jogged up to them with his best smile but lowered his voice when he noticed the twin girls had dozed off. "I was hoping you'd have a few hours free this evening?"

Mona, who'd been away when Arden had first come to live at the clubhouse, was as pretty as he'd been told. Small, with luscious breasts and a pretty face, she instantly drew attention, even in the presence of someone as attractive as her spouse.

Rain frowned and combed back her short hair, standing with her arm around Mona's shoulders. "What's going on?"

"I was hoping you could take me to this one mall in Reno? I'm dying to get my hair done…"

Rain shook her head. "Sorry. Got my wife back after two weeks, I'm staying home. But if it really can't wait, go ask the guys. They know to not give you any shit."

"Ask Leo," Mona added. "He's the nicest and lives with his husband near Reno, so he'll be going back there anyway."

Arden thanked them for their suggestions and walked on, but his shoulders sagged. He'd seen Leo around, and had found out about the guy's bisexuality on his first day here, but had felt too intimidated by Leo's stony exterior to approach him.

There was that weird atmosphere where they were both aware of each other but never spoke even when occupying the same space. Arden got the sense that Leo didn't want to fraternize with him, as if that could somehow affect the way others saw him as a gay man. Ridiculous macho posturing.

But desperate times called for desperate measures, so Arden passed the two buildings that made up the clubhouse and headed for the garage where Leo was hard at work. He was used to being the freak show, but in a town as small and boring as this one, nobody seems to have gotten used to his presence yet. The gawking was making him uncomfortable at this point, especially that the vast majority of people who hung around the club never attempted to speak to him, so he focused on the concrete slabs making up the surface of the yard.

Leo was drinking coffee when Arden arrived. He moved behind the vehicle at the front of the large room smelling of oil and paint, as if trying to flee, but gave up the moment Arden waved at him.

There. He could do this.

"Arden, right?" Leo asked, leaning against the side of the car as if he hadn't tried to get out of sight seconds ago. "What's up?" he asked without much energy. He was good-looking, but way below Mike on Arden's personal hot-o-meter. Maybe because he actually seemed sane and friendly, unlike the men who usually gave Arden shivers and made him draw porn until his pencil went aflame.

"Yes. I'm sorry to bother you, but Mona told me I should talk to you because you're the nicest Heller..." He smiled, letting the fact that they both knew each other's sexuality hang between them unsaid. It was awkward as fuck.

Leo's gaze lifted to meet Arden's. "What?"

"Would you go to a mall in Reno with me? I've got to see my hairdresser. Can't go anywhere close, because my hair is kinda difficult to work with. It will take two hours tops."

Leo took a deep breath, then his face twisted when he glanced beyond Arden's shoulder. Something changed in the air, and Arden's nape broke out in goosebumps as someone entered the garage, their boots scraping against the dusty concrete behind him.

"Leo here can't wait to go back to his husband. But I can take you right away."

That voice. Low and sultry. Delicious.

Arden could just see himself under—

No. He would not think about things that weren't allowed to happen. So despite the shivers running up and down his body, he ignored Mike's presence and smiled at Leo. "Pretty please? I can pay."

Leo rubbed his greasy hands on a towel so dirty it likely distributed germs rather than soaked them in. "I'm really busy. Sorry, but my advice is don't go with him. He's charming on the outside, rotten on the inside."

"Hey," Mike complained. "Don't be a cockblock. My intentions are completely honest. And I can get you wherever you need to be free of charge. I've been meaning to go see a barber myself anyway," he added as his burning hot hand slid along Arden's shoulders, creating invisible sparks. He smelled of some woodsy cologne, and Arden could already sense the fire.

He must have showered after that long drive he'd come from earlier. As he came into Arden's line of sight, refusing to be sidelined, the breeze tangling in his hair transformed him into a music video hottie.

Don't get drawn in. Don't get drawn in. Don't get drawn in.

"And what are those honest intentions?" Arden asked, secretly enjoying the touch. Mike had to be at least twice his size, and his hands were massive. Like a biker demigod gracing Arden with his presence, he had the most golden skin, the bluest eyes, and the whitest teeth. The birds and exotic animals tattooed on his arms looked as if they were ready to move their colorful wings and carry him away from undeserving mortals. Tall and cocky, he could have flirted the pants off anyone in his way.

But he'd zeroed in on Arden.

The filth Arden's mind suggested was like a wave he couldn't stop, no matter how wrong it was to be this shallow.

Mike rubbed his thumb against Arden's chin, as if there was something stuck to it. His beard was thick and a bit bushy, but appeared pillow-soft, and Arden wanted to roll into his sun-kissed arms.

"I want to buy you a drink," Mike said. Again.

Leo offered Arden a stare that could have been meant as a warning, but it was so very hard to focus on logic when Mike spread his outlaw biker charm like spores that wouldn't stop getting in Arden's eyes.

Tight white T-shirt, black leather vest, a belt Arden could just about hear being unbuckled. Would the signets on his fingers tangle into Arden's hair when Mike held him down?

It shouldn't have been so hard to make the right choice, considering that being a stupid slut who didn't know any better was what had gotten Arden into this mess in the first place. "Okay. I'll let you take me to the mall, but only if you buy me a bubble tea."

Mike showed off his strong teeth in a grin as he glanced at Leo's somber expression. "See what I did there, bro? I'm on a roll!"

"What about your future bride?" Leo asked.

Arden perked up at the possibility of a chaperone. He'd need one around Mike. "She can come with us."

But Mike's expression soured. "Don't listen to that idiot. He means the girl I dated for a while. Her family is a bunch of crazies, and they demand I marry her. Not gonna happen. I'm a bird who needs to fly free," he said pulling Arden out of the garage.

"That's code for fuck and run," Leo grumbled, but when Arden stopped and looked back at him, unsure what to make of this, Leo's gaze softened. "Don't worry. He's straight, very bored, and won't do shit."

Mike groaned, as if it was all beneath him. "Who knows if I'm that straight? And you're my date," he said, taking Arden away from the relative safety of Leo's presence.

Mike's hand slipped to the small of Arden's back, and the top was short enough for skin-on-skin touch that sent Arden's imagination into overdrive. He shouldn't be liking any of this. He should be *so* over sex, yet he was following the trail of lusty crumbs straight into Mike's trap despite knowing that this was most likely an elaborate prank for him to laugh at with his buddies over beers later.

"It's not a date."

"It absolutely is. What is that thing you want me to buy you? The one with the funny name? Is that like a girly drink from Starbucks?" Mike asked, leading him through the courtyard, as if he were presenting a prized filly to the girls sitting on a bench by the bar with bottles of Diet Coke in their hands. Almost as if he were teasing them by touching someone else, and Arden could sense his skin going red from all the stares.

And yet he stole glances at Mike time and time again, remembering how firm and muscular his chest was, how cool all those tattoos on his skin were. He bet Mike had a gun and knew how to fight. How to fuck. Kaley had said it herself that he was good in bed. Even if he didn't have sex with men, someone like him had surely tried anal with one of his many girlfriends, and Arden could just imagine their moans when a stud like Mike—

"Hm?" Arden had to take a deep breath. "Bubble tea. Yes. I mean, no, it's not from Starbucks, it's this drink with tapioca balls in it. They do different flavors, if you wanted to try."

A part of Arden wanted to make his point by stepping away, but he didn't feel threatened like he'd had at the store when Mike had taken him by surprise. So he let Mike lead him to the row of bikes standing along the wall of the MC bar. A machine Arden hadn't seen before glistened in the sunshine, recently washed. It was a meaty chopper in shocking orange, the perfect fit for Mike's boisterous personality, and as they approached it, he couldn't help but imagine Mile bending him over the vehicle, pulling down his pants, and spitting on his hole. There had to be a monster in his jeans if he scored so much, and he'd thrust it into Arden's tight hole over and over while everyone watched.

It was definitely time to step away, so Arden did so under the pretense of approaching the bike.

"Wouldn't it be better to go by car?"

"Nah. You're afraid of something if you need protection, and it's much easier to flee on a bike," Mike said and casually lit a cigarette.

"Could you not smoke if we're about to sit so close?" He gave up complaining that his fresh hairdo would be ruined under a helmet, as that would get him ridiculed.

Mike stalled. "Why?" he asked, blowing out smoke as if he hadn't gotten the memo that cigarettes were no longer cool. Yet despite the scent of tobacco, the little deathstick struck Arden as rather tempting when it hung from between Mike's lips. "Does it make you think of something naughty?" he asked and had the audacity to wiggle his eyebrows.

Now that Mike put the image in Arden's head…

"No. It stinks."

"No, it doesn't. It's an aphrodisiac," Mike said as he handed Arden a helmet and put on shades, as if he were the king of the compound. He did kind of look like he was.

Arden chewed on his lips, wondering if this wasn't a bad idea after all. His legs softened now that he imagined them balancing on the vehicle at high speed. "I've never been on a motorcycle."

"And I've never been on a date with a boy. There's a first time for everything," he said, releasing smoke like a dragon about to consume the virgin offered to it as tribute. Only that Arden was no virgin, and as soon as the monster found out, he'd spit him right out.

Arden should have reacted in anger when Mike's foot slid between his, forcing them apart, but he couldn't make himself pull away.

Mike was teasing him. That was all. He was a very straight biker, confident enough in his sexuality to play around. Nothing out of the ordinary would happen, and all Arden needed to do was keep up the facade of disinterest.

"I'm actually avoiding the cops, so... no speeding."

Mike rolled the cigarette with his tongue, so it moved to the other side of his mouth, and he leaned closer, his presence so loaded with sex Arden was getting worried he might embarrass himself on the bike.

"How did you get on their radar, naughty boy?"

"None of your business, just know... I'm dangerous."

"Dangerously sexy. A real temptation with your long legs and that mouse-sized knife," Mike said, and he rubbed Arden's chest, rendering him breathless. The guy really had no shame.

"It's small, so no one sees it coming until it's too late." He approached the bike as an excuse to turn away from Mike. The trail on his chest burned with unwanted sparks of arousal, so he took a deep breath of the dusty air.

Mike tossed the cigarette into the dirt and rubbed his hands before mounting his steel beast with a self-satisfied smile. "It's gonna feel nice. Just clench your thighs on it and hold on to me as tightly as you can."

Arden was losing confidence in this idea by the second, but temptation was too great, so he grabbed Mike's arm when mounting the bike. As soon as he was in the seat, its curve made Arden slide straight toward Mike's ass.

This was bad. Was there still time to change his mind?

Mike chuckled, and as the bike came to life, Arden put his arms around him, trembling along with the revving machine. "Knew I'd get you to spread your legs one way or another."

Any answer Arden could have to the insolence got drowned out by the bike's engine. At least this meant Arden could stop lying to them both because yes, he'd spread his legs for Mike.

Chapter 3 – Mike

All the jokes about hard-ons pressing against his ass passed through Mike's brain on the way to Reno, and he was almost disappointed that he hadn't felt any evidence of Arden's arousal. Sure, they both wore jeans, and the stiff fabric must have held the boy's cock at bay, but it was like a slight. As if Arden hadn't been lying about his complete lack of attraction to Mike. Which couldn't have been the case. Maybe he'd simply been stressed by his first ride.

"And here we are," Mike said as they dismounted in front of the huge mall. He couldn't wait to be inside and enjoying the aircon.

Arden slid off the bike and was flushed when he took off the helmet, his hair creating a frizz of platinum around his head. Every time Mike looked at him, he found something new to consider cute. Which was kinda weird and confusing, because all jokes aside, he wasn't actually interested in fucking a *boy*.

"What?" Arden frowned and pushed back a strand of wavy hair that had slid out of the pink bun.

Mike's gaze was drawn to the slender shoulders. Just as he noticed the lacy trim on something Arden wore under his T-shirt, the scent of cookies baking at a shop nearby hit his nose, making him salivate. His focus got laser-sharp, and the longer he stared, the more obvious it became the undergarment was some kind of *bra*. Did that mean Arden had tits? Was Mike so drawn to him because he was not *entirely* a boy? It wasn't impossible that Arden was intersex, or something.

Mike wanted to sink his teeth into the smooth cream of his shoulder regardless. To pull on the strap and find out whether it carried any weight at all.

"Is that a bra?"

Arden pushed the strap back up and out of sight. Shame. "Don't know what you're talking about."

Mike frowned as they passed the revolving doors and entered the building, which greeted them with shiny floors and a thatch of fake bamboo surrounded by benches. "Hey, it happens all the time with underwear. Remember thongs and hipster jeans? *That* was a time to be alive. Do *you* wear thongs?" he asked, even though something at the back of his mind told him he shouldn't have.

Arden shrugged and entered the bright space under a glass roofing. "Weren't you supposed to buy me bubble tea?"

Did Arden understand that being given the cold shoulder was only spurring Mike on? Maybe he was doing it on purpose. It reminded Mike of that one time he got the hots for his chemistry teacher. She'd pretended to be angry with his constant flirting, but went on to ride his dick every weekend for three months as soon as he'd graduated.

"Are you always this eager to get to the main dish? Because I'm a guy who likes himself some foreplay," Mike mused and draped his arm over Arden's slender shoulders, with delicate bones he now wanted to suck dry. Was it Arden's girly smell that confused him?

Arden stiffened at first, but then looked up at Mike with those big blue eyes. How could a *man* be this pretty? "Are you not afraid of people staring?"

Mike went still, and for the blink of an eye it occurred to him that he did kinda care whether strangers saw him touching a girly boy. Which in turn spurred anger, because why would he be self-conscious about anything he did? He was a stud, who'd fuck anyone he wanted, not one of those pathetic cockroaches who didn't dare to be open with such things. He was Mike Heller, the unofficial Mr. Nevada—too good for bullshit like beauty contests—and if he wanted to fake-date a boy, he absolutely would, and anyone who had a problem with it could go fuck themselves!

So he held his head high and paraded down the corridor while the faceless figures of the other shoppers became the background to his day out. He used to love this place while in high school. Now? Not so much. They always played music he disliked, and the shops screamed at him with large banners advertising sales and new collections. But he wasn't here for his own amusement. He was here to prove Kane wrong.

"No. I don't care what anyone thinks."

"Your abs are awfully chiseled for someone who doesn't care. And your ink—" Arden stalled, looking for words. "Your tattoo artist did a very good job."

Mike stretched, his chest inflated with air. "Yeah. She's very, very good. Told me I was like a tropical bird among sparrows. Poetic, eh?"

Arden snorted. "Whaat? That's so cheesy. She just wanted a tip. And the lion?"

Mike shrugged. "Lions have multiple females and are the graceful kings of the savanna. Basically, I'm a biker lion. And with the way you dress, you don't seem to dislike attention either?"

"I'm used to it, I'm a graceful, unique butterfly. I want to live as my true self, not hide it so everyone else is comfortable."

A surprisingly stern answer from a boy who smelled like a flower and seemed so frail a strong gust of wind could topple him.

Mike liked it.

"What does it mean? What is your *true self?*" he asked, too entranced by the movement of Arden's lips to notice the stores they were passing. So maybe there was no sex at the end of the road they were taking, but this might still be one of the most interesting dates he'd been on.

"I'm a man, and I like that. I like all my *bits*, but since I also like lace and makeup, then I'm gonna enjoy it. I don't even care if it's attractive to others or not," Arden said, leading the way, because Mike had no idea where they could buy the bubble drink thing.

The way Arden lifted his chin proudly like a kid who'd gotten an A for their assignment made Mike snort. Too cute. And yet his brain munched on the words that stood out to him.

Lace. Bits.

Arden was gay, but nothing like Zolt or Leo. He wasn't hairy or butch or intent on proving his masculinity to anyone, and Mike couldn't help but wonder what he looked like naked. Was Arden shaved all over? He would find out about his legs at least once the boy wore shorts.

Mike was a mature guy, but still struggled keeping a wide grin at bay. He needed a different approach with this pretty flower. "How did you know you like that stuff? It's not typical for a guy."

Arden stole a longer glance at him from under impossibly dark eyelashes as he stopped at the end of the line by a small coffee stand that also boasted that they sold bubble tea in bold letters. Mike wouldn't admit it to his brothers, but his heart skipped a beat in response. Then again, this ritual of push and pull was familiar and always got him invested.

Everything inside him longed for an answer to his question, but Arden took his sweet time reading the menu and then ordering two drinks. He didn't even ask Mike what flavor he wanted, and that display of confidence was both funny and endearing.

They sat at a pink table. An outlaw biker with a big milky drink in hand and a guy who wore a bra under his T-shirt. Someone could've said they were mismatched but Mike didn't give two shits about someones.

"Got you the classic one, so you see what the big deal is," Arden said and crossed his long, slender legs, instantly drawing Mike's attention lower. But Mike was here on a mission, and he needed to focus.

"Are you dodging my question on purpose?"

Arden took a long slurp of his blue drink. "You know my sister actually. And yes, I'm going somewhere with this. Kaley?"

Mike stared. He was pretty sure he knew several Kaleys, but his mind didn't produce any meaningful information. "Yeah..." He closed his mouth on the straw and sucked. The beverage tasted like milky green tea. Sweet and tasty but nothing out of the ordinary until drinking became more laborious, and a squishy ball shot into his mouth through the wide straw. Confused, he bit on it only to discover it tasted of nothing, but the texture added novelty. It wasn't something Mike could see himself having often, but wasn't terrible either.

"My parents died very young, and we didn't have any other family around. Not close, anyway. But Kaley was already an adult, and she took care of me. She's an exotic dancer, and I spent a lot of time around her friends when I was younger. They let me play around with their makeup and were generally very open. They helped me find myself within that, never judged me, and I've been through some terrible fashion phases."

"Like... you stopped shaving your pits or somethin'?" Mike asked with a wide grin, his gaze drawn to the lush mouth pursed around the pink straw.

Arden kicked him under the table. "Dumbass. No, I wore these stupid-high stripper heels. Even got detention for it once when I had the not-so-smart idea to wear them to school."

Mike's imagination instantly produced the vision of Arden's slender legs in heels and he might have salivated a little into his drink.

"Not anymore?"

"Not since I broke my ankle."

Ouch.

"Oh right. Happened to one of my exes. She still wore them to bed though," Mike poked, gradually attaching his tentacles to Arden's pert flesh. The boy *would* admit to liking him within a matter of days.

But Arden glanced at his watch, as if the suggestion meant nothing to him. "And you'll never know if I do."

What. The. Fuck. Where did this stubbornness come from?

"So you wanted to be like strippers because...? You saw it attracted guys?"

He must have hit a nerve because Arden scowled and leaned back on the background of a fountain. "I don't know. Did you become a biker because it attracts girls?"

Mike had to bite back a smile. So Arden did consider him attractive.

"Among other things. Why, you expect me to deny it? That Smokey vest"—he grabbed the rim of his cut and showed Arden the patches—"and the bike between my thighs are more of an aphrodisiac than chocolates and flowers." He said and leaned in, placing his hand on Arden's knee.

Arden slapped it away and got up. "You're so shallow. Is that the only thing you care about in the world? Picking up girls and riding your bike? I know you're playing some game here, and I'm onto you."

Mike rolled his eyes behind Arden's back, grabbed his drink, and followed him. "Yeah? And what do *you* care about? Are you writing the next great American novel? Rescuing puppies? Volunteering at a homeless shelter?"

"I... had plans." He pouted and slurped.

Now that Mike knew about the lingerie, he couldn't ignore the shadows of the straps under Arden's T-shirt. Despite the boy's standoffish attitude, he still wanted to see more of his flesh. Wouldn't be the first mean girl he ended up dicking.

Only that Arden was male.

And there would be no dicking.

"What kind of plans? I hope they aren't as focused on your own pleasure as mine, because that would cost you that claim to self-righteousness," Mike said and put his arm back on Arden's shoulders. Most people would just assume Arden was a girl anyway.

And *score*. Arden didn't shrug him off this time.

"You're so pushy. I know this is one big joke to you. I could have developed my own makeup line, or become an Instagram celebrity, but no, I'm stuck with your lot."

Arden's little rant was silly, but Mike still enjoyed the way Arden's slender shoulders fit under his arm. None of his brothers needed to know he was having fun while he fought to win this bet.

Mike hummed. "Right, right. Makeup line and getting famous on your cuteness doesn't sound shallow at all," Mike said but gently squeezed the tip of Arden's nose with his fingers to show he wasn't being mean.

Mike would have watched Arden's Instagram if it involved lingerie shots. Just out of curiosity, of course.

Arden sighed, his eyelashes fluttering like butterfly wings. "Okay, so maybe it wouldn't be anything groundbreaking, but still more ambitious than getting laid."

Mike snorted. "I don't just 'get laid'. I make the girls happy. There's not enough true romantics left, you know," he said as they walked past the food court and into a corridor that featured numerous stands in the middle.

There it was, he managed to squeeze a little smile out of the ice prince. "Oh I bet. Your promises of undying love until the next one comes along must mean a lot."

Mike stilled, something in his brain jarring even when he made himself smile. "I don't fall in love. But when I'm with a girl, I make sure she feels special, because in that moment, she is," he said, and before Arden could have answered, Mike steered them to one of the stalls, which sold all kinds of fun accessories, from plastic jewelry to costumes. "Look at that," he said, pointing to a pair of fairy wings made of wire and thin fabric in pastel shades.

Arden threw away his empty cup. "What about them?"

Mike did not need to share his idea. He pulled them off the stand, handed the seller a ten dollar bill and presented the wings to Arden, whose big, glinting eyes were slowly getting consumed by their pupils.

There. The appreciation he so enjoyed working for.

"For you, little fae," Mike said with a wide smile.

"Are you calling me a fairy?"

Mike's brain halted, but only for half a second. "You said it yourself that you're a butterfly. I'm calling you an out-of-this-world cutie."

Arden took his sweet time chewing on that, but then turned around and reached his hand back so Mike could put the gift on him. He didn't even have to lie. The boy *was* a cutie. At least as much as a boy could be.

He had those slender shoulders, a narrow waist, and an ass of the perfect size for his body—shapely, with a bit of curve. From the back, Mike would have never taken him as a guy.

If Arden, or someone like him, wore lingerie that kept his genitals hidden, would fucking him still be gay?

Mike's brain pulsed with heat as he strapped the costume wings on the boy and rested his fingers just above the tempting hips, sensing the heat radiating through his clothes. When Arden looked up at him over his shoulder, a spark went down all the way to his dick. Maybe the bet hadn't been such a good idea after all?

"Thank you," Arden whispered, as if saying it any louder could have cracked their fragile connection.

"Mike? You're in Reno for the weekend?" A high-pitched female voice he immediately recognized made him swear under his breath. He'd been getting somewhere with Arden, damn it!

For a moment, his plan had been to take Arden by the hand and lose Miranda, but she was way too close, and it wasn't his style to openly ignore women.

He turned around and smiled, hoping to get rid of her soon. She was nice, but... well... underage. "Hello, darling. Yeah, we've come to do some shopping," he said, nodding toward Arden, because the suggestion that he was on a date should send her on her way sooner.

Her teenage entourage was there too, too shy to approach him the way Miranda did but happy to bask in the glow of their smooth-haired queen bee in tight jeans and a crop top. Mike would've given his pinkie that at least three of the Valentines he'd gotten this year had come from his high schooler groupies. He'd even had to warn his brothers to steer clear of them, because not all of them looked as young as they were.

Many dangers came from being as handsome as Mike.

Miranda tossed her long hair over her shoulder with a grin. "With your... cousin?"

There goes nothing.

Mike reached for Arden's hand and squeezed it, rubbing his thumb along his finger. "No, we're on a date. Hope you enjoy your day, girls."

This could be a good thing actually. He'd appear confident in front of Arden, and get rid of his little fan club in one go. Win-win!

"Wait. What?" Miranda asked, but Arden wouldn't let Mike have this little victory and slipped his fingers out of Mike's hand.

"I'll be late for my appointment," he muttered and rushed off.

At least that gave Mike an excuse to lose the jailbait. They'd now heard Arden's voice and surely suspected he was a boy, but with fifty bucks and Mike's pride at stake, he chose to follow Arden.

"Hey, where are you running off to, babe?"

The wings on Arden's back glistened and trembled with every step he took, and Mike couldn't help but chase the colorful butterfly.

"To the hair salon, remember?" Arden reached the door of a bright parlor, the kind where a male trim was fifty dollars, and glanced over his shoulder for only half a second. A little flush had bloomed on his features, but Mike couldn't read what it meant.

"You just left me there, in the clutches of thirsty teenagers," he said, adding an appropriate amount of drama to his voice.

"I thought you were all about pretty girls..." Arden muttered, waving at a stylist, who approached the entrance from the back of the parlor, but Mike would not share Arden's attention, so he took hold of the unusually smooth chin, and turned Arden's head, so their eyes would meet.

"I *am* with a pretty girl."

Arden didn't seem to breathe for a while. "Boy."

Mike nodded. "Pretty boy." The electricity was back in the air between them, and Mike loved the buzz of an impending conquest, even though he wasn't intending to consummate this one.

A clicking of shoes against the tiles made Arden break eye contact, but he didn't pull away.

The stylist whistled, walking through the automatic doors like a whirlwind of black silk. "If this is your new boyfriend, Arden, no wonder you haven't had the time to see me this month. Bet you stopped leaving the bed, let alone combed your hair."

"No! It's nothing like that," Arden said quickly, but didn't try to shed Mike's grip and stared back at him, like a doe that stopped in the headlights of an upcoming truck. He wouldn't know what hit him.

"This is our first date, actually," Mike said and took hold of Arden's shoulders, spinning him around so they both faced the well-built man in a black uniform worn by all the staff beyond the glass walls of the parlor.

"Why waste time on hair if you're gonna ruin it in two hours?" The stylist teased, and Mike was loving all this insight. So the boy was only *playing* hard to get.

Arden groaned. "It's nothing like it. I wouldn't do that. Don't encourage him, Seb."

"Why not? This guy's such a hunk. Don't recall you ever wasting time."

Arden stepped away from Mike and put his hand over the stylist's mouth. "Don't!"

This was too adorable.

"Maybe I should have gotten you the demon wings," Mike mused, gently tapping the accessory attached to Arden's back. Seb caught his gaze, and while Mike deduced he was gay too, not only due to the way he teased Arden, but also his mannerisms, he had a masculine appearance, with a short black beard and smooth hair styled in a fashionable undercut.

Clearly, Seb was more than ready to help his friend—or throw him under the bus, depending which way one looked at it—and grinned, using his height advantage to free his lips from Arden's hand. "Don't believe this coy act, dude. The boy's a trap!"

"I'm almost nineteen, thank you very much." Arden put his hands on his hips with a huff.

"*Now* you are." Seb snorted and glanced up at Mike with a wide grin. "If he's *really* changed his slutty ways, I'm free after work."

Mike stilled. He was an open-minded guy, but Seb was almost as tall as him, had muscular forearms, and a beard. It was a hard pass.

"No offense, but I'm more of a smooth skin and flower scent kind of guy," he said and stroked Arden's neck so gently the boy shivered beneath the touch. And because everyone was free in their mind, Mike imagined pushing his hands under the white T-shirt, all the way to the bra that held nothing.

He wasn't sure if Seb was telling the truth or teasing his friend, but hearing that the boy could possibly be no angel after all, opened up a new door in Mike's head. The room behind it overflowed with filth, and because no one would ever see what happened inside it, Mike allowed himself to imagine Arden sweaty, panting, and pulling his own jeans off just to get dicked by Mike faster. He'd be wearing panties, spreading himself open—

The real-life Arden's laugh was nervous, the glances thrown at Mike shy and fiery at once, and when he let Seb lead him inside, Mike was left with one burning question.

If no one knew he'd done it, would he fuck Arden?

Chapter 4 – Mike

Mike did pop into a nearby barber's where his looks had been cleaned up after the long journey, but he was back within half an hour, and Arden's hair wasn't even close to *done*. Many pretty girls swanned around the pristine space of the salon, but Mike couldn't help but focus on the narrow window between Arden's legs. The boy was having his head washed to get rid of fresh dye, and had no idea he was being ogled.

There was no denying it—Mike could see the outline of a dick in those tight pants, but for whatever reason, it didn't bother him. He could just about imagine walking up to that chair, standing on either side of Arden's lap, and pulling his head close by the damp hair. In his mind, he saw his dick entering Arden's mouth, lipstick stains on the shaft, and Arden choking on the cock as it went all the way in.

The fact that he *shouldn't* want Arden intensified those fantasies, because whenever Mike was barred from doing something, he always wanted it more. His mother had used that against him from early on. When he was a kid, she told him he could only have one piece of broccoli at dinner, and half a carrot. She'd told him vegetables were his special treats, which in turn encouraged Mike to steal them from the fridge instead of gorging on chocolate milk and marshmallows. Mom was a smart woman.

He grinned when Arden returned to the styling chair with a white towel wrapped tightly on his head. Damn, he was adorable. The boy had even painted his nails a soft pink shade that would complement the scratch marks they'd surely leave on Mike's back.

"You sure you're not up for a head massage?" Seb asked with a wide smile, choosing his tools.

Mike shrugged. "I'd take one from Arden."

Arden shook his head, and while Mike saw him rolling his eyes in the mirror, a small smile graced his lips. "I wasn't offering."

Mike raised his hands. "Okay, I'll take any other type of head."

He was expecting a groan, but Arden giggled. "In your dreams."

This was going *great*! And Seb must have thought so too, because he winked at Mike. Lured by the lack of pushback, Mike rose from the leather sofa and walked up to Arden, who dug his teeth into that full lip and watched him approach. Ah, it felt good to be watched like this, like a prized stallion about to mount the best mare in the stables.

"Do you want to hear about my dreams?"

Arden closed his eyes. "No."

But Seb grinned, pretending to make subtle changes to Arden's hair. "Tell *me*, and Arden can plug his ears."

Mike leaned against the counter in front of Arden, staring at the flush spreading over the pristine cheeks. God, they were like ripe peaches. And there was no one close enough to hear the obscenities about to leave Mike's lips.

"I thought you could eat cotton candy off my dick. You'd have to get through all that pink fluff first before getting your savory dessert," he said, shivering at the image in his head.

Arden burst out laughing, but kept his eyes closed. "That's revolting. Seb, please say he's scaring the other customers."

Seb shook his head. "Oh, no, it's all good. Do continue."

Good man.

Mike leaned forward, until he could smell the sweet shampoo on Arden. "I'll save it all up for you. There'll be so much juice in my balls you won't be able to swallow it all. Maybe I should come on your face instead?"

"You're not even gay. You're *bored*." Arden covered his face with his hands, but sadly for him, the gesture only made him cuter.

Mike could already see those pink fingers jerking him off as he took his time playing with Arden's tongue. It would never happen in real life, but in theory he would have loved for Arden to stick his pink tongue out and rock his tool along it, until he came down the boy's willing throat.

"I can be flexible," Mike said. "Mostly ride choppers now, but dirt bikes were my first love."

Seb patted Arden's shoulder. "See? The man's a keeper."

Arden smirked. "What if I'm a top? Are you flexible enough for that, Mike?"

Seb's whisper was hardly a whisper at all. "He's not a top."

"I assumed as much," Mike said, drilling his gaze into Arden, who squirmed in the chair while Seb worked some kind of foamy substance into his hair.

"Have you ever kissed a man?" Arden asked with a groan, but opened one eye. He was genuinely curious, and that pushed Mike's brain deeper down the rabbit hole. Because if he wanted to kiss a guy, he'd want to experiment with Arden. He seemed like the type who'd be nice and pliant in bed. A soft marshmallow Mike could twist and knead however he liked.

"Not yet."

"No kissing until I'm done," Seb laughed, but then added after a touch of hairspray. "I'm done."

He switched on the hairdryer, and its roar cut the conversation as efficiently as a motorcycle's engine always did.

He exhaled and returned to the waiting area, where he kept the fantasies alive until Arden's hair was done. Finally.

And didn't he look like the cutest little bunny. When Seb had pulled Arden's hair out of the buns, it turned out that Arden's hair was quite wild and curly, but after the treatment, not only was it brighter, with the color refreshed, but also perfectly straight. Two tiny buns sat on top of his head, but the rest of the hair reached below his shoulders, so soft Mike wanted to grab the strands and twist them around his hand.

"So what now, babe?" Mike asked, pulling out his wallet.

Arden stilled. "You don't have to..." he mumbled, but was most definitely watching Mike's reaction. Seeing him stand closer was worth the price of the visit. So the cash obtained from Kane upon winning the bet wouldn't cover what Mike was about to pay, but Mike was willing to invest in this new venture.

"Oh, a man should always pay for their date. Isn't that right, Seb?"

"Gets tricky in the gay world, but you'll get the hang of it, I'm sure." The man laughed, taking the money. "See you next month, Arden."

They walked out of the salon, Mike following the scent of Arden's pastel hair. It smelled so good Mike could've rubbed his face against it. While he laid on top of Arden and slowly fucked his tight ass. The fairy wings would come alive with sparkle as it happened and tremble in tune with the boy's moans. Mike just wasn't sure about the role of Arden's dick, but in his fantasy it didn't have to matter.

"Thank you," Arden said after several minutes of walking in silence, but his features, no matter how pretty, were once more an icy façade.

"Why the long face? You don't like how your hair's turned out? Mona gets like that sometimes," Mike said, stepping that bit closer as they walked along the corridor with no clear purpose. Should Mike offer to buy Arden dinner?

"No, I do. I feel really nice, I just..." He glared at Mike. "I know you're playing at something, and I don't like it. I'm just not sure if I'm your freak show for the afternoon, or if you're making fun of me."

Mike stopped and watched him for a few seconds. "I am not making fun of you. I don't have over a hundred dollars to burn on pranks," he said, and the voice at the back of his head once again asked, *If Arden offered you sex, would you say no?*

Nobody needed to know Mike's answer, and besides, wanting to experiment didn't make him any less of a man. Not when Arden resembled a girl to the point where he'd fooled Mike.

"So if you're for real, you need to know I don't do sex anymore. This won't go anywhere even though I'm very flattered."

Mike blinked, only to roar with laughter. "Oh, come on! You can do better than that. Nobody gets rid of me that easily." What did 'don't do sex' even mean? Especially that 'anymore' and the stylist's comments indicated Arden was most definitely up for dick in general.

Despite having just said no, Arden stepped closer and slipped his hand into Mike's, squeezing it hard. "Pretend you're my boyfriend," he whispered in a higher pitch, his eyes wide and frantic.

Okay. That was... weird, but Mike was eager to serve and pulled Arden close, burying his nose in the smooth hair that smelled of candy shampoo. His head spun from the intensity of the sweet aroma, and as he moved his lips along the slope of Arden's skull, he opened his mouth and nipped on the tip of his ear.

"In what capacity? You want a warm popsicle after all?" He said it because expressing whatever his horny brain wanted came naturally to him, but it wasn't just for kicks. He'd love to know what was going through Arden's mind.

"No, that's not the—"

"Arden. Lovely new hairdo," said a deep male voice.

Mike looked up and met the eyes of a man who'd dived so deep into Mike's personal space that his intrusion begged for a broken nose.

The guy was buff, almost as tall as Mike, and as heavily tattooed, but there was a darkness to his gaze and he had stitches going across his forehead and all the way into short blond hair. He looked like bad news, even though Mike had to admit to seeing a certain roguish charm in him.

"Who is this, baby boy?" Mike asked, ready to shove the stranger away, because Arden wouldn't have pushed so close to him if he wasn't worried.

"This is Luke. An old friend." Arden turned around with a tense smile, but his fingers gripped Mike's hand like a tiny vice.

The man spread his arms. "Just that, huh? I'd like to chat again sometime."

"Sorry, no can do. I'm busy with my new job, and boyfriend and stuff," Arden said quickly, on a single exhale. "Hope the head's healing well."

Mike stepped into his new role as if he'd been born to do this.

"A friend my ass! You're *not* meeting your ex behind my back. Haven't we talked about this?" Mike asked in a stern voice before facing Luke with a threatening smile, the kind that either pushed men into attacking him or running with their tails between their legs.

What kind of man would Luke be?

"I advise you to take a hike. Try contacting my boy, and I'll visit you when you're sleeping," Mike snarled.

Luke's jaw tensed and he squinted but didn't risk taking a step forward. "So that's how it is, Arden? Already found yourself a new dick to sit on?"

"Fuck you!" Arden spat, but it was like the peep of a mouse, and the way Arden sought protection in Mike woke a lion in him.

"What did you say to him?" Mike snarled and shoved Luke right out of the invisible circle that should not have been crossed by random strangers. "Treat the boy like the lady he is or shut your mouth."

He had no doubt Luke had stolen a glance at the front of his cut. Yes, fucker, think about your next step, or you'll have a whole biker club on your ass.

Luke was smart enough to raise his hands and step away. "It's not over, tramp!" But he rushed away as soon as he'd said that, and melted into the crowd, disappearing from sight.

Mike hadn't even noticed when he'd put his arm around Arden's shoulders, but the boy was glued to him like a baby chimpanzee.

Mike relaxed and stroked Arden's arm, guiding his stiff form to a nearby bench. Jesus. What the fuck was that guy's problem?

"Are you okay?" he asked as they sat under an artificial tree across from a shoe store.

Mike had thought he'd seen Arden's facade crack before with honest smiles, but it seemed he'd been just scratching the surface. Arden kept panting as if he were on the verge of a panic attack and rubbed his thumbs under his eyes in a bid not to mess up his mascara. "He's an ex who just won't disappear. I'm so stupid. I shouldn't have come here."

Mike exhaled, leaning against the wooden backrest as he watched people pass by with their shopping, his arm around Arden, in case the bastard came back. "If he won't give up, maybe I should talk to him more sternly. Where does he live?"

"No, no, no!" Arden took a few deep breaths, going pale. "Just... it will blow over. If he thinks a guy like you is with me, he'll fuck off. I think."

"You *think?*" Mike asked, raising his brows, but Arden's frantic, shallow breathing told a different story, making Mike itch to follow the bastard and deal with him the only way men like him deserved. "What did he do?"

"Drop it, okay? He just... wasn't a very good boyfriend. Will you pretend to be my new guy or not? It doesn't have to be all the time, just if he comes over."

If Arden didn't want the help, Mike wouldn't force him, but there was opportunity in this...

"I have one condition," Mike said, meeting Arden's gaze.

The boy stiffened against him. "I can pay you, but I'm *not* blowing you," he growled so loudly an elderly couple on a bench nearby ostentatiously got up and walked away.

Mike scowled, took his hands off Arden, and pulled away. "Jeez, what the hell is wrong with you? I never had to blackmail anyone into sucking my dick. If you ever get a piece of this delicious meat, it'll be because you can't help yourself!"

Arden stalled and took a deep breath. "Sorry. Then... what do you want?"

Mike was still offended, but that wouldn't keep him away from his goals. "I want you to tell everyone you're crushing on me. And that I'm a god in bed. Especially Kane."

Arden blinked, and his perfectly manicured brows lowered. "What? You want to prank your friends into thinking you're bi?"

It had only been about winning the bet, but Mike's mouth stretched into a wide smile. "Yes. I didn't know I wanted to do *that*, but now I do. Let's do it," he said and grabbed Arden's wrist, lifting his hand for a loud high-five. "Yeah! Can't wait to see their faces! But first, you have to admit I'm your type. Go on. I've seen your ex. No need to be coy."

Mike was *buzzing*. This would be hilarious.

Arden groaned, holding on to Mike's hand after the high-five. "Okay, you're my type. *So* my type. Hot, hunky biker with a dirty mind. I wanna spread my legs, like, yesterday." He fanned himself sarcastically, and rolled his eyes but the act was good enough for Mike.

"Sounds great, just less theatrically next time for my family."

Chapter 5 – Arden

Arden held on tightly to Mike, but even the scent of his cologne and the touch of his muscular body weren't enough to make the ride pleasant. He wasn't sure whether he was that glad he *hadn't* killed Luke, because while this meant police weren't searching for him after all, he'd gained another massive target on his back.

And Luke would not give up. He never did.

Arden remembered the blood trickling out from the wound so vividly. Dark red against a beige carpet.

He'd never hit someone the way he had that night and could still feel the impact of the lamp hitting Luke's head as a phantom tremble in his arm. He hadn't intended to kill Luke, just to defend himself, but because he was as physically weak as Luke was strong, it had been a fight for his life.

But Mike was nothing like him. He had the strength of a bull and the confidence of a lion protecting his lionesses from invading males. With Mike at his side, Arden didn't have to fear Luke.

Relief softened his muscles as they drove past the sign at the outskirts of Hawk Springs. All of a sudden, the town wasn't a shithole but an oasis of safety and tranquility. This was MC territory, and even a hothead like Luke wouldn't be stupid enough to approach Arden here. He'd moved into the clubhouse two weeks ago, but the quiet streets constantly swept with dust had become his new normal, and today's visit to Reno proved he shouldn't have been so eager to return to old habits.

Many of the inhabitants commuted to work, which made the town seem eerily empty during the day, and the sparse gardens with gravel and cacti rather than the lush greenery that required a lot of watering in the Nevada sun only reinforced the sense that nobody was home. But the closer they were to the MC compound, the more signs of life Arden saw. Two girls in yoga pants on a walk back from the gym owned by Mike's mother. Men arguing over coffee they'd gotten at the gas station where Arden worked.

So maybe the Hellers weren't exactly law-abiding citizens—which was exactly why Kaley had suggested Arden ask them for asylum—but they were at the heart of their community and seemed well-liked in town. They kept this place safe, and therefore Arden should also feel at ease, no matter what happened at the mall.

He was still glad to pass the open gates of the compound and rubbed his face against Mike's back as they drove into the vacant parking spot at the side of the yard.

It was already getting dark, but the lamps attached to the walls provided enough light to showcase all the people gathered for the evening. A man drove his repaired car out of the garage just as Arden dismounted, and Leo waved him off, stretching in his stained overalls after a whole day's work. Rain and Mona were there too, seated on plastic chairs alongside Jack and his wife, Trixie, while all their children miraculously slept in their pushchairs.

People gathered by the unofficial bar to get some beers in, flirted, chatted. It was the kind of normalcy Arden longed to have, but couldn't because of Luke.

He flinched when a tall shape appeared in the corner of his eye, but before he could have rushed behind Mike's back, Axel's expressionless face reassured him that he was not under attack.

Out of all the Hellers, he unnerved Arden most. Kurt, Mike's uncle, and his son Kane were by far the most homophobic and offensive, but Axel? Arden read somewhere bears were difficult animals to work with, because they seldom warned of their intentions before attacking. Axel was a bit like that. Not that Arden had ever seen him attack anyone, but something about his attitude and the cold, expressionless silence he practiced spoke of danger. Arden couldn't shake the sense that if any of the Hellers were to hurt him out of the blue, it would be this one.

Nothing about Axel stood out. He had short dark hair, tanned skin, and eyes that were the definition of muddy brown. His face was flat, with small lips, and while not ugly, it had features Arden found hard to remember.

He didn't know what Axel's opinions were, because he kept them to himself. That stern, oval face barely ever moved a muscle, whether Axel watched pretty girls stripping or lost at cards, which kept Arden on edge whenever he was around. And now, the lizard man's eyes swept over Arden, stopping at his face for a split second too long. He was like a stereotypical serial killer—average-looking enough to melt with the crowd yet odd in his behavior.

He spoke to Mike without otherwise acknowledging Arden.

"We got an anonymous call. The man claimed he saw you and Arden behave like lovebirds. Said he wanted us to know one of ours was 'soiling the nest'," he said and shook his head. "Not my business, but you should know you have an enemy," Axel said in a monotone voice.

"Luke. That stupid fuck." Mike groaned and put his arm over Arden's shoulders as if it was the most natural thing in the world.

Axel frowned, his face gaining the tiniest bit of an expression for once. God, if Arden were to describe this guy to anyone, he wouldn't have a clue where to start. Which would have made Axel the perfect assassin... something Arden should not be thinking about at all.

"Luke?"

Mike pulled Arden closer, forcing his nose against the T-shirt his handsome protector had been wearing all day. It smelled of wood, earthy yet somehow sharp. Arden shut his eyes and stopped breathing, but he didn't feel like pulling away either so he ended up relaxing into the hug while Mike went on. If they were to be fake boyfriends, he might as well enjoy it without Mike having to know.

"Arden's ex. He accosted us at the mall. Told him to keep his dirty hands away from my boy, and the coward was too scared to confront me then and there. Seems like he chose to snitch on me instead. What a little bitch."

Arden couldn't see Axel, but felt the lizard gaze burning into the back of his skull.

"Your boy," Axel said flatly, even though it was a question.

Mike pressed a loud kiss to the top of Arden's head. "Sure is. Look at him. What man wouldn't want to tap that?"

"This one here," Axel said, though there was no judgment in his voice.

Arden slipped his hands into the back pockets of Mike's jeans. Maybe they could just stay like this and not have to face anyone else? Arden closed his eyes with a sigh. He wasn't obsessed with nice butts, but he loved all of the male form, and getting that bit closer to knowing Mike's filled his head with fumes of filth.

"Because you haven't smelled his hair yet." Mike chuckled, stroking Arden's back in a way that made him melt.

Axel's silence extended. "Dad is not happy," he said in the end, and by the sound of footsteps in the gravel, Arden gathered he'd walked off.

"You heard that? What a coward," Mike said, rubbing his hands up and down Arden's back.

Someone whistled. "Get a room, you two!" Jeff, the youngest of the Heller siblings. Of course he found it hilarious that his older brother made a display of hugging another man.

"I'll get a room when I want to get my sausage deep in there, Jeff," Mike called back, with a smile to his voice.

Arden should've been offended. He also should've been uninterested in sex after what Luke had done, but there was no denying that even the most stupidly vulgar mention of sex with Mike ignited sparks he didn't know he still had deep down. Arden had the brains not to act on impulse though. He'd learned his lesson, but since being Mike's boyfriend for laughs was his ticket to safety, he gave himself leeway to play around.

So he kissed Mike between the collar bones, savoring his masculine scent.

But regardless of the narrative Arden was spinning in his own head, it wasn't for show, because no one would notice a gesture so minor without standing close. He pulled away from the tight embrace when he realized that much but was already missing the feel of Mike's ass against his hands when he came face to face with a family that would hopefully not be out for his blood. After all, Zolt and Leo were a couple—both MC members. And Rain was part of it too. A *woman*. The club was progressive enough, but while Leo and Rain were family, Arden was an outsider leading their brother astray. He couldn't count on the same rules applying to him.

Jeff cocked his head, furiously typing on his phone, but it was Leo's gaze that Arden ended up catching in the crowd. Was the frown an expression of harsh judgment?

"You guys want to ask me somethin'?" Mike asked in the end, but he kept Arden close, standing straight, as if he were anticipating a medal on his chest.

"Yeah, I want to ask you to stop making fun of Arden. I think he's got enough on his plate," Leo said, stepping closer to Rain, who left Mona with the twins and came over with hands stuffed deep down her jean pockets.

Arden felt like a shit for lying to her after she took him under his wing and convinced the club president to let Arden stay, but the agreement with Mike was still standing. "N-no, it's okay, we... it's all so sudden." Saying this nonsense to her face stressed him out so much he had to take a deep breath to decompress.

Leo spread his arms, but it was clear his expression of annoyance was meant for Mike. "Is this some extremely convoluted way to get attention from girls?"

Mike took a deep breath, and Arden fought to keep his eyes open, because the crowd of people gathering around them was becoming too much after the shocking interaction with Luke.

"Seriously, Leo? I thought you of all people would understand!" Mike roared, pointing at Leo's chest so abruptly the poor guy took a step away, blinking.

One of the children cried, awoken by the commotion, and Mona scowled at them, starting to gather her things.

"Arden, you don't have to put up with Mike's shit no matter what he told you," Leo said, intent on not letting this go, and as if that wasn't bad enough, Arden spotted Kane's fiery red head at the edge of the courtyard.

Arden took a few seconds to compose himself, but found his voice at last and slipped his hand into Mike's. "It's true though. Mike is exactly my type. I couldn't help myself around him." He looked up at Mike's handsome face, taking in the cocky grin, the blue eyes, and the blond beard... There's never been a truer lie. If Mike really wanted Arden, he'd eventually break Arden's defences with his dirty mouth and confident touch.

It would be inevitable, no matter what Arden thought about it. Which was why he needed to find a solution to the issue with Luke fast.

"Trixie, would you drive Mona home? I'll be back later," Jack told his old lady and rolled out of the plastic chair, heading in their direction like a bald tank with muscles so big they strained the front of his T-shirt. Where Axel was the silent assassin at the Smoke Valley court, Jack was the king-to-be, despite several members being older. He just had that air of authority about him, and Arden hadn't seen anyone questioning his decisions.

The female hangarounds jumped apart to avoid accidental trampling, and the men stood still, once Jack faced Mike. With his thick neck stiff and hands balled into fists, he looked like a bull about to charge, but despite the unease hanging in the air, Arden felt perfectly safe in Mike's arms.

His fake boyfriend didn't even flinch.

"Hey, Jack. You know my boyfriend, Arden, right?" Mike asked in a casual tone that seemed to keep everyone on edge. Over a dozen people gathered around them now, and while Arden appreciated being noticed, he'd have preferred it happened for different reasons.

Jack poked at Mike's chest with his finger. "You are so full of shit. I don't know why you're doing this, but I will find out." He stalled, and then poked Mike several times more. "Wait. It's because of that Harlyn girl, isn't it? You think the Jarens will hear the rumor that you're gay and leave you alone? It won't be that easy, Mike, but you can find out on your own. I'll just watch the performance and laugh my ass off."

Jack must have hit the right note, because Arden noticed several people nod and relax, as if that explanation put them at ease. An elaborate scheme of this sort was far more acceptable to them than Mike actually wanting to be with a man. Which told him *everything* about Mike's love life.

"Dad will still want to have a word with you," Rain said without anger. She watched them as if she were trying to figure out the truth, cautious despite the lack of trust in Mike's story. Arden felt like such a shit about this stunt.

"Oh no, you think he'll ground me?" Mike asked, pulling Arden along toward her.

As some of the people went back to their beers, satisfied with the reasonable conclusion to Mike's relationship status, Kane got in their face out of nowhere, his shoulders squared as if he were ready to throw punches. Arden expected Kane to bark at Mike, but the guy's crazy eyes focused on him.

"You can tell me if he's put you up to this."

Arden wouldn't have trusted Kane enough to tell him that he snoozed on the job the other day, let alone confide in him. "Wow. Can no one see how happy I am?"

Kane's pale green eyes were like those of a wolf, and Arden half-expected teeth on his throat before Mike pushed his cousin back. "Easy. You're scaring him."

Kane pulled his large front teeth over his lip, but his entire face remained scrunched, the red hair like warning coloration. Whatever was at stake here, he was ready to fight for it.

"I do not believe this shit. You've been gone what, four hours? Five?" he roared, and the flush on his face descended down his chest, making his circus-themed tattoos even redder.

"More than enough when you have game," Mike said smugly.

Arden laughed and playfully swatted Mike's arm. "Stop it! They'll think I'm easy." It was so strange, but he found peace in these lies. It was as if he could be himself again under a disguise. Because before Luke, he *had been* easy. He *had been* a lot of fun. And he'd liked to flirt, talk dirty, and be that little bit in everyone's face.

Mike grabbed Arden's chin. His fingers were rough to the touch but gentle, and when Arden met the blue gaze, the roguish grin, the softness in his knees was inevitable. This guy was too hot for Arden's good.

"You're only easy because I'm irresistible," Mike said and leaned in, making Arden freeze while his insides melted in anticipation of a kiss. Their noses met, then their foreheads, and Mike shut his eyes, rubbing his face against Arden's, as if he really were in love and longing for tenderness.

The fake sound of puking coming from Kane didn't matter. In fact, it spurred Arden to let go, and be that bit more like his past self, in the safety of Mike's lack of real interest. "That much is true. Can't keep my hands off you." He slid his hands to Mike's sides. He was so firm. Like Arden loved a man to be.

Kane raised his hands in defeat and walked off. "I'll be talking to you later, Mike!"

"Aaand he's gone," Mike whispered, but just as Arden thought the hot cake would slip out of his hands, Mike's own palms landed on Arden's buttocks and gave them a squeeze. "You're costing me my reputation, boy."

Arden had been jumpy since the incident with Luke, yet there was nothing frightening about Mike's touch. And that made his insides spark with light. Maybe Luke hadn't taken everything from him. Maybe there was a way out of the hole he'd been so brutally thrown into?

This was a big joke, but maybe there could be someone else for Arden one day.

He grinned at Mike, giddy that the physical closeness didn't bother him. "I promise it's gonna be worth your while."

"I'm sure, but I think I need some tips from a pro," Mike said and led Arden away from the bike, toward Leo, who rolled his eyes, pretending he didn't see them.

No such luck.

"Hey, Bro! I have so many questions," Mike said in a cheeky tone, chasing Leo, who sped up, running off to the entrance across from the garage, where he and the other mechanics changed and washed after work.

"I don't have time for your unfunny jokes. Zolt's coming, and I don't want to smell."

Mike's laughter came from deep within his chest. "Right, you need to be pretty for your husband."

"Oh, shut it, Mike," Leo snapped, pushing through the door, but Mike refused to take the hint and followed him inside.

The room was rather small and had only one window covered with broken shutters. Boxes and unused furniture filled the interior while bags of trash cluttered the floor around a sofa that had seen better days. A tall fridge had been decorated with posters of topless women, and the whole space looked like the basement of an unsupervised frat house, with an ugly open bathroom in the back.

"No, this is really urgent," Mike said, cuddling Arden from behind as if he were a giant plushie. "I need to know how to make my boy happy. Tips on giving head, Leo. At least three."

Leo stilled, but his glare could kill. "You got enough blowjobs in your life to have an idea."

Mike slid his hand into the back pocket of Arden's jeans, gently rubbing him through the denim, even though Leo could not see that. What kind of game was he really playing? Was it all just to feed his ego?

"Come on, Leo! Don't leave me with this. You know well enough that it's different to give than receive," Mike fake-complained.

Arden bit his lip with a smile. "Ignore him, Leo. I'll teach him all he needs to know."

Leo shook his head. "Better test that horny dog for STDs."

Mike's face fell. Leo had definitely hit a nerve there. "Hey, I always use condoms!"

"Then go suck on some rubber, and stop pestering me!"

Arden ran his fingers over Mike's tattooed arm. "Let's leave him to it, Mike. It's been a long day."

Mike took a deep breath, as if he were trying to calm himself, and tugged on his beard, glancing Arden's way. "Do you groom down there? Because your forearms are real smooth."

Arden's cheeks went aflame, but the teasing brought out the naughtiness in him. "You'll just have to find out."

"Cause Zolt doesn't, does he, Leo?"

Leo squinted at him, and Arden knew the guy reached his boiling point before he opened his mouth. "He doesn't, *Mike*. Zolt is a big, bad, hairy motherfucker, with a dick that just rams at the back of the throat. So I can't give you tips on how to fuck a boy that smells like a flower."

Ouch.

Mike hummed and squeezed Arden's buttock, making flesh hot with his touch. "I thought as much. So you're the one receiving it?"

Leo shook his head and grabbed a towel. "Mike. Grow up." He looked at Arden. "I can see the appeal. His mental age is the same as yours."

Arden cleared his throat, embarrassed by Mike's behavior, even if they were only *fake* boyfriends. "Mike… I'll be going."

Mike snorted and slapped Arden's ass, leaving behind a pleasant burn. "Let's take your stuff. You're moving in with me."

Leo took the opportunity to flee into the shower, leaving Arden alone on the battlefield. "Um… Huh?"

Mike stepped back and opened the door, gesturing for Arden to step outside first. "Good pranks need to be believable. Plus, I don't want you sleeping on your own," Mike added, though whether he was being honest or trying to scare Arden into doing what he wanted was anyone's guess.

Arden chose to believe Mike was being overprotective. But living together was a dangerous line to cross. From now on, he'd have to stew in his own arousal while on Mike's territory. Surrounded by Mike's scent. Possibly seeing Mike naked?

"Thanks," he said in the end, because that was the truth. Mike could have left him on his own back at the mall, yet he was willing to stick out his neck. Was it possible Mike was one of the good guys? Luke had also been a 'good guy'. Until he wasn't.

The small evening party must have already started, because music was on as they left the sad changing area of the mechanics, but they'd barely made it out the door when Mike leaned in, slid his hands to Arden's waist and knees, and lifted him up.

The move was so unexpected, Arden yelped and wrapped his arms around Mike's neck. His heart fluttered at the ease with which Mike held him. Kaley was right. Mike was a charmer and dangerous to anyone's chastity.

But Arden laughed for the sake of all the onlookers who remained figures on the outskirts of his vision. "They think you're mad," he whispered.

Mike grinned and bounced him in his arms, provoking another yelp. It was very clear he had no issue whatsoever carrying another person's weight, and that aroused Arden more than it should have. "Let's prove to them I'm crazy about you," he said, walking past friends and family, who gawked, confused how to react to this development.

Arden played along and pressed his face into the crook of Mike's neck. But he wouldn't lick the skin. He would not.

"Do you always take things so far?"

"You think *this* is taking things far?" Mike whispered before approaching the entrance to the main building. "Coming through. Jeff, open the door for my sweet boy," he called out, and passed inside the bar without thanking his younger brother.

The walls had recently been painted blood red, and the black furniture completed the look of a cheap strip joint. A girl in skimpy clothes danced by one of the poles, but it was the middle of the week, so there weren't that many people to watch her.

The interior smelled of beer and cigarettes, but the music here was louder, making uncomfortable questions harder to discern. An older biker playing pool with a woman in a leather mini skirt stared at them with a scowl, but Mike's smile only grew wider.

"Hands to yourself, Jag! I see you ogling my piece of sweet ass. Go find your own dick to suck," Mike yelled, and Arden couldn't help bursting with laughter.

And maybe he did lick Mike's neck, but just a little.

"Go fuck yourself, Mike!" Jag called after him, but didn't try to follow them and just pulled his chick closer, as if he needed to cleanse his palate after witnessing *gay stuff*. He had it tough, considering there already were two gay couples around.

"Fuck the holes in the pool table, Jag," Mike said and entered the staircase, leaving behind all the noise.

"Am I not getting too heavy?" Arden asked as Mike climbed up the creaking stairs barely breaking a sweat. He knew what the answer would be, yet still craved to hear it.

Mike smiled at him, so youthful it was hard to believe he was the second-oldest Heller sibling. Sand-colored hair hung around his face in shiny strands, the perfect frame for someone with so much roguish charm.

"Baby boy, this is nothing. You weigh less than a bird," he said, though there was a bit of tension to his voice now.

It was nice to know that despite all this being a stunt, Mike wanted to impress Arden. Maybe if Arden teased his ego enough, Mike would actually go for something more—

No.

No, Arden.

You are done with bad boys covered in tattoos.

"It's 'cause I live on milkshakes." He let the innuendo spark between them, a low-hanging fruit for Mike to pick.

The sky-blue eyes darkened, and Mike sped up, breathing more laboriously now that they were nearing the first floor. "Really? I bet you like reusable straws. What's your favorite kind? Salty?"

The hallway upstairs was nothing special. It had a faded carpet and stains on walls decorated with motorcycle posters no one had bothered to frame, and the air smelled of air freshener ineffectively masking the smell of someone's piss. So it was a bit of a dump, but Arden would be safe here.

Did Mike forget that he didn't have to act anymore, or did he not care?

"Haven't had a salty one in a while." There. He could pretend he forgot what this was about as well. He'd never kissed a man with a full beard, because Luke was adamant facial hair was full of germs, but Mike's smelled so good after the barber treated it with oil. His cologne was in the mix too, even if the choking aroma of cigarette smoke snaked its way back as well, making Arden's smile fall a bit.

Mike made a sudden turn, and Arden yelped when his body got sandwiched between Mike's chest and the wall, and the blond hair swept across his cheek. "Maybe I could treat you?"

Arden snorted. "You know no one's looking, right? You can stop." Yet he couldn't take his eyes off Mike's. This was a disaster in the making, and it would end in tears. His tears.

Mike hummed but wouldn't blink, as if he were hypnotized by Arden's own gaze, so close it felt like their bodies were about to merge. "Yeah. So?"

"So you can put me down now." Why was Arden whispering? His chest was constricting all too fast. He absolutely needed to shift his attention to 'nice' men, or he'd be doomed to repeat the same mistakes he'd made with Luke.

Mike's laughter was quiet, soft, yet rough as if there were wood chips in his throat. "What if I don't want to let go of you?"

Then we might as well fuck against this wall and get that over with.

"Then maybe you're gay after all," Arden teased, hoping it would wake up this straight guy to the reality of what he was doing.

Mike exhaled, his eyelashes fluttered, but just as Arden thought he'd won, the strong, muscular biker shifted, dropping one of Arden's legs, only to press him to the wall this time and pushing his hips between Arden's thighs.

Arden's shock was so great he couldn't catch enough air to speak as Mike leaned in, bringing with him the scent of wood and cigarettes.

"This doesn't feel gay to me."

Arden groaned, desperately thinking un-sexy thoughts. Stacking cans of chicken soup in the shop. Lemon-flavored chewing gum. Steak and beans.

He met Mike's gaze. "It will when I get a boner." He needed to be real here. It was a question of when not if. And yet, despite the words coming out of his mouth, he still trailed his fingers over Mike's shoulder.

Mike blinked, swallowed, and then leaned in closer.

For a moment, Arden's body filled with heat. He opened his mouth, breathed in but—

Oh, hell no! If they kissed, Arden might as well pull his pants down, because he had no doubt Mike was a good kisser.

He pushed at the firm chest away so abruptly, Mike let go of Arden's other leg, leaving him off-balance for a second. He extended his arms, keeping Mike at distance even though the hot biker was now the personification of 'horny'.

"I was trying to give you the benefit of the doubt, but you just don't get the hint, do you?" Harsh, but necessary. "No kissing. Even around other people. A— You stink of cigarettes. B—You're straight. C—I don't want to!"

Mike stalled, then lowered Arden to the floor and took a step away. "Why wouldn't you just say so?" he asked, somewhat flushed as he pulled on a strand of hair and smelled it.

"Because sometimes saying things clearly earns you a slap, and I'm not in a position to take the fallout of a bruised ego." Arden leaned against the wall with clenched fists. 'Just say'. He'd been clear enough with Luke, and it had done *nothing*.

"I *can* stop smoking," Mike said, and when Arden's gaze briefly darted lower, he couldn't avoid noticing that Mike's package had grown. He wanted to see that dick so badly his salivary glands swelled.

And yet he couldn't fucking believe Mike's words. This guy just didn't give up. "Then stop smoking, so we can move on to discuss point B."

Mike grumbled like a kid who hadn't gotten his favorite toy. "Fine. Jeez. You flirted back," he said and led the way only two doors down the hallway. Still disgruntled, he unlocked the door, but instead of stepping in like a normal person, he gestured at Arden to enter first.

Right. Because he was such a gentleman, and Arden was a 'lady'. It would have been funny if it wasn't so tragic, but as soon as Arden walked inside, it became obvious living with Mike would be an enormous step up from a mattress on the floor and using a duffel bag for a wardrobe.

The walls were gray, with the exception of the one behind the massive bed, which had been painted a stark black that served as background to a white mural depicting a motorcycle rider speeding upside down inside the globe of death. A two-seater stood with its back to the bed's footboard, facing an iron coffee table and an entertainment center with a flat screen TV and speakers. The storage furniture was made of metal as well, in a simple, industrial style, and posters depicting motorbikes and cars served as decoration.

Arden was kind of impressed that there wasn't a single porny picture in sight, but maybe by thirty-seven, Mike had learned that those wouldn't impress the women he brought here. No. Actually, one obscene thing was there. It was an ashtray out of all things, acid green and featuring a couple of aliens—one of which had makeup and huge boobs and the other, a huge dick—*in flagrante*. Mike grabbed it before Arden could have said something and tossed the thing into trash.

"An unwanted gift," he said curtly and approached the window.

A half-open door led to a bathroom which Arden eyed with longing after having to wash in the grimy communal shower downstairs. The room carried Mike's scent, but it wasn't choking like some cologne-drenched spaces. And while smoke was present in the air, it was an afterthought, as if Mike only ever gave into his nicotine craving by the open window.

"Give me the key, I'll collect your stuff," Mike said, and for a second Arden worried Mike might have a peek into his sketchbook, but it had a lock, and he never left it out in the open anyway, so he handed over the key to the guest room he'd occupied until now.

He'd appreciate the moment alone to snoop.

Mike smirked, stealing a touch of Arden's hand as he took it from him. "Be right back. Shall I get the mattress?"

Unbelievable.

Arden squinted. "Yes, get the mattress. Unless you're worried that would cast a shadow of doubt on our *relationship*, then a blanket and pillow will do."

Mike rolled his eyes. "I won't let you sleep on the floor. You're so thin you'd get bruises all over," he said and mercifully took his sexy self outside.

Arden groaned and his shoulders sagged the moment he was alone and didn't need to keep up the illusion of confidence. Couldn't Mike have been meaner? It would have been so much easier to hate him then. But there was no time to waste, so Arden checked out the bathroom, which was clean and spacious with a large bathtub designed to fit two people. It would be heaven to take bubble baths in.

He went for the wardrobe next, but as soon as he opened it, his gaze was drawn to a denim vest hanging on the inside of the door. It didn't deserve much attention at first glance, but it was small, most definitely not Mike's size, so he picked it off the hanger to have a closer look, confident some girl must have left it to mark her territory.

Confusion sank its teeth into his flesh when he saw its back. Instead of the club name, the top rocker stated *Property of* and the bottom one *Mad Mike.*

Arden's head buzzed, but he put the vest away. Maybe he shouldn't have snooped after all.

Chapter 6 – Mike

Mike stared at the plastic shelving unit he'd put in the corner so Arden didn't have to live out of a suitcase.

A week had passed since the boy moved in with him, and somehow listening to Arden's unmistakably male voice hadn't dampened Mike's confused attraction to him. In fact, the forbidden fruit smelled sweeter every day. Mike just had to work out whether Arden was the broccoli that only drew him in because it wasn't allowed, or candy from abroad that tasted as nice as the stuff he'd treated himself to all his life.

Challenge was the sweetest aphrodisiac for him, but having Arden sleep there, wash his slender body in Mike's shower, and reject him despite there being obvious chemistry, was slowly pushing him down the road of madness. And the fact that Mike had ditched the cigarettes in an effort to smell nice for Arden didn't make the situation any better, because he didn't know what to do with his hands at times.

He took a step closer to the shelves and looked down at the mattress covered with a lavender-hued blanket Arden had borrowed from Mona. The sheets smelled like Arden's skin did—of jasmine and tea, but if he kneeled to rub his face against the pillow again, he might as well roll into the fluffy pillows that occupied his otherwise masculine room.

But the lowest drawer of the unit? He hadn't seen what it contained yet, but the semi-transparent plastic revealed whatever was in there had *straps*.

A drop of sweat rolled down Mike's back, because he shouldn't invade his guest's privacy, but Arden was still showering, and having a peek at his stuff might prompt Mike to stop thinking about warm water all over the boy's smooth skin.

Because yes, Arden *was* smooth. Mike hadn't seen him naked, but he'd seen enough to know Arden shaved his legs and pits.

Opening the drawer, he felt like a teen again, spying on Jack's first girlfriend, but instead of the simple thongs he'd found back then, Arden's stash was all lace, in a variety of colors. Mike pulled on the first bit of fabric stuffed tightly into the small drawer to reveal a pair of black lace boxers. Heat flooded his head when he realized there was extra space at the front, while the back had a corset lacing that would have showed off half of Arden's ass.

Mike so desperately wanted to see the boy wearing those. He liked nice underwear on women, but the same items would be so *illicit* when worn by Arden. It's been a week since that one time the bra strap had slipped down Arden's arm, and he still hadn't gotten over it.

But there was more to see in the drawer: stockings and even flat bras of thin fabric that would have covered Arden's nipples without the need for holding anything up. His mind did the rest and put Arden in the corset lying at the bottom of the drawer. Brain synapses fried in Mike's head when the imaginary boy bent over, placing his hands on the bed and tempted Mike with the sway of his hips.

And his balls? They were right there, tucked under lace south of the tempting buttocks.

Mike froze when the door behind him opened, and he frantically shut the drawer, the imaginary Arden who kept trying to pull him into sex ripped to shreds by the appearance of his real-life equivalent.

Only then did Mike realize he was still *holding* a pair of lilac panties.

Arden was wrapped in a towel up to his chest, hiding his nipples from view, which made Mike want to see them all the more. "What the hell are you doing?" he yelled and charged at Mike, one hand holding the towel, the other extended like a claw.

Mike shot up and, without having planned it, raised his hand high, taking the piece of underwear far beyond Arden's reach. "Hey there, pretty thing! How was your shower?" he asked without acknowledging that he'd totally been snooping.

"How do you think? It was wet." Arden took the bait, jumping up to reach the stolen item, which was futile and so cute Mike surprise-tickled him under the armpit.

He was so, so smooth there.

"I always imagine water-hands touching me when I'm showering," Mike said, getting weirdly breathless when Arden's flat chest rubbed against his side.

"No you don't! You just smother yourself in that weird-ass sexy rosemary soap your mom made!" He squealed at another tickle and the towel fell just enough to reveal one pink nipple. That glimpse was enough to get Mike's dick to stiffen.

"Are you saying I smell sexy, baby?" Mike teased, leaning in. He had not smoked a single cigarette in the week since Arden had moved in, and wouldn't budge even when the others offered. Would the boy pull away again?

"What? No! That's not what I—" Arden noticed the towel had slipped, and stopped jumping to readjust the covering. Sadly, in doing so, he also took his lips out of Mike's range. "Just give those back." Arden's expression stiffened into a scowl, but it somehow only made him cuter. His face had those soft oval lines, and while the makeup he wore on a daily basis added to the illusion of femininity, Arden's face looked *boyish* without it, and Mike couldn't ignore the fact that this particular *boy* was a stunning person.

"How about an exchange?"

Arden squinted. "What do you want?"

Mike licked his lips, staring at the plump mouth below. "I want you to put them on."

Arden cocked his head. "Fine."

Mike's heart rattled like crazy, but it had to be simply because Arden kept giving him such hard rejections, so any scrap of 'yes' felt like victory. Nothing else made sense. He handed over the bit of lace and watched the boy step back.

The thin panties slipped up the smooth, long legs and disappeared under the towel which Arden so desperately clutched around him as he worked the lacy underwear on with one hand. And just as Mike started revving for a reveal, Arden raised his eyebrows with a smirk.

"There. They're on."

"That's cheating!"

Mike would have stepped closer, tried to tickle Arden out of the towel, but Dad chose that moment to knock on the door. Only he announced his presence by banging on the wood with his entire hand.

Mike exhaled, keeping Arden's gaze. "We're not done here," he whispered, but then called out, "What is it?"

"Rain needs your help at the garage. Leo's off today, and she won't text you 'cause she's too stubborn."

Mike glanced at Arden, then at the door, which he reached in a few steps. "Why would she not text me?" he asked, pulling on the handle.

Dad leaned against the doorframe but his gaze still drifted over Mike's shoulder. "What do you mean 'why'? Because she always thinks she can handle everything herself. How's your *boyfriend*?" he asked in a mocking tone that clarified he saw through Mike's bullshit.

Facing Dad felt weird sometimes. Their features were so alike that watching him was almost like getting a glimpse into his own future. Mike had seen pictures from Dad's youth, and they were like mirror images of him, even though Dad used to wear his hair short. It was comforting to know that since they shared so many physical traits, Mike might be handsome and suave well into his old age.

"He was just about to show me his new lingerie," Mike said, pointing his thumb toward Arden, who shook his head.

"Was not."

Dad nodded. "So it's a chaste relationship. I see. Makes sense, since Mike is saving himself for marriage."

Unlike some of the MC members, who couldn't stop themselves from making digs at Mike, Dad saw the fake relationship with Arden as a stunt and kept humoring them about it. Mike wasn't about to argue, because keeping the reality of his fascination with Arden secret suited him. It wasn't like it mattered. Whether something ended up happening between him and Arden or not, wasn't anyone's business.

"Totally. I was wondering whether Arden prefers traditional wedding dresses or something more modern."

Arden snorted but Dad shook his head. "Get your ass to the garage, Mike," he said and walked off.

Mike looked back. "So, which is it?" he asked, eyeing the smooth thighs below the hem of Arden's towel-dress.

"Big and puffy, but with a slutty back," Arden said, and he must have thought about it before, because this very specific answer came right away.

Mike shook his head. "I knew you were a real lady," he said and shut the door behind him, going off to the shop.

His nape tickled as he made his way through the dusty yard, swaying to the rhythm of the song playing in the bar area, and when he glanced over his shoulder, he did it fast enough to catch a glimpse of Arden watching him from their window. The boy hid the moment he realized he'd been spotted, but knowing his interest wasn't one-sided after all was enough to make Mike smile as he strode to the garage with even more confidence. He didn't know what exactly he wanted from Arden, but he'd find out once it happened.

"Reinforcements have arrived," he said, spreading his arms upon entry.

Rain's long, skinny legs bent at the knees where they stuck out from under a Toyota Corolla. "I told Dad I can handle it," she grumbled.

"And he knows you're losing sleep because of the little girls and need some rest, so here I am. Don't have anything better to do anyway," Mike said and pulled his hair back into a ponytail. He hadn't changed after cleaning his own bike, so he could get straight to work in ripped jeans and tank top. "Do you and Mona still have the energy to *take care of one another*?" he asked, grinning.

Rain laughed, but then kicked the concrete floor and started swearing. "Shit, got oil in my mouth. None of your business, dumbass perv."

"No? But I very much care about the wellbeing of my sister *and* sister-in-law," Mike said, ducking when a damp sponge flew his way and hit the wall behind him. "That's so hurtful."

"You know what? If you're here, I might as well take a break." She rolled out from underneath the vehicle, black hair out of order. "Give me a cigarette."

Damn it.

"I gave up," Mike said, quick to pick up the journal they used to list the chores for a given day.

Rain groaned and had a sip of water instead, wiping the black goo off her face with the sleeve of her overalls. "Since when?"

The decision to lie—or rather, omit truth—was swift. "Oh, you know, I'm not getting any younger. I thought it was time to take care of my health."

It had absolutely nothing to do with Arden's distaste for tobacco. Nothing at all.

Rain snorted. "What next? Yoga? Juicing?"

"Who knows? Gotta keep those hips working like a well-oiled machine until I'm old and gray, sis," Mike said, pushing his crotch back and forth to demonstrate what he meant.

"You moved those hips yet with your new boyfriend?" she mocked, but there was a hint of true curiosity in her eyes.

Mike stilled before rapidly looking over his shoulder, but there was no one there to tease him alongside Rain. She really wanted to know.

Mike cleared his throat and left the journal on the desk, approaching the Toyota. Blood pulsed in his temples as he met her gaze and took a deep breath. "Will this stay between us? And I mean *us*, not me, you, and Mona."

Rain groaned and took her time swiping him with her gaze from head to toe. "Fine. What is it? And it better not be nothing stupid."

"Why would it be anything stupid?" Mike whispered, placing his hands on his hips, but he didn't wait for her answer and spoke as soon as he double checked that the dark corners of the work area didn't hide anyone else. "The thing is that... it's all play, but it also isn't. Do you get me?" he asked, sensing sweat beading on his forehead.

Rain's expression remained stony. "Hmm... not really. Are you talking about Arden?"

Mike groaned. "Who else? Rain, have you been living under a rock? You must see how insanely hot he is!"

Her frown only deepened. "I mean... He's a pretty kid. I guess. So... this whole boyfriend thing *isn't* a joke? I'm confused. You know he's not transgender, right? I asked, and he told me he just likes to be feminine. Whatever you're imagining, he is not a girl."

Mike waved his hand. "I know he's a guy, but he looks and acts like a girl. I mean, *you're* gay. How do you not see it?"

"I don't know, Mike. I'm a lesbian. His face might be pretty, but he does nothing for me. I thought you were all about pussy, and at thirty-seven, you still manage to surprise me, old man. Now I'm mad I can't tell Mona," she grumbled.

Mike rolled his eyes. "I do love pussy. And I bet his is lovely too!"

"That is *such* a wrong thing to say! You guys live together. Maybe you'd get it out of your head if you saw his dick." Despite the crudeness of the words, her voice expressed concern. Maybe out of all Mike's family and friends, she'd be the one to treat his problem seriously. Because Mike had too much of a rivalry going on with Leo to be vulnerable with him.

Mike licked his lips. "He won't let me. But he flirts back all the time, and he watches me like I'm the juiciest steak, but he won't say he does. It's making me insane, Rain."

She took her time gulping more water. "Okay. I get it, shit can get a bit confusing, even for an old dog like you, but Arden's been through some shit. He's vulnerable and half your age. If you wanna experiment with a man, and I can't believe I'm even saying this, then go on Grindr and hook up with some pretty rando. You can't pull Arden into bed, then freak out when his dick rubs against you. It would crush his confidence."

Mike scowled, longing to sense jasmine, not gas. "It's a dick, not a burning iron. And why would you think I want to experiment with a guy? I've never wanted to. He's just so... different," he said helplessly and let his arms drop.

Rain rolled the water bottle across her forehead. "Sometimes I long for those simpler times when you didn't bug me with existential questions and I always won bets over girls with you."

"You did not," Mike said and nudged her foot with the tip of his boot before leaning back against a pillar. "You know most of those chicks were just bi-curious. You couldn't get them the same way I couldn't get any of your hot lesbian girlfriends."

"That much is true, but it was fun watching you try," she teased. "You're not pushing on Arden because of a bet, right? You already won the one with Kane."

"He still hasn't paid up, but no, that's not it. I'm just... really confused. There's something about him. I know he has a dick, and that he is a boy, but he's just so... feminine. I think about him, like, *a lot*."

She laughed. "No surprise there. Your mind's always been in the gutter."

"And I'm not ashamed," Mike said just as his phone buzzed. He met Rain's gaze, frustrated by this interruption, but his face relaxed the moment he saw Arden's name on the screen. He showed it to Rain. "See? He's already missing me."

Mike cleared his throat and picked up the call, proud as a peacock. "Hello, baby."

Arden's voice had never been less flirtatious. "Mike... Some weird people came into the store," he whispered, instantly making Mike's hair bristle. "And they're not the Jarens. Maybe it's just me... but— Please put that down!"

Rain stood up without needing to hear what this was about. "Guns."

Mike exhaled and ducked under the desk, pulling out a secret drawer openable from the leg space. He took out two firearms and tossed one to his sister, who caught it and was the first out of the garage. Mike ran after her, driven by a searing burn at the base of his neck, dashing past Jack and Dad's office. Rain was calling others, but he only saw the open gate and sped toward it as if it were about to close forever.

Nothing had happened yet, but the bad feeling in his stomach made him run even faster. He heard a faint scream from the gas station, then a screech of tires.

His head exploded with fury, but his heart slowed down until he felt as if it had stopped beating altogether, plunging him into unwanted memories he'd repressed for so long.

"No!" It tore out of his throat as if something had punched it past his gullet, leaving it raw, but Mike already fell back and mounted his bike before everyone else, speeding past the gate the moment the engine came to life. A huge truck roared as he dashed right in front of its ugly muzzle, but while split seconds had saved him from a deadly collision, he was fueled by pure adrenaline and made a turn in the sand on the edge of the asphalt before shooting after whoever had taken Arden.

He would not let this happen.

Not again.

Chapter 7 – Arden

Arden yelled at the top of his lungs, and even the hard slap he got from the man who'd shoved him into the back seat couldn't stop him. He stood no chance against his kidnapper, a man twice his size, but if these men were taking him to Luke, he had to fight. A few bruises were nothing in comparison to what Luke might do to him.

"Make him shut up!" the driver yelled as the other one, a freckled bald guy with a peppering of red stubble grabbed Arden's jaw in his massive hand.

"Hear that, you little bitch? Shut the fuck up!" he roared, spitting at Arden's face when he clenched his teeth.

Arden's heart was in his throat, but on the empty road, no one would hear him, and tears spilled down his cheeks when he realized his own helplessness. The car shook as it sped toward the hills, and soon enough, any clue about his whereabouts would be dust.

"I'll give him back the money!"

"No can do," the driver said. "Luke wants you, he paid up, so he'll get to punish you however he wants."

Who were those people? Arden had never seen them around Luke, but it wasn't like he'd been privy to Luke's business. He'd always suspected his ex could be entangled in some illegal shit, because he had way too much time and money, and those two things rarely went hand in hand for people who did honest work. Arden had just never expected this would turn against him.

He'd been so stupid.

"I'm not his to punish!" Arden threw himself at Freckles with all the ferocity of his fear, but a single punch to his jaw was enough to push him back while the shrubs growing on either side of the road passed by at alarming speed. His world spun, and his head still rang from the hit when something banged loudly behind the car, prompting him to scream out again.

"Shit. You should have gotten to him right away. We lost too much time," the driver remarked, and he must have accelerated, because the engine roared as if it were being strangled, and the car shook over every single bump in the asphalt. At this rate, they would crash, and he curled up, covering his head in a vain attempt to provide himself some protection from what now seemed inevitable. The sob he uttered earned him another shove.

"Shut up," Freckles said and leaned in between the front seats. "I needed to make sure it was him, so stop making it my fault. You weren't any faster." Before he could have said anything else, the glass at the back crumbled, and both he and Arden cried out.

"Shoot him. Shoot the fucker," roared the driver, his voice gaining a high pitch as Arden's other captor produced a large handgun and kneeled on the seat, sending bullet after bullet through the empty window.

Each shot was like a blow to Arden's head, echoing in his ears as he scrambled lower, hiding on the floor littered with empty snack packages and condom wrappers. The noise outside was unbearable and he covered his ears, trying to breathe and keep himself in a stable position.

He would die today. He was about to die, whether he reached Luke's or not, and that realization squeezed out more tears, because he was nineteen and still had so much to live for.

He should have yielded and kissed Mike when he had the chance.

Something exploded, and the car sank lower before swerving as if it were about to roll. The driver hit the brakes, uttering a frantic yell, and just as Arden thought he was done for, the vehicle must have left the road, rocking on the uneven ground as it lost speed.

Arden couldn't catch his breath, crying as each shake resonated in his knees and elbows. Too afraid to look up and see whether it was safe to bolt out of the car, he stayed perfectly still as the vehicle came to a halt.

The sound of a motorcycle revving brought his heart back to life and it only hit him then that Freckles could have shot Mike or one of the other Smokeys, because who else would have been on their tail with so much ferocity?

"Let the boy out, and I'll consider not shooting your balls off," Mike said in a voice so sharp and low he barely sounded like himself. But he was here. He'd come for Arden!

Freckles was about to say something, but the driver snarled at him. "There's three of them already and more coming. Open the goddamn door."

The bald head glistened with sweat, but in the end, he squinted at Arden, breathing shallowly while he calculated his chances for survival. "Get out."

Arden didn't have to be told twice, and fell out of the car as soon as he pried the door open, still stunned that he hadn't ended up tied up in Luke's basement.

The sun blinded him after the ride in the dusky interior of the car, and he blinked, stumbling toward the big figure he recognized as Mike.

"Behind me, boy," Mike roared, watching the vehicle with his arms steadied, as if he were ready to shoot at any moment.

Arden was so shaken he couldn't walk straight and ended up falling over into the sand, but he still crawled on all fours just to be farther away from his former captors. The sand and rocks dug into the flesh of his palms, but he would only be safe once he reached Mike.

"It's all good, man," said Freckles, stepping out of the car with his hands raised. "I think it's a misunderstanding."

"Luke sent them," Arden whined without shame, still squinting so the bright sun that made the air tremble wouldn't hurt his eyes.

He could see Mike's face now, and the sky-blue gaze got darker, meaner, as if a different person had crawled out of Mike's body. And this person wasn't there to joke around.

"You're bleeding," Mike said, swallowing as two more bikes approached, roaring in anger. One of the abductors hissed.

"Shit. Fuck!"

"Sorry! It's a fuck up, we got the wrong person," the driver yelled, but agitation was palpable in his tone. "It was just one punch, and then you got here..."

As Arden scrambled to his feet, he realized the coppery taste on his tongue was blood. He rubbed some from under his nose, still shaking. "I'm okay, Mike."

He flinched when Rain and Jack lost speed as they rode off the road and dismounted their bikes a few feet behind Mike.

"Throw your guns," Jack yelled, flanking the car on the driver's side without ever lowering his own weapon. You're outnumbered, so if you wanna live, be good boys and answer my questions," he said, carefully stepping between thatches of dry grass while the sun scorched them from above.

Rain moved to the other side of the vehicle, her expression cold and focused in a way that told Arden she wouldn't hesitate if any of the men disobeyed Jack's orders.

The Smokeys were way more confident and organized than Luke's goon friends could ever dream to be. Even in a small group, they were a swarm of hornets taking on two bumble bees that made more noise than harm.

Sweat was cold on Arden's back despite the heat when Mike kneeled in front of him, thick blond brows lowering as he wiped blood from under Arden's nose.

"*Just* one punch?"

"Yeah, I'm okay," Arden muttered, rubbing his eyes with his inner wrists because there was sand stuck to his fingers, but his gaze was soon drawn to a bruise on one of his arms. Cold dread speared right through him, because that image of fingers imprinted on his tender flesh instantly took him right back to that terrible night with Luke. He sobbed as if he were alone, with no one to see him lose control.

· He realized he'd had his knife on him all along, but had been too shocked and scared to remember its presence and defend himself.

· Mike's lips twisted, but he only had tenderness for Arden, rubbing swollen flesh as he roared, a lion protecting his prey from scavengers. "Out! Out of the fucking car, both of you, or I'll set you on fire."

He rose, hair floating in the dusty wind, breathing hard as if his lungs couldn't keep up with the demand for air. The narrow road behind him was empty and quiet. There would be no unwanted witnesses to whatever happened next.

When the men hesitated for too long, Rain loudly took the safety off her gun.

"You won, give it a fucking rest," the driver grumbled, but did get out, unlike Freckles who eyed Mike from the backseat like a rabid dog.

Mike rolled his neck until something cracked. "His gun?"

Rain showed him the firearm, stepping away from the car, and the moment Mike saw it, he yanked on the back door so hard he could have broken the hinges. Freckles tried to fight him, but Mike dove right in and dragged him out in a chokehold. The bastard didn't relent, as if he hadn't yet realized they'd lost, and kicked about, creating a cloud of dust.

A part of Arden worried for Mike, but he didn't say a word and watched his revenge fantasy unfold through the tears in his eyes. He'd never considered himself bloodthirsty, but now he wanted to see the man who'd punched, who'd almost taken him to Luke's, pay for what he'd done.

So when Mike's signet-studded knuckles hit Freckles in the face and made his bones sing, Arden didn't flinch. The lowlife collapsed, but Mike was on him again before he could have covered his face.

"One punch," Mike said, panting as he pressed the sole of his steel-toed boot to the bastard's cheek and twisted it in a way that made Arden choke with nausea. But for Mike, this was nothing. He was a hard man, with strong muscles, and the desire to keep Arden safe. "Look at the boy. Are you proud of yourself? Do you feel strong now?" Mike roared, but before Freckles caught his breath to answer, Mike rolled the boot off him and kicked him hard in the ribs.

His siblings watched on in silence as more bikers arrived, and even the driver, who'd proven himself a coward, stayed still, watching his companion take the brunt of Mike's fury.

Arden's heart was in his throat when Freckles helplessly covered his head, but Mike pulled the bastard's arm away and smashed his fist into a bloodied face again.

Arden should be disgusted by the violence, yet watching Mike turn his abductor's face into a pulp was satisfying. And the more blood he saw, the safer he felt.

Luke had a rough-around-the-edges charm that used to give Arden a thrill, but Mike was the real deal, ready to take on anyone who crossed him, not only those obviously weaker than him.

Hank Heller, the president of the club and Mike's dad, eyed the scene without a word, his face somber. "Easy now. Unless you want to kill him, I suggest you stop."

Mike grunted and punched Freckles' back, prompting him to whine and curl into a ball, like the maggot he was, but he pulled away, spitting at Arden's abductor as if he couldn't contain his disgust.

"If either of you ever comes close to that boy, I will break all your limbs and leave you in the desert for the coyotes and vultures. Same goes for the coward who sent you," he shouted toward the driver who stood by the car with his hands lifted, pale like sun-bleached bone.

Jack had never tried to hide that he held no love for Arden. A scary man in his forties and tattooed all over, he tolerated Arden's presence because of Rain's wishes, but he spat at the ground in front of the driver all the same. Maybe the fact that the abduction happened on Smokey territory made it personal for him, no matter who it involved. "Get your buddy out of here and do as told," he said through clenched teeth.

The driver rushed over to Freckles as soon as he was allowed and dragged the moaning, bleeding sack of flesh to the car.

On a whim he couldn't explain, Arden picked up a red-stained tooth out of the sand. His jaw still hurt, and his fingers trembled, but he didn't want to cry anymore.

He flinched when someone kneeled right next to him, but then he smelled Mike's favorite cologne, and the goons, nor the desert didn't seem all that scary anymore. Strong arms pulled him close, until his head was tucked under Mike's chin, and they stilled, both gasping from pent-up stress.

"You okay, baby? I'm here," Mike whispered in the softest of voices.

"Now I am," Arden said and hugged Mike tightly, running his fingers over the patches at the back of Mike's vest. He'd never known this kind of safety and he had no idea just how much he'd craved it until today.

The other bikers were busy dealing with the goons, and there might have even been some fuckery going on with helping them change the wheel in the broken-down car, but he didn't listen and didn't care, focused only on Mike's breath and the steadiness of his hug. It wasn't sexual, but spoke of closeness he'd never experienced before.

"I'll take you home now. You need to put some ice on your face."

They got up, and Arden realized he couldn't have risen if it wasn't for Mike's steady grip on him. His knees were like rattles, and while his mind was freakishly calm, aid proved necessary.

He opened his palm and showed the tooth to Mike. "Can I keep it?"

Mike's brows lifted. "I suppose," but he seemed more curious than weirded out as he guided Arden to the orange bike.

The club president watched them while his children dealt with the two goons. "It's been a smart choice to stay with us," he said as Mike and Arden walked past him.

"Thank you so much, sir." Arden made a point of showing his gratitude, because if the club president hadn't agreed to him staying, he wouldn't have had his new sanctuary.

Just last week he'd been complaining to his sister about the clubhouse being a dumpster, but everything had changed since Mike's arrival, and this day hit him with the realization that his relationship with the Smokeys could be the difference between life and death.

So he sat behind the man who protected him with the fierceness of a loving guard dog, and closed his eyes as fatigue settled in, sinking deep into muscle. Pain pulsed where Freckles had punched him, but today could have ended so much worse, and seeing Mike mete out punishment for his suffering kind of made up for all the fear he'd experienced during the kidnapping.

He wasn't even sure how much time had passed, but the ride back to the clubhouse didn't take that long, and when Mike parked in the courtyard, Arden still didn't quite feel like himself.

"Mike? What the hell happened? We just got here, and Mom said there had been an emergency?"

Leo.

Arden slid off the motorcycle under the scrutiny of Leo's husband, Zolt. All the bikers were in good shape. Even Jeff, the youngest, hit the gym every day, but Zolt was a bull of a man with a black beard and dark eyes that seemed to know everyone's weak points.

"You okay, kid? You're bleeding," he observed in his deep baritone.

Arden instantly slid his hand into Mike's. "I've got an ex who won't give it a rest, but maybe now he'll get the memo."

Mike exhaled and squeezed Arden's fingers. "They would have gotten away if Arden hadn't managed to call me from the station. It was real fucking close," he said with an odd strain to his voice.

Leo walked up to them and pulled his brother into the briefest hug, as if it was Mike, not Arden who needed comfort.

"But you caught up. That's what counts," Leo said with a sigh, meeting Arden's eyes for the first time since they'd met.

"Is everyone else okay?" Zolt asked, hovering close to his husband.

Mike waved his hand, while still holding Arden with the other. "Yeah, those guys were fuckups. I need a drink."

Zolt raised his eyebrows and pointed to Mike's bloodstained T-shirt. "What you need is a washing machine."

Mike looked at the fabric with a scowl, and pulled it off, revealing his muscular torso, all shiny with blond hairs that glistened in the sun, making the realistic depiction of a male lion's head tattooed there come alive. The animal's flowy mane transitioned into branches and leaves as it entered his shoulders, creating the backdrop for fantastically colorful birds that also inhabited the skin of Mike's back, around the sepia-brown club tattoo of a skull with smoke coming out of its eyes.

"Yeah, yeah. I'll put it into cold water," Mike said and tugged Arden toward the club bar. He ignored several hangarounds who watched them in silence, acknowledging the signs that Mike had been in a fight yet not asking about it.

Zolt and Leo followed, and Arden couldn't help but notice that despite being the real couple here, they walked behind them without touching one another. It was kinda nice that Mike didn't hesitate to hug Arden, even if their relationship was as fake as the cheap pancake syrup in the clubhouse's kitchen.

"Stop ogling him," Leo warned and slapped Zolt's shoulder, but his husband laughed as they walked through the interior smelling of beer and liquor.

"I wasn't!"

Arden slid his hand over Mike's naked waist, taking advantage of his fake-but-kinda-not relationship and pulling his attention away from the full-figured girl practicing her routine on one of the twin pole-dancing stages.

"Mike's all mine," Arden said.

If only... What was a game to Mike, was a chocolate box filled with razors for Arden. Each sweet treat could be the one to cut him open and make him bleed arousal.

"Zolt, your chances might have hovered around three percent in the past, if I got drunk enough, but now that you're my brother's husband, I'm as off-limits to you as Mountain Dew is to a diabetic," Mike said and spun around, looking at Arden. "Can I leave for five minutes?"

Arden hesitated, and his adrenaline instantly spiked, but he should be fine with Leo and Zolt. "Yes, but please come back soon," he said despite knowing it sounded needy.

Mike leaned down and kissed the top of his head, softly blowing air into his locks. "Sure will. Keep an eye on my boy, will you?" he said to his brother and jogged away, leaving Arden in the empty bar.

The stripper used earphones for music and ignored the gay boys as she sank lower, rolling her ass against the pole until only a thin strip of fabric separated her anus from the rod. So it was erotic, but also rather awkward in the empty space, with no rhythm or melody to create the right atmosphere.

Zolt cleared his throat and pulled on his dense beard. "If it wasn't obvious, I'm not interested in Mike. You can keep him and his ego."

Leo rolled his eyes and opened the freezer. "You're making people uncomfortable."

Zolt shrugged, his grin a stark white against the black facial hair. "That's how you always keep them on their toes," he said to Arden, winking. "Besides, I was actually looking at the ink on Mike's back because it reminded me of yours..."

"Zolt, watch it. He's a kid," Leo warned, flushing to the tops of his ears.

"I'm nineteen." *Almost.*

"See?" Zolt put his massive arm over Arden's shoulders. "Worldly-wise young man with an appetite for life. Give 'im a beer."

Leo rolled his eyes and put some ice cubes into a clean dish towel, which he spun to create a pouch before handing it to Arden. "I think he needs *this* more."

Arden hummed and placed the makeshift icepack on his aching face, relaxing into the chair. "I've had beer before."

"See? He needs something to calm down," Zolt said and squeezed his massive paw on Arden's shoulder, which felt weirdly... fatherly, because Arden was getting no flirtation vibe from Zolt.

Leo put an open beer bottle in front of Arden. "Fine, but I'm watching you until I'm sure you're a hundred percent sober."

"Why do you care?" Arden asked more harshly than he would have liked.

Leo huffed, tapping his fingers on the sticky table top. "Because you don't belong here, and I'm not saying this to be mean. This is no environment for a... man like you, and if you stick around, you'll end up hurt."

Arden met Leo's gaze and pointed to his bruise. "I'm safer here than anywhere else."

"You'd be safer out of Mike's room," Leo said, looking at Zolt rather than Arden.

A deep sigh left Zolt's chest, and he smiled, meeting Arden's gaze. "Don't listen to him. You're only young once. That's the time to have fun. Just don't expect anything more than that from straight boys like Mike."

"That's... grim." Leo mused. "I used to be a *straight boy* too, remember?" he asked, and Arden could have sworn he poked Zolt's thigh under the table.

Zolt spread his arms. "I'm just saying. Keep your heart safe, and use condoms."

"Zolt! Seriously," Leo groaned, and Arden had to giggle seeing an outlaw biker who took offence at any mentions of gay sex. Especially while being married to a man.

"What? He's nineteen, I bet he rode a dick or two by now."

Arden couldn't believe his ears and snorted so abruptly beer came out of his nose.

"See? He's already feeling better," Zolt said and moved his hand under the table, surely to squeeze Leo's. It was kind of sweet really.

"You know what we'll do?" Mike asked, ignoring two hangarounds who followed him from the corridor, like kittens hoping from milk from their momma. In a fresh shirt, he was as appetizing as a warm cookie. "You need to know how to defend yourself," he said and took a beer from the fridge.

Arden took a big swig from his own bottle, feeling weirdly okay around those butch men even though his usual crowd were strippers. "How?"

Mike parked his ass on the table in front of Arden and rested his boot on the armrest of his chair, inevitably drawing Arden's attention to his crotch. "I'll teach you self-defense."

Zolt sniggered and wouldn't stop when Leo nudged him with his elbow. "What? I'm just thinking that the boy needs to pack some weight on.

What are you? A hundred pounds? I bench press twice that. Eat some meat boy, if you want to get stronger."

Arden groaned. "I don't like meat. It's... chewy."

Zolt laughed harder. "You'll have your work cut out, Mike."

Mike ignored him and focused on Arden instead. "Is it just me, or is it too loud here? Wanna chill?" he asked, reaching his tattooed arm to Arden.

Leo scowled. "You okay, Arden? Not dizzy?"

Arden shook his head, taking Mike's hand. "I told you I had beer before." Though it was kinda nice that Leo cared, even if slightly patronizing.

Mike pulled him to his fragrant chest, and Arden didn't hesitate before rolling his face into the dip between his pecs. Despite the joking around with Leo and Zolt putting him at ease, he was still rattled by what had happened today and nothing was as comforting as Mike's arms.

"Don't worry, Leo, if I wanted to intoxicate him, I'd have done it long ago," Mike said. "I like my prey horny and very willing."

Arden sighed as they walked off hand-in-hand. Mike's scent could intoxicate him with more ease than hard liquor.

They didn't speak until they reached the second floor. "I forgot to thank you," Arden said.

Mike snorted. "Really? I thought I deserve some love for coming in, guns blazing."

"You do!" Arden said quickly and turned to him in the empty corridor. "You've earned that kiss I guess." His heart started pounding when he stood on his toes and slid his fingers into Mike's beard. He'd have his cake and eat it. He'd pretend he was only doing it for Mike's sake, and in turn, get to indulge in Mike's lips.

But Mike frowned and gently inched away. "I'm too hot for a charity kiss. When I kiss you, it will be because you asked me to."

Arden stared, biting his lip and falling down a deep dark hole of sexual frustration.

Fuck.

Chapter 8 – Arden

Arden couldn't believe how achy he was. When Mike had said he'd teach him self-defence, Arden had imagined playful tumbling on the bed. *Maybe* going to the shooting range. But instead, Mike had signed him up to an intensive self-defence class run by his mom at the Heller-owned gym.

Two weeks in, Arden was sore, even if growing in confidence. Though the fact that he was the only male member of the class, and that at least half of the attendees seemed to have a better grasp on the techniques than him did chip at his ego. And whenever they exercised in pairs, it was painfully obvious that many of his partners were stronger too.

He wasn't sure whether he'd find the courage to push his thumbs into Luke's eyes if the bastard sneaked up on him somewhere, but Mike claimed the moves would eventually be in his muscle memory, so Arden swallowed his pride, ignored the fact that he got sweaty, and continued practicing kicks in the 'nuts' of a girl whose name he didn't know.

He was intent on at least looking cute doing it, so he sported a pair of unicorn print leggings and an oversized crop top saying *Cardio is Hardio*. He did enjoy the stretching after a tough workout, and since he still didn't like meat, Mike introduced him to a strawberry protein shake. It was... okay.

Most importantly though, his bruise was almost gone, and he hoped that Luke had given up. But the future was still uncertain. Arden paid Mike's Dad a small fee for the protection every week, and he would run out of cash sooner or later, since his job at the gas station contributed to making the price of his presence at the clubhouse smaller without adding anything to his bank account.

It was natural he'd have to learn how to fend for himself because Mike's interest in him would only last so long. Next time Luke came for him, Arden might be on his own.

"Okay, girls, good job. I'll see you in two days," Mike's mom said, clapping her hands. For a woman her age, who'd had so many children, she was remarkably fit. Just like her husband, she had the vibe of a much younger person, and the tight exercise clothes she wore most of the time complemented her figure. Her face hadn't been affected much by the passing of time, though she did look mature.

It seemed to be a family trait, considering Mike was almost forty, and Arden would never have guessed if Leo hadn't told him.

"And boys!" Mona added, winking at Arden.

She didn't take all the classes, too busy with her twins, but Arden could sense her support whenever she was present. They talked every now and then, and he'd learned that she'd been in a similar situation to his once. Well, somewhat. A runaway from the altar, she'd sought refuge at the clubhouse and even lived in that same bare-bones room downstairs as Arden had when he'd first arrived.

It made him imagine a future where he too managed to thread himself into the tapestry of the Heller family and found his place among them. Safe.

Were he a girl, he could have tried to make Mike his, to make himself useful to the Hellers even though he knew nothing about engines or running a bar. Hell, as a girl, he could have gotten pregnant for the sake of staying within the orbit of the club. Not that he wanted kids, but that seemed to be the way to go, since the Heller clan was an army of *nine* siblings and already sprouting a new generation of kids.

But he wasn't a girl, and didn't want to be one.

"You're getting better every time," Mona said, nudging him with her shoulder as all the participants gravitated out of the room and down the stairs. Arden's legs felt heavy after each session, but Mike told him his muscles weren't used to so much strain.

"Thanks, trying to build up those biceps." Arden laughed and bent his arm, knowing very well there was hardly anything there. He didn't mind. He liked being small, but did wish to get stronger, because the classes had showed him how useful it could be.

Mona chuckled and pinched his twig arm before walking off to the women's changing room. Which left Arden as the only person to approach the men's.

He'd been wary to enter it at first, because some guys were overly sensitive to his presence, but he was now positive no one would be stupid enough to pick on him when he was under the protection of the Smokeys. Not at their own gym. So he entered, glad to see no one there.

The changing room was a simple affair with gray lockers and blue tiles, but while it smelled of sweat and cheap cologne, he didn't mind it as long as no one bothered him.

The showers were always the tricky part, as they weren't divided in any way, allowing space for five men to shower at a time. Arden hated the lack of privacy since he was nowhere near as eager to walk around naked as some of the other gym-goers. A lot of the time, Arden skipped the shower altogether and washed at home—it wasn't like he had a job interview to go to after—but since the facilities were empty, he decided on a two-minute refresh.

Arden hung a towel nearby, just in case, and turned on the water. It was still kinda cool when it splashed his head, but within moments the shower heated up, and Arden relaxed, rubbing his face while artificial rain washed off the sweat and grime of the day. The temporary tattoos on his arms were fun to put on, but a pain in the ass to wash off. He still had two he needed to rub off, but he vowed to not get them again.

A secret part of him imagined a hot muscular body approaching from behind, and the droplets became the wandering hands Mike had described one time. Why did Mike have to be so sexy? Arden made a point of avoiding any glimpses of Mike's dick in the room they shared because he might self-combust if he saw it. Whatever the size and shape it was, it would be a thing of beauty, and he couldn't allow himself to admire Mike any more than he already did.

Was there time for a quick jerk off? There was no one—

Arden opened one eye to look around while water streamed down his face and he yelped, scrambling for the towel the moment he spotted the lion tattooed on Mike's chest exhale.

The sneaky fuck stood in the doorway of the shower room in all his tan, inked glory, with only a towel around his hips.

"That's not okay!" Arden pointed an accusatory finger at Mike, yet all he could think of was that Mike had seen him naked, and instead of making his presence known had stood there, admiring the view. Arden was far too concerned with more important matters to be embarrassed over something like this, but... did Mike like what he'd gotten a glimpse of? Arden's dick, while no monster, should have spoiled the illusion of femininity Arden managed to establish.

But Mike kept staring at Arden as if he were a lion eyeing a juicy gazelle, his huge grin showing strong teeth that were ready to sink into flesh. "Why? Are you saying I can't use the shower at my gym?" Mike asked and loosened the knot of his towel, letting it drop.

Arden couldn't breathe. All his dreams and nightmares came true at once. He shouldn't. But he stared. It took him far too long to spin around and face the wall. His head—no, his whole body pulsed with heat of unresolved lust.

"You damn well know... Weren't you..." What? What exactly? Arden's thoughts became a labyrinth, and he was struggling to remember his way out while his only towel became heavy with water, since he hadn't switched off the shower when he hurriedly wrapped it around his body.

His imagination suggested the filthiest fantasies of Mike pressing him against the wall, and sliding his cock in while stuffing Arden's mouth with his thick fingers to stop him from making noise. He'd have ridden Arden like that for endless minutes, and wouldn't bother to stop if someone came in to change. No, he'd keep drilling his cock in until his lust was satisfied and Arden's greedy hole was filled with spunk.

In terms of size, Mike was just above average, which made Arden imagine the endless times he could take it each day without much discomfort. It would have been so easy to offer his mouth to him, have a taste, and be done with it, because Mike would surely lose interest once he got the girly boy fantasy out of his system. But no. He could not allow himself to go there. Mike seemed genuine in his intent to protect Arden, but if Kaley said he was a douche when it came to relationships, Arden was inclined to believe her.

He needed to find himself someone sweet. Normal. Not another badass with tattoos and questionable morals. Especially not one who identified as straight.

"Were I what?" Mike asked as he switched on the shower next to Arden's, stepping in naked, as if he knew no shame. Then again, what was there to be ashamed of? He looked great. A biker demi-god walking the earth for the sole purpose of tempting the likes of Arden—those with frail morals and weak resolution.

"I haven't seen you lifting weights, so you haven't yet had your workout. How are you here already?"

He came on purpose, the sneaky fuck.

When Arden glanced over his shoulder, he made sure to keep his eyes on Mike's face, but it was hard, because the shabby interior was in such stark contrast with the masculine beauty of Mike's tanned flesh that Arden couldn't help himself, and his gaze kept gravitating to the torso painted over with the majestic muzzle of a male lion surrounded by photorealistic birds from somewhere around the equator.

Did Mike not realize what a work of art he already was that he decided to add more layers of beauty to his skin? When he walked into a room, everything else became a blurred background.

"I like being clean before I hit the benches. It's more hygienic that way," Mike said, but the light, teasing tone he used made it clear he wasn't serious. This was an opening for Arden, but he would not take the bait. He'd had enough bad boys to last him a lifetime.

"So it has nothing to do with spying on me?"

Such a muscular ass with cute dimples... *Fuck—eyes on the face.*

Mike shrugged and leaned against the wall, letting the water cascade down the side of his torso while keeping his head away. His hair darkened when wet, and it now hung in dripping streaks, tapping his smiling face as he moved.

"What if it does, baby?"

This again. Mike was relentless in his pursuit.

And he was so good at it too. Every time Mike called him baby, Arden's heart thawed a little, but that was the danger of it all. Once the walls melted, Mike would bite into his chest, rip open the ribcage and leave nothing behind.

"Then you're a perv," Arden said and lifted his chin.

Mike grabbed his wrist, and the warmth of his touch had Arden freezing. "You like that."

He did.

Just like he liked that Mike stopped smoking, and that he was intent on hoarding Arden's attention.

Arden gave him a level stare despite the faint shudders jumping over his skin. "Why would you think so?"

Mike stepped closer, and as he switched off the water, Arden's gaze focused on a droplet clinging to Mike's nipple. His tongue grew hot, as if it wanted to lick the little bead off pink flesh.

"You're still here," Mike said.

Arden pulled away as if scalded with boiling water. He half expected to be tugged right back to Mike's naked chest, but Mike released him, letting Arden flee.

He dripped water all over the floor in the changing rooms, but the locker room area was as empty as before so he dried and dressed as if doing that quickly was his superpower.

He managed to run off before Mike finished and burst into the corridor, stumbling when he realized the door hit someone.

Shit! It was Mama Heller.

"I'm so sorry. Lost my balance, because my legs feel a bit weird after workouts," he said breathlessly, but she rubbed her hip, which was where he must have hit her, and smiled, combing back her short blonde hair.

"That's fine. Maybe you'd like some tea? I have herbal," she said, and when she took hold of Arden's arm, it was clear there was no way out of this.

"I still have to dry my hair," he tried.

"It's a pain, sorry, we still have to install the better hair dryers in the men's locker rooms. But you're free to use the ladies'. They're in a separate grooming area, so no one should complain about you being there. You know what? I'll just go with you."

So there would be no escape.

Whatever she wanted to discuss with him, he'd just have to bear it. Fortunately, while he could hear voices and the tap of showers next door, the small area with mirrors and counters was empty, even though the whiff of shampoo and perfume hung in the air, indicating it had been in use not long ago.

"You're getting better," Mrs. Heller said, taking a seat on a stool by the hair dryers. Nothing here was elaborate or decorative, but the pink tiles around the mirror counted for something.

"I wouldn't have come to the classes if Mike hadn't encouraged me, but I see the merit. I need to at least learn to not freeze up when there's danger," he said and started working his favorite coconut product into the damp curls.

She asked him how he managed to keep his hair soft with all the bleaching, but Arden had a sense there was more coming his way, and he hadn't been mistaken.

"I'm glad you don't feel alone at the clubhouse," she said a few questions later, chewing a protein bar.

"No, it's been such a whirlwind with Mike." And after almost a month, it was anyone's guess why Mike hadn't yet given up on his big fat prank. Maybe he just wanted to squeeze some sex experimentation out of it before telling everyone the relationship had been fake all along.

Oh no. Mrs. Heller's smile was definitely insincere.

"Mike is like that. Very open to new people, new experiences," she said and let that hang in the air for a little bit.

"And he doesn't want kids, so maybe he's not bothered which way he swings." Arden's smile was met with a chilly expression.

So maybe it had been a rude thing to say to Mike's mother, but why should she be free to interfere in Arden's life?

She exhaled and shut her eyes, as if she were about to do some yoga. "Look, maybe you don't see it, because you're very young, but Mike isn't very steady in his feelings. He likes to have fun and experiment, and he knows how to make everyone around him feel special. He's a fantastic son, and I love him very much, but I don't want you to end up hurt. You're so much younger than him."

"I'll be fine, but... thank you, I really appreciate that you care about me."

And he did, though this reminder that he really shouldn't get involved with Mike stung his heart. Even if Mrs. Heller's intention was to get her son back on the straight and narrow, she only echoed warnings Arden had heard before from his own sister. Mike was not the relationship type. He'd never claimed he was, and while he sometimes left girls heartbroken, he apparently never made any promises he didn't intend to keep. He was just the kind of guy people fell in love with, regardless of what kind of relationship they'd agreed on in the beginning.

"Because he's to marry Harlyn Jaren?" Arden asked with a small smile, trying to make light of the topic.

It worked, and Mrs. Heller snorted, shaking her head. "Her entire family is not right in the head. They sell UFO souvenirs, but to be honest I feel like they've come from an alien planet themselves. They think women *have to* get married when they're no longer virgins. It's not like there's a baby on the way. Mike made sure he never becomes a father."

"Are those people... dangerous?" Arden didn't want to end up as collateral damage because of some backwater spat over a girl losing her cherry.

She rolled her shoulder and pouted. "Well... anyone can be dangerous if they're armed. But if we ignore them long enough, I think they'll just marry her off to someone else and that'll be that. Not my business."

A form of speech because Mrs. Heller made everything involving her kids her business. Once Arden started working on his hair with the dryer, the noise made talking impossible, and she left, patting his arm goodbye.

He was relieved that she'd left, but being alone pulled memories of Mike's naked body to the surface, and it didn't matter that Arden hadn't stared for long. The image of that dick and the dark blond hair above it was etched into his pupils and would stay there forever.

Putting his hair in order was like meditation. But he was eventually done arranging it into twin braids and left the grooming room, at a loss. He could go home and enjoy some free time, but after the abduction attempt the short walk back to the clubhouse felt unsafe. What if Luke came for him in person this time? Drove by and pulled Arden into the car, without Mike being there to save him or anyone to witness the abduction?

Arden hated how jumpy he'd become. As if that one night, that one time Luke had crossed his boundaries changed everything about his personality. Not that long ago, he used to be confident, outgoing, and never feared to walk around Reno at night, even though in hindsight, that had been reckless. Luke hadn't just hurt him physically. He'd broken Arden's trust, taken away his sense of safety, and that was what Arden hated him for most. He'd always believed that if he didn't like something his partner did, all he needed to do was tell him. It had always worked before. Even with Luke.

Until it didn't.

They'd had sex countless times before, so why had Luke not been able to wait for that fuck he craved? Why didn't he want to enjoy something else that Arden was willing to give? Why had Luke chosen to force... to *rape* him as if Arden were a dog who needed to perform the desired tricks no matter what?

Arden had thought about that terrible night too many times to count, and the conclusion he came to was that Luke had never truly cared for him. That for him Arden had always been only an object to satisfy sexual desire. Not a partner. Never a lover or a friend. Maybe not even a person.

Arden did have feelings for Luke, feelings that had been torn to shreds within the fifteen minutes between the moment Arden had realized Luke wouldn't take no for an answer and Arden smashing a lamp on his head once he was free. Luke had been his man, and that had entitled him to respect and warm feelings, not sex on demand. Yet no matter how many times Arden raged about those painful moments, he was still left with a sense of loss.

He'd been hypersexual from an early age. He'd had boyfriends, watched porn, and hung out with strippers. His drawing hobby expressed his obsession with dicks, sex, and people entwining their bodies in filthy ways. He'd identified as slutty as if it were a badge of honor, and even now, despite all the anguish he'd been through, his libido was as alive as ever, which was more frustrating and confusing than losing interest in sex would have been.

The itch was always there, but he was now afraid to scratch it. Luke had hurt him only once, but the waves of that pain kept hitting him again and again, as if trying to wash away his identity. He was the same boy he was two months ago, yet at the same time he wasn't.

There was a waiting area at the main entrance into the gym, which must have been renovated not that long ago. The walls and carpet were a pleasant grassy shade, and the gray reception desk added to the serene atmosphere. Arden passed a vending machine selling sports drinks and protein bars and took one more glance at the sun-parched road outside, deciding to wait for Mike after all... which made him walk up to the swing doors to the main gym and peek through the glass partition to find out if he was even still there.

Mike had been exceptionally easy to spot, since it was the middle of the day and most regulars were at work. His chest looked so buff under the tank top, and as if that wasn't impressive enough, he was doing bicep curls with a huge dumbbell.

And Arden wasn't the only one staring. A team of three young women exercised on treadmills, which had been strategically placed in front of the free weights section, and each of them seemed more focused on the hot beefcake than with their own training.

Mike wasn't leaving anytime soon.

Arden was done with exercise. His pastel hair was groomed into lovely braids, he'd put on some basic makeup and looked way too cute to spoil it with sweat. He sank into a gray chair across from the reception desk and opened his sketchbook, intent on spilling his filthiest fantasies on the paper. He might not get the real thing, but this would be good enough for now. Masturbation via art.

He'd start with Mike's dick, because it had low-key been on his mind constantly since the shower. Hell, he could just go for it and draw that fantasy of Mike pinning a boy—okay, him—to the tiles.

His pencil danced over paper ever faster, digging into the lovely lines of muscle, inking tattoos onto skin, tracing Mike's signature grin, which Arden was so hopelessly attracted to. Moments later, the hot, muscular giant pressed the pencil-and-paper Arden to the wall, squashing his cheek against the surface, his dick halfway up Arden's ass, about to slam in and make him go to his toes.

This other Arden hadn't become a repressed hermit because of Luke's actions. He spread his legs wider, and his speech bubble left no room for misinterpretation. It read, *make me your slut, I wanna drip with your spunk.*

His face heated up as his pencil sped over paper at a frantic speed, and he was glad he'd changed into jeans, because those hid arousal a bit better than leggings. He erased the hand on the bottom's hip and moved it to the twin braids instead, making the tattooed hunk pull on them, as if they were reins to put Arden-the-slut in his place.

His brain boiled, and he was about to run for the bathrooms to take care of his raging arousal when something snatched the notebook out of his hand.

No. Not something. *Someone.*

Arden's stomach sank, dropped into a well of terror the moment he noted the angry red hair on Kane's head.

He wanted to shout, to kick him in the nuts like he'd been taught during the classes, but he froze, when Kane let out a raspy laugh. "Oh man. Is that *Mike?*"

"No!" Arden jumped to his feet, spurred into action by sheer panic. "It's not! Give it back!" He kicked Kane's shin in warning, because he didn't actually want to poke his eyes out, but Kane hadn't yet changed into gym clothes, and the thick leather boots he wore saved him from pain. He ignored Arden, eyes wide as he held the notebook high and browsed a catalog of Arden's most secretive sexual fantasies.

"Hey, Mikey! You need to see this," Kane said, laughing so hard he was losing breath as he burst past the door.

"No! I warned you!" Arden yelled and ran after Kane. Like a rabid monkey, he grabbed Kane's shoulders and climbed onto his back in a desperate attempt to reach the sketchbook, while he put his other hand over Kane's face and dug his nails into flesh without mercy.

"Get off me you little fuck!" Kane's squeal speared him with satisfaction that was soon followed by relief when Kane dropped the notebook to peel Arden off. It didn't last long.

Kane took a few steps back and slammed Arden into the wall. As if the post-workout soreness hadn't caused him enough pain. Arden slid to the floor with a groan, but his secrets were safe at least.

"What the hell?"

Mike's voice brought a chill to Arden's muscles, and as he helplessly spun around, Mike was already scooting down by the open sketchbook, his eyes wide. Arden's humiliation knew no bounds, yet as Mike picked up Arden's shameful secret, he still imagined Mike bracing him against one of the exercise benches and ramming him hard as punishment for jerking off to him without permission.

Arden was already scrambling to his feet, but just like Kane had moments ago, Mike turned a few pages of the sketchbook with a silly grin. He whistled and wagged his finger at Arden.

"My, my... There I was, thinking you were shy..."

"It's not meant for you!" Arden yelled, not even caring that he was making a scene. The girls were still on the treadmills, and he could see at least one more guy at the free weights, but the embarrassment of them seeing him act erratically meant nothing in comparison with the contents of his notebook being exposed to *anyone*. Anxiety was a collar blocking his air, and he flinched when Mike sniggered and showed Arden a picture of a boy in stockings screaming in pleasure as two faceless men in biker gear fucked his ass in unison, their huge cocks stretching his tender hole until he could no longer think.

"You are *wild*, baby. I knew you were kinky, but not *that* kinky."

Arden's face was on fire, and the tears streaking down his cheeks couldn't cool it his burning skin. "Fuck you! You can keep it if you want! It wasn't for you to look at!"

Mike's smile dropped. "Hey, baby, I'm only joking," he said, trying to grab Arden's shoulder, but Arden stepped away, choking on air.

One more glance at the sketchbook hanging open in Mike's hand, and Arden saw no other prospect for himself but to flee. No matter what he said, Mike would now *know*.

Unable to fight the sob breaking out of his mouth, he turned on his heel and ran.

Chapter 9 – Mike

The joyful curiosity of Mike's discovery turned into anger like a blue summer sky swelling with clouds and hammering down with hail. He shoved Kane away. Again.

"Why? Why did you take his shit in the first place?"

Kane didn't seem offended and laughed, massaging the back of his head, which had hit the wall upon impact. "Oh, so now it's my fault? You know you loved seeing yourself in those pics. Though maybe it's just misidentification? Your schlong isn't quite so big."

"But my fists are big enough to bash your face in, so don't you dare mention this—" Mike waved the sketchbook in the air "—to him!"

Kane raised his hands. "So the boy's a little perv. What's the big deal?"

Mike roared. "You should have let him perv in peace, Kane! What the fuck? Should I log into your girlfriend's livestream, if it's not a big deal?

He knew he'd hit a nerve when Kane's face went bright red. "Don't you fucking dare!"

"That's what I thought, so stop bothering him!"

Kane pulled out his wallet with a huff, and handed Mike fifty bucks. "I thought you were playing a game, but I guess the pictures prove he really is into you."

Mike threw the note right back into Kane's face. "Go fuck yourself! You tell anyone about those damn drawings, and I'll end you, Kane!" Mike growled, more agitated by the second. The lewd pictures passed through his mind along with the image of Arden's eyes tearing up, and his brain refused to put them into separate boxes. He'd fucked up.

Kane spread his arms. "Fine. I like money," he grumbled as he picked up the bill, but Mike was already on his way out of the free weights area.

"Mom?" he asked, approaching the reception desk with a huff. "You seen Arden? Did he leave the gym?"

"No, but I saw him running that way. Is everything okay? He was crying. Did you break up?" she asked with a concerned expression, but Mike hated the hint of hope in her voice.

"No, Mom, Kane was a shit to him," he said curtly and jogged down the blue corridor, his head pulsing whenever he thought of the image depicting a man who was unmistakably him—and he recognized it by the toucan tattoo on his shoulder—fucking Arden in the showers, which was a fantasy they apparently shared. He stilled by one of the few windows, breathing in the fresh coat of paint on the walls and looked at the cutesy pink pattern on the cover of the stolen sketchbook.

He shouldn't open it again.

But he did.

When asked about his drawing, Arden had claimed they were fashion designs. Mike had no interest in fancy clothes, and would have long forgotten the sketchbook if its contents weren't a secret. When something was forbidden, Mike wanted it all the more. As had been the case with the broccoli, and that had also been one of the reasons why he'd gotten interested in Harlyn Jaren in the first place. His stupid curiosity always got him in trouble, but when he opened the sketchbook again... boy, was he in for a treat.

Page one only featured an elaborate ornamental proclamation.

Owner: Gutter Mind where the *i* was a dick spurting a drop of cum.

Despite lust already boiling inside him, Mike had to first acknowledge that Arden was actually great at drawing. His style wasn't realistic and resembled comic book characters, with exaggerated features, but other than that, the anatomy, and there were *many* bodies, was spot on.

Arden didn't just draw himself, but many different twinks with all sorts of hair or special features like piercings, tattoos, or tentacles and hooves for that matter, but there was a consistent thread of those boys getting fucked by big buff types. From minotaurs, to bikers, the tops in his drawings were big, bad, and horny. Their huge dicks dripped with pre-cum, or were already embedded in tight round asses. The sex was rough, and included double penetration, bondage, lingerie, and toys. There was sex underwater with some kind of shark man on one page, and sex on a pool table with the bottom's expression hazy with desire as he sucked on a cue on another.

Some of the tops had their faces crossed out with harsh strokes of a black marker, but there was no denying that Mike featured prominently in the newer drawings, as the kind of stud he liked to see himself as. His stamina—endless.

Mike sighed, shivering as lust wrapped itself around the base of his dick like a cock ring.

Shit.

He'd never watched any gay porn, but those pictures, with their energy and exaggerated elements were so erotic he couldn't help but imagine himself in place of the dominants, just where Arden wanted him. Topping a slutty boy in stockings and a tightly-laced corset while the gorgeous creature held his ass cheeks open and begged for dick.

And the fact that this boy, who'd already managed to stir so much confused desire in Mike, has created all this, only made his budding need more pressing.

The boy wanted him all right, and now, after seeing those pictures, Mike knew with absolute certainty that he wanted Arden. He hadn't been blind to signs of attraction in Arden. His ego was big enough to ignore Arden's attempts at sort-of shutting down their flirting, but what he saw on the pages proved what he'd known all along, and that made him hornier than ever. Arden was into him.

In one of the pictures, a pink-haired boy humped a pillow in the lower part of the page, his imagination bubble taking up most of the space with a rendition of Mike fucking him over a motorcycle.

But Arden crushing on him posed problems of its own. Mike needed to find the boy and straighten this out. He ran up the stairs, because there was no door on the way, and popped his head into the two exercise rooms, then into the little broom closet, but his gaze eventually gravitated to the two final doors on this story. They were restrooms, and he stepped into the men's.

The violent sobbing echoing inside broke his heart. He shouldn't have joked around with Kane about the drawings. He shouldn't have peeked in without permission.

"Arden?"

The noise came to an abrupt stop, but Arden's breathing remained loud and frantic. "Go away!" he choked out.

Guilt weighed on Mike's neck as if it were an anvil. Each wheeze echoing off the white tiles was a stab with Arden's cutesy butterfly knife, cutting flesh until Mike could no longer think straight.

"I'm sorry," he croaked, shutting the door with his foot, but he was not going to leave, no matter what Arden said he wanted. It wasn't about forgiveness or redemption. He was worried for the boy.

Arden had been cutely pseudo-offended when Mike had walked in on him in the shower, but this was different. This time, his feelings had really been hurt.

"You're not! You just don't want me having a meltdown because we live together."

It wasn't hard to identify where Arden was, because his mint green sneakers were like beacons shining from under the door of the last stall in the row.

Mike exhaled. "Why would you say that? You really think I'm a heartless dick?"

It hurt that Arden took his time to answer, but in the end, he did utter a, "no."

Mike huffed, more offended than he'd have liked, but he didn't voice his feelings and offered Arden the sketchbook through the gap. "I didn't think it was such a big deal to you. Kane promised he won't tell anyone."

Even though Arden had earlier left the sketchbook with them, he now grabbed it as if his life depended on it. "I'm not a perv," he said following another sniff.

"You've got talent," Mike said, getting back up to lean against the door. "Those drawings are quite something."

In fact, they were uncomfortably hot. Hotter than most real-life porn Mike had watched. Or was it because Arden had drawn them? He didn't know anymore.

"You're just saying that because I'm crying."

Mike groaned, staring at his reflection in a long mirror that desperately needed a wash. "Jesus, no! They're insanely hot. It's just..." His mouth dried as he remembered the picture depicting how their short interaction in the shower could have ended in an alternative universe. "You draw *me* a lot. And I'm not gay."

"I know that! I'm not stupid. You shouldn't have seen those. You're the one who keeps flirting with me. And I know it's just a game to you, but I have needs and feelings." He did sound calmer now, thank fuck.

Okay. That was *fine*. The last thing Mike wanted was to give Arden false expectations. But there was no denying the attraction always trembling in the air between them like scorching air on a summer day. There was curiosity too. And Mike never denied himself.

"I'll say again that I'm straight, but that doesn't mean I can't have gay feelings sometimes, right?" He exhaled, imagining what could have happened if Arden unlatched the door and let Mike in. A hot shiver ran down his back and tickled his balls. He could feed that boy cock right here and now if only the desire for that to happen was truly and mutual. "If you want those things you draw—"

"I don't!"

Mike sweated under his clothes, way more than he had during his workout. "But *if* you did... I'd be open to fooling around." The understatement of the century. "Nobody needs to know, if you don't want them to. At the end of the day, bodies are bodies. I won't lie, I am curious. I've never met anyone like you. Never felt like I wanted to throw a guy on the bed and dick him, so if you wanted—"

"I don't want everything I draw! I have… a vivid imagination, okay? And some things, okay, I do want some of them. I'm no choir boy. But I've been burnt, and I'd rather *not*. I shouldn't like you this much, because it's never gonna go anywhere."

Mike had to bite his lip at the way Arden expressed his interest in him with such honesty. Any time he did so in public had presumably been a lie for the sake of their prank. Here, the admission was for Mike's ears only. Raw, sweet like pancake syrup dripped straight on Mike's tongue, and maybe equally unhealthy. Still, Mike enjoyed its flavor all the same.

"You've been burnt? Like… you're not looking for a relationship?" Mike asked, exhaling when he thought of all the things he could do with this boy if Arden agreed on keeping things limited to sex. If feelings weren't involved, he could let loose and experiment without running the risk of hurting Arden. That would have been *perfect*.

"Yes."

Mike exhaled. There was nothing more to say, but the drawings kept circling in his head, and he didn't want this conversation to end. "So… those things you draw. Is it like… art or more like porn?"

Mike's heart fluttered at the little snort from the other side of the door, but Arden didn't need to know that.

"You're such a dumbass. It's both. I like both. It was another shallow career path I was considering."

Mike shrugged. "There's nothing shallow in giving people the entertainment they want. I almost became a pro at motocross. Wouldn't have cured cancer, but it was fun, both for me and the viewers," he said, his voice dropping at the memories.

"You did?" The bathroom door squeaked, and opened as soon as Mike pulled away from it. Arden's face was pink with a flush as he peeked out at him with red eyes, and the sight of him made Mike's heart speed up.

Boy or not, he was a cutie. And to know that he was also horny on top of it pushed all of Mike's buttons.

He wanted to see Arden in stockings so fucking bad, and the glimpse of his ass Mike had caught in the shower only made that need more urgent.

"Yeah, baby. I got real big. I could have been a star by now. But if I continued on that path, I wouldn't have met you," he finished with a smile and gently poked Arden's nose.

Damn, it felt good to see a smile pass those lovely features.

"Why are you so charming, and why do I fall for it every single time?" Arden shook his head but smiled, wiping tears away with his wrist. "It's terrible."

"I'm terribly hot. You're terribly talented. We're a match," Mike said and put his arm around Arden's shoulders, glad to feel his warmth again. And his hair? It always smelled of jasmine.

"The power couple of the Smoke Valley MC." Arden laughed against Mike's chest, cuddling up to him despite no one watching. They were alone in this nondescript restroom and hugged instead of enacting Arden's illicit fantasies. It felt good.

Mike couldn't help himself. He kissed the top of Arden's head and pulled him close, enjoying how his slender form fit in his arms. Unasked questions floated in the air, and the prolonged silence turned the joyful rush in his chest into a frantic gallop.

"So... I have business in San Francisco next week. Would you like to join me?" he asked without thinking, but knew it was what he wanted the moment the words came out.

The big blue eyes brightened, still glistening with dampness. "I won't be a burden?"

Mike swallowed, his mind already in their motel room a week from now. Arden's long legs entangled in the sheets. His cock hard as he opened his legs and gave Mike sultry bedroom eyes.

"No. I trust my family, but I'd rather keep an eye on you myself."

"Is it the kind of trip where you book a hotel but—oops—there's only one bed?" Arden asked, but he didn't seem offended and slipped his cool hand under Mike's top to stroke the small of his back.

"I'll try my best."

Yes. Yes, it was.

Chapter 10 – Arden

Things had changed since the sketchbook fiasco, though in non-tangible ways. Arden had been forced to admit that he did in fact fancy Mike, but he'd also made it clear he didn't want a relationship, so the status quo remained in place. But when Mike flirted, Arden could no longer pretend he wasn't attracted to him. So he flirted back.

They still slept separately, and weren't a couple in any way, shape or form, yet... Mike would kiss his head in passing, or give him those little hugs that made all the butterflies in Arden's stomach flutter. Arden would catch himself returning the affectionate gestures more frequently, the earlier unease gone, as if that restroom conversation had melted the wedge of Arden's fear.

Mike had kept bugging him to see Arden's new drawings, and so Arden eventually caved. Of course he did. One could only deny Mike Heller for so long, and the pictures, while embarrassingly personal, offered a peek into his dirty mind. He could allow that much. At first, he'd feared Mike would tease him, or make the drawings into a running joke with his friends and brothers, but the genuine excitement shining in his eyes prompted Arden to create more, just so he could show the erotic pictures to his protector. His body tingled with heat whenever he had a new piece to present, and the further Arden invited Mike into his secret world, the more heated their flirting became.

He shouldn't get too attached. Mike would get bored with the novelty of a girly boy, with the prank on his family. He'd meet a girl he wanted to bone and break up with Arden. Yet he couldn't help but allow himself more touch, more affection, more conversations... more of Mike.

He'd accidentally-on-purpose let a bra strap slide off his shoulder, or let his pants hang lower to give Mike a glimpse of lace. And Mike *always* noticed. It was exhilarating to feel like a sexual being again without fear of where that could lead.

The danger to his heart grew every day. When Arden had first seen Mike, all buff, tattooed and pushy, he'd thought he knew what kind of man Mike was, but while Mike could flirt the pants off a pastor's daughter, his energy was different to Luke's.

Where Luke had wanted to know where Arden was at all times to control him, Mike wanted the same to protect him.

Where Luke had a need to dominate, Mike was masculine but playfully seductive.

Where Luke pushed for sex until he got it, Mike longed to be desired in return.

Mike wasn't the kind of 'bad boy' Luke had been, and it terrified Arden, because if they weren't alike, then maybe he didn't have to force down his desires. Maybe he could give this fake relationship a chance of becoming real?

Maybe he would have, if Mike wasn't straight. Arden was already in way over his head and didn't need any more drama in his life.

Still, he accepted Mike's invitation to San Francisco because they'd be spending more time together, going on fake dates where Mike treated him like a princess, and hugging on Mike's bike.

The drive had been a leisurely one, with a stop for late breakfast. They spent over an hour arguing what the very best horror movie was over burgers and pie Mike paid for—he even remembered to get Arden a veggie patty—but two hours later, they were almost at their destination, driving along a grassy area with elegant houses on the other side. Some of them were colorful, with siding and white frames around the windows, while others, made for more than one family, had bay windows and decorative ridges.

The sun made the city all look fresh and inviting, but Arden truly relaxed once Mike drove into a large urban park boasting tall trees and bushes, which seemed to stretch endlessly on either side of the wide road. He'd missed this kind of greenery in the parched stretch of land that was Hawk Springs.

Mike then took another turn, and a wide landscape dotted with palm trees and monuments opened up before Arden as they slowed upon approach to an elongated building with a facade covered by rusty-colored metal.

This was the place Mike had business to attend to? A museum? Arden's confusion grew when Mike drove into the underground parking lot, but then again, maybe he was supposed to meet someone at a discreet location in the park?

"Leaving me here for the day?" he asked when the engine stopped rumbling, but he indulged in hugging Mike from behind that bit longer. The cool air that swept over them throughout the journey prevented Arden from enjoying much of Mike's scent, but he'd take any excuse to touch those sturdy muscles.

Mike removed his helmet and combed his unruly hair with one hand, weirdly cute with the flush coloring his cheeks. "Huh? No, I'm only meeting the guy late in the afternoon. Thought we might as well enjoy ourselves if we're riding out this far."

Arden lit up as he got off the bike. "So you're taking your boyfriend out on a date?" he teased, but his heart burst with joy as if they really were together.

"Sure am. What kind of boyfriend would I be if I didn't?" Mike asked and entangled his fingers with Arden's as soon as he was ready to go. "They have a comic book exhibition now. Thought you might like it."

Arden's lips parted when he realized Mike had planned this for him. That was so... thoughtful. Luke would have never gone out of his way to make Arden's day.

He squeezed Mike's hand, bouncing in excitement as he pulled him along. "Oh, my God! I've only been to a few galleries in Reno. I know what you're trying to do. You want to inspire me so that I draw more porn?" He winked at Mike, who looked thoughtful.

"I didn't think about that, but if you want inspiration, I can give you plenty once we get to our hotel. You don't have to draw me from memory, you know," he said, pulling Arden toward the staircase.

Arden laughed, nudging Mike with his elbow. "Are you saying you'd be able to stay still for two hours so I can get everything right? Because I highly doubt you're that patient."

Mike hummed. "I imagine you'd like to put every single detail on paper. Every perfection and imperfection," he said as they emerged behind the museum to bright sunlight hitting their eyes.

There are no imperfections, Arden thought. "You know me, I'm all about anatomy." He winked, sparkling with joy over being able to be loosen up this much.

Mike entwined their fingers, and they walked along the building, toward the entrance. The mood was perfect, the sun kissed Arden's face, and they were like any other couple spending time together. And then, Mike's phone beeped.

He exhaled and picked up the call. "Yeah?"

Arden used this moment to put on his shades, but the scowl twisting Mike's features made him stall. Was something going on? Would they have to speed back home?

"Yeah, yeah, I'll deal with it. See you tomorrow," Mike said and put his phone away.

"Everything okay?" Arden asked as they entered the shade of the building. He couldn't believe Mike planned all this for him. Even the air smelled better around here, and he could breathe easily for the first time in two months. Luke was so far away he felt like a bad dream, and his pretend-boyfriend wasn't ashamed of holding his hand in public.

They would have been perfect together if Mike didn't see their arrangement as a game to startle and shock people.

Mike groaned. "It's the Jarens again. Mom says I need to talk to them, but what is there to talk about? I'm not getting married."

Arden's cheeks tingled when he saw a large poster featuring a bare-chested hunk with very masculine features and a muir cap. He knew what the exhibition was before he saw its title.

Mike sniggered and pressed a kiss to the side of Arden's head. "Thought you'd be interested. Didn't think they showed gay porn in galleries, but you learn something every day."

Arden's heart beat so fast he had to take several deep breaths to settle his nervous excitement. Not only because he was a huge Tom of Finland fan, but also because Mike had taken his time to research local events and found it for him.

"Maybe one day my art will be on display in a place like this?" he mused, pulling on Mike's hand so they'd reach the ticket counter faster.

Mike grinned and paid for everything, like he always did, then picked up the map and led the way. Arden could see himself following Mike like this on many trips to come, being a permanent feature on the back of his bike, and wearing the property vest he didn't dare ask about.

"Your boys are prettier than his. You could totally dethrone him. You just need a good manager," Mike said, proving that he had no idea who Tom of Finland was or why he got so famous. But that was okay. What mattered was that Mike cared.

They were about to enter the elevator when Mike's phone rang again, once more about the Jarens. It was a bit unnerving for the topic to come up so unexpectedly, but Mike calmed Arden by saying that if something serious happened, Dad would have told them to come back. But unease still curled in his heart.

"Are you prolonging the fake-dating me to get them off your back?" Arden asked, his voice quieter than he would have liked.

Mike rolled his eyes and entered the elevator. "I don't give a fuck about them. They can all line up to suck my dick, and I wouldn't have given them the time of day. I just wish they'd fuck off already, but confrontation seems unavoidable."

A member of staff, who joined them in the elevator along with a couple more people, cleared her throat. "Sir, please, refrain from such language."

Mike showed her his palms and apologized.

"Is that girl really so obsessed with you?" Arden laughed, but he scanned Mike from head to toe in appreciation. *Anyone* would have grown an obsession if they tasted a stud like him. The tattooed arms partially hidden by the sleeves of Mike's black T-shirt were so lickable Arden imagined himself tracing each line of ink with his tongue. Right here, where everyone could see.

Unaware of Arden's lusty thoughts, Mike shrugged. "Not really. She was just fed up living with them. She really wanted to skip condoms, so my theory is she's desperate to get married and leave home. She was barking at the wrong tree anyway, since I got the snip. Told her she should just move out, but she doesn't think that's an option. Funny story, actually. Two years ago, Leo was itching to get married to pretty much any girl. But if he succeeded back then, he wouldn't have gotten together with Zolt, and I would have missed out on the juicy opportunities to tease him."

"But he's bi, right?"

Mike shrugged, his brows lowering as the elevator opened and they entered a somber white corridor. "No idea. He was always so desperate around the girls that maybe he wanted to hide something. Doesn't matter, does it?"

"It does to him. It must be hard being perceived as something you're not."

"Oh, come on, we're brothers. We always picked on each other."

Arden bit his lip, glancing at Mike's handsome profile. "If you actually dated me, how would you have handled being called gay?"

Mike opened his mouth, but his frown deepened, and he focused on a modern sculpture decorating the interior. "I guess... it would stop being funny after a while, because I'm not. Damn it," he groaned, shaking his head.

Arden chuckled, lifting his chin up high. "Is it 'damn it, I hate you for making me rethink my offensive ways'?"

Mike dragged his hand down his face. "No. Damn it, I'll have to stop teasing him about it. It was *so good*," he complained.

The conversation quickly changed when they showed their tickets at the entrance to the exhibition and entered the large gallery with walls dotted by drawings. It started with a large panel that served as an introduction to the man and his work, but Mike seemed way more interested in the art itself, since he went straight to the nearest piece.

Arden admired the exaggerated features in Tom's work and couldn't get his eyes off the whole array of big-dicked bikers in leather chaps pictured on the wall. And he couldn't believe a supposedly-straight biker was here with him, leaning closer to avoid missing a single detail.

"Feel like wearing more leather?" Arden sniggered, poking Mike's ribs.

Mike snorted. "Nah. I'm just wondering about the size of those dicks. I know big can be good, but this just looks painful. Care to share?" he whispered, blowing straight into Arden's ear as he pulled him along to the next picture, of a sailor sunbathing in just his hat while another man stole his clothes.

Arden looked around to make sure there was no one close enough to overhear them, and wasn't surprised to note two other gay couples holding hands.

"Very big is... not so good. I draw it like that because it looks fun, and I like the size difference, but it's just fantasy."

Mike hummed, smirking. He was so damn confident in who he was he had no issues coming here, or openly showing Arden affection, and that counted for something even if Mike wasn't serious about any of this.

"Makes sense. Does it feel good? I mean... I know it must, but... you know what I mean," he asked as they passed a couple of the artist's personal artifacts encased in glass.

Arden's face heated up by the second, to the point when he didn't know any more if he'd be able to focus on the exhibition with Mike around.

And Tom *was* one of his favorite artists. "It feels good when done right," he whispered, choosing to forget the night that kickstarted this new chapter in his life and focus on all the good drilling that he'd gotten in the past. "Even the weight of a man on top is exciting." He stole a glance at Mike's face. What guided those questions? Simple curiosity, or was this arousing for him on some level?

"Yeah, I kinda always thought one guy in a couple has to be more submissive or, you know, girly, but then Leo got together with *Zolt*, and he's hardly a blushing flower. Maybe I'll just never get it. This is sexy because of the way it's drawn. But I can't see those men themselves as hot."

Arden squeezed his hand to express that he understood. "I like how guys similar to me look, I know I'm cute and fuckable, but... they don't get me all hot and bothered the way a man like that would." He pointed to a life-size poster of a buff, shirtless biker in knee-length boots, who watched them with a cocky grin.

"Huh," Mike said, and his hand moved up Arden's forearm, eventually settling on his nape. "So you'd only suck my dick if it smelled of leather?"

There it was. The blunt flirting that got to Arden every time. "I'm not a fetishist. That rosemary soap of yours would do."

"So what are you waiting for?" A rasp. Quiet. Sweet and warm at the same time. Mike's touch *burned*. His hold on Arden's nape tightened, flooding his imagination with visions of Mike holding him like this as he fucked Arden's mouth with that gorgeous dick of his.

"A miracle changing your sexual orientation?" he asked to turn the conversation into a joke and slipped out of Mike's grasp. Mike was serious about his attraction, and Arden had no doubt that if he offered, Mike would have unzipped his pants without a second thought. But Mike was also only looking to experiment, and Arden didn't want to get in too deep with a man who only had play in mind.

"Don't we both want the same thing? You said you're not looking for a relationship, so why does it matter what I generally like?" Mike asked.

It matters because I like you too much.

Arden avoided having to answer by fleeing to another picture. Mike followed relentlessly, but something sank inside Arden and tied his feet to the floor.

In the drawing, one of the characters just had a bottle broken on his head and bled. The memory of Luke on the floor, red flowing out of a gash in his forehead was like a bad dream come to life. A reminder of why Arden shouldn't trust boyfriends or boyfriends-to-be.

"Hey, you're not offended, are you?" Mike asked and tapped Arden's cheek with the back of his fingers.

"No, I just... I'm not ready. Luke messed me up," he said, unable to take his eyes off the blood in the picture. "We had a big fight before I left him."

"Messed you up?" Mike asked, but he didn't try to touch Arden this time, as if he realized it wasn't what Arden wanted or needed. He was good at reading cues like that. Maybe that was why women fell for him so easily?

"I don't mean fight as in we yelled at each other. He got violent with me, and I saw no other way but to fight back. I fell over, he was dragging me by my leg. I grabbed an electric cord attached to a lamp. The next time he tried to hit me, I pulled it to me and broke it on his head. There was so much blood, and he stopped moving. I thought I killed him. That's why I told you the police could be looking for me when we first met. I don't know what's worse anymore. I kinda wish he was dead, but I'm also relieved I didn't kill him and won't go to prison..." He had to take several deep breaths, because he'd forgotten to inhale while speaking and exhausted what he'd had in his lungs.

Mike watched him, his chest rising and falling at an accelerated rate. Blots of red spilled over his cheeks, his brows lowered, and he slammed his fist into the wall right next to the picture.

"How dare he!"

The movement must have come too close to the artwork, because something beeped, and one of the uniformed staff approached them while speaking to someone through a mic attached to her uniform.

"Sir, I'm going to have to ask you to leave," the woman said with a stern expression.

"He won't do it again," Arden whined, but he didn't expect understanding.

Mike stuffed his hands down his pockets. "Yeah, sorry. It was just the wa—"

She wasn't having it. "Security already knows. If you refuse to leave, we will be forced to call the police."

Mike stilled. Swallowed. Glanced at Arden like a dog who knew it had fucked something up. "I'm sorry. You'll find me outside, once you're done here."

"No, let's go together," Arden said right away, sensing numerous gazes licking them in judgment. He wouldn't ditch Mike. Even for Tom of Finland.

Mike stilled, as if he wanted to repeat himself, but grabbed Arden's hand instead and went straight for the exit, ignoring the people, who at this point were staring at them openly. At least the alarm had been switched off.

"Sorry," he mumbled as they entered the corridor under the scrutiny of a male staff member who not-so-discreetly followed them to the elevator.

"It's okay," Arden whispered. "Maybe I shouldn't have been talking about it here. Spoiling your date."

"It's *our* date," Mike mumbled once they stepped into the elevator.

"*Our date.*" Arden repeated, fighting the urge to hug Mike. His heart was frantic, knocking on his breastbone with ever more power, and he couldn't even tell why. Was he so *into* Mike? Was this because they'd been removed from the gallery? Or was he nervous about having told Mike such painful, private things?

If *this* angered Mike so much, what if he decided to take revenge in Arden's name? And Arden had barely scratched the surface of what had happened that night. Images of Mike punching his abductor's face into a pulp, passed through his mind, stirring a warm sense of satisfaction, but he didn't want Mike to go to prison. And if he found out the truth about Luke, he might end up doing something rash.

Mike was completely quiet until they left the museum and faced the green open space again. He exhaled as if he'd been holding his breath that whole time. "What kind of scum does things like that? He never deserved your attention."

Arden led him to a nearby bench where they sat together, facing an abstract sculpture. "I didn't know that at the time. Guess I was thinking with my dick. I may be feminine, but I get as horny as any other guy. More even. Sex clouds my judgement."

"Sometimes I think girls have another, stupider head somewhere too," Mike said, flinching when the hot wood touched his bare arm. No wonder. It had been so, so hot since morning.

That was such an unexpected statement, it broke through Arden's gloom and he snorted. "It's called a clitoris, but I wouldn't know much about it." Maybe it hadn't been the best idea to talk about Luke back at the museum, but telling Mike why he'd had to flee made his chest that bit lighter. As if he wasn't alone with his worries but had an ally who truly wanted to support him.

"People are just animals after all," Mike said and placed his hand on the back of the bench, right behind Arden.

Arden pulled his feet up and rested them on the edge of the seat, hugging his knees. "I know the clit is somewhere in the elbow, but is it the left one or the right one?" He winked at Mike.

"In my experience, the key to a woman's happiness can be anywhere," Mike said and dove in. Arden wanted to pull away, but when Mike's nose slid under his jaw, and warm lips rubbed his skin, his lips uttered the tiniest gasp as pleasure danced up his back.

Arden laughed and slid his fingers into Mike's hair. "I don't know if you're romantic or just really kinky."

Their faces were so painfully close. Their lips less than two inches apart. All he'd have to do was lean in, and Mike would have met him halfway. But he shouldn't.

"I'm a man who can do both," Mike said, grinning.

Arden pressed his hand to Mike's face and playfully pushed him away. "Stop it or I'll call the cops on you, and when they ask me why, I'll tell them you're so sexy it should be illegal. And you don't want that, because then they'll arrest me for hoax calling."

Mike chuckled and stretched, staring up into the sky. "There's no other way around it. If we can't be at that museum and watch men deepthroating, I need to get you a big... fat... ice cream."

Arden kept laughing when Mike wiggled his eyebrows. "That sounds acceptable. I'll show you how to eat one. You can look, but not touch."

Mike shifted so his knee touched Arden's thigh, his sandy hair tickling Arden's cheek while the scent of wood and earthy perfume reached him with the soft breeze. "Will you eat it for me in lingerie?"

Arden cocked his head and played with a curly strand of hair that fell on his forehead. "I will," he whispered.

So wrong. I so shouldn't do that.

Chapter 11 – Mike

Mike liked it when their business partners had money-counting machines. It made doing cash-only transactions so much easier. He smiled, packing the bill folds into his backpack. "It's always good doing business with you."

Though while he kept the conversation going, flirted with Mr. Wong's secretary, and exchanged jokes with the man himself, his mind lingered on Arden, who waited for Mike at a vegetarian Ramen place just around the corner. They were far away from Luke, and Mike was positive they hadn't been followed, but he still worried for the boy's safety. A man who hired goons to abduct their former partner may be cowardly but not less dangerous.

Mike wanted to return to Arden's side as soon as possible.

Fortunately, the secretary called to inform Mr. Wong someone had come to see him, so Mike exchanged another handshake, flirted with the woman again, and rushed outside. It was already dark, but tourists were still crowding the streets, and Mike swallowed his annoyance at being stuck behind a group taking up the whole sidewalk despite moving at an inconsiderately slow pace.

But as he stood at the crossroads and breathed in the scent of gas and salty food, he spotted Arden on the other side of the street, oblivious to Mike's presence while he browsed through his phone, slurping something from a tall metal cup.

Sure, Arden was male, and Mike *had* gotten a glimpse of his dick, but the way he presented himself transcended gender. He wore his curly hair down today, and it was like a mint and lilac halo around his pretty face. He'd been much paler when they met, but he'd tanned a bit since then, which meant freckles had bloomed on his nose and cheeks. Some days he powdered his skin and made them less visible, while on other days he embraced them and even drew on more.

He must have taken into account the long trip, knowing he'd spend hours in a helmet, so he had a more natural look going on, with mascara on his already-long lashes as the statement feature. The white sleeveless top with *Sailor Moon,* which he'd paired with pale blue skinny jeans looked both casual and cute. He'd teased Mike that he would have worn a skirt if they weren't going by bike, and that fantasy was still in Mike's head along with that of lacy panties and stockings under such a skirt.

This boy would drive him crazy. At least his nicotine cravings were now mostly non-existent, and he hoped they'd remain so if he didn't give in to temptation *that one time*. Whether he managed to woo Arden or not, he'd end up gaining something anyway. Like, improving his athletic performance through better lung capacity.

He had no idea where this road would lead him, be he sure hoped there would be at least one stop in Arden's bed.

He entered the restaurant and nodded at the server, heading along a row of small booths separated with black lacquered dividers. The interior was simple, with one textured wall and lots of green plants for decoration instead of stereotypically Japanese imagery, but despite the use of square, somber shapes, each table felt cozy. Particularly the one in the corner, where Arden sat, unaware that he was already being ogled.

"Oh hey!" Arden beamed when Mike came into his field of vision, the pink stud in his nose catching the light. "How was your day at work?" he sniggered. He didn't seem to mind that Mike was involved in illegal shit, and that only ticked another box in Arden's favor.

"Good," Mike said, tossing the backpack on the bench as he pushed his ass next to Arden's instead of sitting down across from him like a good boy.

He was nice, but not *good*.

"What about you? Are you on Grindr, looking for real gay men?" It was a joke, but now that it left his mouth, Mike realized he wanted to know.

"Nah, just browsing online stores. I can't use social media 'cause Luke is probably spying on them, like the creeper he is."

Mike exhaled and pulled the metal straw out of Arden's hand to suck out some of the milkshake. *Hm, vanilla and sesame.* "We'll deal with him in due time."

Arden fluttered those gorgeous lashes at him. "One more word, and I'll believe that you're trying to get into my panties for real!" When he playfully shoved at Mike's arm, a lilac bra strap slipped down Arden's shoulder, and Mike stared at it, struck by the desire to lick the uncovered shoulder and pull on the underwear with his teeth.

They'd gone shopping earlier, and while Mike had roped Arden into going to this alternative unisex lingerie store he'd found on the Internet, the boy refused to let him into the dressing room or show him what he'd ended up picking—even though Mike had paid for it. That loose strap took him back to a place full of sexy outfits and pretty underwear. Mike wanted to see Arden in each and every set.

"Is my interest still a surprise?" he asked and pulled on the strap, breathing faster when he sensed the heat of Arden's skin. "Is that a bra?"

Arden didn't push him away, smirking. "A bralette."

Mike repeated after him, with no clue what that was.

"Hm... Maybe I'll show you at the hotel."

Mike exhaled, choking on the hot air, and he gently placed his hand on Arden's thigh. "Such a little tease."

"Or maybe I won't." The boy laughed but didn't move away, instead placing his hand on top of Mike's and stroking it with his thumb.

This was unbearable.

Torture.

Arden smelled so good too, of fresh flowers, and milky vanilla, and desire.

It didn't matter where they were as long as Arden touched him.

"I'm getting hard," Mike whispered.

"Then we better get going." Arden got up, taking away the lovely heat of his body, but glanced over his shoulder and winked at Mike. "Hope the hotel's nice."

Which only reminded Mike they'd be sleeping in one bed, because he had no shame and booked that kind of room.

"You'll be the death of me, baby," He said and followed, willing his arousal down. But then he remembered he'd left behind the backpack with thousands of dollars and picked it up. He needed to stay focused, because he'd definitely not get to see Arden naked if they crashed.

Getting to their destination took almost an hour, because Mike wasn't in the habit of booking overly expensive hotels in the city center when he could get something just as nice on the outskirts. He did upgrade to a much classier place than usual though, because he doubted Arden would have appreciated the cheap motels Mike chose for his own use.

Arden deserved to be treated like the jewel he was.

The hotel didn't look like anything special—an imitation of the fancy houses in the city center, built sometime in the past fifty years, but it was clean, had a restaurant, and pleasant staff at the reception, so Mike was confident in his choice by the time he and Arden left the elevator in the third floor and walked down the carpeted hallway.

Neither of them spoke, and the dense atmosphere conducted the electricity jolting between their bodies with even more ease, but Mike was still nervous in a way he hadn't been in a long time.

What was Arden really thinking? Was he excited? Worried?

He wanted to ask, but words could have shattered the growing tension, so he only smiled once he found the right door and opened it with the key card.

His heart beat faster. His stomach twisted with unexpected cramps, and none of it subsided once the light went on, revealing that the space, while small, didn't look like some dingy by-the-hour motel room. This was the kind of place you brought your girlfriend to, not a hook-up from Craigslist.

He let Arden enter first and followed him in perfect silence, taking in the large bed with tables on either side and the cabinet with a small television and some magazines. The mirror above a vanity/desk faced the bed, hung at perfect height to showcase things that might happen atop the mattress.

It was way classier than rooms Mike usually booked, but what really counted was Arden's assessment. Would he be pleased?

Arden turned toward him with a gasp and covered the bottom of his face, feigning shock, but his eyes sparkled with glee. "Oh no! There's only one bed!"

Something inside Mike relaxed. He would have offered to sleep on the floor if Arden hated the prospect of sharing the double, but he did agree to this trip in the first place, and, well, the underlying tension kept growing, so it would eventually need to lead to a climax.

"Oh, damn. Seems they couldn't give us that twin I asked for after all," he said and dropped the backpack.

Arden pushed off his white sneakers and jumped onto the bed. "At least there's air-con," he said, bouncing on the mattress, and Mike didn't fail to notice that his sheer socks were lilac just as the bra strap had been. It instantly made him wonder about the panties that went with such a set.

A thong? Something delicate and sweet, or kinky? Did Arden wear corsets too? Mike wanted to see him in one, and then fuck him in it, holding on to the lacing.

"There's just one problem. We forgot to buy the ice cream," he said, sitting on the stool by the vanity to remove his boots.

Arden slid his fingers across his chest as he stilled on the bed. "Well, I wouldn't have wanted it to get all over my new bralette anyway..."

Now Mike was sure Arden was flirting back as if his pants were on fire and needed taking off ASAP.

He exhaled, opening and closing his hands to loosen up, but it seemed excruciatingly hard when Arden was right there, flat on the bed, his long legs stretched, as if just waiting for Mike to crawl in between.

"It's a curious name. And I still don't know what it is."

Arden gave him the most sultry bedroom eyes as he sat up, and Mike couldn't take his eyes off his slender form. The conversation from the gallery came back to him. Not the shitty one about Luke, but the one where Arden mused on how good being fucked could feel.

"Will you be a good boy and not touch?" Arden smirked, already reaching to the edge of his top and toying with it.

Christ.

How. How was this so hot? What was it about Arden that made Mike's brain shrink until it made him stupid?

"You know I'm not good."

Arden pondered that, biting his lips. "I suppose you're far enough. And you did take me out on an amazing date…" He was already pulling off the top, and Mike hadn't been more horny to see a bra since he was fourteen and desperate to squeeze some tits.

The bralette lay flat on Arden's chest—a flimsy piece of stretchy lace that covered the hardening nipples, but had no filling, no push-up effect. No pretense at suggesting there was more than a pec in there.

It was lovely. The color looked *amazing* against Arden's skin, but there was something about this skimpy piece of translucent fabric that sent a burning hot chisel into what Mike used to believe about his sexuality, and crushed it all into pieces that needed to be put back together in a new way.

Before this moment, he could have blamed his interest on simple curiosity, but he now realized this was something he'd needed to see all along. Because it was *thrilling*.

"I did," he muttered in an embarrassingly quiet voice.

"But are you ready to see what you paid for?" Arden seemed so at ease, playing with the attraction between them as he kneeled on the bed, fingers hovering over the button of his jeans. He was so tiny, yet held so much power in those smooth, graceful hands. Did he realize what he was doing to Mike?

Did he know that if he asked Mike to hand him over the club money, Mike would have actually considered it? He wouldn't have robbed his family, but he would have entertained the idea!

"I'm always ready for you, baby," Mike rasped and pulled on the leg of his jeans when they started growing uncomfortable.

He wasn't even sure how or when Arden wrapped him around his little finger like that. They were alone in the room with sexual chemistry sizzling like a steak carelessly thrown on the grill, and he didn't dare touch uninvited to not risk spooking the pretty blue-eyed doe.

Arden winked, making a slow turn. "I don't think you are, but let's try." He tugged down the zipper of his jeans and started pulling them down at an excruciatingly slow pace.

He had wide hips for such a slender guy, but once the delicate lilac lace emerged, hugging Arden's buttocks just right, Mike went still, and only his heart rushed, pumping testosterone-dense blood. The panties showed bits of skin between the subtle patterns of lilac fabric, and dove between the pert buttocks, ending halfway, to show off the bottom of Arden's ass.

Christ. Mike loved this kind of underwear.

And on Arden, he loved it more than ever.

"Yess..."

Arden pushed the jeans all the way down to his knees, but then bent forward and supported himself with one hand to pull them off completely. He wiggled his painted toes in the sheer socks, but Mike's attention was right back on that gorgeous ass only half-covered by fabric. Arden held his thighs together for the most part, but whenever he shifted to pull on the jeans, Mike spotted a hint of balls tucked into the panties, and the sight of them was so unexpected when paired with lavender mesh, that he couldn't think straight.

The last time he'd felt like this was when he'd been about to lose his virginity many, many years ago.

"You like what you bought?" Arden's voice was barely audible through the thudding of blood in Mike's head, but he nodded nevertheless, scalded by the inferno raging inside him. He wanted to grab one of the cute feet and pull off the sock with his teeth before sucking on each of the pretty toes.

"Spread your legs," he breathed. "I need to see more detail."

Arden glanced over his shoulder, but then, almost shyly, parted his thighs. His balls and cock were tucked into lace, close to the front of his body, but the bulge was there. Was he as hard as Mike?

He had such smooth thighs, with milky skin devoid of any imperfections, but once Mike saw Arden's balls lovingly encased in the panties, that was all he could see. At the back of his mind, he wondered whether such obvious signs of the male sex shouldn't deter him from Arden, but somehow their presence made it all even sexier. Kinky. Taboo. Illicit. Here was this unique creature, this very feminine man, and Mike wanted him. God, he wanted this boy so much.

"Yes. You chose a beautiful piece. Will you show me from up close?" he uttered, struggling to speak clearly while his mind whirred, causing ever more noise.

Despite Arden's confidence, he now seemed like the frailest piece of porcelain that Mike would need to handle with care so it wouldn't break. Arden made a slow turn, still on his knees. When he presented Mike with the erection trapped behind lace, his face was flushed, and he looked so fuckable Mike had to pinch his palm to not charge in.

What was he to do? He didn't want to scare Arden and rush in like he would have with someone less fragile. Words were the one weapon he had left.

"You are... Baby, you're the hottest piece of ass I've ever seen."

The tension in Arden's features gave way to a small smile, and he stood on the bed, presenting himself in all of his long-legged glory. Mike could already imagine him in stockings, harnesses, or garter belts Mike would hold as he plundered his ass from behind. He was a sexy beauty, and Mike would devour him whole given half the chance.

When that devil in angelic disguise tentatively approached the edge of the bed Mike rose for a better look. He was a statue made of alabaster—so perfect in its beauty Mike felt undeserving of his attention. But when Mike's face was just inches from the bralette so tenderly hugging the pink nipples, Arden put his slender fingers on Mike's shoulders and met his eyes from above.

"Kiss me?" he whispered, and Mike's barriers broke, sending burning splinters everywhere.

"Told you that you'd ask for it eventually," he whispered and pulled on Arden's thighs, but caught him halfway through the fall. Arden's nostrils flared as he looked up, shivering already, but Mike placed one foot on the edge of the bed and held him up by the waist. "There. I got you now, pussycat. And I'll give you all the treats you want."

He placed his open palm between the cups of the bralette, and whimpered when Arden's heart knocked against the ribcage, as if it wanted to break free and feel Mike's touch. But then he moved his fingers lower, along the smooth stomach, eventually tickling Arden's belly button.

"What should I call you? Are you my king? My queen? Princess? My sweet little slut?" he teased, falling forward so his knee hit the mattress. The change of position made Arden gasp, but Mike was still holding him up.

Arden wouldn't even blink, panting as he locked his eyes with Mike's. There wasn't a masculine bone in that cute body. "Kitten?" he whispered, gripping Mike's arms like his life depended on it.

The little pussycat knew what he wanted.

Mike had enough reason to lower Arden into the sheets gently before he straddled him, pushing his fingers into the lush hair. His other hand rolled down to Arden's pec and squeezed it as he leaned down, staring into the pale blue eyes that spoke of complete worship.

"My little sex kitten. My precious sugar figurine. I'm going to eat you whole and suck all the sweetness out of your bones," he said and pressed his lips to Arden's.

He'd have burned less if lightning hit him in the dick.

And now he yearned to have it all. To ravish Arden so completely no other man would ever satisfy him again, to hear the boy begging for dick. *His* dick.

And even now, trembling under Mike's touch, Arden wasn't passive. He slid his fingers into Mike's beard to pull him closer and opened his mouth in invitation accompanied by his hot breath. And as if that wasn't arousing enough, he arched his hips off the bed with a mewl, like a cat in heat desperate to rub against *something*.

Mike rolled his face against Arden's, his tongue diving ever deeper, teasing Arden's and tickling the roof of his mouth as he lowered himself, rocking his raging hard-on against the boy's cute lace-covered dick. His brain sizzled, and even with his eyes closed he could see colors he'd never recognized before. It was madness.

He was crazy for Arden. And loved it.

His kitten moaned into the kiss, but the pace at which he rubbed against Mike left his intentions clear. They were fucking despite their clothes covering all the important bits, and Mike had no qualms about sliding his hand under the bralette to squeeze the stiff nipple. So responsive, so horny, yet so pliant, the boy was his wet dream come true.

He nipped on Arden's lip and pushed the slim thighs apart, settling between them as he moved his kisses to the arch of Arden's throat, lapping at it as he descended lower, already pulling down the straps of the bralette to uncover nipples.

They were flat and small, but Mike couldn't resist and poked the pink flesh with his tongue, rolling his hips against Arden's as his balls grew ever heavier.

He was about to come as fast as a horny teenager.

"You're such a lusty little kitten. I could practically smell it on you."

He realized Arden curled around him when nails bit into his back through fabric, and Arden's feet landed on his thighs, right under his ass. Arden pushed his face against Mike's neck, panting pure arousal.

"It's your fault," Arden uttered, and Mike didn't hate one bit that the boy was basically fucking himself against him, the hard flesh rubbing his time and time again. "So hot. I just wanna... suck you, fuck you, drip with your cum."

"Yes. Yes. I'll give you everything you want and more," Mike rasped, opening his pants when the pressure of underwear became too much to bear. His mind spun when he pulled on Arden's nipple with his teeth, and as he looked between their bodies, to Arden's cockhead popping from under the lace as if it wanted attention, Mike grabbed his own cock and pushed it where Arden's groin met his thigh, under the panties, so it poked Arden's.

Both their shafts stretched the delicate fabric, making it bulge, and he frantically thrust into that pocket of damp flesh and underwear, staring straight into the watery gaze shining at him from Arden's face. "I'll make you drink my cum every morning and night, so you're fattened up by the time I want to eat you."

Arden dug his nails into flesh with more force and bucked his hips, lips parted for a moan as he clenched his eyes shut. The heat between them intensified, and Mike's cock got more hot lubrication to drill into. He wanted to do *everything* to this gorgeous, shivering body.

He wanted to wreck it. He wanted to worship it. He wanted to curl around it every night.

He'd been asleep for so long, but Arden pulled him into a reality where cum smelled delicious and dicks looked tempting in women's panties.

Hot spunk splashed his cock, and he thrust harder, faster, capturing Arden's lips as he came, rolling his hips between those tempting thighs. He would have loved to fuck Arden's tender ass, but he was too frantic to wonder about all the options that lay ahead.

Arden's cock throbbed right next to his, and he couldn't force himself to care whether what they were doing was gay or not. It was horny, fleshy, dirty, and all his. Just the thought that their spunk now stained Arden's lacy panties made Mike kiss Arden with more excitement.

He grabbed the boy, pulled him close, and rolled them over so the lithe, warm body lay on top of his. It quivered in the aftermath of their orgasm, and Mike eagerly soothed Arden with long kisses trailed along his jaw.

Arden lifted his flushed face and shifted with Mike's cock still in his panties, which was so ridiculously hot Mike's gaze got cloudy. His bralette had shifted, revealing one nipple, and the curly hair was out of order.

"Um… so… that kiss got out of hand," he muttered, and Mike grinned, petting Arden's cheek with the back of his hand.

Maybe he should've been horrified that touching another man's bits excited him rather than disgusted, but he really didn't care. At thirty-seven, he'd just had an epiphany, and when his instinct told him to go ahead with something, he never fought it.

"Yeah, well. You're just too hot to resist."

Arden exhaled. "You're not exactly Quasimodo either." He pulled away and sat on Mike's hips, triggering a fantasy of Arden riding his cock even though right now, Mike was so happily spent.

Mike stretched, content despite his cock starting to burn from rubbing against fabric earlier. "True. We're both irresistible, baby," he whispered, placing his hands on Arden's hips.

Arden rubbed his face and kneeled to get Mike's dick out of his panties, but ended up sliding them down altogether, and yep, he was fully shaved.

"But it shouldn't have happened," he groaned, his chest still flushed when he gave Mike's cock a longing look.

Mike frowned.

He caught Arden's hand and pulled to his mouth, kissing the warm middle of his palm. "Why, kitten? We both want it."

"Because I promised myself to stop being a stupid slut and fuck men who can't be in relationships with me." He awkwardly untangled himself out of the spunk-soaked panties and sat his ass next to Mike, but didn't pull his hand away. And while his flush was still sexy, the frown told Mike the boy was overthinking it all.

"You're not stupid. And didn't you tell me yourself that you're not interested in relationships? Neither am I. We could have a good thing going," Mike said, petting Arden's perfectly smooth thigh and stealing glances at his softening cock. Even not in the heat of the moment, seeing it made Mike flush.

"Because I wasn't. But with you, I eventually would be. I really like you Mike, but that's exactly why I can't do this. I'm sorry. We can still be kissing friends like before, right?" He swallowed, and as much as Mike hated what he was hearing, he wanted to wipe the worry off Arden's face more than express his frustration.

This wasn't the first time this had happened to him, but the first time it happened with a person he so desperately wanted to keep in his bed for longer. And it fucking sucked.

"Okay. Kissing friends. Got it," he whispered, trying not to show his disappointment too much, already wondering whether he shouldn't rethink his policy when it came to relationships. There were no guarantees he'd ever meet another unicorn like Arden and... no. No, he should not change anything. He'd chosen to stay single for a reason, and he would not listen to his dick when it came to juggling with Arden's life.

Maybe it would be better that way.

"You wanna shower first?" Mike asked, once more glancing at all that tempting flesh. This one time would have to last him forever.

At least now he'd get to kiss that tempting mouth in private.

"Yeah, if I can. I'm so pumped out." Arden laughed nervously, grabbed a towel, and was off, giving Mike one last glimpse of his gorgeous ass.

He wanted to howl, but whatever he'd discovered about himself tonight could no longer be explored, not with Arden at least, and when the boy disappeared in the bathroom, Mike rolled to his side and groaned into the pillow.

Maybe it *was* better that way. He'd already gotten far too attached to Arden for their own good, but the moment he remembered the dirty underwear lying on the edge of the bed, he sat up and sought it out, shivering at the memory of the glorious moment his and Arden's cocks rubbed together beneath the flimsy lace. It was a wonder the fabric hadn't torn.

Desire was back, faint but already there, prompting him to lean in and hover his face above the damp panties, so he could breathe in the musky scent of their sex.

If he was to ever open his heart again, could he be with a boy? Rain was right about one thing—he shouldn't toy with Arden's feelings if he wasn't sure. Arden's body was deliciously sexy, and Mike was into every last bit of it. This attraction changed his sexual identity. He just wasn't sure how.

While Arden showered, Mike stretched the panties over his softened cock, but it wasn't the same without Arden in there with him.

And besides, he was too upset to get hard again and managed to remove the incriminating evidence from his dick before Arden returned, wrapped in a towel.

Their eyes met, and Mike was hit by a longing so intense he rolled out of bed right away. "I'll leave you to it."

Arden did smile at him though and grabbed Mike's wrist to stop him on the way to the shower. He stood on his toes and kissed Mike's cheek. "I did have fun. It's gonna be okay between us."

Mike made himself smile. "Of course. Kissing friends," he said and swatted Arden's ass before hiding in the bathroom where the damp air left behind by the first shower choked him from the get-go.

Damn it.

Fuck.

Fuck.

Fuck.

His shower would be a cool one. Maybe once he woke up tomorrow, his unexplained attraction to Arden would be only a memory.

He took his time, washing every bit of his body and hair, because despite Arden playing it so cool, things had changed, and Mike didn't feel like facing that fact. By the time he finally left the bathroom, Arden was all tucked in and peeked at him from where he squashed his cheek on the pillow.

Mike would have eaten his own hand to keep him around.

"Look, I know *you know* I lied. I wanted the one bed. So if that's not okay, I can just sleep on the floor tonight."

Arden pushed a pillow at him. "Don't be stupid. It's a big bed." He then proceeded to put another pillow between them. "There. Respectable."

Mike accepted the fluffy wall between them. But somehow, in his sleep, Arden crawled over it, and by midnight, he lay with his head on Mike's shoulder.

Chapter 12 – Mike

Mike had never stopped missing Leah.

He'd been sixteen when he'd met her, and knew he'd want to marry her only a month later. But life—death—had gotten in the way.

She was a bit too tall, a bit too thin, with black eyes and the biggest nose he'd seen on a girl. He'd loved that nose as much as she'd hated it. It was an unexpected feature that some might have called ugly, but it made her even more beautiful to Mike. Yeah, he wasn't blind, and there were plenty of girls, who were technically prettier than Leah, but none of them had her smile, none of them understood him to the point of finishing sentences for him.

Everything changed when he lost her, and while he tried to go through life with a smile, it often remained skin-deep, because he would never let himself forget that she'd still be alive if she hadn't foolishly chosen him.

There had been a few women since Leah who had caught his attention for longer, but Mike wouldn't let them make Leah's mistake, and kept them at arm's length. They didn't know he was doing them a favor when he broke their hearts.

He stroked the patches on the back of the vest that had belonged to her, fondly remembering the night he'd given it to her. *Mad Mike* had been his motocross nickname, and he hadn't even been a prospect, let alone held the right to gift a woman a property vest. But he'd been young and stupid, so he'd mirrored the gestures he'd learned were important. He'd sewn on the patches himself, and Leah had worn them like a badge of honor.

That vest had caused her death, and pointed her out to anyone who cared to look. Mike should have burned the thing years ago, but he didn't have the heart to. Not then, not now. He put it back in the wardrobe so it could serve its purpose as a reminder of why Mike wasn't allowed to love.

Out of his family, he'd been the only one who'd lost a partner to gang conflict, but that didn't mean it couldn't happen again, and the last thing he needed was to pull anyone into danger for his selfish needs. He wasn't a good guy, but he did have a heart.

His gaze drifted to the bed, where he'd slept with Arden since their return from San Francisco. Arden's side always had that faint scent of jasmine that made him want to roll in the sheets and let that aroma cling to his flesh, but he would not do it.

Mike had never been good at lying to himself. He'd fucked up.

He'd allowed himself too close to Arden, because he didn't think it would cause any issues. After all, he was straight and therefore couldn't develop gay feelings, but he had, and couldn't take any of it back.

He still *felt* straight but was falling for Arden as if he'd slipped and was tumbling toward the boy's waiting arms at record speed. He hadn't planned for this to happen, but it did, and the one way forward was to ignore his budding feelings until Arden moved on.

One way to allow that to happen was creating a bit of distance, so he stayed put when Arden went off to do some stuff with Mona, but he'd been itching to text Arden and make sure he was safe every five minutes.

To the world outside their bubble, nothing had changed. After all, they still claimed to be a couple, they kissed, and hugged, and teased each other. But the chemistry between them had changed, and Mike wasn't sure if it was for the better or for the worse. On one hand, he was ecstatic over being allowed more touch, for Arden to admit he was attracted to him, but on the other, it rubbed the already slippery slope with lube.

It was Friday, so their friends had started to gather in the courtyard for the upcoming party. The air already smelled of grilled meat as Mike made his way through the bar, past the girls practising their stripping routine for the night, and he stepped outside, searching for the familiar figure before he could chastise himself for it.

The setting sun colored everything orange, but its light was still strong enough to blind, and forced Mike to squint. His gaze settled on a pair of long legs in fishnet stockings. He knew those weren't tights, because of the strip of flesh between their edge and the hem of a short black skirt. The garment was flared, and for the briefest moment Mike wished for the breeze to lift it just a little and allow him a glimpse of what was underneath.

Only then did his horny brain register the pastel hair arranged into twin ponytails and exploded with two contradicting drives. He wanted to grab a blanket and wrap it around Arden to keep all that sexy flesh to himself. But he also very much felt like walking up to the boy and sliding his hand under the tiny skirt, to cup Arden's package and feel its warmth through satin and lace.

Arden had paired the skimpy bottom with a plain black T-shirt—a very thoughtful move—because otherwise he'd make men self-combust from being exposed to all that sexiness. The fairy wings Mike had bought him the day they met moved with each sway of Arden's body, triggering fantasies of them tickling Mike's torso while he fucked Arden from behind. His boots had a little platform that was taller under the heels, and a wide waist-cinching belt further created the illusion of a female figure. He was *stunning*.

Arden's face lit up when he turned around. The front of his T-shirt wasn't as plain as Mike had assumed, and while it didn't show much of Arden's neckline, the *Miss Kitten* written in bold white letters at the front drew attention to the boy's torso, making Mike wonder what kind of lingerie he was wearing tonight.

"Hey, baby, I like your T-shirt," he shouted across the yard. "Will you hand your man some beer?" he asked, eager to remind everyone that they were fake-really an item.

"Sure thing, babe!" Arden yelled back and made his way to the tub filled with ice cubes and bottles.

Mike could have sworn he wasn't the only straight man watching those long legs work.

After almost two months, everyone was quite used to Mike's displays of affection, and whether they questioned them or not, they didn't do it openly anymore, so Mike strolled to an outdoor furniture set in the corner and sat down next to Leo and Zolt, who played cards with Kane of all people, and another man Mike didn't know. He was muscular and bald, with very strong features that reminded Mike of professional bodybuilders. This was probably yet another man Zolt knew from his daily gym visits.

"You met Theo?" Leo pointed to the stranger. "My brother, Mike."

Mike shook his hand and sat in the vacant armchair, just in time to pull Arden into his lap when he approached with the beer.

What kind of panties did the boy hide under the skirt? How many people would see them? Was there a bra under that T-shirt as well? One with slits for nipples?

Theo's smile widened. "Ah, so you're the gay one."

Leo smirked so hard his face was about to break, but didn't look up from his cards.

Mike remained unfazed, wrapping his arm around Arden's waist, and he rested his cheek on the boy's shoulder. Hell yes, there was a strap under his T-shirt!

He took the bottle from Arden's hand, kissed his cold fingertips and met Theo's gaze. "Our sister, Rain is the gay one. Leo's bi, and I'm straight."

The silence at the table was cut by Kane's hyena-like cackle. "Straight my ass!"

Arden shifted in Mike's lap and put his arms around Mike's neck, pulling him to his chest. "Don't you dare talk shit about my boyfriend."

Kane's eyes settled on Arden. "Or what, pretty boy? You gonna climb me again? That was *sooo* scary."

Mike waved the idiot off, glancing at Zolt and Theo while Arden's cute, jasmine-scented arms settled around him more comfortably. Ah, he could feel the bralette under the thin black fabric rubbing his ear.

He pointed between Zolt and Theo. "*You're* gay. What would you call a man who likes girls and one feminine guy?" he asked and swatted Arden's ass to show how serious he was about his attraction. The gesture was for show. But he wanted to feel the flesh bounce all the same.

Kane shook his head. "Horny?"

The table erupted with laughter, and even Leo chuckled. Maybe he did notice Mike made a point of not calling him gay this one time.

"Doesn't matter. He's just too cute to resist," Mike said and looked up at Arden, gently tugging on his ponytail.

Arden grinned and leaned down for a kiss. All of this affection was for show, yet it felt as real as the meat sizzling on the huge barbeque manned by Axel. As real as the barely-there cellulite on the stripper he could see through the open window of the bar.

"Mike! A word!" Dad yelled from the open door of the clubhouse, and urged him to hurry with a quick gesture.

Mike groaned, rolling his eyes at Leo and the others, but held Arden's chin for a bit longer and licked his sweet lips before gently pushing him off. "You heard your daddy-in-law. Gotta go."

Arden stood and adjusted his skirt. "I'll be with Mona." He pointed to a group of tipsy women dancing in the dying sun. "Sorry, I'm not really a cards kind of guy."

His skirt moved up as he spun, revealing sheer black fabric and Mike couldn't help himself. He slid his hand under the hem and touched Arden's ass, rubbing his fingers over warm flesh. "I bet you're all jealous," he told the other men and pinched Arden, who yelped with a bright smile on his face.

He was so damn cute.

If Mike could do it without emotional fallout, he'd bend Arden over a bar stool and fuck him then and there. Skirt lifted, and panties pulled down. No frills.

But Dad wasn't a patient man, so Mike said goodbye to those fantasies and jogged over to the clubhouse.

The smell of coffee and spicy meat marinade hit him the moment he entered the door across from the bar. The big kitchen was located in the very back, and he could hear his mom there, chatting to Trixie about some baby-related stuff, but instead of continuing down the red-painted corridor, he took a turn left and walked into Dad's shabby office.

It was simple, just tidy enough work in, with an ancient computer on a side desk, and a single filing cabinet next to it. But Dad sat across from the door, behind a desk littered with folders and family pictures, a new motorcycle model attached to the wall behind him as the only real decoration. Unless the little exercise bike in the corner counted.

Mike kicked the door shut behind him. "What's up?" he asked Dad, who looked through the drawer in front of him, longish gray hair falling into his face no matter how often he pushed it back.

"We need to talk. I know it's been fun and all, but this Arden thing is getting out of hand," Dad said with a deep frown on his wrinkly forehead.

Mike's brows lowered. He did not expect *that*.

"Says who?"

"Says me. Is this some misguided scream for attention? Doesn't matter." Dad sat back in the chair and watched Mike like a hawk. "That guy, Luke? He's got a lucrative offer for us, and it would solve this problem. We just need to look the other way next time he takes the boy."

Mike laughed, but then stilled, weirded out when Dad didn't join him and remained serious, leaning back in his chair like a king expecting Mike to nod and leave like a good boy. Mike was *not* a good boy.

"The fuck did you just say? We agreed to protect Arden. Rain made it happen. Does *she* know what you're planning?" Mike asked, squeezing the bottle hard while his brain pulsed, struggling to cope with what he'd just heard. This couldn't be happening. His dad wouldn't have dealt with someone like Luke. The club had once considered something similar, when Mona hid in their clubhouse to escape an unwanted marriage, but at the end of the day, at that time Dad had been negotiating with her family, not with someone who wanted her hurt.

Dad spread his arms. "We did, but his money's running out. Do you know if he's making anything on the side?"

Mike's lungs tightened, keeping him lightheaded. "You're taking money for his protection? The fuck?"

Dad cocked his head. "Since when do we take in strays for free?"

Mike tossed the bottle Arden had given him at the wall. Beer and glass exploded over Dad's exercise bike. "*What* did you call him? How much has he paid already?" Mike asked, burning inside.

Arden was so very afraid of that bastard. How dare anyone even consider handing him back as if he were livestock?

Dad stroked his short beard, squinting at Mike. "A stray. Barely three grand. Fair price, taking into account that some of us almost got shot saving his ass."

Mike exhaled, struggling to keep his fists in check. His feet felt heavy as he approached, the world around him blurred and red. "You will give him back every cent."

"Oh, yeah? Are you gonna pay for him now? Since he's your *boyfriend*? I see right fucking through you, Mike. I don't know why you're continuing with this charade, but it ends right now!"

Mike lost it. He fucking lost it. Within two steps, he grabbed the edge of the desktop and pulled, knocking it over so fast Dad had to dash into the corner to save his feet. Papers, pens, the lamp, and even family photos tumbled to the floor, and Mike stepped right over them, his fists itching for blood.

"We don't do that. We don't sell people! What the fuck is wrong with you?"

Father's blue eyes shone, and he scowled. "Fine. But he should take a hike. This game of yours has gone too far."

Mike grabbed him by the collar, but let go, stumbling back when a hard punch from below snapped his jaws together and popped his head up. His feet hit the desk, but he managed not to fall over and blinked, showing Dad his bloodied teeth. Had he bitten his tongue? Yes, he fuckin had.

Mike could no longer think. He dashed at his father with a roar, grabbed the fist flying his way, and landed a hard punch on his old man's face. "Fuck you! You will not tell me what to do with my life!"

"I sure as hell will, if you have shit for brains!" Dad yelled, no longer playing. He kicked Mike's feet from under him, but wasn't fast enough, and Mike used the momentum to pull Dad to the floor with him.

A cup filled with pens smashed into Mike's head when they hit the filing cabinet on the way down, but he'd taken much harder beatings than that and climbed on top of Dad, slamming his fist into the stomach exposed by the rolled-up T-shirt. His opponent gave a choked cry but didn't give up and hooked his arm around Mike's head, using his superior weight to turn the tables and push Mike to the floor.

"I'll fucking kill you if you don't let me go, *now!*"

Dad huffed, but hit Mike's head against the floor once before getting off him and backing out. He grumbled something under his breath, rubbing his already-swollen jaw.

Mike scrambled to his feet, panting, and only when he saw blood on the floor did he check his forearm and saw a shard of glass sticking out. He removed it with a scowl and tossed it toward the exercise bike.

"You will give him the money back, and if you see Luke, you tell me, and I'll come to twist off his balls!" Mike added in a hoarse voice, his head spinning a bit from the influx of adrenaline. "That damn coward needs to die."

Dad shook his head and rubbed some blood from under his nose. "Luke didn't call. I just wanted to see how serious you are about Arden. Is this a sex thing? Is the girl boy giving you some magic head or something?" he asked in a helpless voice, spreading his arms.

Mike looked around the ruined office, still catching his breath. "What the fuck, dad? Have you heard of this thing called *asking*?"

The door burst open, and Jack rushed in before taking a step back, wide-eyed, almost walking into Mom, who stood behind him, staring at the chaos inside in silent shock. "What. The. Hell?" Jack zeroed in on Mike, but Dad waved him off.

"It's all good, Jacky. Me and Mike... we needed to talk man to man."

Jack's scowl told Mike he wasn't convinced, but he eventually retreated. "I won't be cleaning up all *that* mess," he said and shut the door behind him, already whispering something to Mom. Great.

Mike exhaled, slowly going down from the high of anger. "Why would you care? Leo's literally *married* to a man."

Dad huffed and entwined his fingers at his nape, staring at the mess, as if he hadn't expected any of this to happen. "It's just that... I thought I *knew* you, Mike. I see so much of myself in you. You're the man I would have been if I never married your mother. If you're going gay... I don't even know this world anymore. You know I support you. You wanted to get the snip? I told you which doctor to go to. But as I told you then, I'm once again saying *think it through*. You don't know how reversible this thing is."

Mike couldn't take the stupidity of that argument. "Those two things aren't similar at all! Are you saying sucking Arden's dick would permanently change me? How? I can go back to pussy any time I want. What did you want to achieve here? You think threatening him would change my mind? That I would stop protecting him because of money? Come on, Dad! You know me better than this."

Dad exhaled, shutting his eyes as if he wanted to forget about the inferno he'd caused. "People will talk, Mike. They already do. Right now, you can still go back on this shit and be the prankster of the century or whatever you want to achieve. But if people realize you're serious, women will look at you differently. We all know Leo's bisexual, but you still call him gay. I don't even need an answer right now. Just think about it without being all defensive. You've been through a lot, and I want the best for you."

Mike took a deep breath, trying to clear his brain of all the latent anger. Arden was safe, and Dad's annoyance was focused on Mike's behavior rather than the boy. "Dad, I know you mean well, and you... I guess you said it yourself that you think we're alike. I get it that it's hard to see me not acting like you'd expect me to, but believe me when I say I don't care what people think. I really don't. Remember when people said I could have a prettier girlfriend than Leah? I didn't care either. I don't live to satisfy other people."

Dad lowered his eyes at the mention of Leah, and he nodded. "Fine, but keep me informed on what's going on. It's enough that the Jarens are trying to push their bride on us. We don't know this Luke guy well, so it's hard to say when or if he'll stop being a danger to the boy. I agree to stop taking Arden's money, but if you want to give him back what he already paid, dig into your own savings. You live here for free and don't have kids. You can afford it."

Mike scowled. "Fine. He's mine, and I'll take care of him."

Dad had nothing to say to that, so Mike walked out, but the storm raging in his head was still there. As much as he didn't care how other people felt about him, the problem lay in how he understood himself. Because as much as he liked to look sturdy and relentless in front of Dad, he wasn't sure how he'd feel if girls started shunning him. His relationship with Arden wasn't even real, proven by their sexless bed, and if Arden didn't want to take things further unless they were really an item, and Mike didn't want a relationship, then he shouldn't drag this out. Maybe Dad was right after all?

He should find a girl to have fun with, because the current limbo wasn't good for anyone. Not him. Not Arden. And when something at the back of his mind whispered he'd miss the sight of a cock pushing at lace, he waved it off, and wiped his face with his forearm, leaving the building in a somber mood.

Was he into girly boys? Was that it, and he'd just never met any before Arden? Or was he straight and therefore liked feminine people, regardless of their junk? He wasn't sure it mattered when people like Arden were so few and far between.

His feet dug into the dirt when through the open door of the bar, he spotted one of the strippers rubbing herself against the pole, and realised he hadn't had sex in two months. *Two months*!

When was the last time *that* happened?

The answer choked him, because it had been after he'd lost Leah and couldn't look at other women for a while. But once he was out of mourning? It had never happened since. Mike had always been hypersexual, eager to find new partners, but he'd been so absorbed with Arden's presence of late that he hadn't sought out willing girls, or agreed to liaisons when they were proposed.

He'd been too enchanted, too focused on this incredible creature to even think about anyone else. And that one time the two of them had sex? He'd *exploded*. What did that say about him?

All he knew was that he wasn't gay. The idea of kissing a man like Zolt, one sporting masculine cologne and scratching him with stubble made Mike gag. But Arden wasn't like that. Arden was... somewhere between genders in a way that completely preoccupied Mike. No wonder Dad was worried. Was it possible that his interest in Arden did in fact numb him to womanly charms? He hadn't been worried before, but now that the seed of doubt had taken root in his brain, he needed to know for sure. And Arden didn't have a reason to be offended. It wasn't like they were having sex...

Mike swallowed when his gaze found the sexy boy swaying his hips to music, his skirt close to revealing more than it should. He used to be so isolated, yet there he was, making friends. He didn't *need* Mike anymore.

Arden glanced over his shoulder, as if he sensed Mike's gaze on him. Smiled. Swayed his hips while stretching his arms above his head, wordlessly inviting Mike to dance. Mike wanted to come over, and he would have, but the unpleasant confrontation with Dad made him think too much, and now... he didn't know what he should do about the uncertainty growing in his chest.

When Mike didn't approach right away, Arden grabbed a beer out of the tub and marched his way, jogging for a moment to reach him quicker.

"Everything okay with your dad?" Arden asked, passing him a bottle. The black makeup around the eyes and the mesh wings transformed him into a dark goddess tonight and somehow made him even more seductive. Mike had to act fast if he was to take any action, or he'd forget all his worries and doubts in Arden's magnetic presence.

"Yeah. We had a little disagreement. You'll get back your money," Mike said, pressing the cool bottle to his chest in hopes it would help him stay sane. But it was hard. Arden was just so... it was impossible to focus on anyone else when he was around. An orchid growing in a field of poppies and black-eyed Susans.

"Oh. Were you fighting over that? I'm sorry." Arden's face fell, and he grabbed Mike's hand. His fingers were so smooth, so perfect for kissing that Mike had to let them go.

"It's fine. I'll deal with it. Just..." How was he to broach an uncomfortable topic when Arden was looking at him with so much trust and hope? "Listen, I've been thinking, and this isn't quite working for me. I'm getting restless, and since we're faking it... you know," Mike said and cleared his throat, eager to be done with this conversation already.

Arden's gaze instantly became more attentive, and his body language—alert. "Oh? Wh-what do you mean?"

He was just being honest, but Arden's reaction still made him feel like an asshole. But what was he to do? Arden didn't want to fuck around, and Mike didn't want to be in a relationship. What he wanted was to find out if he was still into girls and get laid. "I mean that we don't have sex, and this isn't going anywhere. I'll still fake it with you, and protect you, but we should tell everyone our relationship is open."

"So you can sleep with women?" Arden asked as if he needed to confirm the obvious.

This shouldn't have been so hard, but the music blaring from the speakers was giving Mike a headache, and the blurred forms of dancing people transformed into demons laughing at his ineptness. "Well... yeah. You said you will only sleep with a guy if you're in a relationship, and I don't want to be in one. So... it only makes sense."

"Okay," was all Arden had for him. He turned around, taking the beer he'd brought for Mike with him, leaving him alone and stunned into silence. He wanted to feel the sting of a slap to his cheek, because this silent anger was much worse.

Arden should have splashed him with beer, not walked off as if Mike weren't worthy of being upset over. Didn't he care? Wasn't he sad?

Mike was.

"Just… stay where I can see you," he called out, desperate for Arden to look over his shoulder again. But the boy didn't spare him a single glance, rejoining the group of dancing women.

Okay. All Mike needed to do was find a horny target. He was used to this. These were his hunting grounds, full of chicks who came to party at the club with the exact purpose of scoring free beers and sucking some biker dick. This shouldn't be hard at all. If the boy's fancy lingerie got Mike so hot, all he needed to do was enjoy that same thing on a woman.

That thought got him back to wondering what the boy was sporting under the T-shirt tonight, and his imagination went off the rails and into the gutter where a pink cock strained against cum-soaked panties right next to his bigger dick. Even that size difference was a turn-on that tickled his vanity.

He was thirty-seven. How come he hadn't discovered this about himself earlier?

It didn't matter. He'd focus and *score*. It had been two months since he'd tried to woo a woman into his bed, and he'd managed to charm Arden's panties off, so how could this task be in any way difficult?

He took a deep breath, relaxed his shoulders, and walked across the yard, into the bar where the pretty blonde stripper taunted him with the sway of her full hips. She was in fancy underwear, her lips were painted red, and she actually had tits.

She'd never slept with him before either. Wouldn't she like to pull a bi-curious guy back to the straight and narrow? Who wouldn't, right?

The wave of heat scorched Mike the moment he stepped through the threshold, and it clung to him with aromas of beer, cologne, and arousal as the beautiful woman on stage tipped her cowboy hat and arched against the pole in a very special rendition of a square dance. The white cowboy boots made the nakedness of her legs more obvious, and the high-cut bodysuit with a print of the Texan flag made her so reminiscent of classic comic book heroines Mike half-expected her to pull him close with a lasso that had the power of igniting uncontrollable lust.

He pushed past Kane, who watched the show with his girlfriend, and stood at the base of the stage, taking in the glorious fullness of her curves. The stripper caught his gaze and winked before sliding all the way to her knees and forward, offering Mike a close glimpse at the stiff nipples pushing at her thin outfit.

Mike grabbed a beer and took his time ogling her dance to 'I love Rock and Roll'. He pondered several opening lines, but decided on what he'd lead with once she was done and the few people hanging around dispersed.

Once the performance was over, the dancer got some wipes from behind the bar counter and cleaned the pole for her next set, no doubt knowing she was being watched, because the way she squatted next to it, pushing back her ass, couldn't have been comfortable.

She smiled at Mike, pretending she only now noticed him lingering, and spoke with a Texan accent, pushing back her long locks. "I'm not ready darlin', but I can be half an hour early if y'all want."

Mike smiled and reached toward her, sliding his hand up her foot, which seemed painfully arched due to the enormous high heels of the boots. Were those the kind of shoes that Arden broke his ankle in? No matter how sexy they looked, when he imagined Arden crying out in pain, he wished the boy would never wear them again.

But this wasn't about Arden. *Focus, Mike.*

"You do private shows?" he asked with a grin and winked at her. "This bull might be in need of riding..."

She burst out laughing. "Oh. You're one of *those*."

"Sorry, m'am," he said, exaggerating his accent to match hers. "Meant no offence, just can't help myself when I see a lady in peril."

She cocked her blond head, squinting. "Peril?"

Mike dropped the accent and climbed onto the stage, using the pole for leverage. "I actually came over to check *this*," he said and grabbed the metal, shaking it lightly. He pointed to the ceiling. "There's a screw up there that gets loose sometimes, and the last thing we need is that beautiful leg broken."

Her expression became softer. "Oh. Okay, thanks. I hate when a pole gets all rickety. This one time in Reno—"

Someone cleared their throat, and Mike turned his frosty gaze to... Leo. Of course. The fucking cockblocker.

"Do you want her to teach your boyfriend how to ride a pole?" Leo asked with a stupid smirk.

Damn it. Mike didn't want to go into *that* yet. He wanted to stop thinking about his problematic non-relationship and just dive in. Have a nice time with a girl and not overthink any of it. It wouldn't be happening.

He gave Leo his most blatant stinkeye. "Our relationship's open."

Leo raised his palms as if he really were sorry. They both knew he wasn't. "Oh. Okay, good to know, 'cause Theo was asking."

Mike's brain jarred, as if it were a clockwork mechanism, and something got stuck between the wheels, creating sparks.

"You have a boyfriend?" the stripper asked, but Mike didn't have time to answer her until he knew exactly what was up with Arden.

"He *what*?"

Leo's eyebrows rose in fake-shock. "Doesn't matter, since you're open. I'm sure Arden told him that much by now."

Mike pushed him back, even though he knew Leo wasn't the one at fault here. "You seem really fucking happy with yourself."

Leo bit back a grin. "I'm just really confused. I thought you were gay now."

A not-very-subtle dig at what Mike used to say to him. Fair enough. Maybe. If Mike weren't so pissed off.

"Yeah, I think I'll have a drink with that guy there," the girl said, indicating Jeff, who had already gravitated their way.

"Fuck yourself with a screwdriver, Leo," Mike said and pushed past him, making sure to shove him with the shoulder on his way to the door. The languid, sexy music no longer affected his mood as he shot outside and turned his gaze to where he'd seen Theo last.

And there the bald fucker was, pulling Arden into his lap with a shit-eating grin while Arden slapped the guy's watermelon-sized bicep, his laugh so bright and sparkly it might as well have been glitter.

Where there should have been anger, Mike experienced a sense of loss so rapid and painful he struggled to keep his face in check. Did Arden not care? Was he not missing Mike already? Had he realized Mike couldn't give him what he wanted and was ready to move on?

Mike had not thought through this whole open relationship thing.

He did want to know how the stripper tasted, but he didn't *need* to. Not when this stranger, who likely didn't care for boys like Arden and just wanted to experiment, was about to take Arden into his comically thick arms and carry him off somewhere where they could be alone.

He was so upset he couldn't even keep his mouth shut for the duration of his way across the yard and shouted. "Theo, right? That's not how we do things here!"

Arden looked up at him from Theo's lap, and Mike could swear his blasé expression was one composed to wreck most damage. In his gothic outfit, perched in Theo's lap, he was a little demon out for Mike's blood.

Theo's bread loaf-sized hand on Arden's nape was only making the agitation in Mike worse. "Hm? What's the problem?"

"Yeah, Mike? What's the problem?" Arden echoed, knowing the answer damn well.

Zolt drank his beer, and Mike could have sworn he was hiding a grin behind a full glass. The traitor.

Mike ignored the boy and focused on the guest, whom he was ready to give the benefit of the doubt. For now. "The problem is that you saw me with him half an hour ago."

Arden crossed his legs and pursed his lips, still in the bastard's lap. "Theo was very polite, but I told him we've got an open relationship, so it's all good."

Shit. Fuck.

Mike could sense the burning heat of eyes on him. If he wanted to get out of this situation without permanent scalds, he needed to act fast. "You clearly misunderstood what I said. Now come here," he said and offered his hand to Arden, itching to hold the delicate fingers in his.

The endless seconds of hesitation were the cruelest torture, but eventually Arden slid his hand into Mike's. He mumbled an apology to Theo—who didn't deserve one—and let Mike pull him up from the fucker's lap and away from his dick.

Mike hated Zolt watching him like a hawk with his glass of whiskey in hand. Did he fashion himself Arden's protector now? The fuck was that?

"So what's the misunderstanding?" Arden asked innocently, but Mike was not having this conversation out in the open and dragged him away, past Leo, who watched it all with a grin that was about to dislocate his jaw, and toward the garage, where he hoped to find more peace. He spotted Dad in the corner of his eye, but since he was the last person whose judgment Mike wanted to hear right now, he just walked forward, squeezing Arden's hand until they entered the shadow of the building, hiding from prying gazes.

Only then, did he trust himself to let go of Arden's hand and look at him again. "You only did it to make me jealous!"

Arden opened his lips, as if to deny it, but took a few more seconds before he spoke. He wrapped his arms on his gorgeous flat chest that was so confusing, and so sexy. "Did it work?"

Mike stilled, no longer hearing music over the frantic pulsing in his ears. There was no denying it anymore. He was lost, and every road led to Arden.

He slowly sank to his knees and rested his head against the boy's stomach, wrapping his arms around the tempting hips.

"It did," he whispered.

Chapter 13 – Arden

So maybe testing Mike's jealousy had been a dirty move, but all was fair in love and war. Arden had been drinking to celebrate his triumph, and might have had one—or three—shots too many, but he felt too safe to care. Not only in the clubhouse, surrounded by people he knew, but with Mike watching his every step. They had become inseparable, and Mike even followed him into the bar's restrooms where they joked about dick sizes while pissing.

They rather liked each other's dick sizes. And Mike got excited about Arden lifting his skirt to urinate.

Mike clearly wasn't in it just for the sex, because he could have had that anywhere, yet he deserted the pretty stripper the moment someone told him his neglected kitten crawled into another man's lap.

He didn't know whether Mike's unwillingness to start a relationship was habitual and he didn't want to give up on the option of sleeping with other people, or if it was an element of his identity, but he wasn't disdainful over others forming couples. There was something to work on there.

Only that Arden *shouldn't* attempt it. The booze in his veins suggested all the things he could do with Mike, how Mike just needed a nudge, but he found it hard to decide whether those thoughts were produced by reason or Arden's misguided lust. Mike was sex on a stick, and Arden was dying to lick him.

When the evening got colder, and the party moved inside, the atmosphere between them became denser with unspoken desire. It didn't help that the clubhouse was a pit of bikers with loose morals, so by the middle of the night the air smelled of booze, cigarettes, and sex. The loud rock music was doing its job of masking the moans of a couple fucking against the pool table, but they were undeniably there, reminding Arden how good wild, careless sex could be. How he used to enjoy losing inhibitions and going with the flow.

The music grew heated, and Arden rolled his head over his shoulders, jumping while other people's sweat clung to him in the tight clump of bodies. He recognized Mike's hand when it touched the small of his back, but he would not give in so easily and swatted it away, grabbing the pole to crawl onto the empty stage.

He was far from a pole-dancing master, but his sister was a stripper, and he'd picked up a trick or two. Right now, he did wish he had the death trap heels on, just to excite Mike more, even if wearing them might cost him broken bones. Mike would take care of him if something happened.

"Mike! Watch me!" he yelled over the music with a grin.

Tonight, he'd allow himself to live in the dreamland where Mike was his boyfriend for real, and where neither of them had a care in the world. Arden slid down the pole, giving Mike a not-so-sneaky peek under his skirt, then got right back up, arching his chest and ignoring the rhythm as he danced on.

Not all of the guests appreciated his efforts, and Mike's uncle outright scowled before one of the older MC members pulled him outside, but there were whistles too, and Kane's girlfriend, who sat on her man's shoulders, as if they were at a rock concert, applauded him, hooting loudly.

But only Mike's opinion mattered. He was the only one Arden noticed, and as he got to his toes and reached out to touch Arden, face relaxed with the booze he'd drank, the sense of triumph filled Arden's heart.

Arden got to his knees, crawling toward Mike like a cat, but didn't bother assessing where the edge of the stage was and almost fell face first to the floor.

Almost. Because Mike was there to catch him and pull him into an embrace while someone else took their turn at the pole to the choir of loud whistles.

"Careful there, baby, or you won't live to get your reward," Mike said, holding Arden to his chest, as if he were afraid to crush him. He stepped away from the stage, and while Arden sensed his legs poking people as they passed, he felt safe under the protection of his loyal guard dog.

"I hope my reward is a delicious shot of strawberry vodka!" Arden giggled and stopped Mike to kiss him on the lips. The new beard oil had a minty aroma Arden lived for, and he rolled against Mike, whose breath shook with excitement as he stumbled toward the bar and sat Arden on the sticky counter.

"Wait for it," he said, pushing back hair that got into his face and opened his wallet before lifting the top of Arden's stocking and sliding a rolled-up bank note under it.

Arden cackled all too loudly, but wasn't embarrassed. Mike had that cocky smile, that easy way about him that could turn ferocious when push came to shove, and all of Arden's senses responded to that with attraction. Like invisible tentacles, Arden's pheromones reached out for Mike, desperate to latch on.

After that fateful night at the hotel in San Francisco, Arden had found it hard to think about anything other than tumbling into bed with Mike. They'd been civil, respectful of each other's boundaries even when waking up next to each other with boners, but being this close set a fire to his panties.

While Mike's attraction to him was as obvious as the fact that the sun rose every day, he didn't try to break Arden's will or emotionally blackmail him into giving in. Even this stupid open relationship idea seemed like an honest attempt at resolving a problem Mike struggled with, and he didn't seem angry over Arden roping him back. He was the mustang that actually knew it was better off lassoed.

Whatever Mike liked to say, he was a good guy at the core, and he didn't take things other people didn't want to give him. So instead of using tricks, he waited, teased, tempted, until Arden's refusal to give in hung by the last threads of willpower.

And those were wearing increasingly thin.

The later into the night, the more his brain nudged him to just have some fun and not overthink this. Mike's smell evoked that night Arden had lost his mind and temporarily forgotten his boundaries. Strong, masculine, it reminded Arden how Mike's weight had felt on top, and how good it had felt to spread his legs for a man without fear.

So when Mike slid between his thighs at the bar, Arden had no other way out but to back out farther. This time, he was aware of the edge on the other side, as well as the whole wall of unmanned alcohols he could still infuse his brain with.

"Where are you going? That area is staff only," Mike said. A blatant lie, since people got behind the bar and helped themselves to the liquor all the time, but Arden might as well go with it.

"You see, I've just gotten this job," he slurred, leaning against the counter with a broad smile while the party around them blurred into neon colors.

Mike snorted. "Aren't you too young to work with alcohol?"

"No. I'm an old soul." Arden said, hovering his fingers over the bottles, unable to make his choice. "I offer other services than just bartending though. This is just a side gig."

Mike took the bait. His eyes grew less focused, and he licked his lips, resting his muscular forearms on the counter. He no longer noticed all the skimpily-clad girls, as if only Arden existed in his innermost fantasies.

"What kind of services?"

Arden glanced over Mike's shoulder, but no one was paying attention to them. "Illicit, so shhh..." He put his finger against his lips, tempting Mike closer with his gaze.

He didn't manage to finish the shushing gesture before Mike jumped onto the counter and rolled to the other side, facing Arden. His gaze was pure heat, and its touch triggered shivers all over Arden despite others around them. Kane was loudly arguing with Axel, who didn't seem to be listening, and Mona was the one showing off her skill on the pole.

Nothing happened. Yet. The calm before the storm.

"Yeah?" Mike breathed, stepping so close it took Arden's breath away. Mike smelled of bourbon, but he kept his hands to himself.

Arden scanned their surroundings conspicuously, but they were alone behind the bar, with no one heading over. When faced with Mike's wide shoulders, the tattooed arms, the hands adorned with signets that would pulverize anyone trying to hurt Arden, it dawned on him through the haze of booze that he wanted this man. More than anyone before.

No matter how Mike identified, and whatever his relationship hang-ups were, the itch to serve this stallion in his prime on hands and knees was like a red hot poker against Arden's face.

He slipped two fingers under Mike's belt, looking up. "That was a lie," he whispered, and guided Mike's hand to the top of his stocking. "I'm just always horny, so might as well take money for it," he teased to make Mike question what part of it was true and what wasn't.

Mike swallowed and opened his wallet with one hand before offering it to Arden, his fingers slipping under the elastic band at the top of the stocking while his face grew darker. "What's on the menu, you little slut?"

Arden teased the large belt buckle open and stood on his toes to give Mike's lips a lick. "Close your eyes."

Mike bit back a smile and waved his wallet in front of Arden. "Are you saying that you won't charge me?"

Arden snatched the wallet, but realized he had nowhere to put it so he dipped it under his T-shirt, into the bra he wore tonight. "You might be a stud, but I'll still take your money." His head was overheating from the closeness that shouldn't have been happening and he cupped Mike's cock through the jeans.

Rock hard.

Arden's eyelids fluttered with excitement at the bad choice he was about to make.

Mike shut his eyes and leaned against the counter, throwing his head back already, his mouth catching air as if there wasn't enough oxygen in it to keep him conscious.

"Oh, baby... it's all yours."

There was enough time to pull back. To make it into a joke and tease Mike. To open his wallet and claim there wasn't enough inside.

But Arden got to his knees instead, because he was the one drawn like a kitten to fresh catnip. He struggled for breath as he unzipped Mike's jeans, his ears filled with muted rock music. He got tunnel vision and craved to suck on that stunning cock like his life depended on it. Rational thinking was for losers.

So he leaned in to breathe in the scent of Mike's arousal and looked up when warm hands cupped his face, thumbs petting his cheekbones. Mike's face was shadowed, but his chest pumped air at a slow, languid pace, taking it in big gulps each time. He was so there with Arden, so very grounded in this moment.

"My sweet little kitten."

He'd been right. They both wanted it so bad. Arden only had so much self-control around this man with steady hands, who carried him with ease and had a cock Arden had wet dreams about.

With his heart pounding like crazy, Arden pulled down Mike's underwear and jeans just enough to set his cock free, and now that Arden got to see it up close for the very first time, he knew there was nothing he'd change about it. A perfect size to fit into Arden's hand, it wasn't large enough to cause discomfort but would still fill Arden's holes so nicely. The head, dark and glistening, was the best kind of lollipop, and Arden imagined it popping out of his slick ass after a job well done.

"Do you even know how stunning your cock is?" Arden rasped, but didn't wait for an answer and dove in with his mouth wide open. One day he'd savor it. Tonight, he wanted to devour, because his whole body throbbed with desire for Mike.

His pre-cum had such a clean, pleasant flavor, he squeezed his hand more tightly around the girth and pumped, in hope of getting more of it on his tongue. Mike's pubes tickled his hand when he reached for the warm sac, and Arden couldn't even begin to think about techniques that might give Mike an earth-shattering experience. This was all instinct.

He sucked on the head, moaning when the rough fingers tightened on his head slightly, and pushed on, shivering as the hard flesh pushed down his tongue. It triggered electric sensations that trailed down his body, making his own dick harden in response.

Arden was only now realizing how much he'd needed this all along. To feel sexual again, and to exert his agency. That kiss gone wrong at the hotel had given him a lick of freedom, but he was ready for much more than that. He was in heaven, and he could swear the wings attached to his back glowed with happiness.

He inhaled deeply through his nose, loving the scent of Mike's arousal, then relaxed his throat and allowed the cock deeper. He wanted to hear Mike moan for more, wanted to tie him to the bed and ride his dick so his wild mustang knew to whom he belonged.

Music and the furious pulsing of his own heart trapped him in a bubble of lust, and when Mike moved his hands into Arden's hair, gradually taking control of the blowjob. Arden let him, clinging to Mike's firm legs as the rock-hard length slid in and out, massaging his palate due to its curve, his warm balls slapping against Arden's chin at each steady yet gentle thrust.

Mike would stop and pet Arden's cheek, encouraging him to take over if he wished, and his silent suggestions fed the fire of Arden's arousal, making him bob his head and tighten his lips, groaning as he explored the delicious shaft with his entire mouth.

It slid over his tongue, leaving behind delicious, salty pre-cum, and Arden shivered at the taste, locked in a world where just the two of them existed. Here, all fantasies came true and labels like gay or straight didn't exist. All that mattered was that this tattooed hunk wanted to stuff Arden's mouth full of cock, and Arden was dying to be the cum-slut of Mike's dreams.

The party was noisy as hell, but somehow Arden heard Mike hiss, "Oh baby.... You're so fucking hot." Even if he imagined the words, the tone of Mike's voice was one of praise, and he wanted to drink it up. He opened his mouth wider and forced his throat open, pushing until his nose was buried in fragrant pubes, and the cockhead pulsed at the back of Arden's mouth hole, taking ownership of his entire body.

He was too afraid to open up his legs to a man again, but he could have *this*. He groaned in pleasure as Mike's cock rammed into his throat again and again, gaining momentum now that Arden showed his prowess at blowjobs. He wanted to give it all the attention it deserved. Pet it, caress it, make it spurt cum until Mike was convinced Arden's mouth was the only place capable of giving him satisfaction.

Arden tightened his fingers on Mike's belt on both sides on his head, heart fluttering with joy when he sensed tremors going through the shaft. Mike squeezed his hand on Arden's hair, pulling out despite his face twisting. "I'm almost—"

"I want it," Arden groaned impatiently, but just as he put his lips back to work, Mike came, splashing Arden's chin with spunk.

It kept coming, and Arden closed his lips around the cockhead, milking the hot dick while the first gush cooled on his face. Mike's entire body trembled, and when his balls ran dry and there was no more for Arden to feed on, Mike pulled him up, his scorching tongue gathering the fresh cum off Arden's skin before diving into a deep, forceful kiss.

His hand found its way under Arden's skirt and pushed between his thighs, rubbing against the painfully-hard cock. Arden moaned and arched against the fingers like a cat in heat, so desperate to get off he humped the hand without a single thought in his brain that wasn't pure filth. Mike's fingers dove under his T-shirt and into his bra, pushing Arden to the verge of orgasm.

A light so bright he saw it through shut eyelids pulled Arden out of the zone, and he blinked, staring at a smartphone that took one more photo with flash. Shay grinned at him, her dark lipstick smeared as if she'd been passionately kissed moments ago, and turned her phone, tapping something on the screen.

"Do continue! You guys are so hot!"

"Hey!" Arden yelled, stumbling back from the hand that had almost made him come. He distinctly felt the wallet sliding out of his bra along with Mike's hand but the prostitute joke was long forgotten. "Are you fucking posting it somewhere?" He frantically rubbed cum off his face, at loss, plunged into a reality so cold he froze on the spot. What had he done?

Mike seemed confused for a second, his face still relaxed in bliss, but the moment his gaze captured the phone in Shay's hands, he dashed at her like a wolf protecting his cubs. "What the fuck? This isn't for your enjoyment," he roared so loudly even people who hadn't yet been aware of the action behind the bar counter looked their way.

She yelped when he forced the phone out of her hand and slammed it against the edge of the counter, bending it out of shape.

Kane chose that moment to emerge from the crowd with the roar of a bear, ready to protect his female. "Hands off my woman!"

But Arden just stood there, watching the mayhem, with a confused boner and Mike's taste still on his lips. He was *so* sober. His brain had used all and any excuses to let his body take the lead, but now he was faced with the reality of what he'd done.

He once again broke his own vows because he was a dumb slut whose brain was under the control of his dick, and the one way out of this was to stay away from Mike. He'd been lying to himself when he decided to sleep in Mike's bed, because the end result of such stupidity had been obvious from the start.

When the phone flew across the room and a stampede of fists followed, Arden took the opportunity and fled.

Chapter 14 – Mike

Mike was furious.

So maybe having sex in public hadn't been the best idea when your partner was a bit out of the ordinary, but he couldn't resist Arden's seduction and had counted on the unspoken social contract that whatever happened at club parties stayed there. Maybe Shay hadn't quite gotten the memo, considering she was doing amateur porn for a living, but most people did not want compromising videos to exist, much less so on a stranger's phone. She gave a shriek and covered her mouth when Mike had reduced the offending device to a piece of broken junk, but of course Kane was there, claws and all.

"Did he touch you?" Kane roared, but Shay shook her head, still too shocked to speak.

"He wrecked my phone!" she screeched. "The fuck, asshole?"

Kane swung his fist Mike's way, but his drunk ass failed to judge distance right, and the counter got in the way.

Mike slammed the broken thing on the counter and pointed at her. "Your woman filmed and photographed me having sex with Arden. What's up with that, huh?"

"I just thought you looked cute together!" she yelled, trying to get through Kane with her long nails ready to become claws, but Kane had enough brain cells to hold her back.

"You can't just record people in here!" he said, tension making liquor evaporate from his body. He bit his lip and grabbed her shoulder, shaking it gently so she'd focus. "Did you do it to anyone else? You can't fucking do that!"

She blinked, staring between the broken phone and Kane, shocked he wasn't defending her any longer.

"I'm assuming she's sorry," Mike barked, looking around to pull Arden under his arm now that the offending device was out of commission.

But the boy was nowhere to be seen.

Shit.

Shit. Shit. Shit.

"Arden?" He turned to see his mom, of all people, and her face, without the usual smile, told him about the depth of her disappointment.

"First you give your father a black eye, and now *this*?" she asked in a curt tone, adjusting her neon pink tank top.

Which meant that she'd watched him get a blowjob, and while this wasn't the most embarrassing experience in Mike's life, he definitely wasn't happy about it. "Not now. Have you seen where Arden went?"

At least it wasn't like the whole party died down to witness his shame. The music was still going, people hung out by the pole, Axel was following twins who kept baiting him for attention, and Jag was still going at it with the girl on the pool table. The fucker was Dad's age and still had so much energy. Good for him, but he had to be taking Viagra or some shit—

Distraction. Mike needed to focus.

"I haven't seen him," Mom huffed. "And if you want to know my opinion—"

He didn't.

"With all due respect, Ma, I'm all grown up. I know what's good for me, and I don't need advice about my love life. And if you're angry over Dad's face, ask him why it happened before coming here to chastise me. See you later," he said before she managed to get a word in, his gaze searching the crowd that seemed to have gotten far denser in the past fifteen minutes.

He looked behind the bar, in the restrooms, outside, becoming increasingly frustrated. He wanted his kitten back in his lap. He wanted to see Arden's pretty mouth stuffed full of cock again, and once more hear him beg for cum. Considering what the blowjob meant in terms of their relationship could come later, once he found Arden.

He spotted Leo crossing the room with a large bag of Zolt's favorite potato chips, and since he had nothing to go on, he jogged up to him, maneuvering between little groups of people, and pulled on his brother's shoulder.

"Hey, did you see my boy?" he shouted, dragging Leo to the room next door, where the noise wasn't nearly as sharp.

Leo's expression got serious. "You think someone took him?"

Mike's shoulders dropped, and he realized that not everyone had seen what happened. "I… I don't think so. But we finally had sex, and Shay filmed us, and he was gone by the time I dealt with her," he blurted out on one breath.

Leo covered his face with his hand. "Jesus, Mike... How do these things keep happening to you?"

Mike pushed at Leo's chest. "So it's my fault now? I did everything right!"

"Just saying. Maybe you could have had sex somewhere private." Leo looked through his fingers. "How... how was it for you? Because if you're saying 'finally', I'm guessing nothing actually happened before, despite him boasting to anyone who'd listen about his boyfriend's dick."

Mike scowled, rolling farther down the well of desperation. "Not exactly. We dry-humped once, but it doesn't matter, okay? He's sensitive, and I don't want him to feel bad about this."

Leo's shoulders fell, and he scanned Mike's face like an emotional X-Ray. "You need help looking for him?"

Mike glanced at their surroundings, but they were on their own in the small space filled with additional alcohol and snacks, and the noise beyond it would make it impossible for anyone to overhear their conversation.

He looked up, more than aware that he rarely spoke to his brothers about sex in a serious manner, but his conversation with Dad had triggered doubts he needed to tackle. "How did you know you wanted to be with Zolt?"

Leo assessed him, squinted, waited for a punchline, but relaxed when none came. "He made me feel like I was hot shit, like he had eyes just for me. No woman ever made me feel that way. From there, it didn't matter that he was a guy, because he gave me what I was looking for. But also, Mike, I've always been bi, just never thought I'd take the plunge."

That was how Mike felt about Arden, even though, unlike Leo, he didn't see men as appealing overall. He'd never experienced chemistry quite so unexpected. It was a constant hunger only Arden could satisfy. Only this boy who needed him more than anyone.

But if he actually chose Arden the way Leo had chosen Zolt, he'd have to treat him like any other partner, and that would involve doing new things. Things he wasn't quite sure of, no matter how many times he saw them in Arden's sketchbook.

"H-how does it feel to suck dick?"

Leo dropped the chips when he spread his arms too abruptly. "Seriously? It's always like this with you. I'm sharing some profound shit here, and you ask me about cock-sucking?"

Mike couldn't help himself and looked over his shoulder. "Keep your voice down. I'm being serious!"

Leo cocked his head and eyed Mike as if he were a ticking time bomb. "What do you think? It's hot if you like dick. You're doing it with someone you're into, and they're excited too. What more do you want? Find out for yourself. It's just a body part, not toxic waste. What's the worst that can happen?"

It made so much sense Mike was embarrassed over asking in the first place, and he dug the heels of his hands into his eyes. "Arg, Yeah, I suppose. But I don't like *dick*. I like *his* dick. It looks so damn hot in lacy underwear, Leo. He's making me crazy. The one time we fucked before I came into his panties."

Leo shook his head. "You're so weird. Talk about TMI. There's only one way to find out whether you'll like this or not."

Mike rolled that around in his head, and there was no arguing with Leo's conclusion. But first, he needed to make sure Arden was safe. "Will you help me then?"

"To find him? Yes. To blow him?" Leo snorted. "No."

*

An hour later, Mike was truly getting anxious. They'd even checked in the garage and on the rooftop, and in most of the rooms Arden could have entered. The boy had either gone off the clubhouse property, or had become a moving target aware of their search, which would have been an extremely shitty move on his part.

Zolt, who joined the hunt as well, returned from a tour of the parking lot empty-handed, and just as Mike was about to shut down the party and put everyone to work, Rain called his phone.

He was annoyed at first, but had the good sense to pick up and ask, "Have you seen my boy?"

"Your *boy* is at our place. Sort it out tomorrow when you're both sober. I don't wanna be in the middle of this drama."

"I'm coming there right now," he said, fear dispersing like air from an opened balloon. He swatted Zolt and Leo's shoulders, showing them a thumbs-up before swiftly making his way toward the open gate. It was fortunate Rain lived close by, but it still unsettled him that Arden had walked there on his own in the middle of the night.

Mike hadn't drunk that much either, so Rain's suggestion that he needed to sober up was worthless. What he needed was to see Arden, kiss those gorgeous lips and make sure his kitten was okay.

Mona, Rain, and their twins lived in a bungalow with the only neighbor being their cousin Melody's family. It provided the kind of privacy the Hellers needed. No one would spy from nearby windows when shit hit the fan.

It took Mike all of fifteen minutes to reach Rain's home on foot, and he walked past the fence he and Dad had put up for the children's safety, accidentally kicking a toy in the dark before reaching the door.

He knocked, on edge like an addict missing his next hit.

Rain opened the door slowly, glaring at him. Her black hair was a bird's nest, and she wore just a tank top and pyjama pants. "Seriously? What part of *tomorrow* do you not understand? But since you're already here, let's get this over with. He's in the guest room down the corridor. The kids are sleeping for once, so keep it down."

Mike showed her his palms, gaze already drawn to the door that had some kind of picture attached. He shook his head and stepped across the threshold. "Three people searched for him for over an hour," he complained but kept his voice quiet, because the twins had very healthy lungs, and he didn't want to risk attending their next concert. Not so late at night.

Whatever Rain might have said next would have only been a comment and couldn't influence his decision, so he rushed down the hallway and stopped to wave at Mona, who watched him from her elegant vanity chair with a discontented expression. They'd travelled together, so he'd seen her take makeup off before, no need to get prissy.

The picture on the door depicted a Mediterranean landscape, so maybe the room was meant for visits from Mona's family members, but Arden was in there now, so Mike rested his ear against the door and knocked.

"Come in," Arden said, but as soon as Mike opened the door and peeked in, the invitation was revoked. "No, not you!"

Mike pressed his finger to his mouth, wordlessly asking for silence as he slid into the spacious room with a set of simple furniture, decorated with yet more watercolor landscapes and some artificial flowers. Arden sat on a double bed, twisting his lips with a miserable expression. He still wore the outfit that had provoked Mike's lust, minus the wings, which lay on the side table like a symbol of lost innocence, but he'd washed off the dark makeup, and his curly pastel hair was set free. The tiny crystal stud in his nose was the last bit of glam left on him, and he still looked beautiful.

"Mike, I'm sorry, okay?"

The door shut with a quiet creak, and Mike rolled his shoulders, trying to relax them when they unexpectedly went rigid. He didn't mean to accuse Arden of anything, but now that he faced him, the hurt deep in his heart was impossible to deny. "I've been so worried. Why did you run off like that?" he asked, keeping his voice down.

Arden wouldn't meet his eyes at him, head hung low. "Because I can't help myself around you. I'm so ashamed. I was the one to tell you I don't want to go into sex, and I did again. Just like last time, I pulled you into it. I'm such a fucking sex pest."

Mike snorted. This was too ridiculous. "*Sex pest*. I like that," he said, approaching the bed in slow steps, like a predator knowing its prey couldn't run. But that was okay, because his little lamb secretly wanted to be devoured.

"No, it's *not* okay. I put down boundaries, and then broke them myself. It's fucked up. That's how I ended up with Luke, and that's how I'll end up being a fuckbuddy to a straight guy who will break my heart, whether he wants to or not."

The uninhibited pain in Arden's voice made Mike stall, and the lusty thoughts spurred on by Arden's words evaporated. He stood still, taking in the boy, who looked so vulnerable without makeup and with his hair down. As if he were made of the most delicate porcelain and could shatter if Mike said the wrong thing.

His feet grew into the floor when he realized this was the final crossroads, and whatever he chose would put him on a course he could not return from. His gaze slid up the long legs disappearing under the flared skirt, the frail arms, the glistening eyes that would cry hot tears if Mike left, and realized how little his identity mattered when it came to Arden.

Straight was only a label to describe how he usually felt, not a prison. He wasn't required to stay within its bounds, because this was about him, and about Arden, nothing more.

His feet tingled as they moved at last, carrying him to Arden's hunched form. "I don't know what this is, baby. But I want you."

Arden looked up at him, the big blue eyes filled with hope he didn't dare voice. "You know... there's people who call themselves heteroflexible. Mostly straight. But sometimes not. It's a thing..."

He left the question of *could that be for you?* hanging in the air.

Could it? It did sound weirdly appropriate, considering that women were still Mike's primary interest when it came to sex, but then again the flexibility part made the word sound like something incidental, which his attraction to Arden was very much not.

"Do we need to call it anything? It's been two months. I've not touched anyone else in that time, and I like you more every day. I think... maybe I just like feminine people, not just women, you know. Because I don't see you as a girl, only as *girly,* and I find it so damn hot," Mike explained, letting his arms drop.

Arden dared a little smile that was cuter than the fluffiest kitten could be. "If that's how you feel, we don't need to call it anything. Are you saying it's not just an experiment?"

Their relationship had already gone so, so far beyond experimenting.

Mike kneeled on the floor in front of Arden and rested his elbows in his lap, staring straight into the cute heart-shaped face. He did look more like a boy without the illusion provided by makeup, but Mike's body still knew what it wanted, and he captured Arden's dainty hands to give them a little squeeze while his heart trembled with hope.

"No. Not an experiment, baby. I have so many thoughts about you all the time."

Arden bit his lip as his smile widened, and he squeezed Mike's fingers in return. "I hope they're dirty."

His words were a red flag waved in front of a bull, and to Mike they felt like a punch of heat. "Spread your legs."

Arden watched, hypnotized, a healthy flush spreading on his face just like it had when he'd sucked Mike off. His chest moved faster, and he opened his thighs without a word.

The thick, heavy fabric fell off the thighs, bundling up in the middle, but the fact that Arden was willingly offering him access was like a match thrown into the dynamite box that was Mike's head. He placed his hands on the boy's legs, stroking him through the stockings, but while neither of them moved, Mike's brain played out whole scenarios with Arden as the lusty porn star.

"Listen to me. You're the only man I ever wanted this way, but that doesn't make this any less real to me. You're my sexy kitten, and when you're close to me I barely notice anyone else. You are the sexiest fucking person I've met," Mike said, letting his hands move up Arden's warm thighs. Very slowly. Past the stocking and to smooth, warm skin. Then, under the skirt.

"You're my wet dream," Arden rasped, shivering. "Dangerous, horny, cocky... with a dick I think about sixty thousand times a day. But I also feel so safe with you." He pulled up the edge of the skirt, revealing his growing cock hugged by sheer black panties, and Mike just—

He leaned in and kissed it. Such a simple gesture, yet when he breathed in the musk of pre-cum, he shivered as if Arden had held him by the nape. "Jesus. You're this perfect storm of innocent and dirty."

All Mike wanted was to hear Arden moan like that time in the hotel, to keep him close and talk dirty.

"Are you sure you want to have a taste?" Arden whispered, struggling to catch his breath as his face bloomed with a deep flush. He had such soft, lovely features, and that made the cock starting to strain the femmy underwear look illicit. Unexpected. Yet also hotter than a Carolina Reaper. Mike's desire for Arden made him ache inside, but he also craved its burn more than anything else.

Leo had told Mike he'd know whether he wanted to do this or not when the time came, and he did.

Mike leaned forward and rubbed his bearded chin along the curve between Arden's neck and shoulder, making the boy shudder so rapidly he was compelled to hug him with one arm. His tongue traced Arden's ear, his teeth pulled on the lobe, and he kissed the warm shell, savoring the scent of jasmine on male skin.

"I loved the scent of your cum. I want to smell it again."

"I love it when you talk filth." Arden ran his gentle fingers up Mike's arm. "I want you to wreck me."

He might as well have given Mike a testosterone injection straight in the dick. "Oh, yeah? That's what you want? For me to roll you over and drill your tight ass until my balls are empty?" He asked, ripping off Arden's T-shirt to see a bralette made of sheer black mesh to expose his cute little nipples. He pushed him back, climbing on top while his hands squeezed on Arden's pecs, rubbing the sheer fabric against skin.

Arden slipped his fingers into Mike's beard, whimpering when Mike pinched his nipple. He was a vision. "Yes and no? Not ready for *that* but… tell me about it. Tell me what you'd do to my hole. Would you leave me dripping? Or splash cum over my ass and watch it drizzle to my balls?"

Arousal ate through Mike's remaining gray matter. He put his weight on top of Arden and twisted his nipple, salivating when the boy squirmed in response, the other pink bud hardening under the mesh cup. He pressed his nose to the pale skin above and rolled his tongue over the thin fabric, teasing the boy. "Oh, baby, the day you let me dick you, I'll stay in bed all day. You'll draw me porn of us, and I'll follow your instructions. I'll fuck you each time my cock gets hard, and you know what that means? I'll dump *so* many loads in you. And if you try to suck me off on that day, I'll still finish deep up your ass. I've fucking dreamed of this since we met," he rasped, rocking his hips against Arden as lust washed over him beyond control.

Arden's nails dug into Mike's shoulders, and he wrapped his legs around Mike's hips, rocking against him. "I'll wear a plug as you recover just to keep your spunk in for longer. My ass will be yours, available at any time. And how will you get me off?"

Mike gasped for breath, pressing his lips to Arden's for a hard kiss that had them both lose breath. He rubbed one of the thighs squeezing around his hips and held on to it tightly while his own dick filled. "How about we find out, baby?"

Arden greedily licked Mike's top lip one more time before Mike pulled away. There wasn't a hint of anxiety in him over what he was about to do, just the excitement of trying something new with the person that drove him crazy with lust.

"Just don't force yourself, okay?" Arden said, which only spurred Mike on.

'Force himself'. What a concept. If anything, he had to *stop* himself from not going in face first.

Mike shook his head. "Baby, when was the last time you saw me force myself to do anything?" he asked, kneeling between Arden's thighs, and since they remained locked around him, he maneuvered them both into a more convenient place on the bed. Images of their lusty future spun through his head like a tornado, and when he exposed Arden's small cock and saw it was now completely hard, desire was impossible to restrain.

He pulled away, guiding Arden's legs to the sides and touched Arden first with the back of his hand, sliding it up and down the mesh-encased shaft while the boy, very unsuccessfully, tried to keep still.

And it didn't feel gross or in any way unnatural. Leo was right. A cock was just flesh. If he and Arden had sex, how was this any different from giving oral sex to a female partner?

"You're not gonna last long, are you?"

"No," came in an honest rasp. "I didn't jerk off after I blew you at the bar. Can't believe I did that. I'm such a slut."

Mike grinned, cupping the pulsing shaft and balls with his palm. It was warm and filled his hand so nicely, as if there had never been doubts whatsoever whether this was something he wanted to do. "It was so damn hot. You're a wild one, kitten. Don't usually do it so publicly either, but what the hell? You only live once, right?" he asked and pulled on the waistband of the sheer boxers, listening for suggestions as he pulled them off. After all, Arden knew best what he liked, and Mike was, for all intents and purposes, a gay virgin.

"Yesss," Arden hissed, glancing down at him, and the pretty pink cock twitched in excitement. "Can't wait to feel your beard down there."

"Are you saying you want to come in my beard?" Mike asked, thrown off guard even as he pulled the panties off Arden's long legs and swatted his ass when the boy raised it off the mattress to help him. This wasn't the strangest request he'd gotten from a sexual partner, but he would not do it until he found out whether the door in the corner of the room led to a bathroom or a walk-in closet. Because he would not walk around with sperm clumps somewhere he could meet Rain or Mona.

"Yes," Arden said breathlessly. "Didn't think I did, but yes. I want to see it dripping down your chest. Take your shirt off," he demanded. Mike loved him like this. So eager and confident in what he wanted despite being the submissive one in their relationship.

"That a bathroom?" Mike asked and tossed his shirt at the door, breathing softly as he stroked the lovely thighs up and down. "Because if it's not, you're gonna have to lick it all off me."

"It is, but I'd still lick you any day."

Arden's eyes overflowed with lust as he sat up, kneading Mike's shoulders. Despite there being no breasts in the bra, the hardened nipples under the fabric were impossible to look away from. There was something so arousing in his clothed nakedness that Mike found himself pushing Arden right back, their lips meeting for a kiss as he moved his palm down the soft plane of Arden's stomach, until he found the warm shaft and touched it, without anything in the way this time.

Arden's stifled moan made Mike's brain fog up. And yet despite all of his agency, Arden gave in to the dominance of Mike's tongue and settled on squeezing his biceps.

Mike set out exploring first, squeezing the shaft before going lower to roll Arden's balls in his hand. They were so smooth Mike wondered where he found the time to constantly rid himself of body hair, but it didn't matter. What did was that the soft texture of bare skin, treated with fragrant moisturizers, burned Mike's inhibitions to the ground. He offered Arden a final grin before descending down his body.

"Watch me, baby," he whispered before trailing his tongue down the middle of Arden's chest.

The boy wouldn't even blink, rising on his elbows to see better, thighs wide open in invitation. "I'm gonna fucking burst the moment you put your lips on me."

Mike hoped it was an exaggeration, because he intended to savor his first time as cocksucker for more than a few seconds.

"Hold your horses. Let me have my fun," he joked, pumping the rigid length that felt surprisingly natural in his hand. Smaller than his own cock, it was a comfortable size to hold, and he didn't expect any issues when it came to accommodating it at first try either. But as he saw the clear pre-cum drizzling down his fingers, any and all logical thoughts were consumed by fire.

He didn't test-drive the whole fellatio thing by teasing Arden with his tongue first or licking off the liquid. He sucked it right in.

The moan that came out of Arden's lips was more beautiful than the roar of a bike on the open read. One day he'd be riding Arden too. When he hollowed his cheeks, imitating what had been done to him many times before, Arden had to cover his mouth to keep down the noise, and Mike stilled, squeezing his fingers around the base while the flavor or Arden's cock, salty and somewhat tart, spread over his tongue, making him salivate.

It was like nothing he'd ever felt, but the girth in his mouth seemed so alive he sandwiched it between his palate and tongue in a slow, deliberate caress. He got bolder with Arden's balls too and squeezed them gently as he started to suck, bobbing his head over his first dick at a slow pace.

"Fuck... so good," Arden whispered, but then bit down on his hand when Mike sucked harder. "I'm not... I'm almost..." He rubbed one stocking-clad leg against Mike's arm, driving him wild.

Frantic with lust, Mike held on to Arden's thighs, and as they closed him in their warm embrace, he went all in, sucking in the meaty juices of Arden's arousal. He rocked his own hips against the bed, seeking friction as Arden's legs shuddered. The boy squeezed the deliciously-pink face, arched his hips off the bed, and his dick throbbed before releasing a jet of cum. Mike swallowed it right away before taking another, and another spurt while his boy thrashed in pleasure, muffling his moans for the benefit of their hosts.

Swallowing cum was a bit like drinking saltwater, but knowing it had originated in Arden's smooth, lovely balls had Mike shiver and grab at the boy's flesh as he released the spent cock and licked it clean of its juices.

"Jesus fucking Christ," Arden whimpered, gasping for breath, his spread legs and heaving chest now made the most obscene picture. He watched Mike from under lowered eyelids, so sexy and vulnerable at the same time.

Arden was perfect in all his dualities, and Mike wanted to have him. Have him. *Have him.*

He opened his pants and spat a slick mixture of spit and semen into his hand before rubbing it over his shaft, which at this point reacted to even the most delicate touch.

"You make me so damn horny," he rasped, staring at Arden down the tunnel of his vision as he grabbed the boy's ankles and rested them both on his left shoulder.

Tension furrowed the pale eyebrows when their eyes met. "I—I told you, not my ass," he whispered in a tense voice as his legs trembled.

Mike gave a low exhale and spat into his hand again, shoving it between Arden's squeezed thighs, above the stockings. "No, baby. Here. That okay?" he asked, just to make sure.

Arden's pupils widened, as if he'd snorted coke. "*Yes*! Do me like that."

That was some enthusiastic consent right there, and Arden's eagerness made Mike smile. "You're such a dirty boy. Wearing stockings to lure me in," he said in a low voice but didn't wait any longer and pushed his dick into the tight cavity formed by Arden's thighs. The painted toes curled inside black stockings, and Mike pulled them closer, rubbing his face against Arden's dainty feet, which smelled of talcum powder and leather.

His head spun as he thrust into the fake hole again, but he had to smile when he sought Arden's gaze, only to find it plastered to the thick cockhead pushing its way through flesh over and over.

"I'm gonna leave friction burns, but don't worry. I'll soothe them with my spunk."

Arden threw his arms over his head, and showed off his chest, arching it up as he watched Mike perform, all spent and beautiful. "Do it. I want to feel it. Want all those juices on me. I won't shower until tomorrow."

Damn it.

Mike bit Arden's heel to stifle the wild grunts pushing at his lips, but the next push he made between the lovely thighs propelled his cum so far it splashed even Arden's neck and chin. He squeezed the long legs together and thrust so fast his stomach muscles ached, riding his orgasm until seed glistened all over Arden's chest, beads of cum on the sheer black bra.

"Ohh, baby," he whispered, empty-headed by the time he let go of Arden's legs and dropped next to him, spent as if pieces of his brain left his body along with love juice.

Arden gave him a mischievous smile as he gathered some of the cum on his fingers and licked it off. "That was so hot. I've got cum all over my skirt. Gonna be a walk of shame tomorrow." With his other hand, he rubbed some of the spunk into his bra, and it was so arousing Mike's empty balls ached with the need to produce more, just so he could give it to Arden to play with.

For now though, he leaned in and licked his own cum off Arden's chin. It didn't taste unpleasant either, and while he'd have never done this when in bed with a woman, he rather liked the fact that Arden was as aroused by this as him. So he kissed him again, pulling Arden's leg over his hip. "You could borrow something of Mona's. Or I could get you fresh clothes."

Arden leaned into the hug with a lazy smile. "Gentleman. But we really did the whole boyfriend thing ass-backward, didn't we? At least you won't have to introduce me to your family."

Mike grinned, perfectly relaxed now that he had Arden in his arms, safe and satisfied. "So... would you really want to skip condoms, or was that just dirty talk?"

"Oh. I... I want to. Turns me on. But I hate hospitals?" Arden groaned.

Mike rolled his eyes. "I'll hold your hand, but if you wanna skip them, we'll both get tested. And then... we'll be ready and see what happens," he said, pressing a kiss to Arden's forehead.

"I'm so happy," Arden said, but was already closing his eyes as he yawned.

Mike didn't even bother to cover them with anything, since it was so warm. He kissed Arden's cheek and hugged him, resting his head on the pillow.

So was he.

Chapter 15 – Arden

Arden rolled over on the mat to get a look up Mike's legs. Private self-defence practice was so much more fun than group classes.

He ran his fingers up Mike's calf. "Oh no, I lost... What's my punishment?"

Mike's brows rose, but he shook his head, smiling as he tied back his unruly hair. "If you want your fantasy to happen, you need to draw a comic about it," he said and tapped the middle of Arden's chest with his bare foot.

Arden groaned but teased Mike by picking on hair sprouting from his big toe, his best puppy eyes in place. "You sure a break isn't in order, teacher?"

The last two weeks had been a whirlwind including the trip to a clinic to get tested where Mike had promised Arden a 'lolly' for good behavior. Arden's sexuality, which had been so painfully repressed since that traumatic event with Luke, was blooming again, even though he still wasn't ready to go all the way and sometimes flinched when surprised by touch. Mike was there with him. All in. Dick deep in Arden's mouth whenever it pleased them.

Doubts about Mike's intentions had sunk so deep into the waters of Arden's mind he hardly acknowledged their existence anymore and continued testing his lover. Mike wasn't nearly as appreciative of gay porn as he was of Arden's erotic drawings but still willing to explore, and Arden helped him out with his mouth more than once. Though he suspected Mike was way more into the blowjobs than the hot tough guy-on-twink action playing out on the screen.

The real-life Mike snorted, rolling Arden with his foot. "A break? Your mouth is just hungry for a plowing, baby."

Arden groaned. He couldn't get enough of Mike and anyone who cared to look would spot that. "Am I really that easy to read?" His fingers trailed up the muscular calf, over the knee, reaching to Mike's thigh...

He loved being smooth all over, but there was something irresistible about body hair on other men, so it was a shame the fabric of Mike's joggers was in the way.

"Yes. Now get up, you lazy ass. This lesson is so serious you should call me *Professor* Heller," Mike said, spreading his feet on the edge of the mat. He took a deep breath and clapped. "Move. Move. Move."

Arden whined but got up. He already knew that tone in Mike's voice. This was Trainer Mike, and he wouldn't give in to Arden's pleading for cum. Which was frustrating, because he was a snack in the simple joggers and tank top thin enough to show off Mike's pecs and nipples. "Why is it serious? Don't I have you to protect me now?" Arden fluttered his eyelashes with a smile.

A frown passed through Mike's usually smiling features. "I can't always be there, so you need to know how to act in moments of danger.

Don't you see how important that is? What if someone came for you again?"

Arden flexed his bicep for Mike. He hadn't developed much muscle, but his arm was still bigger than when he'd arrived almost three months ago. "I'm buff now. I can take on anyone." He was joking, but he'd learned quite a few moves a small guy like him might utilize against a physically stronger opponent if push came to shove.

"Oh yeah?" Mike asked, as he grabbed a well-used body shield from one of the equipment hangers. He stepped closer and handed Arden a pair of boxing gloves.

Arden pushed his hands into the hot pockets that still held other people's dried sweat and looked first at the target image on the body shield, then at Mike, who patted the shield, as if inviting Arden closer. "Hit me like I'm Luke."

Hurt passed through Arden with a sudden intensity, the familiar face lurking at the edges of his vision like a shadow circling him to find all the weak points. Arden's hands curled inside the gloves, heat flashing to his face at the memory of the motherfucker, who'd taken so much from him. Who'd broken him to a point where he still didn't feel completely at ease when having sex with his new amazing boyfriend.

He punched the dense shield with everything he had, but Luke would have remained standing, so he attacked again, a lump rising in his throat. He used to regret breaking that lamp on Luke's head, afraid that it made him a killer. But the world would have been better off if that bastard had bled to death. He kept punching even when he lacked air, even when his arms ached from swinging.

So he added kicks to the punches, grunting each time.

"Fuck you!" he growled, landing a kick hard enough to make his opponent take half a step back in a flurry of blond hair just a shade brighter than Luke's own.

Arden wouldn't give in when the tall man in front of him stepped off the mat and chased him. There could be no peaceful resolutions here. No truce. No forgiveness.

His head pulsed with dense, boiling hate that drove him forward until it became crystal clear that he would either see this through or choke on his own grief and anger. So he pushed on, screaming until his throat was raw while the shadow in front of him moved back, toward the edge of hell, where he belonged.

"You had no right! I trusted you! I hate you motherfucker! Hate you so much for messing me up like this!"

Tears stung his eyes, but he punched his big target again and again.

"Stop it," Luke said, triggering the memory of how he'd held Arden down and told him to stop wiggling.

"No! I'm not fucking stopping until I'm done!" Breathless, Arden charged at him shoulder-first, but Luke grabbed him and pulled Arden flat to his broad chest. Heat parched Arden's skull until he could no longer think, trapped and afraid of what might happen next. The giant only let go when Arden elbowed him in the stomach. He could smell and taste freedom already, but big, strong hands grabbed his wrists again. Yanked him to the wall.

The scent of wood was unfamiliar on Luke, who preferred denser, sweeter cologne, but there was no time to assess why that was. Arden's vision was so blurry he could barely see Luke's shape anyway.

Arden put all his strength into trying to pull his arms away, but the hold on his wrists was like steel cuffs. "Let go! Let go! Let go!" he cried, gasping for air, but knew that he was on his own.

He struck the moment strong hands released his to cup his face instead, but Arden kept punching until he realized a warm voice cooed to him.

"Shhh, it's all right, baby. Calm down."

Arden stared up at Mike through a blur of tears, but reality began trickling back, washing away the fear. He'd had a fit. A full-on rage fit in front of Mike, whom he'd punched repeatedly.

"I'm sorry," he whispered, at loss when he saw a small trickle of blood under Mike's nose.

He'd completely lost it. Stepped into a different reality and forgotten where he was. And with whom.

Mike exhaled and pulled him close, his face stiff, with deep wrinkles on the forehead and set lips. "It's fine, baby."

Arden latched on to him in an instant. Mike was his umbrella in pouring rain. This man. This wall of muscle made him feel safe in a way Luke never had, and Arden had paid him back with violence. "Did I hurt you?" he uttered when Mike's arms slowly tightened, enfolding him in a careful embrace.

His heart beat fast against Arden's ear, but its rhythm was so even, so comforting Arden found himself melting until his legs gave up and Mike slid down to the floor with him.

"You did. I'm impressed. Were I any shorter, you'd have clawed my eyes out," Mike said.

Arden curled up in Mike's lap with his arms around his *boyfriend's* neck. He could still hardly comprehend their relationship was real. Every night they cuddled in bed as if they'd always belonged together.

"You just... You said 'Luke', and I kinda lost it. It's so complicated with him, you know?" He pressed his forehead to Mike's hot neck.

Mike spread his legs to accommodate Arden with more ease and pressed a soft kiss to the side of Arden's head. The scent of woodsy cologne, which seemed so alien in Arden's daymare now felt comforting, and he leaned into the firm chest.

"How is it *complicated*? You just had some... some kind of weird panic attack because I mentioned him," Mike said.

Arden let his fingers settle over Mike's heart. "Because it wasn't always bad. I was like... fifteen when we met, and I got to have all this sex, and felt so grown up when I saw that this hot guy wanted me. And then we were kinda on-off, but he was always around, and so generous with money when I had none. I thought we were actually becoming a *thing* when everything went to shit." He had to pause, unsure if he wanted to go *there*, but when he looked up into Mike's attentive blue eyes, he knew he'd either tell this man, or forever shut down about it.

"We met up at his place, and he was just... really horny and up for it, but I wasn't in the mood. I don't even remember why. I think it was something stupid like wanting to talk about some show I was watching, and it pissed me off that he didn't want to listen. He said we'd just cuddle, but then we didn't, and he held me down, and I had no chance to fight him. He's twice my size. Maybe I could have done something, but I froze..." He had to stop when his lungs refused to work and deprived him of oxygen.

Mike held his breath, his gaze wandering off as his fingers tightened on Arden's flesh. "You don't have to tell me about it if it's painful."

"I just... I'm so angry I put myself in that position. I should have seen it coming. My sister warned me he was shady, but I'd just think with my dick."

Mike's exhale was long and laborious, but he met Arden's gaze, biting his bottom lip so hard it was painful to watch. "It's not your fault.

You might have trusted the wrong person, but no one should use your inexperience against you. Not to mention he shouldn't have touched you at fifteen in the first place, whether you wanted it or not."

Arden slid his hand under Mike's arm, seeking his warmth. "But it happened, and now I'm this broken thing. Afraid of something I was always horny for. It's like he took it away from me, and made me nervous. I wasn't like this before. Why would he do that? If he'd only been more patient, I would have fucked him eventually."

Mike swallowed hard, his gaze darting to Arden's as his cheeks burned with a flush. The small wrinkles around his eyes kept twitching, as if his brain hadn't yet decided how he felt. "Why didn't you tell me? If you're scared, why didn't you tell me? I'd have gone about things differently if I knew."

Arden rubbed his eyes. "I thought... I'd be over it. Why can't I just wipe it away and be back to normal? I *do* want you."

Mike's jaw set. "I'm gonna rip the fucker's balls off."

"No! That's the other thing... I saw you obliterating that guy who hit me. You'll end up killing Luke if you go after him."

Mike stalled, his mouth paling as he pressed his lips together. "So what? He fucking deserves it."

Arden put his hand over Mike's clenched fist, but then slowly teased it open so their fingers could entwine. "But you don't deserve to go to prison over that piece of shit."

Mike remained silent, but he didn't push Arden away and hung his head, constantly blinking. "I wouldn't."

He said it with such confidence Arden's heart skipped a beat. The seed of revenge shouldn't have been sown, but there it was, sprouting its ugly rotten bud in Arden's chest.

214 | Gutter Mind

Arden leaned in to place a gentle kiss on Mike's swollen lips. "You're the only person I told," he whispered, surprised by the comfort of sharing his burden and feeling understood.

Mike hummed, gently stroking Arden's back as they both clung to the safety of the wall in the quiet gym room, to the background noise of someone punching a sandbag downstairs. The air smelled of sweat and cleaning products, but that only reminded Arden how far away he was from Luke.

"You know we'll only do the things you want, right? What we're doing now's great," Mike whispered into Arden's hair.

"Yes," Arden whispered, hugging Mike in relief that Mike had been grabby from the start, but he'd been more than accommodating in bed, and it was easy to feel comfortable in his presence. "I probably shouldn't, but I trust you."

Mike shook his head and offered Arden a small smile, rubbing his cheek with the back of his hand. "I wouldn't hurt you. You only deserve good things."

"Is that why I get to have your dick?" Arden winked at him, more at ease by the second.

Enamoured with his bearded knight covered in tattoos Arden leaned in for a longer kiss. He was still embarrassed that he'd lost it and hit Mike, but it couldn't be undone, and led to a new level of understanding between them.

Mike snorted and teased Arden with a couple of light pecks, relaxing against the wall. "Sure thing. And all the delicious cum you can eat, baby."

Arden straddled Mike's lap for more comfort and let himself enjoy their little make-out session, realizing that maybe truth had been the first step for them to take things further. If Mike knew where Arden was coming from, he could act accordingly, and chip at his uncertainty until it crumbled. Because Arden's mind knew Mike was safe. It was his body that needed to catch up.

"I could suck that dick all day and all night," he murmured into Mike's lips as he slid his fingers into the beard. "And I want it in me eventually. So much."

Mike's breath trembled in the back of his throat, making Arden smile, but they both froze at the sound of broken glass. Something tumbled over the floor, and Mike rolled Arden off, stiff as if he were about to fight a fully grown gorilla.

The thing looked like a soda can. Until it made a strange noise and exploded.

Chapter 16 – Mike

Mike could barely see. His eyelids had puffed up, but whenever he tried to pry his eyes open, the burn was worse than having liquor poured on fresh wounds. So he stumbled forward blind, holding Arden in his arms as if his life depended on it. He pressed his shoulder to the wall for guidance, but cries from downstairs were what steered him to the staircase.

His nose and throat ached as if he'd been attacked by a swarm of wasps rolled in ground pepper, and he found it hard to breathe, his lungs tightening in response to the unfamiliar odor. Arden clung to him like a little bird, trembling as he wheezed, setting off all the alarms in Mike's head.

He would survive this—of that he was certain—but what about this frail boy, who'd puked the contents of his stomach before they'd managed to leave the training space?

Mike's skin itched most where the two of them touched, but he didn't have the time to worry about possible irritation and stalled only when his foot hovered above empty space. He stiffened, realizing he could have toppled all the way down, and taken Arden with him, had he stopped a split second later.

But the stairs were familiar, and he sped up, whispering to Arden while nausea rose in his own throat. He would make it outside. He would. He would.

The door ahead swung open and hit the wall, but just as he stiffened, torn whether he should try to reach for his gun or not, Axel's voice brought such relief even Mike's eyes stung a bit less.

"He's here! Mike, put him down."

Mike's skull was filled with the peppery fumes, and his initial reaction was one of protest, but Axel pried Arden out of Mike's arms and forcibly placed Mike's hand on his shoulder. This made sense. They'd be guided to a safe area.

Arden's cries and wheezing were like stabs to Mike's heart. He saw him as a blurry shape in Axel's arms, but the inability to relieve his pain was agony, and he shuddered, squeezing Axel's shoulder.

"He needs..."

"I know, water."

Mom spoke out, as if out of nowhere, her voice muffled. "You're almost there, Mike!"

Fresh air hit him like a pillow, and while it was dry and desert-hot, it brought the scent of dust, not pepper spray. More people cried, shouting for help. He could hear words of comfort, but the one sound that stood out and drew him in was that of running water.

He sped up, pulling on Axel rather than the other way around until droplets splashed his burning skin, and he spun, forcing his eyes open despite tears blurring his vision in the scorching sun. "Arden?"

He pulled his boy close as soon as Axel put him down, trying to rub the chemicals out of the lovely face despite his own flesh aching as if he'd inhaled chili powder. Someone touched his back, but he didn't bother to see who it was even when his tank top was cut open and removed from his body, leaving his torso bare.

"It hurts!" Arden wheezed, but Mike was there with him, blinking away the blurriness in his eyes.

Mike was reminded of what Arden had told him just before this attack, and couldn't bear seeing him in pain. When someone made Arden squeal and pushed Mike away, he almost punched them—but stopped himself when it turned out to be his own mother.

"I know, I know," she cooed to Arden as if he were a baby, snipping away with scissors. "But we have to get the clothes off you. They're contaminated by the gas. Mike, pants off!" she added much more sternly. This wasn't their first rodeo with tear gas, but Arden had to be terrified.

"Cut his shirt first. *His*," he rasped, already blinking with more ease due to the water Axel was hosing them down with. Several people were getting the same treatment at nearby homes, but Arden was the only person who mattered to him, so he got down on his knees and pulled off the boy's shoes and socks, exposing his painted nails, and then yanked down his shorts and lacy underwear, hissing in sympathy when he saw how red the usually-pale skin was.

At least Mom knew not to argue with him and cut Arden's top off as he squirmed like an electrocuted puppy, whining and trembling all over. Seeing him like this filled Mike with so much rage, but also regret. None of this would have happened to Arden if he weren't associated with Mike.

Memories of Leah passed through Mike's mind, as vivid as they were unwanted. They were worse than the tear gas, because no amount of water could wash them away. He'd never forget her final scream. Never unsee the light dying in her eyes.

"Mike! What's... going on?" Arden cried.

"It's fine. Must be tear gas. Keep blinking," Mike said and pushed Arden's forehead back so the fresh water could wash the agent off his face. He kicked off his pants and stood naked, grabbing a bottle of liquid soap the moment Mom handed it to him. Pouring a copious amount into his hands, he went on to rub the coconut-scented liquid into Arden's hair, into his face, neck, shoulders, his chest.

But the boy kept struggling for air as he leaned forward, unstable on his feet. "I think he needs a doctor," Mike said as worry tightened around his neck.

"Get a sheet from the massage room!" Mom yelled to someone as she soaped up Mike's hair in rough no-nonsense motions. "Jeff's already called the doc to come over. This is some fucking bullshit," she growled through clenched teeth.

"Who was it?" Mike asked, holding Arden closer and closer to his chest, finally able to look at him without outright discomfort. His eyes and throat were itchy, sore, but no longer kept him incapacitated.

Arden shivered under the cold water, but he pushed into Mike's arms as if he wanted to crawl under his skin for protection. With the pink leggings and the workout top gone, his face red, hair unfolded from the bun he'd worn, the one feminine thing left on him were the painted nails.

Mike had seen him without makeup many times, since Arden didn't sleep in it, but then he'd still wear cute pyjamas or the like. Right now, he stood in front of Mike the way he was—a scared naked boy—yet Mike's feelings for him wouldn't change because of such details. The vulnerability with which Arden sought shelter in Mike's arms only made Mike's heart pump faster, and with more fury.

He'd break the arms and legs of whoever thought it was a good idea to fuck with them.

"The Jarens," Axel said through clenched teeth, still holding the hose over them.

The fucking Jarens. Words couldn't describe the extent of Mike's hate. But as he held Arden, gently petting him with soapy hands, Memories of Leah's final moments passed through his brain over and over, leaving burning tyre marks at the backs of Mike's eyeballs.

"We'll pay them a visit. Call everyone," he rasped as Mom approached and wrapped Arden's slender body with a sheet to preserve his modesty. He loved her so much for this unexpected gesture. "Thank you," he whispered.

Arden tried to speak too, but coughed instead. He held the sheet around him like a shield, clutching the front so nobody could have an uninvited peek at his body.

Axel nodded, rubbing his hand over his short hair. "They'll regret it."

"Arden? Are you fine staying with my mom?" Mike asked, only now realizing he stood naked in a puddle of soapy water in the middle of town. Oh well, nothing the people hadn't at least *heard* of.

Arden's red eyes darted from Mike to his mom as he wheezed trying to say something, but eventually nodded and kneeled on the ground.

Every fibre in Mike's body wanted to stay here and comfort him, but if this was to never happen again, retribution needed to be swift and painful. "I'll be back soon, okay baby? Mom will take care of you," he said but was already tying a towel around his hips when Axel handed him one.

Arden stared up at him, red-faced and with his nose swelled up. Mike didn't want to imagine how much worse this could have been.

"Take one more soapy shower. We know where they live," Mom said, stroking Arden's back when he gagged, bending over.

Mike bit his lip, stuck on the crossroads, but she nodded at him and led Arden toward her SUV. She'd be taking him home.

"Fuck," Mike rumbled and spun around to have a look at the broken windows of the gym. "Who's gonna talk to the police?" he asked, walking barefoot on the hot asphalt that burned the soles of his feet.

"Jack. He's got a kid in the same nursery as one of the cops," Axel said. He'd been at the back of the building when the tear gas had been thrown inside, but his eyes were still red, and he coughed every now and then.

People peeked at them through windows as they hurried along the empty road with single-family bungalows on one side and the desert on the other, but he ignored them, feeding off his anger until he and Axel reached the clubhouse

The gates were shut to protect those inside, but all the MC members present already knew what had happened and were ready for action, waiting on their bikes while Dad barked orders. His blue eyes, so similar to Mike's, focused on them the moment they stepped through the gate.

"This has gone too far! Customers were affected."

"Maybe we should send all of their green figurines flying?" Kane barked and held up a bundle of explosives in his hand, prompting grunts of approval.

"There's kids in that compound," Rain noted, and that curbed everyone's initial enthusiasm. Nobody wanted children injured, no matter how detestable their parents were.

"All the women and kids will hide in that bunker of theirs once we get there anyway. Though maybe if Harlyn got caught in the crossfire, Mike would finally breathe freely," Uncle Kurt noted, patting Kane's back.

Jesus.

"Fuck you," Mike said, pulling off the towel protecting his modesty, only to toss it into Uncle Kurt's face. "We don't do that."

Kane spread his arms. "I say we go and take whatever opportunity arises."

"Three minutes," Mike said and ran into the clubhouse, straight for his room. Dressed in fresh clothes and armed with his favorite guns, he shot outside and hopped onto his bike, joining Dad at the front of the group.

They were off with an angry roar of engines.

He could have sworn he saw Mom's SUV parked at the gas station, but he trusted her and Jack to keep Arden safe. The memory of how Arden had helplessly clutched at his hand added fuel to the fire already burning in Mike's heart.

He sped up, leading the whole swarm of Smokeys out of town, through a tunnel under the highway, and then down the dusty road pointing between the sandy hills. The sun was on its course toward the horizon as the column of bikers made its way along the winding road, but as they neared the place where those scumbags lived, Mike spotted a flare shot from somewhere nearby.

Kane and a few of the others sped past him before the road turned, on the heels of a truck that drove out from behind a boulder with a roar, leaving clouds of dust in its wake. Something glinted in the air and scattered over the asphalt behind it.

Mike choked, moving to the side of the road. He slowed down just as Kane's front wheel burst with a loud bang. His vehicle swerved and its back went up, effectively catapulting Kane into the air.

"Fuck!" Mike yelled, fearing that others might meet the same fate, but none of them fell off their bikes despite two more tyres going flat. He jumped off his bike along with Kane's dad Kurt, eager to help, but the crazy fucker was already picking himself out of the dust.

"Motherfuckers!" Kane yelled, limping their way and pulling a bit of metal out of his skin. Caltrops were scattered over the asphalt, but Mike's gaze shot up, along a dirt road leading steeply to the top of the nearest hill. He'd been here to secretly meet up with Harlyn more than once and knew that it led to the back of the Jaren compound.

His face tensed. "You make some noise. Draw them away from the farm in the back," he said and gestured at Axel. He needed some reliable muscle, and with Leo, Zolt, and Jack not present, his brooding brother was the best bet.

"What's your plan?" Dad asked while some of the others started kicking the rusty caltrops off the road to clear their passage.

Mike ran up to Kane's fallen bike and grabbed the explosives out of the back with fresh determination. "You just wait and see."

Axel watched him in silence, a drop of sweat trailing from under his helmet.

"Slow," Mike told him as he mounted his orange vehicle again. "They can't know we're about to squash them."

A nod from Axel was enough of an answer.

Mike's bike came back to life, and he led the way along the narrow path uphill, taking care not to come too close to the edge. Dry trees and rocks would hide them from sight, but as they reached the top and saw the compound tucked between the hills, anger flared inside Mike again.

The settlement was a collection of mismatched buildings congregated between a large workshop from the side facing the asphalt road, and a small farm with a pig pen, chickens, and some greenhouses, where the Jarens produced some of their food.

Its remote location, surrounded by the desert and elevated ground was likely why the Jarens hadn't bothered to build any walls around their property and only had a barricade of concrete blocks and used tyres at the front. Armed men swarmed like bugs behind an old bus, which they used to block the entryway into their front yard, but the back remained unprotected, as Mike expected.

Slowly, they made their way downhill, passing behind bushes and rocks until they reached the strip of cultivated land and two greenhouses. Twin green figures of aliens dressed in rags and straw hats stood in the fields instead of traditional scarecrows. As tall as an average woman, the statues were one of the Jaren's more expensive products, but they didn't look too great from up close, with clear mold lines and unsophisticated features. But hey, maybe those two were just prototypes?

With the explosives in hand, two guns, and Axel to flank him, Mike was thirsty for mayhem, but as furious as he was, he didn't want to harm any innocents, and he'd found out from Harlyn that the Jarens had *many* children. That was actually when Mike dropped her like a hot potato. They'd been having a bit of fun, and she started talking about their future kids' names. Who did that?

"What's the plan?" Axel asked, pulling out his gun as they scooted behind a shed just off the small field.

"We wait for the others to draw their attention," Mike said to buy himself some time, but Axel was relentless and instantly asked again.

"And then?"

Mike wanted to growl that he wasn't sure yet, but the moment he caught a whiff of pig shit, the light bulb went on in his brain and his mouth spread into a manic grin.

"I know where to plant the explosives. You stay on the lookout in case any of them have the smart idea of coming back. If they do, hoot."

He circled the greenhouses, sweating into his clothes, but once he picked up the distant roar of motorcycles, the quiet compound came to life. Men and women shouted to get in position, whatever that meant, and as Mike peeked from under the shed that smelled of farm animals and heat, he caught a glimpse of familiar red hair as Harlyn sped inside an unplastered brick hut along with three other women and a little boy. The entrance to their shelter? It no longer mattered, because the metal door shut behind Harlyn the moment gunfire erupted at the front of the compound.

As far as marriage proposals went, this one was especially unappealing, and he'd make sure to let all the Jarens know what he thought of their prodding.

It was shit.

He snuck the explosives into a pile of manure and compost close to the pig shed. In the desert heat, it stunk so bad breathing through his mouth couldn't help, and he hoped for a warm evening that would send his never-family the right message. Sweat beaded on his forehead, because despite the shootout at the front, someone could still be patrolling the rest of the compound, but he had Axel to look out for him. This brotherhood deeper than blood was what he'd joined the Smoke Valley MC for, and even though club members were annoyed with the mess Mike had started by dating Harlyn, they would also stand by him for as long as it took.

One more glance up, and he lit the fuse of the dynamite Kane was so fond of. This was for Arden, but also for Kane who'd acted tough but might have broken something in his tumble over caltrops.

He ran, gesturing at Axel, whose eyes went wide just before he rushed straight into a glasshouse. Damn, what a great idea that was.

Mike followed his example, rushing into the damp space that smelled of tomatoes, and closed the door behind him, capturing Axel's gaze.

"How powerful are those explosives anyw—?"

The blast made both of them sink to the ground, and as he glanced through the misty glass, spotting fire and smoke, several globs of dirt and shit splattered the roof and wall. He thought the fun was over, but another explosion shook the ground under their feet and triggered the shit fireworks to rain manure all over the Jaren settlement.

Mike grinned when brown globs landed on the glass roof above them, but shouting and... cries of disgust erupted a moment later. Axel opened his mouth and cackled like a hyena, which was so unexpected from someone as stoic as him it could only be compared to a rattlesnake playing *Jingle Bells* with its tail.

Mike patted his arm, drunk on victory. "Now. Let's go."

The air outside was perfumed with the contents of pig intestine and undigested food, which prompted Mike to cover his mouth with his sleeve and run, but he froze when a figure stepped from behind one of the houses.

Brad Jaren, Harlyn's older brother had brown goo all over him, and while he was bleeding from his hand, he didn't seem seriously hurt, even if shocked.

"What... what the fuck, man?" he uttered, staring at Mike without bothering to look for a weapon.

Axel grabbed Mike's arm, predicting the inevitable. "Come on, Mike, you'll just get dirty."

"Hell no!" Mike pulled out of the grip and charged at the fucker despite the stench. "You fuckers think you can come for my boy and not suffer for it? Next time I'll blow the whole goddamn place to pieces!"

"What boy?" Brad frowned, but didn't manage to avoid a punch in the gut.

Mike picked up a fallen toy bucket, which miraculously seemed free of manure splatter and tossed it at Brad. "I will never marry Harlyn, so give it up. I've just come out, and I'm with a guy. So this marriage you seem to want for some reason is not. Going. To happen. Now fuck off. Happy cleaning," he said, pointing at Brad before storming off toward the path leading to where he and Axel had left their bikes.

"Say the fuck what?" Brad yelled, but didn't chase them. Smart move, because Mike was itching for his gun every time he thought of Arden's tears.

Axel was right behind him when they reached the bikes, catching their breath despite still riding the adrenaline rush. "You ever think before you talk?"

"Huh?"

Axel clenched his teeth and pushed at Mike's chest in an attack so sudden and unexpected it took Mike's breath for a second.

"You just put a target on Arden's back!"

Mike's eyes met Axel's, and the sinkhole in his chest deepened as if it didn't have a bottom. The sound of far off sirens meant there was no time to say anything more. Not that there was a need. Axel was right.

Mike jumped on the bike with the victory of the explosion overshadowed by fear of what his stupid mouth might have caused.

Fuck.

Fuck. Fuck. Fuck.

Chapter 17 – Arden

"You don't understand. They had to undress me there and then, in the street. Everyone saw I was wearing panties." Arden groaned into the phone, cuddled up in a comforter on the bed he shared with Mike.

He'd called his sister once he was done with his drawing of Mike. Weirdly enough, this one wasn't even all that porny. Sure, Mike was naked on it, all his birds of paradise on show, but Arden had missed Mike so much he just drew them hugging.

Kayley snorted. "I'm only laughing because you're fine now, okay? And people know you wear them because you let them peek out of your pants."

Arden ran his fingers through his hair in frustration. "It's not the same as standing butt-naked and being hosed down with water." He bit his lip at how terrified he'd been. "But you know... Mike's mom was really kind to me. She covered me with a sheet and stayed with me throughout. Even spoke for me when the doctor arrived... I wasn't expecting it, because she'd been giving me the stink eye before, but I may be growing on her."

"Whoa, whoa! Back up. What's that even mean? What's going on there, Ardy?"

Arden lay his head down on the pillow. It was about time to come clean. Mike had called and said that he'd dealt with the Jarens, but that Kane needed to go to the hospital, and that he'd be out with his brothers until late. Arden would stay up and wait for him. The attack should have scared him off from Mike, because this might be the beginning of more mayhem, but instead of faltering, his feelings for Mike only became stronger.

Mike had been so understanding when he listened about the assault, so caring and protective as the tear gas had hit. It was a blur in the moment, but Arden remembered Mike carrying him out of the gym when Arden had been unable to walk and panicked so hard he'd curled up on the floor instead of trying to get away.

"I'm in love with him, Kaley..."

The long silence made his guts twist.

"Well, shit. That's really bad, honey," she said, soft where he'd expected loud berating. "I told you not to fall for his bullshit."

"But it's not bullshit! He wants to be with me. He told his whole family we're a thing, and... we've kinda been living together."

"I'm gonna kill him."

Arden rubbed his face in frustration. "No! This is serious, he's nothing like Luke."

She gave a loud exhale. "No. He's not like Luke. He won't physically hurt you, he'll just leave you heartbroken once he gets bored. I'll come over and pick you up."

"You don't have to. It's not like that. *He's* not like that."

"No? Everyone always falls for his charm. Don't be *that*, Arden." She cleared her throat. "So are you like... sleeping with him? You must know he's straight."

Heat flushed his face but at least in the dark room no one would see. "He's... not so straight. He likes me the way I am."

"Arden! You can't be so gullible! Don't believe a word coming out of his mouth."

"I don't want to never trust anyone again because of Luke," he whispered. "We've been through stuff with Mike."

She exhaled, and Arden rolled over in the double bed, pushing his face into Mike's pillow, which still faintly smelled of his cologne.

Kaley spoke again. "I'm not saying he is a bad person. He has a good core, but he's careless when it comes to other people's feelings. He thinks the fact that he makes no explicit promises makes everything okay, and then you're left heartbroken while he suddenly withdraws all interest and moves on."

But he'd made a promise to Arden, hadn't he? This was different than the fling Kaley had with him years ago. Mike had committed, and fought for Arden.

"Okay, okay, I'll think about it." He wouldn't. "But I wanted you to know what's going on. Oh! I think they're back!" Arden sat up on the bed when he heard more noise and voices downstairs.

"Arden, do me a favor and stop thinking with your dick."

"I will. I have! Bye! My boyfriend's back."

He giggled at her deep sigh and disconnected. How was he to not think with his dick when he had the most amazing guy in his bed every night? Arden slipped off the strap of his satin pyjama top to appear casually disheveled.

The sound of motorcycles outside died down, replaced by loud conversations. Would Mike stay downstairs and chat about how everything had developed out there?

Should Arden change and join him?

He froze in the middle of the bed when the door handle lowered. For a moment he was uncertain whether he should have left the room unlocked, but tension evaporated from his muscles when Mike's blond head popped in.

Arden wouldn't wait for the sake of looking demure and sexy. Mike had already seen him vomiting and naked under a hose today, so all was out in the open. He rushed off the bed with a smile.

"Everything okay with Kane? With you?"

Mike stalled, as if he'd been expecting to find Arden asleep and locked the door behind him in silence. Arden couldn't see any obvious injuries, but his man was unusually somber.

"Kane's leg is fucked up, but it'll heal eventually. No one else was injured."

"Are you just playing it down?" Arden walked up to Mike and put his hands on his man's waist.

Mike was so muscular, so strong, yet still human. He could have been hurt and now trying to hide it for Arden's sake. He was considerate that way, always thinking of Arden's needs first. Like he had earlier, in the minutes following the vicious tear gas attack.

Mike licked his lips, weirdly pale. "No... I really... I'm fine."

Something was wrong. Arden pulled on Mike's T-shirt. "Show me. Did you get into a fight with the Jarens? Are you hurt? I'll believe you're fine when I see it."

Mike took Arden's hand to prevent him from lifting the garment. "You don't need to worry. Haven't landed a single punch today."

Arden glanced at Mike's fingers, and saw that the knuckles weren't bruised. "I was worried that you might have gotten carried away because of me."

Mike swallowed, his gaze holding Arden's for a second as he opened his mouth. "I might have put explosives in a manure pit. Their home will smell of shit for weeks."

Arden laughed out loud and only stopped when the soreness in his throat made him cough. "Oh... my god! Serves them fucking right. I scrubbed myself raw several times just in case. Smell my hair." He leaned in to give Mike a sniff of the cherry shampoo.

For a moment, Mike stood against the wall as if he wanted to become a part of it, but then Arden heard him take a whiff, and his big fingertips rested on Arden's hip.

"You smell nice."

Arden pushed his face against Mike's shoulder with a smile. "You must have taken a shower too. Why didn't you come back here to do it? I would have scrubbed your back." He slid his fingers under Mike's T-shirt and up the firm stomach he loved so much.

Mike exhaled. "Mom told me you were okay, so I stayed in the hospital with the others. Needed some time to think," he said, once again meeting Arden's gaze head-on.

"And now you need to rest." Arden got to his toes to kiss Mike. He smelled different after showering in some strange place. A mix of mint and... raspberry? Not Mike's typical choice. "You smell so good I wanna eat you up."

He didn't get to press their lips together, because Mike pulled him in and placed his chin on top of Arden's head. His embrace was warm, as if there was a fire pit inside him that would constantly protect Arden from the cold and any wild beasts that might wish him harm.

"Yeah? I might use feminine scents more often then."

"Soon enough you'll be borrowing my panties." Arden giggled and kissed Mike's shoulder. Having him close was such a relief, but Arden needed to learn to live with worry if he wanted an outlaw biker for a partner.

Mike snorted. "You wish. But I didn't want to smell like a pig once I came back, and the nurse who lent me her soap only had this and cinnamon vanilla, so... yeah. I can get you the same one if you like it so much." He spread his arms and shrugged.

"Or... you could just rub it all over me." Arden pulled on Mike's hand, tugging him to the bed.

Mike took a shivery breath, his palm getting sweaty in Arden's, but he let himself be pulled. "Didn't think you'd be up for it after today. That stuff could have killed you if I wasn't there to help," he said in a low voice that sounded the tiniest bit choked.

"My throat's a bit raspy, but my hero carried me out very fast. The doctor was impressed that I recovered so quickly. Thanks to you and your mom. Though I'll probably never forget that our neighbors saw me naked." Arden looked up at Mike in the dim light of the bedside lamp. Everyone strived for happiness, but Arden secretly thought he'd always have to get by on scraps of people's affection. What Mike had given him... that complete acceptance of who Arden was? So much more Arden had ever hoped for. His life now had two very distinct phases. Before Mike, and after. A clean cut starting his new life.

"If anything, I want you more."

Mike's chest expanded, and he cradled Arden's hand against it, gently squeezing while ghosts of emotion passed through his unusually rigid features. "You're not afraid?"

Arden shook his head, lost in the depth of Mike's eyes. He felt so seen, so acknowledged for all he was, not just a curiosity to fool around with. "No. I trust you. And I think I... I want to go all the way with you. If you want to that is. You listened to everything I said, and I know you won't hurt me."

Mike chewed on his lip and stepped closer, his eyes wandering before they settled on Arden's. "Oh, baby. I never want to see you hurt again."

Goosebumps tickled Arden's skin and he reached for Mike's belt, heart in his throat. He'd never felt like this about sex. Like it was so much more than a filthy, exhilarating exchange of fluids and arousal. With Mike... it was all that but also a way to communicate, be the closest they could be. Even back in San Francisco, in that kiss-turned-more, Arden had already been overwhelmed with his feelings for Mike.

"And you won't, because I've got a big bad protector, with an even bigger dick." He grinned at his man, his lover, his future.

Mike chuckled. "Oh, I like to think I am bigger than my dick," he said and nudged Arden's chest, making him fall flat on the bed. From down there, Mike always looked magnificent, like a tamed beast who only listened to Arden. He pressed the sole of his boot to the edge of the mattress between Arden's legs, and while it was to make the process of removing his boots simpler, Arden still felt a pang of arousal trail down to his toes.

"It's hard to say from this perspective. I need a closer look. But wait. I think this is in the way..." Arden winked at Mike and pulled off the satin pyjama top, his nipples already stiff. He couldn't wait to have Mike on top of him, pushing that stiff rod in until he came. They didn't even need to use rubbers since they'd gotten tested, and he longed to feel Mike's juice warming him from inside. Marking him as Mike's own.

Mike sighed and removed his other boot before leaning over the bed, his palms resting on the insides of Arden's spread thighs. Long hair fell against his tanned cheeks, trembling along with Mike's body, and Arden enjoyed the thought that it was a sign he was struggling to control himself in the face of Arden's proposition.

"It definitely was in the way. You have such cute little nipples," Mike breathed, placing his knee on the bed at last and lowering himself at a pace so slow it could only be in order to tease.

"And they taste even better than they look." Arden reached up to get his hands on Mike's sturdy shoulders faster. Mike was such a hunk. From the irresistible blue eyes, to the beard, the fantastically colorful tattoos, he was the biker wet dream, and Arden had loved riding on his bitch seat from that first time he'd put his arms around Mike's waist.

Mike hummed and crawled on top of him, still clothed, a big grin spreading his lips as he pressed his forehead to Arden's, and his dry hair fell around their faces. "Yeah? Are you offering me dessert for dinner?" he asked as his fingertips traced the sides of Arden's body, painting intricate patterns over his ribs.

Arden slipped his fingers into Mike's beard, combing it before stroking his way to Mike's ears. He'd kiss every inch of this man. "I'm offering you everything you want," he whispered, overwhelmed by the sense of security that came with Mike putting a controlled amount of weight on him, even though the belt buckle dug into his hip.

Mike gave a shuddery exhale, and pressed a kiss to Arden's forehead. Then his nose. Both eyelids. Rubbed his soft beard against Arden's jaw. When he rolled his head, their lips finally met. A jolt of heat spiraled up Arden's body, making him arch as his blood came to a sudden boil and left him unable to think for himself.

"I want to give you the best sex of your life," Mike whispered, and squeezed Arden at the waist, only to trail up, pushing him into the mattress as they settled just under Arden's pecs.

Heat flushed Arden's face, and he nodded, already spreading his legs wider. He couldn't wait for Mike to press the ignition. His whole body throbbed in anticipation of touch, tingling as if tiny needles teased every bit of skin.

"Leave me breathless," Arden murmured, without a hint of nervousness. He wasn't afraid anymore. What Luke had done to him hadn't been his fault and would remain in the past. He still craved sex with a man who wanted him more than anyone else in the world. He wanted the kind of passionate, tender yet filthy sex he had with Mike.

When the blond head lowered, and Mike rolled his head over Arden's chest, tickling his nipples with the beard, Arden was taken right back to that time Mike had the unexpected idea to decorate his nips with whipped cream. He'd eaten the entire contents of the can off Arden's flesh, deliciously shameless in his desires even when he sucked the stuff off Arden's cock.

There were no sweet toppings this time, yet when Mike closed his mouth on Arden's nipple and sucked, Arden got to his toes, arching against him as his head floated into orbit.

He whimpered when pleasure was followed by a bite and a pinch to his other nipple. His cock was already hard under the satin of his short boxers, and he couldn't wait to rub against Mike, flesh on flesh.

Arden gasped. "How are you this handsome? This skilled? It's too much in one man."

Mike winked at him, moving his attention to the other nipple while he rubbed the one he'd just bitten with the palm of his hand. The sensation it produced was somehow both delicious and uncomfortable, causing Arden to squirm while his man played.

When Mike reached to the nightstand, Arden already knew what was coming, but his face burst in flames regardless when he saw the pink nipple clamps again. They weren't very tight or in any way extreme but allowed Mike to keep teasing Arden's chest even when he was busy elsewhere.

"Gee, I don't know baby. Maybe I've gained this talent after getting licked by a pretty boy. You know, kinda like Spiderman."

Arden's eyes glazed over, and he curled his toes when the first clamp bit down on his nipple. If he knew one thing, it was that Mike loved to see him wanton and squirming with lust. Arden didn't have to play it up for him, because it came naturally around Mike.

Coming up with a witty answer was impossible.

"The Ardenman," he said, but words turned into another whimper when Mike pinched his other nipple with the clamp and dropped the little chain with heart-shaped links to his skin. Arden had no doubt he was leaving a growing pre-cum stain on his shorts.

Mike snorted and gave Arden a sweet yet fast kiss that made Arden's heart gallop for a split second. "Behold. I'll show you all *my* superpowers," he said and tore his own T-shirt off, revealing the firm chest that, thankfully, showed no signs of injury.

Arden was such a sucker for tats, and Mike had a magnificent display of them on the sturdy muscles. "Fuck. I think I felt that in my nipples. You have no idea how much I want you."

Mike grunted, as if he were buried in Arden already, and gently tugged on the chain, teasing his nipples. "You just wait," he said and looked at the tenting at the front of Arden's pajama shorts, the purple satin stained where the tip was. "But first, take them off," he decided, unbuckling his belt as if he couldn't bear staying clothed anymore.

Arden had no energy to tease Mike, and arched his hips to pull off the shorts. His heart pounded like crazy when he leaned in to kiss Mike. Mint and raspberry, as alien as they smelled on him, grew on Arden as he petted and caressed his lover, ready to throw away his fears.

Mike leaned over him, a living statue of gold and pleasure. The room had no sound other than their breaths and the rustling of Mike pulling down his jeans. The sight of him rendered Arden breathless until Mike grabbed his hand and placed it around his dick. "You feel that, baby? It'll be so, so deep inside you soon."

Arden had no idea how much he longed for it until Mike said those words. The yearning inside him was like a physical presence he couldn't contain. It wanted out, to bare itself to Mike and hold him. Arden stroked the thick cock in reverence, already greedy for the cum it would offer.

"Yes. Yes. Do you even know how hot I am for you? It was so hard to resist you when I had to pretend not being interested. All I wanted was to lick you from head to toe."

Mike snorted and cupped Arden's cock and balls in one hand, confident as if he'd been living the bisexual life for years. "I think it's my turn to do the licking, "he said, massaging Arden's throbbing flesh at a slow pace, testing the waters. "Roll over."

Arden would. But not before he got another kiss. Still tugging on the throbbing cock in his hand, he pulled Mike down by the beard and closed his eyes, indulging in the meeting of tongues and lips. He wanted to eat this man up like the human equivalent of a fly trap, to never let Mike out of his grip.

Only when he was satisfied did he pull away and turn to his belly, presenting his naked flesh to Mike.

The chain dragged over the sheets, transferring the tiniest vibrations to his nipples, but it was the sound of the drawer opening again that made Arden moan and wiggle his butt in anticipation. For a moment there, he thought that maybe Mike had changed his mind about giving Arden oral, or that maybe he wanted to finish them off once he came deep inside Arden's ass, but when a soft brush of both hands down his ass was followed by hot air that made goosebumps erupt on Arden's buttocks, his stomach turned into goo.

He forgot how to breathe, and only realized it when he mumbled a yes and barely had enough air to do so. He pushed his ass up, smelling the pillow that carried the aroma of Mike's usual cologne. He'd indulged in the fantasy of being eaten out many times in his drawings where a bearded guy had his face buried between the ass cheeks of a squirming twink. Now the dream would come to life.

Now it would be him and Mike, the god of sex, champion of consent, and his tender protector.

He bit his lip, starting to gently rock his hips in the air as he sensed more heat on his ass. The first touch was dry—a finger gliding between his buttocks but not yet pushing in. "I've thought about it so many times," Mike whispered, his voice throaty as if he'd just given Arden head. "Every time I saw you wearing those panties with a gap at the back. Especially the ones where the gap is heart-shaped. I fantasized I'd bend you over, sit down behind you, and just eat your ass for ages, until you came in your panties."

Arden's cock twitched at the vision. He wanted that too. "I love teasing you. Love the lust in your eyes. It turns me on to be an object of your desire. I'm gonna milk your dick so good."

"Oh yes, baby." It was a whisper this time, but Mike took hold of Arden's ass and moved his thumbs along the borders of smooth, sensitive flesh, until they rested on either side of his hole, keeping it open so Mike could watch. "You are irresistible."

"All yours," Arden whispered. "Make me nice and ready for you..." A shiver went up his spine at the first lick. It was slow and deliberate, but by no means cautious, and he curled his shoulders, already sweating as pleasure spread its tentacles through his body.

Mike hummed, teasing the sides of his buttocks with gentle licks. Over and over, as if he had all the time in the world before he buried his dick in Arden's body. Or so Arden thought, because once Mike got down to business, the stars above fell from the sky, flashing at the backs of Arden's eyelids.

He hugged the pillow with a soft whine as Mike teased the sensitive pucker of skin, then slowly drilled his tongue into Arden's hole. The clamps on Arden's nipples created tiny sparks of pain as if to remind him who was in charge even as Mike gave him pleasure by licking and nipping Arden's flesh with just the right amount of pressure. As if he'd done this many times before and wanted to savor this moment, soften Arden's flesh until he had no choice but to beg for a hard fuck.

The tongue was eventually joined by Mike's thumb, which kept poking the hole while Mike teased Arden's balls and cock with the rest of his hand, and by the time Mike pushed the whole digit in, Arden was hopelessly rolling against the sheets, dragging the nipple clamps against fabric, his balls ready to burst.

None of the bad memories of what Luke had done mattered anymore. He was free to enjoy his sexuality and be himself with Mike.

Arden groaned when Mike pushed his thumb in up to the knuckle. "Mike? I need you to ride me like I'm your Harley right about fucking now."

Mike roared with laughter and rolled Arden over, l licking his lips as if he'd had a most delicious meal. He didn't care about people's opinions, always true to himself. It was so bold Arden couldn't help but admire him for sticking to his guns and being with him like this. Not just in bed but put in the open too, and when Mike pressed lubed fingers to Arden's ass and pulled on the nipple clamp chain, for a moment orgasm was so close Arden let out a frantic yelp, trying hard to not explode all over his stomach before he got to feel Mike inside his ass at last.

He pulled his legs up to his chest and presented his entrance. But his lustful gaze wouldn't meet Mike's eyes, and instead wandered over the tattoos depicting colorful birds, and to the one of a roaring lion in the middle of Mike's chest. This one truly expressed who Mike was—a fierce yet gentle beast that deserved to feed on Arden's flesh.

Mike greased his dick next, his thumb going in and out of Arden's hole as they stared at one another while the bed was consumed by fire. "Your body is made for sitting on this dick. I'm gonna pump you so full of my spunk you'll feel its flavor all the way in your mouth," he rasped and stuffed a pillow under Arden's hips.

Arden's face was hot enough to fry eggs on. "I wish I had another you so I could suck your cock at the same time." He held his legs under the knees, wide open to Mike and ready to give him the ride of his life.

"Maybe next time I'll have you fuck yourself with a vibrator as you suck me, and you'll imagine my doppelganger is the one doing you from behind."

Arden let out the softest mewl when the head pressed against his hole, and Mike looked at him, his eyes lowering as if he were worried, but when Arden dragged his palms down the lion tattoo, the pressure increased, and Arden's body opened to it, letting Mike in.

He'd missed this kind of sex, but it also felt new. He had a connection with Mike that he hadn't shared with any of his previous partners. He wanted to join emotionally as well as have this man's flesh deep inside and give him pleasure.

"Yes…" Arden whispered, but he'd have said yes to anything at that moment, because all he could focus on was Mike's tool slowly drilling into him. "Hard and fast, Mike. Don't hold back. I wanna drip with your spunk."

"Yeah? That's what you want, baby? A flesh jackhammer?" Mike asked, pushing his arms under Arden's head to cradle him as their hips kissed. Sweat shone on his cheeks, and Arden could taste it on Mike's lips too, but all those sensations melted into a sense of joy when Mike held him, and nothing about that felt threatening.

He'd have bet his right arm that if he said he changed his mind, Mike would have pulled away. He was considerate that way. But he wouldn't tell Mike to stop. Because he wanted this—this sense of warm fullness and Mike's eyes on him. He wanted it more than anything in the world.

"Fuck yes." He wrapped his legs around Mike's hips and held on to his shoulders. "You have no idea what you started here," he whispered into Mike's ear and licked it. "My hole is so greedy for a plowing." Arden clenched his ass to drive that point home, and Mike pulled back, dragging his meat through Arden's hole until it almost felt as if he might pull out altogether. He thrust back in before Arden could have voiced a word of protest, the firm move triggering fireworks inside Arden's skull.

Mike's eyes remained wide open despite the growing flush on his cheeks and torso, his gaze pinning Arden in place as he entered him faster next time. He did it at an angle that didn't stimulate Arden's prostate quite right, but he would learn how to fuck a guy in due time, and the penetration itself felt so good he wanted Mike to just enjoy himself.

"You've neglected yourself. You're gonna go all crazy now and lift your skirt every time you have an itch," Mike whispered, somehow with both tenderness and lust.

Arden pulled on Mike's lip with his teeth. "Let's just hope you're there to scratch it or I might have to use someone else to jackhammer my tight, greedy holes." He loved talking dirty with a lover, but he had to feel safe to do that. Some guys took things too literally, and that created problems for him more than once in the past. But Mike understood what this was, and Arden could unleash his mouth and leave self-consciousness out the door.

Mike gasped. "What if I watched?" he whispered and kissed Arden's lips as he thrust again, so hard Arden's body got dragged closer to the headboard.

As the thrusts sped up, Arden's speech was interrupted with moans, but the fantasy turned him on too much to give up on letting his mouth loose. "You wouldn't. You'd be too horny watching me pounded. You'd come over and fuck my mouth while the other guy had me from behind, legs spread wide."

"Fuck, baby. I would have. I so would have. You have the tastiest ass I've ever eaten. The best mouth hole. The cutest dick. The prettiest face," Mike whispered, leaning forward so he trapped Arden folded like a pretzel and used gravity as leverage to slam in even harder.

Arden wanted to spin the tale further, tell Mike how he'd turn around after the stranger was done and let Mike fuck his hole too, but he couldn't speak anymore, reduced to a moaning mess. He held on to this man, who was so strong and brave, a hot head always up for a challenge, yet also tender and sweet in the most surprising ways.

His man.

Mike's dick was like a piston, fucking Arden with all the force of a man in need of an orgasm. Arden couldn't wait to give him one, but wondered whether his own wouldn't come sooner, because Mike changed the angle of his thrusts at some point, to one that made Arden's insides shiver with pleasure, and continued jabbing into him so his cockhead teased Arden's prostate over and over.

Breathless, he kept kissing Arden's face as he pinned him down, words escaping his mouth in a delicious *staccato*. "I'm gonna have you dress in the shortest skirt, and stripper shoes, and fishnets, and I'll watch everyone's eyes on you. And then I'll have you against the wall, ripping open your tights to get to your ass."

"With... others watching?" Arden mumbled, lost in the fantasy world existing in both their minds. "Once you're done fucking... you'd pull the skirt down and just let cum drip down my legs..."

"Yeah. And have you ride in the bitch seat of my bike on the way home. Legs spread wide and wrapped around me," Mike uttered and bit Arden's neck.

One more thrust, and Arden shook, filled with insane heat. The orgasm made him clench his eyes, and he didn't even care how much noise he made as he held on tightly to Mike, his ass throbbing around that hot tool inside him.

His sticky cum spurted between them, relieving the unbearable pressure in his balls, but he still had enough brain power to enjoy knowing some of it would be marking Mike's skin.

He floated on the wings of endorphins, his world pink and golden as Mike thrust into him faster... then stilled, pumping cum into the depths of Arden's body. They pressed together, but the afterglow couldn't switch off Arden's desire, as if Mike's spunk was amphetamine.

A panting heap of limbs, he went straight for Mike's mouth, kissing him with the force of his love for the man who made him feel safe, accepted him whole, and desired his gutter mind as much as Arden did his.

Curled up under a sheet Mike had to have pulled on them, Arden wrapped Mike's arm over himself. "I love you," he whispered with his heart pounding.

Mike hugged him but stayed silent for a while. "We'll talk in the morning, okay?"

Arden hugged Mike tighter, too sleepy to deconstruct Mike's lack of reciprocation. Maybe Mike just didn't hear him. Arden could repeat his declaration tomorrow.

Chapter 18 – Arden

Arden opened his eyes to a dusky sky. It was still very early, but the noise that must have woken him wasn't incidental. A rustle nearby, just beyond the bed, sent a shudder down Arden's back. Had someone broken in?

The person used a phone for illumination as they shuffled through the contents of the bedside drawer. It only took Arden extending his arm to know Mike was gone from the bed.

"Mike?" he muttered, then yawned, blinking away sleep.

The silhouette stalled, and the glow of the cell phone illuminated the tangled strands of hair before distorting the contours of Mike's face by casting shadows.

"Ah... didn't want to wake you," Mike said softly.

"What's going on? Is it the Jarens?" Arden sat up and rubbed his eyes into attention.

Mike shifted his weight, but while his body language expressed uncertainty, he wasn't in a hurry.

"No," he said. The bedside lamp went on, revealing Mike had dressed in fresh clothes and pulled his uncombed hair into a messy ponytail so it wouldn't get into his eyes. Behind him was a large duffel bag. And behind that—the emptied wardrobe.

Alarm bells went off in Arden's head, but he had no idea what the alert was for.

"So... where are you going?"

Mike's face was pale in the warm glow of the lamp, and he crossed his arms on his chest, watching the tips of his boots as he finally spoke. "This relationship is not safe for you. I come with too much baggage."

Arden's reality glitched. This had to be a different dimension, because no other explanation made sense. He'd caught Mike, his beloved boyfriend, packing his shit and fleeing in the middle of the night.

What. The. Fuck.

Arden's mouth was dry as he spoke. "What are you talking about? Is it 'cause I said I loved you? I'm sorry. I should have known it was too soon. You don't have to say it back!" He got off the bed with panic choking his throat.

Mike swallowed several times as he pressed his back against the wall. "No... Arden, this isn't about something you did. Yesterday... that attack reminded me why I decided not to do this kind of thing in the first place. I don't want to put a target on your back."

Arden's instinct had been to grab Mike and hug him in reassurance, but facing him naked didn't feel right, so Arden pulled on his pyjama shorts, painfully aware that he hadn't showered after sex.

He looked up at Mike, still unsure whether he understood this. "And you made that decision *after* you fucked me?" It came out much louder and harsher than he'd intended. A bullet where he'd meant a punch.

Mike's body went tense, as if the word projectile hit him right where it hurt, but he met Arden's gaze without delay, pale cheeks gaining color. "No. I wanted to talk to you about this last night. But then you said you finally felt good about having sex again following that awful... thing your ex did, and I thought I wanted to give you a good experience, you know? So you can move on."

Arden grabbed his own throat and curled his shoulders, unable to speak for several seconds as he processed this monstrosity. What was this supposed to mean? That Mike had sex with him out of some ill-conceived obligation? Last night's life-altering experience had really been a pity fuck for a broken boy?

"A good experience?" Arden whispered. "Are you really dumping me like this?" One more chance for Mike to back out of this and say that he just wanted a break, or... something. Arden would accept it like the self-respect lacking sucker he was, because he couldn't stand the idea of losing him forever.

But Mike swallowed and cupped his own head with both hands before moving them to the back, to hold onto hair. His chest rose and fell quickly, as if he were struggling not to hyperventilate. "It's not you. I can't be with *anyone*. What happened yesterday could have been so much worse. What if someone abducts you, or hurts you just because you're with me?"

Arden watched, shocked as if Mike had declared he was about to join a monastery, but then he pushed at Mike's chest, hoping for a reaction. "It's not your choice to make! I know who you are, I know you do illegal shit, and I still chose to be with you! Just like it wasn't your choice to try and 'give me a good experience'! It's now forever tainted by this. You think your dick is magic or something? It was never about the sex itself, but trusting someone, and you... you wrecked that trust! I can't believe this shit!" Despite fighting tears with all his might, they still spilled down his face, proving he was far more fragile than he would have liked.

Mike stilled, his mouth twisting as he chewed on Arden's pain, surely trying to work out the best thing to say so he'd get the outcome he wanted. Kaley had warned Arden Mike did things like this, but, like always, he hadn't listened.

"I'm sorry. Maybe you're right. Maybe I should have told you last night, but I'm no saint. I thought I was doing the right thing," Mike said in the end, spreading his arms in a wordless plea for his innocence.

Arden shoved him again, even though it was like punching a brick wall. "No, you didn't! You just wanted to see if it's any different to fuck a boy, didn't you? Just that one time before leaving me. And now I feel like some fucking broken Fleshlight! I literally still have your cum inside me you motherfucker!" Anger was a bright red light pulsing under Arden's eyelids, but it was the only thing keeping him sane. If it wasn't for his anger, he'd be shattering into a million pieces.

He grabbed the little switchblade hidden in an oversized key, the one he'd failed to use when kidnapped. He'd learned since then.

Arden snapped the knife open and charged at Mike, but the fucker turned when Arden aimed for his chest, and the blade sank into Mike's arm, into the blue parrot tattoo. Regret flooded Arden as soon as he saw blood, but he still screamed at Mike.

"I hate you so much!"

Mike touched the fresh wound, then stared at the blood as if he couldn't believe Arden had stabbed him. "I—I'm really sorry. You can have my room and stay with us. That's why I was packing my stuff. I really care about you!"

Scraps from the table for the kicked dog. Mike might 'care' for Arden, but he didn't love Arden. Never had and never would.

Arden was drowning in the quicksand of his own making. There had been warning signs. He should have never trusted Mike. Yesterday, he hadn't only felt comfortable and at ease enough to give Mike his body. He'd shared all of himself, with complete trust, and now he was finding out it had meant *nothing* to Mike.

"You don't! You're leaving with some half-assed excuse about my safety. Then go! Fucking go! What are you waiting for?" Arden yelled and pushed him toward the door. The blood trickling down Mike's arm only spurred on his exasperation.

He didn't have the strength to force Mike into anything, so the fact that Mike was letting Arden herd him out into the corridor, was just that. Mike was *letting* him. Because he wanted to leave, and dealing with Arden's fury was another hurdle to overcome before he could sigh in relief and drown in *all* the pussy again.

Arden locked the door the moment Mike backed into the corridor and pressed his forehead to the cool wood as hot tears spilled down his cheeks. The room was too big for a single person, and with Mike out, the emptiness of the tidy space might consume him whole. If he was to stay here, he needed all traces of Mike gone. All of them. He'd wash the sheets and spray the mattress with upholstery cleaner. He'd scrub every surface so it no longer smelled of his masculine cologne.

That bastard was not worth his tears, so Arden was intent on turning his sadness into pure hate and never give his heart to anyone again, regardless of their pretty words and even prettier actions. How could he have been so stupid *again*?

Mike hadn't packed all of his clothes, though of course he had taken the property vest he never spoke about. Arden pulled on a T-shirt and went to work on this toxic place. If he couldn't hurt Mike, at least he'd wreck his shit.

He opened the window, and threw the first batch of clothes out into the empty yard. His one regret was that in this desert there was no mud or puddles to chuck it all into.

He didn't bother to mess up the stuff Mike had already packed. He grabbed the open bag and hauled it outside. It tumbled into the dust, spilling its contents. But he wasn't done. Next came the shoes, which Arden tossed with such ferocity they all hit the wall of the building across the yard, and one tumbled across its roof and fell on the other side.

"Fuck you!" Arden said as he threw one of the alcohol bottles from Mike's collection to the ground. Even the sound of smashing glass wasn't able to soothe his pain, but it numbed it for half a second, so he threw another.

A figure loomed outside, and Arden knew it was Mike before he heard the familiar voice. He threw the next bottle, trying to hit the pile of Mike's clothes, so it would soak in the bourbon and become a trap due to broken glass. He didn't quite manage that feat.

"Hey, what the hell are you doing?" Mike yelled, running up to face Arden from below.

"What do you *think* I'm doing? Getting rid of your shit! You wanted to leave, so take it all!" His voice was a razor slashing through his throat, but he would not curl into a ball and die. Even if he never loved or trusted again, he would live on and fight lying scum like Mike.

Mike looked around, spreading his arms as he took in the damage already made.

The sun wasn't yet up, but it already colored the clouds in a brilliant palette of pinks, oranges, and purples, as if there was another beautiful day ahead, and Arden's heart hadn't been shattered.

"Just put it all into the damn corridor!" Mike shouted, leaping away when Arden sent a facial cream his way.

"You don't get to tell me what to do!" Arden screeched louder and threw lube Mike's way, followed by a blister pack of condoms that fluttered in the air like an unusual bird. "You'll probably need these where you're going!"

Mike dragged his hands down his cheeks. "Arden, please!"

"What the hell is this about?" Jeff asked, rolling out of the office area with messy hair, in just a pair of black boxer shorts and flip flops on his feet.

"None of your business!" Arden yelled.

Mike gave a frustrated noise. "Stop waking people up!"

Arden didn't care if he woke up the whole goddamn compound, and all the coyotes in the desert behind it, because his suffering needed an outlet.

Jeff grabbed Mike's arm. "You're bleeding. What happened?"

"I happened!" Arden cried, his voice thick with emotion. "I could have stabbed you a thousand times over and you wouldn't know how much I'm hurting!" His voice became a rasp on the last word when he choked on tears.

Mike's mouth shut, and he stared at Arden despite Jeff hissing something at him.

Arden choked on the bitterness in his throat, but the sound of the lock pulled him right back to reality. He spun around to face Axel's massive form storming at him in shorts and a tank top. Before he could have considered a mode of defense, Axel yanked him up and carried him out of the room as if he were a bounty hunter delivering a criminal to the Sheriff's office somewhere in the old West.

"You ungrateful piece of shit!"

"Let me go! You don't know what's going on!" Arden cried, but Axel's arms were steel, and he knew exactly how to hold Arden so that none of the moves Mike had taught him worked.

Axel carried Arden down the stairs with terrifying efficiency, and by the time they reached the door to the yard, Mike ran straight at them, blocking the way.

Jeff pulled on Mike's shoulder, as if he smelled mayhem already. "He's fine, I just told Axel to go fetch him. Jack is coming too. I called him before I knew what was going on."

Mike blinked. "What? Why get him involved?"

"You clearly don't have your boy under control," Axel grumbled and let go of Arden so abruptly, Arden barely saved himself from falling into the dirt.

The bastard might have as well cut Arden's heart open. Arden eyed Jeff with the ferocity of a cornered scorpion. "Oh yeah? And *now* you know what's going on? You know shit! Did he tell you what he did?"

"We're no longer together. I don't want you guys involved, or Jack, or anyone else," Mike said and offered Arden his hand.

Arden couldn't slap it away fast enough, even though the sound of the motorcycle outside the gate made him shiver. Jack didn't live on the premises, so it had to be him arriving, and despite their uncle Kurt being the club VP, it was Jack who served as Dad's right hand man and seemed far more responsible.

He was also strict and ruthless, so if Arden wanted to get one more punch in, it had to be now, before the gate opened. He took on the stance Mike taught him, with fists in front of his face. "Fight me! You wanted to date a man, deal with the consequences and fight me!"

Mike took a step back. Jeff sniggered, but Arden would be no laughing stock and pounced forward, swiftly enough to land a punch on Mike's chin.

Mike's teeth clattered, but he shook his head, and instead of hitting back, massaged his jaw before pushing back his hair while his two brothers watched. "Did that make you feel better?"

Arden sniffed, struggling to catch his breath. His ears thudded with adrenaline, but he still heard the gate open and Jack yelling something their way. "No, but maybe *this* will! Fight me!" He demanded, continuing his onslaught, but all he got was Mike shifting to avoid most of the hits.

"That's enough!" Jack yelled, dismounting. He must have come straight out of bed, since he wore a T-shirt and running pants—not his usual day attire. "The fuck's going on?"

Arden was about to climb Mike like a tree and scratch his face off when Axel once more stepped in with his death-grip and held Arden's arms back.

"Calm the fuck down," he growled.

Arden took a deep breath, but fury was a constant simmer, on the verge of boiling over. "Okay, okay!" Another deep breath. "I'm done."

"Don't hurt him—"

The moment Mike stepped closer, Arden used Axel's hold for leverage and kicked Mike square in the groin. There. *Now* he was done.

Mike's eyes opened so wide they almost popped out of his eyelids, and he grabbed his crotch, folding in two with his teeth grinding to stop a yelp from coming out.

Jeff hissed in sympathy, but Jack approached with the subtlety of a tank, and slapped Arden on the face hard. "Whatcha think you're doing, boy? Huh? You think you can run rampant 'cause you have some breakup drama?"

"Don't fucking touch him," Mike warned, red-faced, and while he moved with legs comically pressed together, he still managed to shove Jack at the wall.

Jack blinked and shook his head. "So soft. Maybe you deserved that kick after all."

Arden hung his head, but the burn in his cheek wasn't half as bad as the ache of his heart. He'd let Mike plow him like a fucking field last night, and got betrayed in return.

Jack tilted Arden's chin up with his thumb, as if to make the point that he would indeed touch Arden if he wanted to. "If you're not Mike's, you don't get any special treatment. Understood, snowflake? Get your shit together, clean up the mess here, and tomorrow you'll wash every single car in the garage. This is me letting you off with a slap on the wrist. Got it?"

Arden bit his lips and nodded, deflating in the face of such stern words.

For a moment, Mike's face kept twisting, as if he wanted to say something, but in the end he settled on, "I'll pack my other things. He stays in the room."

None of his brothers said a thing as he headed inside the building.

Axel let go of Arden's arms, and Arden detested the touch he still felt so much, he didn't even want to look at the Hellers. He got on with the task at hand and started gathering items that had fallen out of Mike's duffel bag. He stilled when the vest that must have once belonged to someone Mike cared for far more than he did for Arden emerged from between T-shirts.

'Property of Mad Mike', it read.

Something he'd never be.

Chapter 19 – Mike

Mike had barely slept. The bed in his new room wasn't comfortable, and he'd gotten so used to having his own bathroom that the necessity of using the shared facilities hadn't been the greatest experience. Especially since Jeff and Axel didn't care to keep them tidy. He didn't feel like having breakfast and went straight for coffee, emerging with a cup into sunshine so bright his sluggish mind boiled only a few minutes into the lazy pacing along the courtyard.

The mess had been cleaned, and while the places where his liquor bottles had broken had a faint odor of alcohol, it was almost as if the early morning confrontation never happened. It was near midday now, and while the day started slow for most of his friends and family on Saturdays, many of them already gravitated to the clubhouse, with some hangarounds sharing gossip over watermelon, and a few of the bikers congregated on outdoor chairs in the shade.

To them, it was a day like any other, but Mike's gaze kept straying to Arden's window upstairs. The blinds were open, which meant he was up, but Mike hadn't seen him yet and kept glancing toward it in hopes of getting a glimpse of the boy.

Seeing Arden's tears had been far worse than the minor stab Jeff had dressed for him. His chin still ached a bit from the punch, but any bruising that might be there would remain obscured by the beard. Had he fucked up? He had by getting so close to Arden in the first place, but his intentions last night had been pure. Arden had been so badly hurt by his goddamn ex, and Mike had envisioned that a good sexual experience would free Arden of some of that burden.

And then Arden had confessed his love and made Mike remember what happened last time he felt so deeply for another person.

"Watch where you're going," Mike snapped at a hangaround who bumped into him.

She wore a black bikini top under a fishnet T-shirt, and the garment barely covered her big breasts. Any other time he would have taken this as an opportunity to flirt but he wasn't in the mood.

"Um. Rude? I brought you a beer," She tried, raising her dark eyebrows.

He clenched his jaw, mumbled an apology, and took the bottle out of her hand. He was done with the coffee anyway. "Have you seen Arden today?" he asked just as she was turning on her heel.

Her face fell, but she stopped. She must have heard the gossip by now. "No. Why? Everything okay?"

What was her name? Sammy? He was pretty sure it was 'Sammy'.

Mike shrugged. "It's fine. Just wanted to know."

What if Arden had already vacated the room? What if he'd gone to the bus station and returned to Reno, where Luke could easily target him? What if he'd hitchhiked and became prey to some perverted serial killer?

He might be ferocious when angry but not ready to take on a serious opponent.

"Thanks for the beer," he said, heading to where the guys were seated, enjoying their own drinks while a radio placed on the plastic table in the middle played sports news. The air couldn't have been any drier, scratching Mike's throat with every breath he took, and he longed for the shade, because the heat was making his brain fry.

Kane sat in a rickety armchair with his leg in a cast, but made the effort of leaning in to clink his bottle with Mike's. "Heard about Arden. Only uphill from here, eh? You're now free to marry Harlyn," he teased, but Mike wasn't in the mood and ignored him.

"Did any of you see him today?" he asked, carefully sinking into the old sun chair that was so hard to get out of.

So maybe he was a bit paranoid, but when he thought of Arden out there on his own, of someone else flirting with him, being his shoulder to cry on, just to then use the boy's vulnerability against him, he itched all over to go and knock on Arden's door.

"He's not left the premises," Axel said as if he could read Mike's mind without as much as glancing at him, busy setting up the grill nearby.

Kane snorted. "Wow. There I was, thinking you decided to just go back to all the pretty girls gagging for your dick."

"Shut up, Kane," Jack said from behind his glass of iced coffee before Mike could have.

"He probably didn't get much sleep with all the clean-up," Mike mused instead, his mind stubbornly returning to that moment Arden had stared at him in the dark, his eyes shining with love and hope.

And he'd ruined it.

He should have never gotten attached to someone so vulnerable and sweet. He should have kept it in his pants and had fun with girls who didn't want anything more than that from him. But no, he always had to go for what was being denied to him. Stupid fucking brain.

Jack shrugged. "He got what he was asking for. Doesn't matter how small he is, he can't throw your shit around. It's disrespect."

Mike glanced at Jack's big tattooed hand, the same one that had slapped Arden with such ease. It was the size of Arden's whole face. He knew what Jack was saying was right but still longed to rub his brother's nose in gravel. Would it be so bad to provoke him into a fight?

"That's between him and me. None of you fuckers should have gotten involved," he said, his tongue sharp as a razorblade and ready to cut.

Kane stretched. "Sure. Let's just let the girls run wild and do whatever they want. Because *that's* gonna end so well."

Axel snorted, prompting Kane to slap his leg, so this likely had something to do with Shay having clipped his claws since their relationship started.

Jack smirked, putting on his shades. "Should have leashed your little pup then, Mike."

That was it. Mike was done with this shit. He got up—or rather rolled out of the sun chair—ready to throw the first punch, but a whistle drew his attention, and all blood drained from his head.

Arden walked out of the clubhouse and into the dusty yard as if he were about to star in a music video. He strutted toward the cars with his chin held high, curly hair tamed into soft waves of pale fluff, but what really changed the way he walked was the pair of sky-high stripper heels—blood red like his lipstick and so glossy they seemed to shine in the glow of the sun. His denim shorts weren't too tight, so they didn't accentuate his package, but short enough to give anyone who cared to look a glimpse of the bottom of his butt cheeks. Same ass Mike had so eagerly bitten into yesterday. The icing on this cake drizzled in sex appeal was the tiniest bikini top that held no breasts but covered Arden's nipples. One of the cups featured a pattern of stars, the other—stripes.

"Damn... If I didn't know he was a guy—" Jeff started, but Mike cut him off, breathless.

"Do yourself a favor and don't finish that stupid sentence," he said, hypnotized by the even gait in tall heels that made Arden's hips sway so deliciously he wished he could press him against Jack's black Ford Mustang and forget the terrible things that happened since last night.

But he couldn't. Because he'd done what he'd done, and Arden now hated him with the kind of intensity that only someone who loved before could wield.

Mike had made the choice to distance himself. And now Arden wasn't his.

He watched from the sidelines, like every other dog without a bone. Every single man around him knew Arden was a guy, yet when Arden bent over the car in those impossible heels to wash the windshield, even Axel crooked his neck to see that curved butt better. If they knew how sexually explosive Arden was, maybe they too would have become more flexible in their desires.

Maybe as long as Arden kept on the cute underwear, his cock tucked into lacy panties, they could forget it was there and want him the same way they wanted a hot girl?

But Mike wanted that cock too, and when he watched Arden lift his knee to rest against the front of the hood, his fantasy developed further, into him stuffing his hand down the front of Arden's shorts. Within several fast-paced images, streaks of cum shone on Jack's car, and Arden rubbed them into the metal while Mike dry-humped him from behind.

He'd always liked to see other men appreciating his dates, but it struck Mike that Arden might fuck someone else to get back at him. What if he did that in public? Or in the bed they'd made love in yesterday?

Mike would have killed the motherfucker with his bare hands.

"Mike?" Kane pushed at Mike's elbow. He must have been repeating himself, because Mike had spaced out for a little. "Did you actually *fuck*-fuck him?"

"None of your damn business."

"He didn't," Jack said, waving his hand. "That's why he's so pissed off about the whole thing."

"You know what? Fuck you all," Mike said and headed for the bar, but was distracted halfway when his brothers and cousin hooted. When Mike glanced Arden's way, the boy squeezed a sponge over his flat chest and rocked his hips as the water dripped into his shorts.

Torn between looking away and staring, he stood there, unable to move. If he went to the bar, he wouldn't be there if Arden chose to do something more outrageous. This show was meant to make Mike miserable, to show how fast Arden had bounced back from yesterday's upset and didn't care. Mike knew him too well to believe it, not after seeing Arden at his most vulnerable and holding him through nightmares. This was just a masquerade, presenting the world a distorted image.

Arden leaned against the car as soapy suds dripped down his long legs. "Guys? Can I get a drink? It's scorching today," he yelled from afar.

Even Jack was entertained despite this hardly being the punishment he'd intended to mete out for Arden's behavior.

Sammy smiled and grabbed a beer from the cooler. "I'll get it."

Jeff stretched and whistled after her. "Maybe the two of you could give me a private show?"

She showed him the finger but winked, and strode toward Arden, who dipped the sponge inside a bucket before all but climbing on the hood as he pushed back his ass and rubbed the shiny metal in smooth strokes.

"I should ask my Trixie to wash the car like this for my birthday," Jack said, drinking his beer, as if it was all a big joke, while Mike simmered in his impotent juices.

Kane wouldn't give it a rest either. "Shay's already asked him if he ever considered camming. Maybe now that he's single, he'd give it a whirl. That way you could still perv on him." He wiggled his eyebrows at Mike, who was too focused on wondering why Sammy was lingering around Arden to deflect those suggestions.

For the briefest moment, he sensed tension in the air as Sammy stepped far too close to Arden, getting into his face. The next thing he knew was Arden pouring the entire bucket of soapy water over the top of Sammy's head. Mike moved before laughter and sounds of disbelief could have died down, breaking into a run the moment Sammy punched Arden so hard the boy spun around and lost balance in the killer heels.

"Hey! Stop!"

"Catfight!" Kane yelled from his old-man chair, and Mike almost turned around to break his other leg for encouraging this.

Arden wouldn't just take the punch, and despite blood spurting out of his nose and down his lips, he screeched like a madman and tackled Sammy into the puddle.

Mike reached them within a few leaps and pulled Arden back, dragging his thrashing form all the way up. "Stop! What the hell?"

Sammy, who was completely drenched and had foam clinging to her sparse clothing, rolled to her knees and stood, her damp lashes blinking over and over. "Didn't you see? The sissy poured water all over me when I only tried to be nice!"

"*Nice*, my ass!" Arden yelled and spat blood at her. "You're a fucking cunt!"

Mike touched Arden's nose to see if it wasn't broken, but the boy slapped him away, so Mike shook his head and glared at Sammy. "What is this about?"

"Nothing!"

Sammy showed Arden the finger, while the boy bent over to look at himself in the car mirror, leaving Mike at loss. All he wanted was to gently wash the blood off Arden's face.

"Wrecked my fucking lipstick," Arden growled through clenched teeth.

"What did you tell him?" Mike asked Sammy, who inhaled and avoided his gaze. *Ha*.

"Why do you assume it's my fault? Still playing favorites?"

He rubbed his face. "You know what? I don't care. Give me your cigarettes and get out of my sight."

Sammy took her sweet time, pouting and shifting, but in the end, she slapped the packet into Mike's palm and walked off, making a show of the sway of her ass.

Arden rushed off behind the car, as if afraid to stay on his own with Mike, but he must have forgotten what kind of footwear he was wearing and stumbled. Mike was there to grab him before he could even think about it.

"Careful! Didn't you tell me you already broke your ankle in those once?" he asked and picked Arden's damp body up, pulling him to his chest.

He smelled of soap, but the scent of jasmine Mike so loved was still there, a reminder of what he'd given up.

Arden went limp in his arms, no longer fighting the touch. At least they were out of everyone's line of sight behind the car. Still not as private as Mike would have wished, but it was good enough for now.

"You said they were hot," the boy whispered, the pain in his voice stabbing Mike in the heart.

"You're just as pretty without them," Mike whispered and carried Arden into the corner of the garage, where he sat him on a short stool and pulled a package of tissues out of the desk.

Arden wouldn't meet his gaze, his shoulders curled. "Sammy said you'll be balls deep in her by evening. I need to stop losing my shit like that. It's inevitable, and I should get used to it."

Mike handed him a tissue and grabbed the leg Arden had placed wrong earlier, but the ankle seemed to work as normal, so maybe the boy had just slipped? He gently took off Arden's sexy heels for good measure, admiring the cute painted toenails.

"I... I doubt I'll be in anyone anytime soon," he said in a soft voice and placed Arden's foot on the floor the moment the desire to stroke up the long leg became too insistent to ignore.

He pulled out Sammy's cigarettes and lit one, knowing there was no point in denying himself anymore, because no one but Arden demanded that from him. As warm smoke filled his lungs for the first time in ages, it tasted as bitter as his feelings.

Arden took his time rubbing the blood off along with lipstick until barely a hint of the red was left. "That makes two of us, because I'm never having sex again."

Mike shuddered and closed his eyes, fighting the desire to give in to what he selfishly wanted. To take Arden back. Make him his. Love him. But he'd done enough damage already. "You'll see. A few months from now, I'll be only a bump on your road."

"You won't be. You don't understand what I feel," Arden whimpered and tapped the tissue on his bottom eyelids to spare his makeup.

Mike's heart tightened, aching as his head became uncomfortably light. "I do. I miss you already."

"Then why dump me? This 'safety' thing is such a cop out. It's something else about me and you don't hurt my feelings by saying it. You can't hurt them any more than you already have." Arden looked up at Mike, sniffing. More blood dripped from his nose, so Mike held the cigarette in his teeth and quickly rubbed over Arden's lip with another tissue.

Being close like this, it felt only natural to take care of Arden.

He *wanted* to take care of him. Always. Every day. And that was precisely why he shouldn't.

"No. It's nothing about you. You're... you're the most perfect... person I've met in a long, long time. But I can't be with anyone. It's too risky."

Arden hesitated, but reached out and squeezed Mike's hand. "What do you mean? Why not?"

Mike swallowed, his throat so tight he distracted himself by sitting cross-legged and having another hit of the smoke. Everything around them was trembling like muddy swamp water, which could at any point reveal a predator. But Mike took a deep breath and spoke.

"I had a serious girlfriend when I was still a kid. Her name was Leah. We met in school, and she wasn't really into the biker scene. She just liked me a lot, and we were such a good fit. I was doing motocross at the time, and she always supported me. I was about to go pro. We were just kids but already planning to marry. I felt like she'd be the one for me. That we'd be together forever."

He had all of Arden's attention, and the squeeze of the slender fingers was exactly the support Mike needed. He couldn't recall ever telling this story to anyone. His brothers, his parents, they *knew*, but he'd never *told* them. This bit of Mike's past made everyone uncomfortable, but Arden was there to listen.

"What happened?" Arden asked softly, prompting a shudder to run all over Mike's insides. He didn't want to remember it himself, but the dark past he tried to obscure with smiles was always there, traveling wherever he went.

"The club was fighting for turf with another gang at the time. And they... targeted us," Mike said in a breaking voice. He could no longer look at Arden and focused on the end of the cig instead, silently hoping it would burst into flames and consume him too. "They thought I had information. They hurt her to make me talk. But I really didn't know, I wasn't even a prospect yet," he said, his throat closing as tears slowly dampened his eyes and made him hang his head. "I would have told them everything if I knew. But I didn't. They killed her, and her only fault was loving me."

Arden slid off the stool and to kneel in front of Mike. He wrapped his arms around Mike's waist, and slipped his hand all the way into his hair without a hint of sexual intention. He was just there for Mike despite all the pain he'd gone through himself.

So slim, half Mike's size, yet when Mike threw away the cigarette and hugged him back, Arden wasn't the one trembling. He stroked Mike's back and gave him more solace than he could know. He offered the kind of softness that could cushion the sharp edges of Mike's heart. The kind of softness a man needed to let go and cry.

"I'm so sorry, Mike."

Mike's insides were so sore now he imagined them all bleeding as he leaned into the hug, trying to keep his shit together. It had been years since he'd cried in someone's arms like this. His granddad's death. "I joined the club and took my revenge, but it couldn't bring her back. I can't go through this again. I can't put you in danger."

Arden let out a shivery breath. "I would have taken the risk for you, but I understand. I'm sorry I didn't want to listen."

Mike let his body relax into the hug, even though it was yet another dip into the comfort of Arden's sweet presence. He needed this closeness too much to reject it. "You had no reason to believe me, and I kinda see I made the wrong choice. I should have been more upfront about my intentions."

Arden groaned, but stroked Mike's back, as if he deserved this care after hurting Arden's feelings so badly. "Yeah, it was fucked up, but I see where you were coming from."

"I'm still on your side. Whatever happens, you know?" Mike whispered, staring at the open doors of the garage. Someone walked past, not-so-discreetly peeking inside, but he didn't care anymore.

This might as well be the final time he got to smell jasmine on Arden, and he wanted to make it count.

Arden gave him the gentlest, non-sexual kiss on the cheek. "Thank you. I really need a friend too, not just a lover. And... You got a few hours?" His laugh trembled between them. "'Cause I've got a lot of cars to wash and could use some help."

Mike smiled and pulled Arden's hand to his mouth, kissing it gently. "I'll get you comfortable shoes first."

Chapter 20 – Arden

Chicken soup. Snickers bars. Canned beans.

Stacking shelves had a calming quality to it that helped Arden focus on the now instead of what really gnawed at his insides.

Washing powder. Tissues. Popcorn.

Mike loved this one. Coated in toffee and very crunchy, Mike had once teased Arden over him not liking anything too hard and crunchy. Arden had flirted back that he very much liked hard things. The movie had been forgotten, the popcorn had landed on the floor…

No. No more thinking about Mike.

At least since their breakup Mike started stinking of cigarettes again, so at least that was a deterrent.

But how was he supposed to pretend Mike didn't exist when every interaction in the clubhouse had him as the context? Everyone knew Mike and Arden had been involved not that long ago, and even when they weren't outright asking what happened, they watched Arden whenever he spoke to Mike, when he opened the window of Mike's former room, and stayed quiet, just staring at him while their brains whirred, producing electricity Arden could sense in the air.

A week on, there was no end to the gossip, and he had no doubt some of the club members and hangarounds had wagered bets over them getting back together. Even Mona had prodded at Arden to try and work out if this break-up wasn't another prank of some sort.

Arden sat on the floor in front of the shelves packed with chips and barely held back from rubbing his itchy eyes. He had glitter on his eyelids, and if he weren't careful, his dewy complexion would soon sparkle.

A customer entered, but he didn't bother to look at the screen showing the image from the camera at the front of the shop and picked up another bag of popcorn when a familiar silhouette loomed at the edge of his vision.

"Ardy!" His sister was dressed in a pink T-shirt dress with an abstract picture at the front and fringing wiggling at her knees. He was up before she stepped close enough to hug him.

"Kaley! Why didn't you say you were coming?" He hugged her tight, shocked at the relief of her presence. She smelled of sweet flowers and had put her lush blonde hair into a bun, so casual in comparison to her glamorous exotic dancer persona that most people wouldn't have known the two to be the same person.

"I didn't want you to hide somewhere with Mike just so you wouldn't have to face me," she said, gently nudging his ribs.

Arden laughed and nervously pushed back his curls. He'd been embarrassed to confess that he'd fallen into Mike's clutches. Just a week later, he'd have to bear the shame of admitting they'd broken up. Why was his life so shitty?

"Um... yeah, about that... No more hiding needed."

The playful smile fell from her face, and she tightened her arms around Arden, pulling his face to her shoulder. "I'm sorry. Why didn't you say anything?"

He clutched at her in an instant, like a baby kangaroo seeking safety in its mother's pouch. "Because it's humiliating. I barely told you about me and him, and it's already over."

A low sigh escaped Kaley's mouth, and Arden knew she wished to say she'd warned him it would happen. He was glad she didn't.

"What did he do? Did he say it's not you, because it's all on him?" she asked instead, rolling her eyes.

"No... it's complicated. He's got his reasons, we're still friends. I don't like his reasons, but I get it, he has to make his own choice. I told you where I stand. But... it hurts so much, you know?" Arden stepped away when his throat tightened. He didn't need *this*. Hadn't he cried himself to sleep enough times already?

"That's bullshit. You should just come home. Let's pack your things right now. We could drink margaritas on our couch by evening!"

The elderly lady living nearby chose this moment to enter, surely on the lookout for her favorite cookies, so he shushed Kaley when she hadn't dropped her voice.

"I can't because of you-know-who," Arden said through clenched teeth but the customer still eavesdropped.

To make matters worse, Mike strutted into the store with Arden's favorite milkshake from the diner in the next town over.

"I picked this up for you," he said with a wide smile that dampened at the sight of Kaley. He cocked his head. "I know you... right?"

Kaley's eyes went wide. She grabbed the nearest packet of popcorn and threw it at him.

"Yes, you fucking know me, you ass!"

Mike grabbed the bag and smiled when he realized it was his favorite. "Don't be so touchy. Lots of people come and go," he said, approaching with the shake. Strawberry. Arden's favorite.

"I heard that applies to my brother too." Kaley put her hands on her hips in a combative stance.

This time, Mike seemed hurt, and while his smile didn't drop, it looked artificial. "I see you're busy. So... here's your drink, and I'll be out," he said and placed the cup on an empty bit of shelf, already stepping back.

"Sure Mike, run from all responsibility," Kaley said. "You don't have to worry about either of us anymore. I'm taking him home."

Arden picked up the delicious drink and sucked some in through the straw. Milky and sweet, with a hint of tartness, it was perfection in a cup. He'd said that once, and Mike had regularly picked one up for him since. He was so thoughtful, even now, after they'd split. "It's not like that. Stay. My shift's over in a bit."

Mike stuffed his hands down his pockets, teeth digging into his lower lip. "I don't know."

Kaley frowned. "I'm not sure it's such a good idea either."

"Just wait," Arden said, conspicuously pointing to the customer with his chin, but she must have noticed the tension and strutted back to the counter with her pack of Oreos.

"Oh, don't mind me, I've seen my fair share of drama." She laughed and started lazily pulling out low value coins as if she were a human-sized sloth.

Arden was glad to be out of the line of fire between Mike and Kaley, but his brain burned, his synapses sparking a battle between reason and emotion.

Going with Kaley would be the reasonable thing to do if it wasn't for Luke. But he hadn't heard from Luke or about him since the abduction attempt, so maybe he'd gotten the message and moved on? Luke knew the club would retaliate if he got too close to Arden, so giving up on revenge would have been the smart thing to do. And despite all his faults, Luke wasn't an idiot. *If* he'd in fact given up, there was nothing stopping Arden from getting back to a life in Reno. But couldn't that wait a month or two? Or at least until Mike found himself a new girl to sleep with and Arden couldn't bear to witness them together anymore?

The customer took her time making small talk about her cats, but Arden was back to the silent warzone the moment the elderly lady left the store.

"You didn't mention planning to go home tonight," Mike said in an even tone, but Arden knew it was actually an accusation.

Kaley clapped her hands. "You're *not* his boyfriend anymore. Why would you care?"

Arden hid behind the massive milkshake cup and made puppy eyes at Mike. "I didn't know she was coming. And I'm not going anywhere with Luke out for my blood. You still remember that he hired some goons to abduct me, right?"

Kaley shook her head. "I do, but it's been weeks. His plan backfired, and the club knows where he lives, just in case. I'm sure he cut his losses and moved on."

As reasonable as that sounded, there was always a chance Luke remained a threat and would come for Arden once all suspicions have died down. If Arden wanted to be safe, he should stay here forever and stew in his own unrequited-love juices. Sounded like a plan.

Mike licked his lips. "I can pay him a visit. Or us both. Make sure he knows not to mess with you. That is, if your sister lets you stay one more day," he added in a lower voice seeping with annoyance.

One more *day*? And then what? He'd see Mike once a month? Mike wasn't a facetime type of guy. Arden's heart helplessly rattled its cage for a way out.

"I'm not my sister's property. I do what I want. Speaking of which, no, I don't think it's a good idea to agitate Luke. It will blow over in a month. Or two."

Kaley frowned. "And what, stay here forever? I actually agree that confrontation isn't such a bad idea. He'll steer clear of you if he gets a nighttime visit from the right kind of people."

Mike shrugged and crossed his arms on his chest, his gaze drilling into Arden, waiting for his decision.

Arden slurped to give himself a few precious seconds to consider the right tactic so he could have his cake and eat it too. "Of course I wanna leave... at some point, but I'm scared to go back to Reno. I mean... he's still out there, and I will know that whether he approaches me or not."

Kaley glared at Mike. "And Mike can't help with that? It's the least he could do if you ask me."

Arden shook his head in panic. "No, no, Mike has all this other stuff to do. I couldn't possibly engage him in some crazy vendetta when he's already given me so much—"

Kaley coughed. "Dick."

"So much *support*," Arden said through clenching teeth.

Mike exhaled and opened the popcorn bag Kaley had thrown his way earlier. He offered some to Arden first but started eating when Arden shook his head. "No, let's go. We should have gone after him long ago."

"But you were too busy fucking Arden," Kaley said, and Mike clicked his fingers, eyes wide.

"Oh my God! You're the girl with the pentagram pubes!"

Kaley's face and neck turned a deep pink. "It was a *star*, you idiot!"

Mike wiggled his eyebrows. "Isn't a pentagram a star?"

The stupid argument went on while Arden stood frozen in icy sweat. Once Luke had been dealt with, he'd have no more excuses to stay. Did Mike just want him gone already? Of course he did. They were so tender to one another, but Arden's presence served as a constant reminder of what could never be. Maybe it really was time to rip off that Band-Aid.

Mike snapped his fingers at Arden. "Baby? You okay? You look pale."

Kaley spread her arms. "Why are you still calling him pet names?"

"I... I just... What are we actually planning here? That you'll kill Luke?" Arden choked out.

Mike went quiet, his gaze moving to the camera, but they both knew it didn't register sound, so he spoke once he turned away from it. "I'll do whatever you want me to do. Or whatever's necessary so you can feel safe. I know you said you don't want to get me in trouble, but I've lived and breathed trouble my entire life, I've got a good handle on it."

For once, Kaley agreed, and her eyelids lowered. "Fucker deserves to die after laying his hands on you."

"I guess there's no point in putting it off..." Arden muttered, relieved at the sight of Teona, another young cousin in the extended Heller family. She was taking over the store for the next shift, which meant Arden could flee to his room for a moment and *think*.

Mike cleared his throat and nodded at Teona before glancing Arden's way again, his face tense with determination. "I'll change and fuel up the car. In case I need more room."

If he needed to move the body, he meant. Arden was going to be sick from the stress of it all. Not because he felt sorry for Luke, but because this was the beginning of the end. The true end of their misguided love story.

Once Luke was gone, he could no longer lie to himself about needing to hide at the clubhouse. Mike would slip out of his life forever.

Mike shifted his weight and leaned in as if he were about to touch Arden, but ended up crossing his arms and taking a step back instead. "So... yeah, just chill. I'll let you know when it's done."

Kaley pulled Arden into a hug. "And when it's done, we'll celebrate you coming home."

Arden's whole body tingled, and he almost gagged, overwhelmed with nausea. "Y-yes. Sounds like a plan... I need to change after work. And you know, rest. Maybe you could have some fun at the bar tonight?" He gave her his best puppy eyes, signaling that this was a depressing decision for him, and that he needed space. She got the point.

"You're gonna take a long bath, aren't you?" She ruffled his hair just as Mike disappeared from sight, triggering anxiety that Arden might lose him if he dragged his feet too much. "Fine. I'll find out where Rain is. Call me once you're up for socializing."

"I like my bath bombs, okay?" he laughed, and the sound was surprisingly honest even though it wasn't. "You can show me your new pole moves when I'm back."

Arden's heart beat like crazy, and he could hear nothing but its thudding in his ears as he walked through the storage room of the shop and toward the back door leading inside the compound. What could possibly stop Mike from going after Luke now that he'd made his decision with such ease? For Mike, scaring people into submission and beating them up wasn't as big of a deal as to the average person. And maybe Arden was crazy, but it gave him a sense of safety no one could replicate.

He emerged into the courtyard in time to see Mike enter the bar. With his mouth dry, Arden strode after him, trying to avoid any and all glances, because if someone caught his gaze, they might—

"Hey, Arden," Axel said, grabbing Arden's wrist from the chair he sat in.

Kane tried to stifle his laughter, rubbing Shay's thigh as she slept next to him, spread out on the sofa, a small towel covering her eyes to make the day a little bit darker.

Arden's tactic clearly hadn't worked this time.

"W-what is it?"

Axel licked his lips, his permanently-somber face tense. "It's... it might be a weird question..."

"A Tinder date left him hanging again," Kane said, biting his lip to avoid laughing too loudly.

Axel's cheek twitched. "Is there something wrong with me?"

Arden dared a smile. "Try looking a bit less like you wanna peel someone's face off?"

Kane burst with laughter, prompting Shay to shove at him with a groan. "Some solid advice right there."

Axel hummed, and the corners of his lips lifted, revealing his teeth, but his brows were still drawn together. Arden wasn't sure what that expression was supposed to be, but it sure wasn't a smile.

"Yeah, like that," he said to free himself from this impromptu dating advice moment.

He managed to avoid any other interactions on his way upstairs, but when he stood at the door to Mike's new room and sweated into his T-shirt, he stalled. He hovered his hand close to the wood, took a deep breath, but didn't get to knock, because the door opened, smacking Arden with a gust of air, and Mike froze mid-step.

They stood almost chest to chest, and Arden had to use all of his willpower not to lean in and kiss Mike.

"I... You're leaving already?" Arden eyed Mike's backpack. Small and green, it looked unassuming, but whatever items it contained, Arden was happy they weren't meant for him.

Mike nodded. "Don't leave the clubhouse until I call you, okay? I just have to talk to Axel, and I'm off."

Arden's lips itched as if ants were crawling on the inside of his skin, but he would not kiss Mike. That ship had sailed.

Mike locked his door, smiled, and went off, leaving Arden to his chaotic thoughts. But one thing he knew—he didn't want to be out of Mike's life yet, and there was only one thing that would keep Mike here. He took a deep breath and sped for the other staircase, intent to reach the kitchen as soon as humanly possible.

He just hoped it was empty.

But no. The small space filled with dirty pots had to be occupied by Sammy, who was the sluttiest dishwasher Arden had ever seen. To be fair, she did have a juicy ass to fill those leather shorts, but Arden wouldn't be complimenting her.

"Hey, Sam? Axel wanted to talk to you," he said to drive her out.

She groaned but pulled off her rubber gloves. They'd remained in a state of cold war since that fight during car wash, but that was still better than scratching each other's faces off.

"What the hell does he want?" she said, throwing the gloves on the counter with a wet slap.

Arden shrugged when she passed him, but his brain was boiling with adrenaline. There was only one thing he could think of to keep Mike here for at least one more day. He approached the stove with his heart in his throat and tried not to think too much, because there was hardly any time for doubts.

"For Mike," he whispered to get psych himself up, but as he turned on the gas, and the flames came alive, cold sweat still dampened his back.

This would be painful, but Mike would stay if Arden got injured. Because Mike cared for him like that, and he'd never leave him behind.

Still, Arden's stomach turned, causing nausea as his bristled forearm hair neared the purple flames, but just as he expected them to catch fire, quick footsteps made him spin around in fear. He didn't get to say a word before Mike grabbed his shoulder and pulled him away from the stove.

"What. The. Fuck," he uttered, breathless, staring at Arden with wide blue eyes that expressed... hurt?

Arden held his hand to his chest, even though the flames had barely gotten a sniff of his skin. The burnt smell hung in the air like a badge of guilt. "Um... What are you doing here?" he whined despite knowing he'd been caught red-handed. He had no alternative plan.

Mike reached behind him, switched off the gas, and pushed Arden against the counter, his hair hanging wildly around his face. "Sammy said Axel wanted to see her. A lie. The question is, what were you trying to do with the stove?"

Arden couldn't watch the fury burning in Mike's gaze and hugged himself, defeated. No lie would have saved him now. "I don't want you to go..."

Mike let go of him and slouched against the counter, squeezing his hands into fists as a whole array of emotion passed through his face. "Arden..."

"I know. It's stupid."

Mike pulled Arden against him and pressed a kiss to the top of his head. "He's not gonna hurt me. And once I'm done with it, you won't have to be afraid of him either."

"It's not that... I know you can handle it, but a part of me doesn't want him gone." Hugging Mike was his second nature. He'd fallen asleep next to this man so many times, and if he only could, he would sleep in his bed every night.

Mike went stiff and pulled away as if Arden's skin was on fire. "You can't still have feelings for that bastard," he said, struggling to hold back his anger, going red.

Arden groaned. "Hate is a feeling. What I mean is that... if he's gone, there's nothing stopping me from going back to Reno. No excuse to be around you." His voice dropped when he said those last few words. It was out in the open now. He'd laid himself bare and had nothing left to protect him from the consequences of such sincerity.

Mike stared at him, gasping for air. They both flinched when someone turned on loud music next door, and Mike dragged his hands down his face, as if the noise snapped him out of a trance. "You can stay here as long as you want, baby. Nobody is chasing you away on my watch."

Arden stroked Mike's sturdy, tattooed arm, even though he shouldn't have. This was the problem, wasn't it? His heart beat fast to celebrate every moment of Mike's closeness, sang at the notion of Mike's protection. Mike would be his anchor here, which seemed romantic in concept, but meant Arden could never move on.

It dawned on him how insane his behavior was. Had he really tried to burn himself to have an excuse to stay around a man who didn't want to be with him? What had he been thinking?

He was out of his mind in love, and if he stayed, he'd only fall deeper, until all walls around him became impossible to climb.

"I want to go with you," Arden whispered, tracing the fair hairs on Mike's forearm.

Mike chewed on that for a second, then asked, "Are you sure it's such a good idea? A lot of things might happen, and it won't be pretty."

"I've seen ugly, and he deserves it. He might have given up on me like the fucking coward he is, but he'll just hurt some other boy. You'll be doing a public service." Arden scowled at the harshness of his own words, but he meant them anyway.

Mike's nostrils flared as he frowned, staring at Arden for so long the thudding of the music became background noise. "You want him dead?"

Arden understood the weight of his words, so he took his time before answering. "Yes. But only if you're sure you're beyond suspicion."

Mike shrugged and met Arden's gaze with unnerving calm. "I know what I'm doing."

And yet despite being such a dangerous man, Arden had no doubt Mike would never hurt him.

Maybe he was naive.

Maybe he was in love.

Chapter 21 – Mike

Mike wasn't a born killer. He'd never enjoyed watching life leave someone's twitching body. Even seeing light die in the eyes of Leah's killer hadn't given him the satisfaction he'd hoped for. Closure? Perhaps. But that man's death couldn't have brought her back anyway.

No. Death was utilitarian. It was the means to an end. Ensured the safety of Mike's friends and family. And while the stink of urine made him gag as Luke writhed, fighting for breath while Mike blocked him from getting air, he didn't have any negative feelings about this act.

Luke could have made any promises he wanted, but he wouldn't have been the first man who ignored reason and broke restraining orders, whether those were of legal nature or not. Arden would not be safe as long as Luke lived, and even if the bastard had enough brains to give up on any retaliation against him, Arden was right—he would still target other boys.

He was a weed and needed to be removed.

Arden had refused to wait in the car, so he sat in an opposite corner of the dusky room, watching Luke die despite being pale as a sheet. Mike hadn't thought it was a good idea at first, since Arden wasn't accustomed to violence, but Mike had eventually agreed. As the victim, Arden had the right to see the execution if he so wished.

The house was on the outskirts of Reno, private, with the nearest neighbors far away. It had shielded Luke's dealings from prying eyes, but it would now make his disappearance harder to notice. It would be days, maybe weeks before someone questioned Luke's whereabouts, since he had no family, and given the nature of his assumed business, any associates would be unlikely to contact the police. He'd be gone for good.

The struggle became less violent, and Luke finally stopped kicking about as his oxygen-deprived mind shut down.

"He deserves this," Mike said to reassure Arden, who sat on the other side of the room, clutching the front of his T-shirt.

Arden opened his mouth but ended up staying quiet as he nodded, wiping away a tear that rolled down his cheek.

Minutes later, Luke was dead, and Mike only broke his neck as a precaution before dropping his lifeless body to the large plastic sheet he spread in the living room to minimize the chance of leaving traces of their presence. It had been almost too easy to get in with Arden as bait, but why take unnecessary risks?

"Are you okay?" Mike asked, stepping away from the still-warm corpse to change into fresh clothes.

"Yes," Arden rasped, but his fingers trembled as he shifted in the wooden chair. "I'm just sorry when I think of the *years* he hovered around me and I failed to see what a terrible person he was. I was like a puppy begging for his attention."

Mike glanced down at Luke. While kind of generic in appearance, he was quite handsome and rather tall, which explained why it had flattered a teenager that someone like him showed interest. "To be fair, you really were only a puppy when you met him," Mike said, pulling on a fresh pair of pants.

Arden's hair was tied back into two braids and Mike fondly remembered a time when they'd been together and he'd gotten to pull on those.

The boy shrugged but stayed still otherwise, as if he were afraid to move. "Too young. I can see it now. He was hot so he didn't seem like a creeper. Kaley warned me, but I wouldn't listen."

Mike covered the body with a sheet, so Arden wouldn't have to watch his rapist's face anymore and approached him, offering his hand. "It's over now."

The pretty fingers slipped into his with such ease. And even though Arden had just watched Mike end someone's life, he got up and hugged him so tightly it had Mike's brain racing.

"Thank you. It won't get traced back to you? Are you sure?" he demanded

Warmth bloomed in Mike's heart, and he allowed himself to enjoy the embrace a while longer, shutting his eyes as Arden pushed the tips of his shoes against his, molding their bodies together. For the briefest moment, he imagined that they were still a couple, and that there was a future in which they traveled far away from Hawk Springs and the club. Where no one knew of Mike's past, and where it could pose no danger to Arden. But the MC was Mike's home, and regardless of his feelings for Arden, he wasn't able to desert his whole life and all his other loved ones.

"If it somehow does, I won't have any regrets."

"Don't say that. Do I need to help you… move him? What do we do?" Arden looked up, his cute face tense in the darkened room.

Mike swallowed, smiling when he noticed faint light catching the shimmery highlighter on Arden's cheek. The pretty baby didn't need to lift a finger. Mike was here to handle everything for him, so Arden didn't have to stain himself with dirty blood. Unable to help himself, he petted the smooth skin with the back of his hand. "I've got this, baby."

It's been days since their breakup, and Mike still instinctively called Arden pet names. It would have been much easier to stop if Arden confronted him about it, but he never had. It was the sweetest, yet most painful limbo, like being stuck in a thorny bush while his mouth was full of vanilla milkshake.

Arden had confessed his love just once, but whenever his big blue eyes watched Mike, those three sweet, smooth words echoed in Mike's head in the way they had been uttered in the dark, for only him to hear.

"I'll never be able to repay you," Arden said, lowering his gaze.

"There's no need. I'll be happy knowing you're safe." Mike exhaled and pulled out his cell phone to type a message to Zolt, who knew the best body disposal guy in the area. The message was coded, of course, but once Zolt confirmed, it was a done deal.

Arden's fingers danced up and down Mike's side, as if he too couldn't stay away despite it being the reasonable thing to do. In the week since their breakup, Mike had been thinking about their relationship a lot, and the reckless part of his brain tried to come up with excuses to crawl back to Arden. To pretend there was no danger and fall into the boy's willing arms.

Maybe he could have kept Arden safe from the Jarens, but once those crazy fuckers were dealt with, there would be someone else with a grudge. And Arden, being a boy, would have a much larger target on his back than Mike's brothers' female partners.

The club had taught Mike to be ruthless, because the people they sometimes dealt with had no inhibitions. Keeping Arden close would have put his life at serious risk, and Mike couldn't have that no matter how much his heart selfishly longed to make the boy his. But he'd rather bleed on the inside than see his boy become a casualty of his family's lifestyle.

Yes, he desired Arden more than anyone, but he cared for him even more.

"You're too good to me," Arden said with a small smile that pushed invisible needles through Mike's ribcage. He was so close Mike could smell the jasmine on him, and if he didn't pull away, something might happen. Something that would chip at Mike's resolve.

"Let's go," he said and put on fresh gloves, so he wouldn't leave any prints on the way out.

His bottle-green Dodge was parked behind Luke's home, since a neighbor could've noticed an unfamiliar vehicle, but even once they settled in the front seats, adrenaline refused to settle and kept buzzing in Mike's veins with each inhale of Arden's perfume. It was dark. Quiet. Only the two of them and the cooling corpse in the house next door. Yet the air felt so dense in Mike's lungs it might as well have been jelly.

"I will need to eventually leave. You know that, right?" Arden said out of the blue, hunched in his seat so Mike couldn't see his face.

Mike swallowed, trying to discern some plants and the outline of the barbeque in front of the hood, but the tall fence blocked the moonlight and made it difficult.

He didn't want to think about Arden leaving at all. It made sense, of course, because the boy couldn't put his life on hold forever, but something deep inside Mike refused to accept that, regardless of what he knew was right for him. "I suppose."

The thought of someone else, someone who could hurt Arden, putting their hands on the sweet, trusting little guttermind made Mike's blood boil. So it made sense Arden would have to move, because otherwise Mike would find it hard to contain his jealousy. He wasn't even sure if it was fear for Arden or the fear that he'd shatter if something happened to his precious boy. Was he selfless or selfish?

Arden gave a low exhale. "A few hours ago, I thought I'd do *anything* to stay even one day longer, but it's prolonging the agony of it all, isn't it? Kaley said I can move back in with her."

Mike clenched his teeth, his insides twisting as if there was a parasite eating him from the inside. "I—ah… I will be sad to see you go," he said, twisting his fingers together.

Understatement of the fucking century.

"I know I could never be what Leah was to you, I can see it—"

"This isn't about Leah," Mike said, squirming in the seat so he faced Arden, whose pretty face remained in the shadow with the exception of one glinting eye. "I loved her so much. I still remember her, but she has nothing to do with the feelings I have for you."

Arden turned to him with a deep sigh. "I need to leave while I still have a heart."

Mike swallowed hard and reached out to grab Arden's hand. His heart ached with need, but confessing how deep his emotions ran would have been selfish, so he kept them in and just kissed the smooth hand before curling his face against it.

"I understand."

Arden licked his lips, his pupils wide in the dark. "But if I'm leaving anyway, and no one needs to know… would it be so bad if we got close one more time?" He shifted in the seat, and the air in the car turned from jelly into dense caramel—sweet but somewhat bitter at the same time.

Mike's body felt heavy, hot, and he trailed kisses down Arden's forearm, to the warmth of his elbow, up his arm. Their eyes met in the dark, and the need that pushed him to come here in the first place now drove him forward, until his lips pressed against Arden's.

"I'll take all I can get, baby."

Arden opened his lips as if he'd been waiting for this forever, leaning over the gearshift to grasp at Mike's T-shirt. Pain speared Mike's heart the same way it had a week back, when he'd selfishly decided to 'heal' Arden with sex. It had been so heartbreaking to make love knowing it would never happen again. This time, they'd both be aware of it at least and share the pain.

Mike would have only memories left after this. Three wonderful months of sweetness and self-discovery kept forever at the back of his mind.

"Back?" he whispered, massaging Arden's neck with his palm.

Arden nodded, eager to be Mike's kitten one last time. He crawled through the gap between the seats, but Mike would be better off moving in a more conventional way and swiftly left the vehicle. He yearned to touch Arden again. The week that passed since their last kiss felt like a lifetime, and he wanted to be the center of Arden's universe again, even if just for a moment.

He dove into the sofa at the back of the vehicle, pulling Arden's fragrant body in, so they clashed, hands already grabbing at clothes and tearing them off.

Who needed to think about future consequences when there were so many things they could still *feel* in the now? They didn't have to explain this to anyone, because this touch and these kisses were only theirs.

"You smell so good," Mike whispered into the skin of Arden's neck.

"I'm all yours."

Arden grabbed Mike's hair, his luscious nipples already stiffening under Mike's caresses. His eyes were so bright, like two fountains filled with champagne, and Mike would drink from them until he passed out.

"Yes, me too," he whispered, pulling Arden to straddle his lap as soon as the tight T-shirt was gone, revealing a smooth chest he instantly kissed in the middle, before rolling his face between the cute nipples.

Arden wrapped his arms around Mike's neck, his slender hips rocking in fervent desire, as if he wanted to rub their clothes away. He was always as eager for sex as Mike, a kitten in permanent heat. His excitement was like strokes to the ego Mike could feel all the way in his dick.

His skin, so smooth, so warm, was everything Mike ever wanted, and he pulled Arden close, sliding one hand into his hair while their lips pressed together over and over. It was such a sweet, gentle moment, even if simmering with latent passion, and he pulled on Arden's ear, rubbing his beard against the long neck.

"What do you want? You can have anything."

Arden ran his hand up Mike's arm, adoring him with the touch of his fingertips. "I want you to fuck me so good I forget there's a tomorrow."

Arden's kiss was a match, and Mike—a pool of gasoline. The moment their mouths clashed again, the flames scorched everything they touched.

"Yes. Oh yes. I want you so fucking much, baby."

Arden would soon be gone from Mike's life, but they'd have this one more time to enjoy being together without consequences. A final goodbye to the boy whom Mike would never forget.

Arden pulled on Mike's T-shirt, his movements gaining pace, as if there was nothing he wanted more than Mike's flesh. The light was faint, but Arden's pretty face regained its color, and his lips seemed to darken with each quick exhale.

"That last time? It was everything. I felt so good when you fucked me."

Mike grunted, pulling on Arden's nipple and lifting him with his hips. They both gasped when their dicks touched through denim, and Arden wrapped his arms around Mike's neck, rolling against him with fervent excitement.

"Yes, baby," Mike said, nodding as he cupped that pretty, wonderful face that he wanted etched at the back of his eyelids, so he could at least dream of Arden every night if they couldn't be together in real life. "You were the sexiest filly I've ever had."

Arden smiled as if reality didn't matter. As if he hadn't just witnessed his ex being killed, as if he didn't know they'd part forever tomorrow. He must have truly decided to live in the now, and Mike would be here with him every step of the way.

"*Filly*. So wrong. But I love it so much." He nipped on Mike's lips and stroked his beard, gently twisting some of the hair in his fingers. "You rode me so well that night. So big, strong, heavy..." He slid his other hand down Mike's stomach and cupped his crotch with a huff.

Mike's balls swelled, and he rocked against that small, lovely hand that was so wickedly good at handling a dick. His brain lit up with warmth when he met Arden's gaze. "I love you too," Mike whispered, his throat choking up as he rubbed his hands up and down Arden's ribs before settling them on the boyish hips. His entire world pulsed, even his lips, and he could only be soothed by Arden's sweet, pillow-soft lips.

After Leah, he'd promised himself to never fall in love again. He told himself it was for his partner's safety, but in truth, he was also afraid he wouldn't survive the heartbreak again. It was too late for holding back with Arden, because love had snuck up on Mike when he wasn't looking.

Arden stilled for a breathless moment somewhere beyond time, but then granted Mike the kiss he was so desperate for. Sweet as candy,

290 | Gutter Mind

addictive as cocaine. Arden didn't need to say anything for Mike to know that his feelings hadn't changed since last week.

Who had the time for words when mouths and tongues communicated so much more with touch? Deep, wet and hungry kisses promised pleasure but also emotions Mike hadn't allowed himself to feel in years. He was like a man awoken after ages of death-like slumber, and now his heart beat all too fast, unable to comprehend what it meant to be alive again.

With a low growl, he rolled Arden onto the seat and lowered the zipper of his pants, desperate to get the skinny jeans off Arden's long legs. He needed to taste him this final time, to once more pretend he hadn't let fate fool him into feelings he shouldn't have.

"I'll never forget you, baby." Mike regretted the words as soon as he'd said them and pain flashed through Arden's features.

"Don't say it like I'm gone already. I'm still here. Still yours." The intensity of Arden's voice, the way his thighs opened in invitation were the reassurance Mike needed.

"I know. But I already miss you," Mike whispered and rolled Arden's pants off, revealing cute lacy panties dampened at the front, where the cockhead leaked pre-cum into the fabric.

He'd been such a fool.

Leah was gone forever, and he was at peace with that, but if he were selfish, he could have Arden. He could get a home for them, as did all his siblings once they married. They could have a huge closet for Arden to fill with clothes. And a garden with a pool where Arden could sunbathe and swim in his Americana bikini. They could have watched movies together. Dined together every day. Like a normal couple. As if there was no target on Arden's back. As if they were safe.

The little smile Arden gave him as he pushed his thumbs under the panties melted Mike's insides with both lust and endearment. He had no idea when exactly he'd fallen for him, but it didn't matter anymore. For thirty-seven years he hadn't even considered touching another man in a sexual context, but along came Arden, and everything changed. Mike didn't care what label people put on him as long as he could live true to how he felt. He salivated as soon as the dark cockhead peeked out of the lowered panties, still confused over the fact that his brain sizzled with excitement the same way it did when Mike interacted with a hot naked woman.

More. Because this wasn't about a dick, or about the beauty of Arden's slender yet soft body, but about Arden sharing his sexual side with him. Really *being* here with him, not just sharing pleasure.

"Is that for me?" Mike whispered, unzipping his pants to relieve some of the pressure, but what he wanted was to taste Arden's pre-cum this final time, so he leaned in, obscenely rolling out his tongue.

Arden nodded, his eyelids falling as he pushed off his underwear, naked and ready to be devoured. "Yes. All yours. Will you suck me? I love it when your beard tickles my balls."

"I love sucking your dick. I love touching your balls. You're the most magnificent creature in, like, existence," Mike whispered and pressed his nose to the shaft, breathing in the musk of arousal with notes of jasmine. How a dick could be *feminine*, he had no idea, but Arden's was. His mouth watered, and he pushed his tongue under Arden's smooth balls, letting himself enjoy this moment of closeness.

Arden let out a long sigh of pleasure and slid his fingers into Mike's hair. "You got good at it too." He giggled before uttering another moan when Mike sucked on the cockhead, tasting the savory essence at the slit.

"Nn, that's because you always demand good service," Mike mumbled and sucked the cock deeper, his hand reaching into the pocket at the back of the front seat. And bingo. Lube in the car was an absolute must.

Arden stretched his body for Mike's viewing pleasure, legs spread, one foot on the floor, the other on Mike's shoulder. In the faint illumination coming in through the window, he was a vision painted with light and shadow, a mix of cute and sultry.

"And yet, I'm kept waiting…" he teased.

Mike groaned and handed Arden the lube, offering him one hand while he shut his eyes and sank lower, until Arden's cockhead sat close to the entrance of his throat, and his mouth tightened around the base. He loved how compact it was. How easy he could fit it into his mouth, and he hollowed his cheeks, shivering when cool gel pooled in his palm.

"So good…" Arden's whimpers became needier, making Mike's cock twitch in response. All he wanted was to satisfy Arden, to know that all the slutty boy squirmed for was Mike's cock inside him. He sucked harder at the shot of lust spreading through his body.

Mike wanted to tell Arden how he loved seeing him like this. So raw, so relaxed, but with a mouthful of dick keeping him quiet, he kept lusty thoughts to himself. Lovely, slender thighs trembled on either side of his head as he rubbed the lube against Arden's pucker, rolling his slick thumb against the warm sac while his mind overheated.

He'd gotten good at this, and there were times when he imagined himself in a gay club, going down on Arden for everyone to see just how into this boy he was. He still thought of himself as mostly straight, but he'd suck cock if he felt like it. And he wasn't ashamed of it.

"Push it in," Arden rasped, bending forward, as if he couldn't stand their faces being so far apart. "I'm so hot for you I just want to be ready to take your dick."

His words turned into a moan when Mike pushed two fingers inside Arden's hole, twisting them gently in the smooth, tight channel as Arden rocked his hips with a stifled gasp and pushed his shaft deeper into Mike's mouth. So damn hot. It didn't matter what parts Arden had. He was the person Mike wanted, a beautiful fae spread open for devouring.

Arden clamped down on the fingers the way he would on Mike's cock, and the unspoken promise filled Mike's balls with yet more lust and triggered his imagination as he pushed his tongue against the ridge of Arden's cockhead. He'd fuck Arden for all he was worth. He'd milk his hot dick and only come once Arden's spunk dripped between his fingers.

Such a juicy ass. Relaxed yet tight and warm. With Arden looking at him with glossy eyes, he didn't need to hear invitations to know how welcome he was inside him. Mike always tried to tune in to his partners—that was what made him so addictive—and the first time they fucked he'd found out Arden had a pleasure spot of his own, deep in the tight hole. Mike rubbed it, gently at first, to gradually apply more pressure. A grin spread on his face when Arden's body bucked, shivering in anticipation. *Score.*

"Fuck! Fuck! Oh... fucking God!" Arden whined and leaned forward to grab Mike's shoulders, his nails digging in. "I need your dick inside me right the fuck now. I'm not coming until I feel it in me."

Mike loved to see Arden so free with his words, flushed and without a hint of shyness. He wasn't the kind of guy who got off on chasing virgins. No, he wanted a partner who was just as horny as he was and vocal about it.

"Yeah? You want that big drill inside you?" Mike asked, dragging Arden's hand to his crotch, hot and ready to go.

"Yes. I want us to steam up the windows like it's the fucking *Titanic*..." Arden huffed and stroked Mike's cock with so much awe it twitched in his hand like a happy pup.

Mike saw red. He rolled Arden over, exposing his delicious rump, but he no longer had the patience to worship its tempting curves. Arden's knee dropped off the seat, and Mike got into a similar position, kneeling on the rubber mat while his other leg remained on the seat, supporting him as he leaned over Arden and pressed the cockhead to the molten heat where flesh dipped at the hole.

"Yes, please... push it in..." Arden begged, only arching his ass higher, and reaching back with one hand to pull his butt cheeks apart in invitation. His eyes seemed unfocused when he looked over his shoulder, biting his lip as if it were chewy candy. Mike could not deny him anything. He pressed his hairy thigh to Arden's smooth leg, and as his gun popped into the tight, warm holster that clung to him as if they'd been made for one another, he had to take a deep breath to keep from shooting his load right away.

Mike's vision blurred as pleasure sank its claws into his brain, and he hooked his arm under Arden's shivering body to bring them closer. "Ah, fuck... If I wasn't snipped, I'd want to make babies with you."

Arden's raspy laugh was the stuff of lazy Sunday mornings twenty years from now. "Try your luck. Go extra deep." The mischievous glint in Arden's eyes as he pushed back on Mike's cock made the blood in Mike's veins boil with the need to pump faster, and as soon as his balls slapped Arden's buttocks, he withdrew his hips and thrust in again, holding on to his sexy lover and plowing him harder. Faster. When Arden moaned, rocking back as if he'd never felt better, Mike got more thorough, feeling sweat drip down his temple as he tried to enter his boy at the right angle.

"Ah... I'll plant my cum so deep you're gonna carry it inside you forever," he whispered, tugging on Arden's ear with his teeth.

Mike didn't care that the car rocked with them when Arden's sweaty back was so hot against his chest, and he fucked Arden faster, overwhelmed by the way his boy became putty when touched right,

"I might just not let your cock out," Arden said after a long moan. "You feel that?" He clenched his ass and turned his head to just about catch Mike's lips with his own. "Who's fucking who, hm?"

Mike's brain vibrated, and he forced his dick in even harder, slamming Arden down on the sofa and crawling on top of him. "Tonight? I think it's me after all," he said and rocked his hips ever faster, until the friction made his dick burn and his balls tighten. His skull was on the verge of exploding.

"Okay... It's you. It's you..." Arden gasped for air, his legs open, the hot, slippery hole welcoming Mike's dick with its soft tightness.

Arden's moans and whimpers filled the car, and when Mike smelled his hair, the faint scent of jasmine made him almost come on the spot. He had to stop moving when he faintly remembered wanting Arden to finish first.

"Why'd you stop?" Arden complained, wiggling his greedy ass against Mike.

Mike didn't bother answering and slipped his hand under the boy, thrusting again the moment he started working his boy's cock. Beyond rational thinking, he hoped the hard, desperate thrusts hit the right spot, but the shamelessly vulgar yelps coming out of Arden stifled his doubts.

"Love that thick cock in me," Arden mumbled without much cohesion. He writhed against Mike, so smooth and hot, getting jerked off while Mike stabbed into him time and time again.

If Luke had had neighbors, they would have known the exact moment Arden came. Hot spunk drizzled over Mike's fingers, and that tight ass clenched so hard, he saw white under his eyelids and bit down on Arden's shoulder, rutting like a beast focused on planting its cum inside his mate.

For a moment, it felt as if the car was floating on the golden waves of the warmest ocean, but once his orgasm was over, Mike was left too exhausted to move and stayed on top of Arden, hugging him as they both calmed their breathing.

And somehow, in the dark car that had gotten duskier now that all windows were covered in condensation, tears seemed only a step away, because it hit Mike like a hammer to the skull that he would never feel this complete again. But it wouldn't have been fair to burden Arden, so he rubbed his face against Arden's sweaty back and just listened to the boy breathing, to his heart beating in tune with Mike's.

"They're done," someone said all too close, and Mike jerked out of his pleasure slumber, frantically searching for his gun.

He rolled out of the car with his dick swinging in the air and pointed the gun at

... Zolt.

The guy bit his lips, as if he were struggling not to grin, but the smile was there in his eyes when he raised his hands. "You might wanna put that away," he said, but it was unclear whether he meant the gun, or Mike's dick.

Zolt's buddy, still in the shadows, snorted. "We thought it was polite to not disturb you."

Arden uttered the tiniest whisper from the car. "Everything okay?"

"Yes. Just... get dressed before you get out." Mike stared back into Zolt's grinning face, kinda itching to throw a punch. But it wasn't worth it. "The package's inside the house."

"Oh, we already have it in the truck. Just wanted to let you know so you don't freeze your dick off waiting."

"Has to be some woman in there. You didn't even hear the van," Zolt's buddy said from the shadows, and Mike dragged his hands down his face.

Zolt barked a laugh and retreated toward the bushes, patting his friend on the shoulder. "I'll tell you on the way back."

Mike sighed.

Zolt wouldn't leave Leo in the dark about what happened here. Of course. Gossip had a way of burning through the Heller family like fire in dry grass watered with gasoline.

Well, Mike wouldn't be explaining himself to anyone.

Not tonight.

"I don't want to go to sleep yet," he said as soon as the noise of the truck died down. "Hungry?"

Arden was already pulling on his clothes, but knowing he was marked with Mike's cum was still a thrill. His smile looked as innocent as the two braids suggested he was, but Mike knew the truth and loved the dichotomy of it.

"Milkshakes? All-night cinema?" Arden suggested, pulling on his T-shirt.

Even their minds worked in unison now. As long as they were away from the clubhouse, they didn't have to deal with tomorrow's reality.

Chapter 22 – Mike

Mike's nails shone as if Arden had covered them with pearl dust, but it was only varnish. So it didn't fit with Mike's image, but it was something he'd have with him to remember his boy by for a bit longer.

"All packed up," Kaley said loudly enough to tear Mike's gaze away from Arden's face. He chewed on his lip and offered Arden a smile, still holding on to his small, elegant hands.

"So... remember to take a nap. You didn't get any sleep last night."

Arden's eyes were puffy, but it somehow made him look cuter. "I doubt I'll be sleeping for at least a week, Mike." He got to his toes, as if to give Mike a kiss, but then ended up hugging him instead.

The need to call everything off and take Arden back to their room was overwhelming, but Mike had promised himself he wouldn't be selfish and pressed his nose into the crook of Arden's neck one last time. The fresh scent of jasmine was sweet on the boy's skin, and so intoxicating he couldn't bear letting go. So he held Arden until Kaley cleared her throat.

Still upset over them disappearing on her last night, she clearly wanted her little brother to move on. And she'd been right in suggesting it would never happen if Mike stayed in Arden's life.

"If you have any issues. Anyone stalking you, or just being a douche, you let me know. Promise," Mike whispered.

Arden stepped back, his eyes full of unsaid emotion. "I promise. No one's gonna fuck with me from now on. Look at my guns." He flexed his biceps which, while less skinny than three months ago, were still hardly a curve under the skin.

Kaley snorted. "There, there, Schwarzenegger, let's go."

Mike squeezed Arden's hand and led him to her car in the eerie silence of the early morning. The commuters were already away, but the town seemed asleep, and only the wind howled above, carrying away the dust from Mike's heart.

"Have a good life. You deserve everything."

Arden opened his mouth, as if he wanted to say something more but then just rolled into the passenger's seat. Kaley gave Mike a sparse wave, but once she started the engine, Arden looked back at Mike like a puppy being taken to the pound.

His eyes begged *keep me*, but Mike didn't know whether he'd survive another ordeal like the one with Leah. Parting was best for both of them, even if Arden didn't understand it yet. So he smiled, waved, and watched his boy disappear from sight. Out of his life, forever.

Several moments passed until Mike was certain he could no longer see his kitten, and he slid back into the compound, closing the gate behind him. All he wanted was some bourbon to kickstart this first miserable day without Arden.

He should've felt relieved that the responsibility of caring for him was over, but instead all he could think of was that he wouldn't be there to protect Arden if someone were rude to him because of his looks, or when a guy tried to hook up with him, or in the millions of situations that might put Arden in danger. He lived his life so boldly, dressing in a way that could attract violence, and Mike hated to think that one day someone might hurt Arden for just being himself.

Mike's stomach clenched with anxiety even as he poured the bourbon in. Didn't he have a heart of steel? He'd killed someone last night for fuck's sake. Yet here he was, a ball of stress and sadness.

This would pass. It had to.

"Impersonating Sailor Moon?" Rain asked, appearing by the empty bar out of nowhere to poke him with an elbow. How did she manage to sneak up on him with all the bottles, cans, and other trash littering the floor after last night's party? Come to think of it, it was kinda weird the hangarounds hadn't taken care of it all yet.

"Huh?"

She raised her eyebrows. "The nails—never mind."

"Just... Arden's idea," Mike said, trying to focus on the now as he walked behind the counter, where Arden had blown him that first time. He needed something between him and his nosy sister, regardless of her intentions.

Rain snorted but watched him with the sharpness of a razor slicing his brain open for dissection. "Do you even know how to get it off?"

Mike closed his eyes when the sharp liquid burned its way down his throat. "Don't know. Don't care."

Rain's face fell. What was her expression? Pity? "Mike, come on. It can't be that bad..."

"What is it to you? Don't you have a pretty young wife and kids to bother?" Mike grunted and turned away from her, toward the broken mirror still miraculously sitting in its frame. "I don't wanna talk about it."

Rain's reflection frowned and started tapping something on her phone. "Well, we think you *should* fucking talk about it, because you've been sulking all week and no one knows what to do with you anymore."

"Fine. I'll just take a vacation and go camping somewhere in Washington state if it bothers you so much," Mike said and grabbed a little bag of peanuts from a drawer in a cupboard next to the bar before walking to his favorite leather chair, which offered an excellent view of the stripper poles. He hadn't sat here in ages. Maybe that's what he should do? Visit all the stripper bars in Reno and drink until he forgot about Arden?

The moment he considered that scenario, his brain whispered that he might as well pop in to Arden's for a courtesy visit. And if he wasn't home, Mike would likely stumble upon him by accident at the strip joint Kaley worked in.

He frowned when people started pouring into the empty bar. And not just hangarounds on a late clean-up quest. His dad, mom, Leo, Axel, Jack... they all headed straight for him, grabbing chairs on the way. The fuck was this?

"Err, okay. I'll be in my room if you need me," he said, rising from the seat, on the way to the open door, but Dad pushed him right back down.

"Sit and listen."

"What is this about?" Mike asked and hugged the bottle, weirded out by the subdued glances he was getting.

The way his family sat around him in a circle of chairs reminded Mike of that one time he'd taken Granddad to an AA meeting, and he didn't like that fact one bit.

"Zolt told me about last night..." Leo started, rubbing his hands together with a worried expression.

Of course Zolt would have told him.

"Is that it? You want to talk me out of my misguided gay relationship? Weird for *you* to do that, Leo, but okay, whatever. You'll be happy to know it's over," Mike said, pouring out the bitterness boiling inside him.

Rain shook her head, leaning against Mom's armchair. "No, we all care about you, and Arden seems more important to you than any other partner in a while. Actually, you've only had flings, as far as I recall."

The silence after her comment was almost eerie, but maybe it was because only his parents and siblings were there. Nothing was ever quiet in Kane's presence, or when someone from the old guard was around.

"What's it to you, Rain? All of you spent two months discouraging me, and making fun of me, and now you're on board and actually *want* me to be with Arden?"

"We just didn't think it was serious. It's never serious with you," Dad said, raising his voice, but Mom quieted him with a squeeze to his hand and cleared her throat. She hadn't washed her hair today, which was a ritual of hers, and that prompted Mike to sink deeper into the chair. Shit was about to get serious.

"Your dad means that it took us a long time to realize that whatever was happening between you and Arden was different. But then I saw you during that tear gas attack and I knew how deeply you care for him."

"Why are we having this conversation?" Mike asked, agitated like an injured animal prevented from hiding in the safety of a den where it could have licked its wounds. "I told you it's done. I don't want to be dissected, so leave me the fuck alone!"

Jack squinted at him. He might have taken after Mom's family in terms of features, but the stern expressions often appearing on his face made him resemble Dad more with each passing day. "Stop being a big baby. You can't stay away from the boy, and everyone can see that. So you're afraid of commitment. Boo hoo. Get your shit together and stop being so wishy-washy. You're lucky a pretty thing half your age even wants your sorry undecided dick!"

The silence extended, but even though Mom cleared her throat, she didn't say a thing.

But Jack had no fucking idea what he was talking about.

"Of course he wants me. I give a mean blowjob and fuck like a machine. What more can a boy want?" he asked, challenging Jack with a sharp gaze in hope it would send him out the door.

But Jack took a deep inhale of air and rubbed his face. "Can somebody get through to this idiot? Mike, you're not getting any younger!"

"So what?" Mike snapped, avoiding all the invasive stares by watching the bottle in his hand. "I don't want kids anyway. It doesn't matter."

Mom put her hand on his forearm, and he itched to shrug it off, but had too much respect for her to do that. "You know we support you in whatever decision you make, but you don't seem happy, Mike. Jack is trying to ask if there's something else going on? Why did you break up with Arden when you clearly like him so much?"

"You know what I think?" Axel spoke out, drawing everyone's attention to his somber features. "You're wasting your life. All those girls throw themselves at you, and you just go through them without ever considering that there will come a time where you won't be able to attract them at the snap of your fingers anymore. And you'll be alone, because you won't have anyone to love you. And this thing with Arden? I also thought it was crazy at first, but you really like him, man. I know you do. What the hell are you doing with your life? Do you know what I'd give for someone to look at me the way he looks at you? And you just turned him away."

That was the longest few sentences Axel had willingly said in his entire life, but the jabs pulled at all the wrong strings in Mike, triggering an explosion of anger. He tossed the bottle at the wall, standing up just as the glass broke. "You don't fucking know anything! Yes! Yes, I like him! I want him! If I was someone else, I'd have taken him in a heartbeat, but I won't put his life at risk!"

A tense vein appeared on Dad's forehead. "So this *is* about Leah?"

"Everything in my life is about Leah!" Mike roared, spreading his arms wide. "I wouldn't have become a member if it wasn't for what happened to her, and you know it."

Mom exchanged a glance with Dad and got up when he nodded. She rolled up her top, revealing the protruding scar under her navel. It had been there since Mike could remember, and its appearance had never improved

"See this?" She asked, pointing it out to Mike. "I never had a Cesarean. During the worst times for the Smokeys, when some of you were still babies, and most of you didn't even exist yet, your dad's enemies came for me."

Leo held his breath and grabbed her hand. "Mom..."

She shook her head and squeezed his fingers in the deathly silence that filled the room at that revelation. "It's okay, I survived. I knew what I was in for when I married your father, even though we were very young at the time. Doesn't mean I didn't suffer, but I chose him. I was always willing to face the danger for my man, and I don't regret it. So ask yourself, Mike. Are you rejecting Arden for *his* safety, or to protect your own feelings? Because if it's the former, then you need to leave that choice up to him," she said in a steely voice, meeting Mike'd gaze head-on.

He stilled, his lungs emptying as he dropped back into the armchair and clutched his knees. How was he to fight an argument like that? Arden had been ready to stay with him. That boy, with his lack of care for what others thought about him, wasn't afraid of anything. He wasn't afraid to wear makeup and girly clothing, despite knowing it might draw unwanted attention. And because he loved Mike, he wouldn't have given up on their relationship because of fear either. Mike had been the one to break their bond, and even though his brain told him it was the right thing to do, maybe Mom was right? Maybe his choices were guided by fear and would only lead to suffering? Since when was he a coward?

"Sorry, Mom."

Dad exhaled and rubbed her back, his expression grim as he leaned toward Mike. "I know it's hard. But the truth is people get hurt all the time. You don't need to be in an MC for that to happen. Remember Giger, my friend from Louisiana? He was such a crazy bastard, doing all those extreme sports, getting into fights. But he got paralyzed in a simple car accident. His own mother was driving them to church. Shit happens, Mike, but we need to live hoping it won't happen to us."

Leo let go of Mom's hand when she sat down, but wouldn't look up, too focused on his own fingers. "And it goes both ways, Mike. By being with you, Arden is not just willing to live with the risk of being targeted as your partner. You might get hurt, and he'll fear for you every time you leave on club business. Sure, he can't 'protect' you the way you think you should take care of him, but isn't that even more frightening in a way? If something happens to you, he won't be able to do anything, but he's still willing to take a chance on you. You shouldn't take that choice away from him."

It was something Leo knew a lot about since he and his husband were both MC members, and he'd been out of his mind when Zolt had gotten shot that one time. Mike had thought that their situation was different because they both took on the danger equally, but the longer he thought about it, the more he could see truth in what Leo was trying to say. It was as if a door opened in his mind, shedding light on shadowy corners full of dust he should have gotten rid of long ago. Love was all about trust, and if someone chose a partner who did any kind of dangerous work, they needed to believe their loved one wouldn't take on unnecessary risks.

Leo surely struggled with this every day, but his relationship with Zolt had changed him. He seemed more at ease with himself and just… happier with his life overall.

Could Mike allow himself to have that too? After Leah's death, he'd promised himself to never fall in love again, but twenty years on, it didn't feel like he'd gained anything by sticking to that policy. In fact, right now he felt like he'd lost something he could not live without.

He looked at his painted nails, remembering the careful way in which Arden had applied the varnish earlier, even if it was just for fun. *Everything* was fun with Arden around. The simplest of things gained a deeper meaning when they were together, and Mike felt different at his side. Truly free, because no obligation to Arden ever felt like a chore. Mike wanted Arden. In his life. In his bed. He wanted to be a part of Arden's life.

"He's something else," he whispered, rubbing his palms as his throat closed up. "He's this precious, wonderful creature that came into my life by surprise and changed everything."

Rain put a cigarette between her lips and snapped open a lighter. "See? I told you he needed an intervention."

Jack spread his massive tattooed arms. "So what now? You gonna at least talk to him? I never thought I'd be supporting you going gay, but I prefer that to you sulking like some snubbed prima donna."

Mike groaned. "I'm not gay."

Leo sniggered. Okay. Mike deserved that.

Rain frowned and walked toward the open door as she picked up a call, but Mike's brain was fogging up with the need to call off everything he'd said this morning, get on his bike, chase down Kaley's car, and apologize. Or, better yet, get their address from Rain and apologize with an amazing arrangement of jasmine flowers forming the first letter of Arden's name. Or maybe both their names? A ring? A property vest? His brain sizzled with grand gesture options, and his heart came alive again.

Would that... could that actually work out?

"Fuck!" Rain exclaimed and dropped the cigarette to snuff it out on the tiles with her boot. She turned around to face everyone, but her eyes zeroed in on Mike. "The Jarens. The fucking *Jarens* have Arden. They must have waited for him to leave the compound without club protection. Kaley just called me. They blocked her way, took him, and told her Arden's staying with them until you marry Harlyn. That girl's out of her fucking mind!"

The floor crumbled under Mike's feet, but Mom grabbed his hand, and when all his brothers rose, their words of comfort turned into a cacophony that couldn't quite get to Mike through his fear. And yet, he wasn't changing his mind about Arden.

He swallowed, took a deep breath, and spoke.

"Let's get my boy back."

Chapter 23 – Arden

Arden tried to rock the chair again, but the Jarens must have seen all the abduction movies in existence and ensured it was stabilized with ropes on either side. Crates of fruit and vegetables stood tall around him, three chest freezers hummed in the back, and the metal shelving units were filled with all kinds of canned and dry goods. A ridiculous decal featuring aliens dressed as cowboys stared at him from a fridge. He chose to ignore it and took in the space, looking for weaknesses.

This could have been a small store. And it smelled of the produce, which was pretty pleasant, considering the situation.

A strange sense of calm had overcome Arden after the initial panic. As if he were in a movie and watching himself in an out-of-body experience. When Luke had been after him, he'd feared death. Rape. Torture. But he didn't think these abductors wanted to hurt him. He was a bargaining chip, worth more in good condition.

But while he felt relatively safe due to the severity of the revenge Mike would unleash on the Jarens if a hair fell from Arden's head, he wasn't a princess, who'd just await rescue. He refused to let those people use him against Mike and if there was anything he could do to free himself, he'd jump at the opportunity.

He usually despised it when people underestimated him, but it paid off to be non-threatening sometimes. Unbelievable as that was, none of the men who'd blindfolded and taken him from Kaley's car bothered to search him. And he was still armed. Granted, the keychain switchblade hadn't impressed or scared Mike when they first met, but it was sharp enough to cut the rope binding Arden to the wooden chair.

Breathing in the scent of raw potatoes, he wiggled his hands, trying to loosen the knots that kept him in place, but while that did nothing to improve Arden's situation, his legs were free, and he pushed his hips up, climbing to his toes until his fingers could reach the front pocket of his jeans.

Sweat beaded over his lip as he gasped from the effort, imagining the key slipping from his sweaty hands, out of reach, but he'd made it! Unfolding the switchblade with his teeth wasn't a pleasant experience, but once the small knife was out, freedom seemed within reach.

A door nearby screeched open, and he got back into position, squeezing the knife in his hand. It was small enough to hide this way but his stomach still tightened with worry. He half-expected for the sounds to die down so he could resume his attempt, but the door to his makeshift cell opened, and a young woman walked in with a bottle of water and a sandwich wrapped in paper.

Dressed in cut-off shorts and a yellow T-shirt with a wide neck that uncovered one tanned arm, she seemed way too wholesome to be a part of this family of abductors. She was the sexy girl next door who managed to look stunning while hardly wearing any makeup, and she even had a smile for Arden as she glanced at the bread and bit her lips.

"Oh boy. I forgot this will be difficult to eat in your position. I should have made you a protein shake."

The fact that his captors hadn't bothered to gag him suggested there would be no point in screaming. Arden's breathing picked up, his mind calculating his options. Maybe she could become his ally if he played his cards right.

"You don't want to be a part of this," he said softly.

She placed the water and sandwich on a counter above two rows of shelves filled with soap and cleaning products, and applied some lip balm.

"I'm sorry, you're getting this all wrong. You're the boy Mike's been sleeping with, right?"

Arden was no prude, but a flush still burned his cheeks. "And you are...? Wait. Are *you* Harlyn?"

She smiled, and while one of her canines protruded from the otherwise even, white teeth, it didn't take anything from her attractiveness. "Yeah. I just wanted you to know I made my brothers promise they won't hurt you. It's not personal."

That had to count for something, though it felt damn personal to him. "He doesn't love you," Arden said, trying to sound compassionate. He didn't plan on slapping her on the face with that fact, since that much was obvious from Mike's reluctance, but he needed to know where she stood on all this.

Harlyn pushed her long silky hair over the shoulder. "It doesn't matter, okay? I need a way out of this dump. I want to be wild and free, and ride on the back of his bike with his name on my vest. Don't take this the wrong way, but Mike likes girls. He'd lose interest in you sooner or later, so you're really not losing anything, but I can have a new life. My family would cut ties with me if I ran off, so the only way I can have what I want is to marry him."

Arden blinked several times, struck silent.

What. The. Fuck.

All this time, he'd thought—everyone did—that Harlyn was obsessed with Mike, but what she actually wanted was a different lifestyle and an excuse to have it while remaining in touch with her loved ones.

She smiled again, as if she hadn't just told him the stupidest plan he'd ever heard and unwrapped half the packaging. "Sandwich?"

Arden shook his head.

"You sure? I could cut it into bite-sized pieces," she suggested and smelled the food. "You could find yourself another biker, if you dig all that leather and motorcycles. We'd be like sisters," she said, completely oblivious to the craziness of this suggestion.

Maybe you *find yourself another biker*, Arden thought in frustration, even though her words stung him to the core. Mike wasn't his anymore.

His chest filled with stones, but that couldn't kill his will to act. He and Mike might no longer be together, but their feelings for one another were strong, and Mike had to be going out of his mind with worry, especially given what had happened to Leah. That experience had been the reason for their parting, and now another person Mike loved was taken, turning his nightmares into reality.

Fuck.

The moment he was alone, he'd cut himself free and run.

Unaware of his thoughts, Harlyn went on, sipping water from the bottle she'd brought for Arden. "They have such a close-knit family, the Hellers. I met most of his brothers, and the ones who are married treat their old ladies like queens! I want that even if my marriage has a bumpy start."

She blinked, freezing with the bottle at her mouth, and moments later Arden realized why. The roar of motorbikes used to stir no emotions in him yet now it proved that the cavalry was coming for him, and his heart fluttered.

Harlyn grinned. "You hear that, right? Don't want to be too enthusiastic, but I can't wait to feel those vibrations between my legs again," she said, digging her teeth into her bottom lip as she gravitated farther away, to the single door, and poked her head out, letting in more of the noise.

This was Arden's chance.

He turned the knife in his hand and put it to the rope holding his wrist, cutting, cutting, cutting even when his muscles ached from the unnatural position of his fingers. He kept peeking at Harlyn every now and then but he could sense the little threads in the rope breaking, and every passing second made him sweat with worry that he might end up discovered.

"I want a mini dress for my wedding. But with a long train at the back," Harlyn said dreamily as the roar became ever louder. As did the beating of Arden's heart.

The rope snapped and, taking advantage of Harlyn's preoccupation with the noise, Arden freed his other hand. Lightheaded with fear that she might notice his escape and lock him in before he reached her, he got up, imagining himself as some kind of cross between a cobra and Liam Neeson, a creature who moved without making a single sound, leaving its victims ignorant to danger. He wouldn't hurt Harlyn, of course, but he'd make her believe he would if necessary.

"Would *you* wear a dress or a suit to your wedding?" she asked, about to look back, when Arden wrapped his arm around her and put the knife against her throat.

"I'm small, but I will slit your fucking neck open if you try to fight me, understood?" He didn't know where such harsh words came from, but he was high on adrenaline and her bubblegum perfume.

Harlyn stiffened, and when Arden came closer, twisting back her arm, it became clear that they were very similar in size. Which made this whole thing that much easier.

She choked and grabbed his wrist, trying to push his hand away, but when Arden reflexivity pulled it back, and the blade met resistance, she gave a frantic yelp and sobbed. "Oh God… oh God…"

Arden's heart froze, and for a moment he feared he might have hurt her, but she kept mewling, so her windpipe was clearly fine. The fact that he'd managed to overpower another person like this gave him no satisfaction, but he did think she deserved those moments of uncertainty for being so callous when it came to other people's lives.

"Forward. And stay quiet," Arden said as the engines died down, and she gave a nod, stepping into the scorch outside, into a sandy path between small buildings of wood and metal. Arden blinked, noting they were in some kind of valley surrounded by barren hills. Dust was everywhere, and the air carried a sharp scent of farm animals, but the voice Arden knew well, Mike's voice, made him urge Harlyn in the right direction, toward a metal structure dwarfing the settlement. Its sheet metal roof reflected the bright sunlight, forcing Arden to squint and turn his head away. A cat stared at him from the nearest window, but before he could have worried that it might alarm its human, Mike's voice made him walk faster, to where the alleyway opened into open space

"Where. Is. The boy?" A roar worthy of a lion. It made Arden choke with emotion, but as he pushed Harlyn toward the sandy yard and walked alongside a large truck toward a barrier of cement blocks and tyres, he wanted to shout. To reassure Mike he was fine.

"Nobody move!" Arden yelled, and the group of strangers—the Jarens, he presumed—turned to face him, shotguns ready to fire.

His instinct was to freeze, but he fought through it when he saw Mike among the other Smokeys, standing in line like the alpha wolf leading his pack. Their eyes met, and Arden's heart rose in his throat. He'd known Mike would come for him, yet his presence, from the heavy boots to the blond hair messed up by the helmet meant more to Arden than he could ever express. He'd be important to Mike forever, regardless of the past trauma dividing them.

"This whole bullshit marriage thing ends today!" Arden yelled at the top of his lungs, so intensely angry his throat ached, making the last syllable barely a rasp.

Everyone was here. The whole club, with the exception of Kane, who still nursed his broken leg, and they'd all come here *for him*. Warmth soaked through his chest when Mike waved at him, his mouth opening in a small smile, but as the Jarens melted into blurry figures, Harlyn let out a high-pitched screech, making Arden's ear bleed.

"You can't stop me, Dad! And neither can he! I'm gonna get married. This month. I'm gonna ride out of here on a bike, and have *so* many babies!" she rambled, digging her nails into Arden's forearm. She must have gotten more confident of her position with her family within sight.

Arden's chest filled with fury and he pushed the knife harder against her neck. "You sure as hell won't be having Mike's babies, because he's had a vasectomy, dumbass!"

Everyone went so silent they could hear birds singing nearby, and even Harlyn stilled, though Arden stayed alert as if he were restraining a human-sized porcupine.

Axel cleared his throat and raised his hand as if he were a student wanting to ask the teacher a question. "I have a bike and a working penis," he said, and in that moment Arden knew exactly why his Tinder dates weren't going well.

Mike slapped the back of Axel's head, his mouth twisted. "Hey, my dick works!"

"It's just the pipes that don't," Mike's dad said with a grin worthy of a ten-year-old hearing an adult joke. His face twitched when he looked toward Arden and Harlyn, as if he were trying not to laugh into her face. "Always wanted you as a daughter-in-law, Harlyn, I like a girl who knows what she wants, but I think you bet on the wrong Heller."

One of the strangers took a deep breath of air, showing his teeth as if he were ready to jump across the fence and go for the club president's throat. "Are you mocking my daughter?"

The man wore a shirt several sizes too big for him and was rather bony, which explained why he compensated with the two rifles he had on him. "Your son lied to her. He should take responsibility for his actions!"

Mike spread his arms and approached the fence despite several guns pointed at him as if he carried a bunch of grenades. "That is such bullshit! She told me she wanted to have fun with a biker. I never told her it was anything but that!"

"You said I could stay at the club!" Harlyn didn't fight Arden anymore, standing still even when his hold on her loosened.

Mike shook his head. "Yeah, but not as my *wife!*" He turned to Axel and said something too quietly for Arden to hear, but Axel nodded, determination making his expression sterner than usual.

Mike patted Axel's arm and pointed to him as if he were presenting a particularly fat pig at the market. "Look at him, Harlyn. Is he not a fine piece of biker? You should get to know him better. Hell, I'll even pay for the wedding cake if the two of you hit it off."

Arden took a deep breath, his brain glitching at the ridiculousness of this proposition. But he still whispered in her ear, "He's actually really nice."

"W-what?" Harlyn asked, too shocked to immediately understand the offer, but whether Axel was serious about this thing or just bluffing, the scheme could be Arden's way out.

"Axel just proposed to you."

"Oh... he did?" she asked while the Jarens stood perfectly still, as if Axel were Medusa and had turned them into stone.

Jeff and Zolt spoke to Axel, but he only stood straighter, cleared his throat, and joined Mike at the front of the group, staring straight at Harlyn. "I always thought you were very pretty. Do you want to go for a walk?" he asked in his dull voice, but this was still better than his initial proposal.

Harlyn's father shook his head. "I warn you, Mike. If this is just a ruse to get the boy out, I will bring the wrath of heavens upon you!"

Talk about being dramatic.

Arden led Harlyn toward the makeshift barrier of rubber and concrete, closer to the Hellers and safety, but the Jarens were now at arms' reach, their eyes on him as if he were toxic waste. His heart beat faster at the danger of their proximity, but Mike would surely protect him if anything went wrong. Once he was out, it wouldn't matter that they'd broken up. They'd hug, and he'd ride *home* on Mike's bitch seat one more time.

When had he started thinking of the clubhouse as his home?

"Just say the word, Harlyn, and I'll fuck them all up!" yelled one of her brothers, but she waved at him dismissively.

"Let me go on my date, okay?"

"Supervised!" her father huffed, scowling at Arden as if he were a piece of rotten meat. But as soon as Axel stepped past the old car blocking the driveway into the compound, hands raised to show he wasn't going to attack, Arden pushed Harlyn forward and leapt to the other side, scrambling over the tyres making up the fence.

His skull boiled with worry that someone on the Jaren side might lose their patience and send a bullet his way, but moments later he was on the other side. Safe.

Mike ran up to him right away, and as Arden choked up, jogging forward, the familiar chest was the solace he needed. It smelled like it had in the morning too. Of wood, and a hint of jasmine.

"It's okay, baby. I'm sorry," Mike whispered, panting.

Arden had kept his cool before, as if his body had been pure adrenaline, but his knees buckled the moment Mike's arms closed around him. "I didn't know what they'd do," he uttered, barely able to speak with his trembling lips. "I was so scared they'd hurt me and you'd have to suffer because of it."

Mike sank low with him, sitting in the dust while Arden caught his breath. "It's my fault they took you. I'm so sorry," he said, petting Arden's cheeks, his face tense with anger. Mike didn't even need to profess it, Arden had no doubt he'd drive headfirst into the tyre fence for him if need be.

"You can't control everything," Arden said, settling into a hug as the most awkward date in history began somewhere behind his back. "It's their fault, because *they* abducted me."

Mike hummed, tightening his hold on Arden. "Yeah. But they did that because they knew I care about you. This will always be a risk," he whispered, resting his chin on Arden's head.

Arden pulled away to look into Mike's eyes and slid his fingers into Mike's beard. "And you teach me self-defence. I'd take that risk ten times over to be with you. I still love you." It was an embarrassing thing to admit to someone who had pushed him away, but he needed to say it. He'd been through enough to know safety was never a given. Any relationship could end badly, one way or another, but he couldn't live afraid of ever trusting again.

Mike blinked, his gaze turning away as he chewed on his lip, anchored by Arden's fingers in his facial hair. The Jarens and Hellers were shouting in the background, still arguing some points despite the temporary truce, but Arden only saw Mike and the way his features relaxed.

"I know. But are you ready for this danger to always be there?"

Arden stroked the soft facial hair, pondering the question on a deeper level than just yes- because-I-love-you.

"I've been the little queer boy at school, I've dated and hooked up with men like Luke, and I live with the knowledge that someone might target me for being the way I am. Are you ready to live with *that* danger? Because for me being with you means more safety, not less."

Mike swallowed and pulled himself up, dragging Arden with him. "Nobody in their right mind will touch you," he said, leading Arden past the Smokeys waiting for the weird arranged date to end, to his bike. "I'd go after them, and fucking impale them on streetlamps," he said, anger oozing out of his voice as he opened the saddlebag and pulled out a bundle of denim. He seemed strangely nervous when he unfolded it, revealing Leah's old vest. Bleached denim. And those patches.

Property of Mad Mike.

"Be mine?" Mike asked, his voice as intense as his blue gaze in the bright sun above.

Arden's lips spread into a smile, and he hadn't realized when tears blurred his vision. "Always," he whispered through the rock in his throat

Mike's shoulders hunched in relief. "I can... like... get you a new one, if you want. Or we'll add the club patches to this one."

Arden shook his head and turned around, spreading his arms so Mike could put it on him. "This one's perfect."

His heart was so light he felt as if his feet might leave the ground at any second. He used to worry Mike saw him as second-best, but he no longer harbored such ignorant fears. By wearing Leah's vest, he'd be honoring the memory of a girl who Mike once loved, and maybe this way he'd make the awful memory of her death a little less painful.

Mike's presence behind him was enough to send a shiver down his back before they even touched. When the vest was in place and Mike hugged him from behind, he felt so utterly complete. As if in the moment that denim touched his shoulders he'd found his true home.

"My family staged an intervention. Can you believe that?" Mike asked, smiling against Arden's neck while they faced the naked hills surrounding the only road leading to the compound.

Arden snorted, tickled pink that Mike's family approved of him so much. "Guess you needed one, huh?" He lifted Mike's hand to his lips and kissed the center of his palm where Mike would forever hold his heart. The vest was the symbol of Mike's love and protection. Everything a boy could want.

Mike turned them around to face the others, and while the Jarens were still there, clearly not a hundred percent happy with the situation, Arden focused on the smiling faces of his new family.

Mike held his arm over Arden's shoulders, and it was the sweetest weight, only emphasizing the fact that he now belonged with Mike, and everyone needed to acknowledge that undeniable fact. He grinned at the pearly nail polish on Mike's fingers. Maybe they'd make that an ongoing thing. Something to mark Mike as *his*.

Rain patted Mike's arm on the way to her own bike. "Axel's staying with Dad to polish out the details."

Mike's mouth fell open. "Wait... he's really interested in marrying her?"

Rain snorted, rolling her eyes. "I've got no idea what he said to her on that five-minute *date*, but they'll be tying the knot."

"I'm Mike's property now," Arden boasted to her in case she hadn't noticed.

Rain straddled her Harley, snickering. "Get ready for the ride of your life then."

A soft warmth filled Arden's chest as he stood on his toes to kiss Mike. "Ride me as often as your bike?" he whispered with a wicked grin.

Epilogue – Mike

Mike didn't think he'd ever say that, but the Jarens knew how to throw a party. He'd been full of doubts when Harlyn's father insisted the bride's family should always be the one to organize the wedding, but he was changing his mind fast.

The Jarens served a whole roast hog as the main meal, its meat more succulent than any Mike had ever tasted, and alcohol flowed freely as if it came from a bottomless well. Guests danced around a huge bonfire set up in the middle of the Jarens' front yard while others sat on long benches in and out of the workshop, which had been converted into a wedding venue for the occasion. The wedding favor was a small plastic figurine depicting aliens as the bride and groom, and if that didn't describe Axel and Harlyn's relationship, he didn't know what would.

Mike had been worried his brother had made a grave mistake getting hitched to a girl who seemed to treat marriage as a way out of an uncomfortable situation, but Axel had been more excited than Mike had ever seen him be since the unexpected engagement during the standoff over Arden, so maybe there was method to this madness. Tinder had not worked for Axel. Two months later, the two of them acted like complete lovebirds, and despite Axel always claiming he hated dancing, they'd even done the whole first dance thing at the start of the party. Harlyn got what she wanted, but Axel seemed happy to serve.

Maybe life would finally work out for him?

"Embracing *being gay*?" Leo asked, approaching Mike out of the blue, and when Mike stalled, not sure what this was about, Leo pointed to the painted nails of Mike's left hand. Despite the casual nature of the wedding, Leo still wore a jacket and shirt, even if without a tie.

Mommy was surely proud.

"Embracing being sexist?" Mike shot back but was already grinning. Those jokes had seemed funny as hell when he'd directed them at Leo, but they'd lost their dubious charm.

He'd hit the jackpot, because Leo stilled with his mouth open, desperately searching for a snappy answer that wasn't coming. Leo never was good at those.

"I... didn't mean it that way," he grumbled.

"Everyone has nails. No reason not to decorate," Mike said, even though he'd have considered it a waste of time if he were to do the manicure himself.

"So... Arden's staying, huh?" Leo sipped from his beer bottle and stood closer, watching the dancing crowd from the outskirts.

Mike's boy was dressed to the nines, and was dancing with Rain, who'd just tilted him back. They made the most curious couple with her wearing a shirt and tie under the leather jacket, and him in a lavender bridesmaid dress. Because yes, despite Arden leaving a mark on Harlyn's neck with a knife, she'd offered Arden a spot as a bridesmaid. That girl was crazy, but maybe her energy would balance out Axel, who so rarely smiled.

The lavender dress had been adjusted for Arden's size, but the whole outfit consisted of white stockings, a fitted bodice laced at the back, and a puffy tulle bottom barely longer than a tutu. It was hard to take eyes off Arden's long legs as he twirled on the dancefloor. He'd worn small heels for the event, but had swapped them for good old sneakers now.

He was the cutest girl out there, despite not actually being a girl.

"This is it for me, Leo. My wild days are over," he joked, but there was truth in what he was saying. He still enjoyed the lifestyle he'd led so far and wasn't intent on giving up on parties, but he would settle on the tail he already got instead of chasing a new one each night.

Arden kept him satisfied.

Leo snorted. "For real? You're saying he's not wild?"

Mike snorted. "Oh, he definitely is. And territorial too. What do you think the nails are really about? He's claiming me with those," he said, glancing at his thumb, which matched the color of Arden's dress. "It's his version of the property vest."

Leo shook his head. "That's actually kinda cute. How are you... um... coping with this whole identity change?" It seemed that after two years with Zolt, Leo still had far more hang-ups than Mike.

Mike shrugged and took a sip of his beer. "Not much changed, to be honest. It's weird how I never discovered this part of myself before, but it feels good. Dunno, Arden felt *right* from the moment we met. I was never the overthinking type. There's no need to label me or Arden. But I know it bothers *you*. I kinda see how I'd been a shit to you over Zolt. Sorry."

Leo did a double take at Mike with a smile. "Whoa. Mike apologizing? You really have changed. But yeah, I guess it does bother me a bit. At least now I have you to take half the burden." He glanced at Zolt who was talking to a group of men on the other side of the room. With his thick beard and arms covered in hair revealed by rolled up sleeves, he couldn't have been more different than Arden.

Mike considered that for a second and smirked when Arden finished his dance and strutted to where Zolt was standing, squeezing past him to get a drink. "That's how you think about it? That it's a burden?"

Leo shrugged. "Isn't it? Dealing with people's shitty attitudes. I used to want to stand out more, but now that I do, I'm 'the gay one'. It's fucking annoying, but what can I do? I married Zolt for a reason, so that's not changing. You're really not bothered, are you?"

Mike draped his arm across Leo's shoulders with a sigh. "No. Don't like the idea of others defining who I am. It helps that I can beat the stubborn ones to a pulp. Even this," he said, showing Leo the varnish, "is Arden taking care of me. I personally can't see what you see in all that hair and muscle, but Zolt is a good guy at heart. And he's changed for the better since you two got together. But you never touch him in public. Is it because he doesn't like it?"

Leo tensed under the touch, but didn't shrug off Mike's arm. "No, I... I'm not like you. I don't like the attention, people staring at me and judging. *Making comments.*" The last line was delivered with a glare.

"I know, I know, I'll be better, okay?" Mike said, raising his hands. "And me beating people into a pulp extends to those who make comments at you from now on. That shit's not on. Just look at Arden. That boy's fearless, but I think the more you put yourself out there, the less it must hurt when someone doesn't accept you. He doesn't give a fuck, and I love how bold that is. He'll be himself even if that means judgement from others."

"Thanks, Mike. I really appreciate it. It's gonna be important for my daughters to have an uncle like you growing up." Leo clinked their bottles.

Mike blinked. "That's the first time anyone's told me a girl's lucky to be around me."

"Well, I know you don't want kids, but I've got no doubt you'll be their lion and spot all the horny hyenas circling my girls in fifteen years. You know all their tricks." Leo laughed and waved at Zolt when his husband gestured for him to come over.

"Maybe you should learn a trick or two from Arden?" Mike asked, gently nudging Leo forward, to their partners who chatted over drinks, as different as night and day.

Leo smirked as they approached. "Hey, Arden? Mike's saying I should get knives for my daughters like the one you have. Sure won't hurt to teach them early." He seemed hesitant about something, but then slid his arm around Zolt's waist.

Zolt stilled, his mouth going slack with surprise only to stretch into a smile. He placed his beefy arm on Leo's shoulders and pulled him close. "Appropriate size for their tiny toddler hands."

Mike shook his head, grinning, and placed his hands on Arden's waist, standing right behind his jasmine-scented self.

Arden pushed back into him, as if he couldn't wait to get closer. "A sparkly diamante-studded knife will go well with a tiara. Speaking of crystals... Wanna show you something, Mike. Talk to you guys later." He turned and pulled on Mike's hand with an eyebrow wiggle. His makeup was especially flamboyant tonight, with silver glitter on his temples and fake lashes for days.

He was prettier than the bride and all the other bridesmaids combined, though Mike sure wouldn't be mentioning that to Axel, who at this point was feeding his new wife grapes as if she were a Roman empress.

"Show me something?" Mike asked, slotting his fingers between Arden's as they made their way through the crowd of guests and along the wall of the workshop. He finished his beer and tossed it onto a trash can on the way, but his gaze focused on Arden's neck, exposed by his classy updo dotted with stars and flowers.

Arden winked at him and pointed to the back of a shed far away from bright light and people. "Yes, it's just up there."

Arden led the way to a ladder left behind after all the decorations had been put up. He swiftly climbed the steps, and Mike was instantly more interested in staring up the long legs clad in stockings than in whatever Arden wanted to reveal.

The boy got to the top and bent forward, giving Mike a show all the way up his frilly skirt. "See how it sparkles?" He giggled.

Mike looked up to the roof, but his attention got drawn right back under Arden's skirt, and his face flushed when a pink glow lit between Arden's buttocks at a click of something in his hand. The tulle layers of the skirt turned into the fitting backdrops for one of the most arousing sights of Mike's life. A LED light was inside a round pink... crystal, illuminating both the fabric and the heart-shaped opening at the back of Arden's lacy panties.

Mike's brain was turning liquid. "Is... is that what I think it is?" he asked with a rasp that hurt his throat.

"I don't know. How dirty is your mind? As filthy as mine? You might want to check." The boy grinned over his shoulder and pressed some button, switching the light off.

Mike reached up to grab Arden's hips, his face hot, dick already pushing at the front of his jeans. "How long has it been there?"

Arden leaped into his arms with a squeal. "When did the party start?" he teased, and all Mike could think of was the plug stretching

Arden's hole, keeping it ready for a fast fuck. Mike just needed to choose *where* the inevitable would happen, because he had no doubt his boy was up for it.

He could barely think, and the little fae knew it, judging by the devilish smile he was giving Mike. "You little slut. It should be criminal to tease your man like this."

"What's the punishment?" Arden got to his toes to kiss him, guiding Mike's hand up his skirt. They were in the shadows, but still far too close to people for what Mike wanted to do.

He glanced at the people gathered around the bonfire, cupped Arden's warm cock and balls, and leaned in, rubbing the tip of his nose against Arden's while their gazes met, sparking fire. "We need to be alone for *that.*"

Arden eyed the party once more and pulled on Mike's hand. "I know a place."

Mike heard fireworks, and while they could be a part of the wedding celebrations, he was positive they erupted everywhere in his body. He'd hit the jackpot with Arden. His little minx would never stop surprising him. Never stop teasing. Never stop loving him.

He was all in. Not afraid to love anymore.

The end

Thank you for reading *Gutter Mind – Smoke Valley MC.* If you enjoyed your time with our story, we would really appreciate it if you took a few minutes to leave a review on your favorite platform. It is especially important for us as self-publishing authors, who don't have the backing of an established press.

Not to mention we simply love hearing from readers! :)

Kat&Agnes AKA K.A. Merikan

kamerikan@gmail.com

http://kamerikan.com

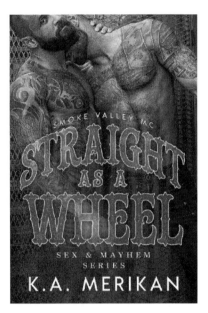

Straight as a Wheel – Smoke Valley MC

"Your secret's safe with me, Leo Heller. Whatever happens here, nobody will know. Ever. Do you understand?"

Zolt. Gay. Player. Predator. Fetish: Straight guys
Leo. Straight. Biker. Prey. Fetish: True love

Zolt knows what he wants from life--cold hard cash so that he can enjoy an early retirement in the Carribean as rent boys serve him drinks on the beach. Meanwhile, he's got his pawn shop as a front for illegal operations, and a baseball bat to deal with troublemakers.

When it comes to men, Zolt loves the chase, and his favorite, most elusive prey is curious straight guys. He goes out of his way to seduce and devour them. If he can be their first, all the better.

His next mark? A biker. And not just any. An outlaw, Leo Heller.

Leo's got his future all figured out. A wife, two to four kids, maybe a dog. If love was as easy as others make it seem, Leo would have been married already.

A string of failed relationships leads him to the one person he shouldn't be crushing on, shouldn't be admiring, and most definitely shouldn't be touching. Because a man like Zolt Andorai won't give Leo the family he wants. Hell, Zolt doesn't even do boyfriends. But what Zolt does offer is no-strings-attached experimentation, and Leo is only human.

After all, if no one ever finds out Leo's secret, it's as if it doesn't exist. One kiss leads to another, lines blur, and before Leo knows it, he's in over his head.
In love.
Helpless.

Themes: Outlaw motorcycle club, organized crime, homophobia, hurt/comfort, forced proximity, coming out, seduction, forbidden attraction, first love, greed, player, family ties
Genre: M/M romance, suspense
Length: ~110,000 words (Standalone novel)
Contains hot, emotional, explicit scenes

Available on AMAZON

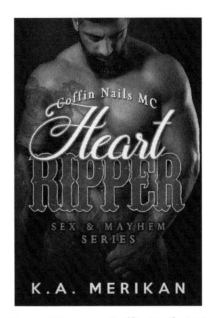

Heart Ripper – Coffin Nails MC

--- *You always want what you can't have.* ---

David. Catholic. Gay. Set on keeping his purity ring.

Raja. Biker. Manwhore. Never refuses a bet.

David has always tried to be the best son his parents could dream of.

Always at church on Sunday.

Always eager to help with the garden.

Always trying his best at school.

Prim, proper, innocent, and kind.

But deep inside of him, there is a yearning planted by the devil himself, and when a cocky, foul-mouthed biker pulls him a step too far, David doesn't fall into the abyss. He leaps.

Raja is all he's ever dreamed of, yet didn't dare voice. Older, dangerous, a wall of muscle with a grip so strong David can't resist him no matter how hard he tries.

As a freshly appointed president of a motorcycle club on the verge of ruin, Raja has a lot to live up to. Being gay doesn't do him any favors in terms of commanding the respect of his men. He has his way of compensating though.

Always first in a fight.

Always bragging about his sexual conquests.

Always up for a bet.

Daring, tattooed, sexy, and unapologetic.

After he boasts he can have any man he wants, he gets challenged to hook up with the preppy guy wallflowering at a party. Raja can't wait to pop the innocent cutie's cherry. But when he finds out the guy is his friend's younger brother, life gets a whole lot messier.

Why is the one guy who should be off-limits always the most tempting?

POSSIBLE SPOILERS:

Themes: Outlaw motorcycle club, organized crime, religion, homophobia, bet, good boy meets bad boy, coming out

Genre: M/M romance, suspense

Length: ~100,000 words (Standalone novel)

WARNING: This book contains steamy content and graphic violence.

Available on AMAZON

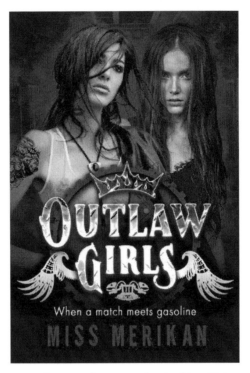

Outlaw Girls – Smoke Valley MC

--- *When a match meets gasoline.* ---

Mona. Mafia princess. Rebellious Italian beauty. Runaway bride.
Rain. Motorcycle club president's daughter. Androgynous biker goddess.

After her sister was forced into an arranged marriage, Mona vowed she would never suffer the same fate. She would do whatever she had to, even set the church on fire, catch the first bus to nowhere without a dollar in her pocket while still wearing her wedding dress.

Away from her controlling family, Mona intends to fight for her financial independence on the stripping pole at the Smoke Valley Motorcycle Club.

Her plan is to earn enough cash for further travels, but once she gets closer to Rain, and becomes more comfortable on the back of her bike than she ever was in the world of privilege, staying in the middle of Nowhere, Nevada no longer sounds so bad.

Rain doesn't do girlfriends. Her biker lifestyle means secrecy and unsavory deeds no girl she's met would roll with. Her only goal is to smash the glass ceiling of her family-run biker gang and become the first female member. She does do flings though, and the Italian beauty who crashes her birthday party is perfect for one of those.

But Mona sticks around. Rain can't stay away, and all rules go out the window when Rain finds out Mona is the runaway daughter of a mafioso. Maybe she could just be the kind of woman who understands living outside the law

When the mafia comes after Mona, Rain has to choose between loyalty to the club and the woman of her dreams. One thing is certain - there will be no escape without mayhem.

POSSIBLE SPOILERS:
Themes: mafia, organized crime, marriage, forbidden love, danger, motorcycle club, biker chick, family, rebellion, independence, first relationship, self-discovery
Genre: F/F romance, suspense
Erotic content: Explicit scenes
Length: ~60,000 words (STANDALONE novel)

Available on AMAZON

AUTHOR'S NEWSLETTER

If you're interested in our upcoming releases, exclusive deals, extra content, freebies and the like, sign up for our newsletter.

http://kamerikan.com/newsletter

We promise not to spam you, and when you sign up, you can choose one of the following books for FREE. Win-Win!

Road of No Return by K.A. Merikan
Guns n' Boys Book 1 by K.A.Merikan
All Strings Attached by Miss Merikan
The Art of Mutual Pleasure by K.A. Merikan

Please, read the instructions in the welcoming e-mail to receive your free book :)

PATREON

Have you enjoyed reading our books? Want more? Look no further! We now have a PATREON account.

https://www.patreon.com/kamerikan

As a patron, you will have access to flash fiction with characters from our books, early cover reveals, illustrations, crossover fiction, Alternative Universe fiction, swag, cut scenes, posts about our writing process, polls, and lots of other goodies.

We have started the account to support our more niche projects, and if that's what you're into, your help to bring these weird and wonderful stories to life would be appreciated. In return, you'll get lots of perks and fun content.
Win-win!

About the author

K.A. Merikan are a team of writers who try not to suck at adulting, with some success. Always eager to explore the murky waters of the weird and wonderful, K.A. Merikan don't follow fixed formulas and want each of their books to be a surprise for those who choose to hop on for the ride.

K.A. Merikan have a few sweeter M/M romances as well, but they specialize in the dark, dirty, and dangerous side of M/M, full of bikers, bad boys, mafiosi, and scorching hot romance.

FUN FACTS!
- We're Polish
- We're neither sisters nor a couple
- Kat's fingers are two times longer than Agnes's.

e-mail: kamerikan@gmail.com

More information about ongoing projects, works in progress and publishing at:

K.A. Merikan's author page: http://kamerikan.com

Facebook: https://www.facebook.com/KAMerikan

Patreon: https://www.patreon.com/kamerikan

Twitter (run by Kat): https://twitter.com/KA_Merikan

Goodreads:

http://www.goodreads.com/author/show/6150530.K_A_Merikan

Pinterest: http://www.pinterest.com/KAMerikan/

Printed in Great Britain
by Amazon

48044845R00194